selected stories

ALUN RICHARDS
selected stories

seren

seren is the book imprint of
Poetry Wales Press Ltd
Wyndham Street, Bridgend, Mid Glamorgan
Wales

A CIP record for this book is available at the
British Library Cataloguing in Publication Office

ISBN 1-85411-117-5

*The publisher acknowledges the financial assistance of the
Arts Council of Wales*

Cover illustration:'Phyllis, 1957' by Will Roberts
Transparency supplied by Oriel Mostyn, Llandudno

Printed in Plantin
WBC Book Manufacturers, Bridgend

Contents

Biographical Note

Alun Richards was born in Pontypridd in 1929 and has lived there for most of his life. His previous books include six novels and several collections of short stories — most notably, *Home to an Empty House*, *Dai Country*, *The Former Miss Miss Merthyr Tydfil* and *Ennal's Point*. He is the editor of *The Penguin Book of Welsh Short Stories* and *The Penguin Book of Sea Stories* (volumes 1 and 2). His collected plays are published under the title *Plays for Players* and he has written extensively for radio and television including early contributions to the long running BBC TV Series, *The Onedin Line*. The first part of his autobiography, *Days of Absence* was published in 1986 and followed the widely praised memoir of his compatriot, Welsh rugby legend Carwyn James. The first volume of his short stories received the Welsh Arts Council prize for 1974 and he was awarded an Honorary Fellowship by the University College of Swansea in 1985.

The Widow-Maker

It was a day when there was hardly a ripple on the water, such wind as there was, a nodding breeze from the South-East, and out beyond the headland, a long line of orange lobster buoys glistened in the early morning sunlight. It was also a day for fine thoughts. On such a morning, princes in golden finery rode glistening Arab stallions to greet pining maidens on turreted balconies and carried them away with one fell swoop, Dr Huw Pugh-Jones thought fancifully. He had neglected to listen to the marine weather forecast, but in a good mood, he was inclined to give a literary dimension to things.

It was incredible to think that only six months ago, he was a complete stranger to the sea. In the brief space of a year, all his eggs seemed to have hatched; a senior lecturer's appointment, a new house in a new place, Rian's pregnancy, then his Aunt Rachel's legacy, all of which added up to a year of bouquets when everything had gone right. It stemmed from two things, he was fond of saying, his decision to move South to a little seaside town on the most anglicised coast of Wales, and stranger still, his friendship with the local Gas Inspector.

'You won't like them down there,' his mother'd said, scowling in the gloom of his father's manse, bleak slate outcroppings visible on the bare mountain behind.

'Nonsense!'

'Mark my words, they're not to be trusted and clannish.'

But they weren't, not at all, and his very presence at this moment, feeling the rounded edge of the little fishing boat's mahogany tiller under his hand was enough. He could even remember the very first conversation with Ernie Smalls, his wizened ferret face tanned under his cap, the faintest smell of fish bait coming from an official satchel.

'Just moved in, have you?'

'Yes, we have, yes...'

'Nice house?'

'Yes, we liked it.'

'Doctor, is it? Medical?'

'No, I'm in the Polytechnic.' (Was there a moment then, a brief gleam in Ernie's shaded eyes that indicated some relief, that said, 'Oh, the Polly? Another one of them College lot!')

But then Ernie smiled broadly.

'Like a bit of fish, do you? Fresh?'

'Fish?'

'Well, I used to have rare old chats with the people here before you. Mr Jefferson? Did you er... before he...'

'No, we never actually met him.'

'A prince of a man, he was. A real loss. Very knowledgeable about the sea and boats. I used to come up to the house to chat with him. We was going into partnership. Lobsters. Boat called the *Sully Maiden* up for sale. I'd do all the running around and he'd just put up the... Well, I don't mind telling you, I come up the drive that day and I seen the blinds drawn, and my heart was in my mouth. Wept, I did.'

That was one conversation. More followed since there was a major relaying of gas pipes in the district, and Ernie Smalls seized any opportunity to call, advising them on matters to do with the house since neither Huw nor Rian, his wife, were very practical. Like the tides across the road, he occasionally brought gifts, wanted and unwanted. In the autumn, he brought fish, some sewin that had 'fallen into a net', as he said with a wink, later crabs, one small lobster with a claw missing, and some sand dabs in a plastic pouch, once the property of the Post Office. If they were not in, he left his presents on the doorstep with a printed note in large childish handwriting, 'Courtesy of E. Smalls'. In the winter, learning that Rian was pregnant, and seeing how inept Huw was with a shovel, he also cleared a good part of the drive of snow, and even brought milk when the milkman found it too difficult.

Rian, however, had reservations.

'There's something I don't like about that little man,' she said one night when they had entertained some friends, including Huw's Director of Studies to whom he had spoken all night about Ernie as the indispensable local man.

'Oh, Ernie's just Ernie.'

'You spend half your time outside talking to him.'

'He's a very interesting and knowledgeable person.'

'Have you seen the way he looks at my underclothes on the line? He picked up my slip the other day. I saw him rubbing it against his face. I had to wash it again.'

It was quite unreasonable, Huw thought. If Ernie looked at anything, any garment or piece of cloth, it was to test its utility, in this case as a duster. Perhaps Rian was clearly feeling her pregnancy. He'd been warned by his mother that she was likely to get a bit strange. But Ernie did have the most sharp and penetrating eyes which fixed upon you like a stoat's when there was something he wanted.

A few days later, Rian went away to spend a few weeks with her mother in the North and when Huw drove back alone, he found Ernie hovering in the driveway.

'I didn't know you was going away? At first, I thought, something's happened to the Missus? She's been looking a bit peaky.'

'She's gone to stay with her mother.'

'That'll be a relief then. Six months gone, is it? Another month, she'll be right. They can drop then, fit to bounce! Wonderful mother she'll make.'

Huw smiled. Ernie had seven children and regarded himself as an expert. He would report that when Rian telephoned.

They had a cup of coffee and a chat.

'Pity you got no interest in the sea?'

'I just haven't had the opportunity, that's all.'

'It's not just the fish, it's the feeling it gives you.'

'Isn't it dangerous? There's such a rise and fall of tide around here.'

'Oh, you gotta be careful. But as long as you knows the ropes.'

'How does one learn those?'

'Well, you gotta have someone to show you.'

A day later, Huw was strolling around the little harbour of the seaside town when two lads got into difficulties launching a dinghy near the yacht club slip. Although holding a rope attached to the dinghy, they were clearly not prepared for a wave that caught the stern or the ominous crunch as the keel grounded on the edge of the concrete slip. Without fully understanding what was happening, Huw watched, as did a number of the yachtsmen who had heard the sound of wood splintering. Nobody, however, seemed prepared to help when suddenly Ernie appeared wearing a pair of thigh waders, hurried down the slip and with a few deft movements, shoved the dinghy back into the oncoming tide, allowing the boys to complete what they had set out to do. Then Ernie, ever obliging, brought the metal trolley back up the slip. It was a small event but Huw could sense the rightness of what Ernie had done and the sight of him in thigh waders and worn fisherman's guernsey with a red bobble cap was somehow as reassuring as his uniformed self. He looked, as ever, a man who knew.

Seeing Huw watching, he grinned.

'See that? Bits of kids. They'd have had the bottom out of her.'

Huw noticed that everyone seemed to know Ernie and by chance, while they were talking, a middle-aged man wearing a yachting cap interrupted them to ask Ernie's advice. Behind them, a newly painted dinghy stood up-ended under a FOR SALE sign.

'What d'you think of that, Ernie?'

Ernie looked down the long line of the dinghy's keel and noticed a tiny cluster of paint bubbles in a barely discernible crevice in the wood. With a furtive look over his shoulder, he produced a pen knife, opened the small blade and tested it gently against the wood of the keel. The point of the blade went easily into the wood.

'Ripe,' Ernie said gravely and shook his head.

'I'd never have thought of doing that.'

Later, strolling along, Ernie nodded at a larger boat covered by a tarpaulin which stood on a wooden bogey, its varnish gleaming, obviously of a stout construction.

'That's her,' Ernie said. '*Sully Maiden*. All boat, she is, and going for a song. What couldn't we do with a boat like that? Pay for herself twice over in a season.'

That was on a Monday. On the Tuesday, Huw already knew that the *Sully Maiden* had been built across the channel in Appledore by the same craftsmen who were entrusted with the replica of the *Golden Hind*. Nothing had been spared in her construction. She had a metal shoe to take the beach. Stones, Ernie said. This was a boat built by fishermen for fishermen. None of your fibreglass rubbish, all cabin and toilet, all right for giving your secretary a quickie and put the kettle on after! Oh no, this was the boat of boats, old, traditional, but she'd been looked after, rubbed down each year, varnished up after, not a drop of paint on her, you could see the wood. And what was more, Ernie had a near brand new Yanmar diesel engine and all the fittings in a shed at the back of his house. Insurance job. Bought up cheap. New, the engine cost four times as much as they were now asking for the boat.

'How much is that?' Huw asked.

'Four hundred quid.'

But Ernie could get it for three.

Considering the expense of the re-tiled kitchen, the new washing machine and the dishwasher, purchased after Rian had received her aunt's legacy, it was a ridiculously small amount. On Wednesday, Huw had a coincidental chat with his Director of Studies who asked how he was settling in and said how much they enjoyed the meal and how everyone hoped they'd put down roots in the locality. Next year Huw might give his mind to the popular courses they were

going to be forced to put on to attract mature students. Would Huw
give his mind to something like, 'The Literature of the Sea'? In his
mind's eye, Huw saw Ernie in his thigh waders, guernsey and bobble
cap and he recalled a detail he had once noticed on an oil painting
of Drake's crew returning after the sack of Panama. There was
something timeless about the expression on their faces, the merest
strokes of the artist's brush which reminded him of Ernie's pinched
face, somehow always hungry, something hard and immovable
about it, a toughness that you did not see in the countryside.

On Thursday Rian rang. Instead of being looked after, she'd had
to do some looking after. Her mother'd sprained her ankle stepping
off a ladder after cleaning the guttering of the bungalow. It so
happened that Ernie had advised against Huw doing exactly the
same job on the house, and they'd got a man in to do it and Rian
remembered this. She was in a good mood. All was well. Only she'd
be away another week.

'Are you sure you're not doing too much?'

She was quite sure but she had a query of her own.

'How are you managing?'

'I'll tell you when I see you. Look after yourself.'

On Friday, Huw had begun to understand Ernie's difficulties.
With seven kids, and a small council house, one of them was the
lack of physical space. And the amount those robbers from the
Corporation charged to keep boats on the Hard all the year round
was half the price of the *Sully Maiden*. 'Bloody rent,' Ernie said. If
he could have kept it at home, he'd have bought it and had the
engine installed in a day. The same with lobster pots. There was
nothing he couldn't make himself, but again, there was the problem
with space.

They now sat outside on a bench left behind by Mr Jefferson, the
previous owner. Behind them lay the large untended garden which
was mostly rough lawn with a dilapidated shed at the back. Huw
had been meaning to do something about it, but now that the
weather had turned fine, he hadn't got around to it. At best, it only
needed a lick and a promise with a lawnmower. But he wasn't a
gardener. It did not interest him, and while for years he had been
gently chided on his lack of outdoor leisure pursuits, he had never
minded. But now an idea took shape. Why shouldn't he purchase
a share in the Sully Maiden?

'I must say I'm tempted Ernie, but what would Rian say? That's
what's uppermost in my mind.'

'Who?' Ernie blinked.

'Rian — my wife.'

'Oh, yeah, it's short for something, isn't it?'

'Arianwedd.'

'Lovely name for a boat,' Ernie said unblinking.

'If I came in shares, what would be the maximum outlay?'

'Three hundred quid flat.'

'Three hundred?' Somehow he had expected to pay half of that.

'Well, I'm giving you the engine, all the fittings, and all my time putting it together.'

Huw hadn't thought of that. He bought the boat, Ernie provided the engine.

'I don't know, Ernie. If I came into partnership, shouldn't the boat be surveyed? — like a house, I mean?'

'We're not buying the Royal Yacht! Listen, suppose we tried it for a year, if you didn't fancy it, I could always buy your share, couldn't I?'

Huw nodded, somehow hypnotised by Ernie's intent stare.

'That way, you'd have the experience. And with a nipper coming, very soon, you'd want something of your own, just for you and the Missus. By then, you'd have won your spurs, wouldn't you?'

It was the educational aspect of the proposition that decided the matter in Huw's mind. Ernie would show him the ropes. He wouldn't always want to be dependent on Ernie. He smiled. It had been a marvellous year. Why not?

'All right,' he said grinning, his normally austere, serious face suddenly made more youthful. At thirty, he looked ten years older, but now a quiff of thick black hair fell over his brow and he brushed it back, amused.

'You'll come in?'

'Yes, Ernie.'

They shook hands, Ernie's grip firm and prolonged, his eyes softening, a pale sliver of tongue licking nervously around his thin lips, more relaxed now than Huw had ever seen him. It was a funny thing to notice, but normally, when he spoke, Ernie seemed to have a peculiar caged unease, one eye warily on the move as if he expected a trap to close behind him. But now, he moved his cap jauntily to the back of his head. There was just one proviso. He had to have cash since cheques took a long time to process through his Post Office Account. Huw agreed and then events moved with bewildering rapidity. Before he had time to telephone Rian, Ernie was back the following day with a carved mahogany name board, indented letters carved and illuminated with gold leaf, spelling out Rian's

name in full, *Arianwedd*. Ernie also had a company satchel full of
large stainless steel bolts wrapped in greaseproof paper that had
somehow come his way. They would save them a small fortune, he
said with a wink. As Huw was admiring the name board, three men
whom he had never seen before arrived with a lorry, lowered the
boat on to its bogey and expertly manoeuvred it up the driveway,
completing the task manually so that very soon the *Sully Maiden* lay
neatly parked alongside the garage. By this time the light was fading
and it was not possible to make more than a cursory inspection but
Ernie saw to everything, and the men kept their distance from Huw,
although he could not help but notice that they tended to speak in
low, conspiratorial voices.

The following morning, he had to leave early but when he
returned, he could not get into his own driveway because a huge
Gas Company repair van was drawn up alongside the boat, a diesel
engine suspended on a small crane at the rear as Ernie expertly
supervised the placing of the engine inside the boat. There was
another squad of overalled men present and Huw had to reverse his
car out on to the main road and park elsewhere, returning on foot
to find Ernie waiting for him half way down the drive.

'I thought I'd get her in before you got home — surprise you!
Won't be a jiff.'

Huw had the first feelings of disquiet. He knew at once that if
Rian had been home she would not have allowed it. Ernie was
clearly at fault for not consulting him, but he did not quite know
how to articulate his reservations. And his uneasiness remained.
Ernie always seemed to be carrying parcels, or satchels of some kind.
He knew there had been a spate of prosecutions for various kinds
of misappropriation of official property locally, and in a neighbouring town, two mayors had ended up in prison for financial miscon-
duct. That was South Wales for you. And now, for the first time
since he had come south, Huw remembered his mother's warning
about the South Welsh, and while he said nothing, his face must
have reflected his unease.

'They'll be out of here in two shakes,' Ernie said with a wink.

In the end, Huw went into the house by the front door, saying
nothing further and surveying the operation from behind the curtains of an upstairs bedroom. The engine was soon fitted and the
gleaming stainless steel bolts made fast with a special spanner. All
the time, Huw wondered what he would say to Ernie, and by now,
his reservations multiplied. Although the house was detached, they
were overlooked by neighbours and it was quite unrealistic to

suppose that a van of that size could arrive unnoticed, or indeed that it was performing its proper official function. Then there were the stainless steel bolts. Huw couldn't remember exactly, but he was sure the greaseproof paper in which they were wrapped bore the insignia of some Government department. When he came to think of it, Ernie's helpfulness in so many matters seemed to be based on what he could lay his hands on. Now Huw had the feeling he was being drawn into a web of half-understood happenings on the verge of legality and it disturbed him. He was about to go down and remonstrate with Ernie when the telephone rang. It was Rian. She'd be coming home at the end of the week. At the end of the conversation, she surprised him.

'Is there something wrong?'

He hesitated.

'To tell you the truth, I've planned a little surprise for you.'

But he wouldn't tell her what it was and her excitement relieved his anxiety. When he put the telephone down, he changed into a pair of slacks and a sweater and delayed further, making himself a cup of coffee before he went outside to see Ernie. But when he actually went outside, Ernie was gone, following the van down the driveway. But there, gleaming in the afternoon sunlight was the boat, her new name visible on the transom, so that it would be the first thing Rian saw when she returned. Somehow this seemed to make all the difference and his reservations slipped to the back of his mind as he ran his hand over the varnished woodwork. There was no doubt about it, the *Arianwedd* was a substantial acquisition.

But as it happened, it was not the first sight which greeted Rian on her return home. Again, when Huw was at the Polytechnic, the mysterious team appeared and took away the boat, depositing her in the little harbour so that before he left for the long drive North, there was the briefest of conversations with Ernie.

'Don't you worry, I'll have her right as rain before you get back. Then I'll give her trials, couple of weeks we'll have you in it.'

'I'm just a little concerned about the use of your employer's equipment,' Huw said stiffly.

Now there was a moment when he thought Ernie would explode. Underneath his cap, his face coloured, tiny red veins about his nose and mouth suddenly making it seem as if his face was on fire.

'Look here, Dr Pugh-Jones,' he said in an unnaturally high pitched voice. 'I've give my life to the Gas lot, my whole life, and there's not a day when I don't save 'em thousands. So when I wants a favour, I tell you, I only gotta raise a finger and I'd get the whole of Engineering out, drop of a hat, if I wanted. They owe me, they do.'

'I just thought I'd mention it,' Huw said evasively, conscious of his inadequacy but at the same time hoping that he had given the impression that he would draw the line at any flagrant dishonesty. Ernie had previously called him Huw or Hughie, and the formal use of his name and title now was completely unexpected but perhaps indicated that he might have made the desired impression.

But Ernie still bristled. He was very red indeed and his breathing came in short pants.

'You can bring the Missus down Sunday. About twelvish. But tell her to watch where she's walking. There's a lotta rope and rings and that on the harbour wall. Very slippery.'

And with that he went off, one shoulder hunched, his face still inflamed, his small figure tense as he muttered to himself. He was clearly offended and for the first time in their acquaintanceship, he looked unhealthy, suddenly older than his fifty years.

Huw shrugged his shoulders. What had been said wanted saying but there remained the problem of telling Rian and he changed his mind about surprising her, mentioning it casually on the long drive back from her mother's home.

'A boat?'

'Only a small one.'

'When am I going to be ready to come out in a boat?' Rian pouted.

She did look huge suddenly. For some reason she had stopped wearing make-up. Her hair was lank and her high colour gave her full face the kind of irascible invalid's look that had suddenly appeared on Ernie's face when confronted in the driveway.

Huw remembered that all her family suffered from abnormally high blood pressure. He tried to sound reassuring.

'Not this year, of course, but we'll have a share of the catch,' Huw said, at the same time suddenly aware that he had discussed no such thing with Ernie, just presumed that they would share. 'Anyway, it's only a few hundred pounds, nothing to what we spent on the...'

'Very soon, we'll have two to think of,' Rian said, pouting.

He bit his lip. Did no one say anything that was not painfully obvious?

He tried to smile.

'We've called it *Arianwedd*. Your name's been carved in the most attractive gold letters.'

Rian was unimpressed.

'It's the first time you've never consulted me.'

He was about to say, 'Very well, I'll sell it!' when he realized how difficult that would be. He had no bill of sale, and the fitting of the engine somehow seemed to be such a major and final act that he wouldn't know where to begin to separate his share. One thing was clear, he would have the very greatest difficulty getting the money back from Ernie, and, not for the first time, he regretted very much that Rian hadn't been present when the matter was discussed.

'I wish you'd been home,' he said finally. 'I just wanted to surprise you. You always said I should take up some other interest.'

Rian did not reply.

On the Sunday, they walked across the promenade down to the little harbour but they did not venture on to the jetty itself because of the ropes and obstructions which Ernie had warned against. Instead, they stood high up at a vantage point and watched Ernie who had the boat alongside a pontoon down in the harbour. Unaware of their presence, he was coiling a stout white rope, laying it in hanks into the foreward locker. Everything about the *Arianwedd* now looked brand new, even the gleaming silver buckets that were stacked in a plastic container that bore the name of a well known sausage maker. That too had a bright newness about it and the engine box, a new addition, had mahogany struts over a marine ply base, all newly varnished so that the entire craft seemed to sparkle. Ernie wore his thigh boots and the old blue guernsey with a new, jaunty red stocking cap. Huw thought he looked every inch a seaman of the old school, whatever the old school was, but when they went close to the edge of the harbour wall and Ernie looked up and caught sight of them, Rian flushed and clung to Huw's arm, drawing down her skirt which flapped in the wind.

Ernie indicated that they should come on down and gesticulated towards some steps but Rian said, 'You go'.

Huw did so, carefully treading on the steps which progressively became more slippery.

'What d'you think of her?' Ernie said, extending the palm of his hand.

Huw had to admit, she looked a picture.

There followed a month of high comedy when Ernie was not to be seen, or if seen, appeared always to be hastily moving away, gesticulating from fast moving company vans, disappearing on the nearby site into inaccessible places, and not once calling at the house. Huw realized he did not even know where Ernie lived, and although he thought he recognised some of Ernie's children whom he saw hanging about the harbour, they too seemed never to stay long enough in one place to be confronted. Once, Ernie's wife, a small exhausted woman in a drab raincoat, appeared with a croco- dile of four small children, then disappeared around a corner into an old van, and drove off, their eyes pointedly avoiding him. As the weather grew finer and Rian entered her seventh month, Ernie seemed to have disappeared, and Huw was well into the summer term which involved a good deal of marking and other assignments, and the weeks slipped by without him being able to give thought to the matter. He had made one or two enquiries of various workmen who seemed to be part of a conspiracy in never seeming to know where Ernie was, but once he made a deliberate journey to the little harbour when the tide was in and just got to the jetty as Ernie put to sea with two of his children, the *Arianwedd* piled high with lobster pots, the bright red plastic traps at the mouth of each one bearing a marked resemblance to the plastic bollards used by the police to deter parking. Ernie also wore a fluorescent yellow oilskin with the letters of some organisation crudely erased from its exterior, the two children similarly dressed. Now the *Arianwedd* chugged out of the little harbour, her bow lifting to the tide, Ernie standing relaxed at the tiller, the two children already busy baiting the pots. Again, Huw thought, there was something of the last century about the sight of the little craft and from somewhere at the back of his mind came the phrase 'about their lawful occasions'. He grinned wryly. All except for the part-owner, he thought. He had a notebook and pencil with him and clambered down the the jetty where Ernie had a small dinghy tethered. He wrote a brief note asking him to call and made sure it was visible and firmly secured. Ernie was clearly going to be a long time at sea and he did not feel like waiting, but he made his way home, the little boat visible from the promenade as it made its way to a distant headland. At the back of Huw's mind was the thought that Ernie had said that he wanted to put the vessel through her trials before he was allowed aboard, but there was now a month before Rian entered the final period of her pregnancy and he was more available than previously. He would have to make a firm stand. He had found out that Ernie made an early morning visit to a site near his house and now determined to be waiting there when the workmen arrived. Accordingly, he set the alarm but when it went off, he was not quick enough and it woke Rian and the sight of her face heavy with sleep upset him.

'Where are you going?'

'I'm going to have a word with Ernie.'

'Don't you think of anything else?'

He frowned. He knew he had been preoccupied. The more he thought about it, the more he realized he was being made to look a fool, and the faces of the workmen of whom he had made enquiries indicated that they knew exactly what had happened. Well, it would have to stop.

'There's no need for you to get upset.'

'When you've thrown three hundred pounds down the drain?'

Huw selected a formal suit, washed and shaved and was about to go downstairs when there was a sharp hammering at the front door. When he opened it, Ernie stood there with a smile, as round and false, Huw thought, as the caricatures you saw of children's drawings of the Man in the Moon. But before he could say anything, Ernie put a bucket of crabs on the step. They were still alive, bubbling evilly with claws waving.

'Thank Gawd I caught you,' Ernie said. 'The pots are out. I was going to ask you to come with me tomorrow. Looking forward to it, I was. Nine sharp at the hard. Don't want to worry about wellies, I got them, and a suit of oilskins. All for you.'

As good as his word, Ernie was waiting the following morning, and from then on, despite his reservations, Huw entered a magical period of partnership and his misgivings went away. From the moment he stepped aboard, he sensed that he was entering a new phase of his life, and there followed a period of tutelage under Ernie's watchful eye which opened up a new world for him. The little craft moved like a live thing under the slightest pressure of the tiller and when your feet were braced against the bottom boards and the bow lifted to meet the oncoming waves once you rounded the pier of the little harbour, it was as if the *Arianwedd* was an extension of your own body, so compact and perfectly shaped was she. With the wind in your hair, the spray flying and the full expanse of the channel opening up before him, Huw became aware of the immensity of the horizon, a feeling no landsman ever had. He was not, he told himself, getting romantic about it — his feelings were quite genuine — but with Ernie beside him, knowing the boat and the various pulls of the tide, he had such a feeling of security that it was as if he could feel himself literally glowing, almost becoming a different person in the space of a few weeks when the sun shone and constant light breezes came and went. He also looked different, developing a handsome tan, feeling muscles he had not previously been aware of, his appetite keener, his sleep heavy and undisturbed while Rian shifted uneasily in bed beside him as he now began to keep what she tersely described as British Gas hours, often leaving the house with the dawn, and returning with fish scales embedded in the new blue guernsey he had purchased. About him, and the car, was the pervading smell of fish, an odour that was not compensated for when Ernie, unasked, produced a grubby account book, with pencilled entries relating to the sale of lobsters and crabs since the venture had begun. There were deductions for certain expenses but diesel fuel, ropes, and an endless supply of the sausage maker's plastic trays were not amongst them. Ernie, as he said with a wink, still had his connections, and at the end of the first week, he handed over forty soiled pound notes, Huw's share of the season's catch to date. Huw gulped when he received the money, and reporting it to Rian, expressed his regret for the suspicions which he had harboured.

Rian, huge and increasingly silent, made no reply. Earlier, she'd reported that the cleaning woman whom they'd engaged had confirmed her vague suspicions of Ernie's sexual predilections. He had a conviction for indecent exposure and a few years ago some mothers kept their children away from a park near his home because of him.

Huw was speechless. He couldn't believe it. In all their many conversations together, there had not been a hint of irregularity that he could detect. He was inclined to put it down to gossip, the malevolence that the idle had for the hardworking. He did not, of course, know, but he was unwilling to upset Rian in her present condition, and Rian continued to exist in a kind of withdrawn blankness that he associated with her final months of pregnancy. He thought it politic not to argue, and besides, he was somehow busier than he had ever been.

As a teacher, Ernie was a hard taskmaster. When it came to picking up the lobster pots, the instructions were precise.

'Now remember what I'm bloody telling you, always go up to the lead buoy bow-first, then slip her astern if the tide's got any poke in her. Never put the prop' to the rope, otherwise you'll have a yard and a half of sodding terylene wrapped around the shaft. It gels, it do, goes as hard as iron, and you'll have to go over the side with a saw in your teeth like bloody Action Man to get free of it. Got it?'

'Yes, Ernie.'

'Well, you bloody remember it then. Keep the prop' away and knock right down on the revs.'

'Yes, Ernie.'

Ernie had this way of talking, attributing the feminine gender to everything pertaining to the boat and Huw found it amusing. When the time came for him to take the boat out on his own, he fell into the same habit, and even picked up some of Ernie's phrases as he went through the drills he had been taught. Asked about the engine, Ernie regularly said, 'She done good!' And Huw agreed 'She was a little beaut'. Ernie had also explained the importance of listening to the marine weather forecast and frequently gave a general warning about the easterly winds which did no one any good locally. 'Easterly-beasterly' Ernie said. But when Huw suggested purchasing a portable hand-held marine radio transmitter between them, Ernie was scornful. They were expensive, corroded easily and were barely audible in an open boat at sea. 'No,' Ernie said, tapping his forehead. 'It's your loaf you gotta use.' Huw acquiesced but tuned in to the weather forecasts at home whenever he remembered, an action that caused Rian further annoyance.

Rian, in fact, had not changed her mind about Ernie, and grew increasingly irritable. It was a very trying time, and when she began to express fears for Huw's safety, they came at a moment when he was beginning to feel supremely confident. Under Ernie's sharp eye, he had mastered all the drills. Daily, he checked fuel, and took care always to sieve new fuel through a pair of Rian's tights in order that no impurity might reach the engine's injector. He had learned not to hurry, to do things slowly, to use the tide and to take his time. Whenever he came around the pier, he gave it a wide berth, following bearings and a course which Ernie had given him so that there was no danger of a collision with the youths whose speedboats sometimes went at criminal speeds. Once, he had even towed one of them into the harbour after a breakdown and he'd felt a thrill of pride, with waiting Ernie's watchful eye upon him. 'You done good,' Ernie said, and it was manna. He'd even invented a maxim: if you could teach, you could also learn, and Ernie nodded approvingly. So far, he had fulfilled all his promises, but Huw sometimes felt as if Ernie was his only admirer. Of course, it was a very bad time for Rian, but she never strolled down to the little harbour to see him come in as many of the other wives did, certainly for the yachtsmen. From the beginning, she had been against the whole idea as he well knew and he had already decided that he would dutifully have absolutely nothing to do with the boat during the last month of her pregnancy.

'I've told Ernie, June is out, and very probably July as well,' he said one night after a very successful catch. He was unaware that he spoke as if he were making a substantial concession and by now, he was quite wind burnt. He looked altogether sharper and healthier, his thick black hair had begun to curl again, and the paunch that had previously been visible had vanished. It was quite absurd, but although much taller than Ernie, he often seemed to have taken on Ernie's stance, a habit of hooking one thumb into his belt and cocking his head to one side as if straining to hear in the wind, while Rian, pale and swollen, looked much older and moved as little as possible. On some days, she hardly spoke at all and while he made it his business to do as many of the household tasks as he could, she seemed to be retreating into herself, at ease only with the cleaning woman, or one of the neighbours, also pregnant, whom she met at the clinic, a silly, scatterbrained creature in Huw's view, who also subscribed to the general local distaste for Ernie. By now, Huw discouraged any gossip whatsoever, and once, when he had come home unexpectedly, he entered the kitchen to find the three women seated having coffee, an awkward pause immediately descending on the conversation so that he had no doubt Ernie was being discussed. Then, and later, it seemed as if there was a female conspiracy to exclude him, a feeling that was reinforced by Rian's silences when they were alone. It was very odd, and upsetting too, but he put it down to her condition.

On the night before he was going to make his last trip, allowing a full month to prepare for the baby's arrival, Rian suddenly came out with a strange sentiment. He had explained that it was imperative that he brought in the lobster pots on the following morning as Ernie was going to be away, but this would be his final involvement for months. He had begun by trying to explain to her how happy he was, how much his involvement meant to him, how fit he felt, but now — for her sake — it was time to make a change.

'I know you resent it, but I've never felt fitter in my life and when you're better, I'm sure you'll enjoy it too.'

She looked across at him, her eyes unblinking, their paleness giving her an almost albino look. She suddenly seemed a total stranger, as if, he thought uneasily, she was sitting facing him across the compartment of a train and he had made an indecent suggestion.

'You'll regret it,' she said flatly.

'Regret what?'

'Tell him to go himself.'

'He can't. He has to go away. It's his work.'

Now her eyes narrowed and the hostility in them was incredible.

'I wish you'd finish with it altogether.'

'But everything's working perfectly?'

'I'm not going to say it again.'

'It's so unreasonable.'

'It's up to you.'

'I know it's up to me, but...'

'Remember, you didn't consult me at all in the first place?'

He shook his head at the absurdity of it.

'Oh, very well. But I have to go tomorrow morning. It wouldn't be fair to Ernie if I didn't. But after that... Well, if you insist, I'll stop it.'

Rian did not answer.

On that last golden morning when the sun began to cloud over, he noticed there were no other boats out. By eight o'clock, a much stiffer breeze brought bigger clouds from the East, making a stir on the water as Huw fished the first string of pots, the engine in neutral, hauling them up one after the other and laying them inboard on a string of canvas which he placed over the engine box. They were all empty save for the numerous starfish which lay inert below the untouched bait. He opened the trap and threw them out gingerly, noting that the boat was now wallowing on its side and he could hear the sound of the waves slapping against the transom. On such a day, Ernie would say, 'Getting a bit cheeky!' but it was not alarming since, once the engine was started and the bow brought back to bisect the oncoming waves, the unpleasant wallowing motion ceased.

Placing the pots on the forward locker, Huw began to move closer inshore towards the second string whose marker buoy was showing beside a rocky ledge where white water was clearly visible as the wind and tide built up the waves. When he put the stern to the tide, the speed of the boast increased and he felt himself to be rushing forward, the bow sinking further into the troughs as the wind seemed to grow stronger very quickly. The expanse of white on the water around the rocks grew larger and although he was mindful of Ernie's instruction always to approach the rope bow first, it did not seem so sensible with the wind and tide pushing him forward faster than he intended. One wave rose behind him and the *Arianwedd* surfed forward so that for a few seconds, she seemed to stand up on the crest, then plunged downwards and onwards almost out of control. He eased the throttle back but it seemed to make no difference. He had half a mind to abandon the pots but he could see Ernie's scornful face and he knew that the pots closest inshore were the most likely to be lost if he did not retrieve them.

He was still being swept forward and the closer he went, the louder was the noise of the wind and the more menacing the turbulence in front. He actually felt his hand trembling on the tiller as a third wave picked up the boat and continued with the headlong sweep forward. Then, seemingly without any conscious decision on his part, his hand began to move the tiller and he had the feeling of watching as a spectator as his hand began to act independently, exerting increasing pressure, then panicking until the *Arianwedd* spun around in her own length, great gouts of water shooting up above the gunwales, causing the iron framed lobster pots on the locker to fall off like so much hardware. Now the propeller, suddenly thrust towards the lobster buoy, immediately became caught in the loose rope, in a second, winding it around the shaft and bringing the propeller blades to an abrupt halt. The boat gave a final shudder and stopped like a log, as if lassoed. And then lay silent, dead, and motionless. But in an instant, the stern became a sounding board as further gouts of water smacked against it, sending spray flying into the boat and very soon he heard the evil swishing of water in the bilges.

He felt like crying aloud in protest. But he had done everything he was told not to do and now he was caught. He sat down abruptly like an out-patient told to wait and for a long time, he did not move. First he was sick, then angry. He put his head between his knees in an attempt to relieve his nausea. It did not work. Retching, he continued to look at the bottom boards, avoiding the sea. An insane rage began. If only Rian hadn't insisted on going to her mother's, he would never have even contemplated buying a share in the boat without a bill of sale. There was nothing seriously wrong with her mother. Now as the spray continued to fall into the boat and the vomit washed away below him, he began to see her mother's face, bloated and puffy as she opened a box of Turkish Delight, spooning the glistening cubes with a wooden fork. He retched again, then looked up. The sky had become an ominous grey. A seagull came in a low sweeping dive over the boat, then rose again, its eyes beady, beak cruel, shrieking as it left him. Then he heard more water swishing in the bilges. He would have to do something. There were distress flares in the forward locker. He went forward, crouching in a panic, fumbling with the locker door. The bright coloured cardboard cylinders lay in a plastic pouch, and he read the instructions with shaking hands, drawing out the largest. He was required to unscrew a plastic cap and advised to shield his hand with a cloth. But there was not a cloth to hand. Holding the flare away from himself, he twisted manfully. Nothing happened. He drew out another flare, aware of the dampness inside the pouch. Again, no result. He tried them all to no effect. Soggy! Then he saw an unmistakable sign stamped on the side of the last cylinder. USE BY 1984. All out of date, the one item Ernie couldn't purloin.

Very soon he lay face down on the bottom boards. He wanted to blot out the sea and sky. Ernie Smalls, he thought; Ernie Smalls — widow-maker. Strangely, he felt more the victim of some unspecified financial disaster yet to come, than a marine casualty. He couldn't believe he'd been so thoughtless — to put himself at such risk, to be so hoodwinked. And it was not just his life, it was his character that was compromised. He should have known that the irregularities of the past month must offer evidence for countless prosecutions for the misappropriation of goodness knows what official property. He should have drawn the line at the outset. His mother was right. These people down in the South were very different, shifty, evasive, sly. They corrupted you with their nods and winks and smiles.

And now he would never see his own child.

Preoccupied, he did not notice that the wind had eased, and laying there in a prone position, he did not realize that from the beach, the boat gave every sign of being abandoned. Had he done so, he might have reasoned further. Bobbing there, close in shore, it represented not so much a casualty, as every local longshoreman's dream — something for nothing! Indeed, two surfers, strolling along a distant beach spotted it and launched a canoe to investigate. One of them, a ginger larrikin with a broken tooth and a wide slash of a mouth, put his head over the gunnel and looked down at him with evident disappointment, his thick, fleshy lips falling open.

Huw sat up shamefacedly. Fortunately, they both wore wet suits. He pointed out the trouble. The ginger youth took a knife and released the offending rope easily. Slowly it dawned on him that they did not regard him as being in any danger. The tide was making, the wind had dropped. Even if the engine had failed, he would have been washed up on the beach. As it was, the engine started at once, and he drew away immediately with a muttered 'thank you'. He'd be home at his usual time and would say nothing to Rian in view of her condition. He was finished with the sea, but not with Ernie Smalls.

Ernie came round the next day. He'd heard, of course, promptly informed by the mysterious local grapevine. And Ernie was on the attack. When he saw a weakness, he went for it.

'D'you think I haven't had people keeping their eyes on you every day? Off out with the wind going East? You want your head read!

And another thing, I been down the boat, all the flares gone, three strings of pots lost and not a penny to show for it. The one day I left you on your own.'

They stood at the back door. It was early and Huw had gone to answer it in a dressing gown. Rian stayed in the kitchen. Although surprised by Ernie's attack, Huw was not unprepared and he chose his words with care, finding a curious formality of speech that was somehow a pointer to the future. It might have been a new Director of Studies talking.

'I have one or two things to tell you, Ernie. From the moment I was inveigled into this mistaken enterprise, one irregularity has followed another...'

Ernie's lips seemed to be trying to close on the long words, framing them like a child struggling with a primer.

'In the first place, d'you think I haven't noticed all those parcels?'

'Parcels?'

Huw itemised them, the stainless steel bolts, the new white rope, the buckets, oilskins, then the illegal use of the Company's van, the fuel, finally the absence of receipts, the crucial bill of sale. There was also an ultimatum. Huw was getting out. His share was to be repaid at monthly intervals over a period of twelve months. And he did not want to see Ernie personally. It would be done through the bank. Otherwise, he would inform Ernie's employer and he had no doubt Ernie would comply. Before Ernie could protest, Huw moved closer and looked directly into his eyes.

'I understand you have a particularly unsavoury reputation locally,' he said, mindful of Rian listening inside the house.

Ernie's mouth opened and closed. Once again the red veins about his cheeks became inflamed and the caged look returned. But this time his breath became audible. With a trembling hand, he clutched his chest, and his face now conveyed a hatred that had clearly never been far away. But Huw went on coldly.

'And as for the flares, no one in his right mind would put to sea with emergency equipment that is quite so out of date.'

In the end, Ernie said nothing, just turned away, still clutching his chest. Huw breathed more easily. He felt he had avenged his moment of humiliation, the horror of laying in that prone position along the bottom boards. When he shut the door and went into the kitchen, it was as if he was returning to family life and his proper place in it.

It was Rian who noticed the column inch in the evening paper several days later.

DEATH OF LOCAL BOATMAN.

Ernie had suffered a coronary shortly after leaving the house, and died several days later.

Huw flushed. He remembered Ernie's hand clutching at his chest, the puffiness of his cheeks, the sudden difficulty in breathing. Perhaps he had been too severe. But then nothing he'd said was untrue.

'You can't possibly blame yourself?' Rian said.

He considered it, then shook his head. If anything, he felt an enormous sense of relief. He remembered the hatred in Ernie's eyes. They were the eyes of a man who, in the last resort, would stop at nothing, he finally concluded. Very soon, they discussed whether or not he should attend the funeral. The boat would have to be sold and they would have to negotiate with someone. But he thought not. And if anyone said anything, there was always Rian's pregnancy. The people who mattered would understand. He stretched his hand across and Rian took it, holding it gently on her lap. There was an expression of such contentment on her face, anyone might have thought he had just been returned to her, courtesy of E. Smalls.

Cherry Trees

Do me a favour? Don't sound so married!'
'I have to go, Moira. Really!'
'Yes!-Yes! Be careful with your collar — it collects hairs! — and
you had a much thicker knot in that tie last night.'
'Next Monday?'
'No.'
'Tuesday then? I'm in the studio the rest of the week.'
'No.'
'I can't make the weekend.'
'I know. They all go home weekends.'
'*They*'?'
'You don't think you're the first, do you?'
'I can finish early on Tuesday?'
'No.'
'Very early. We could go...'
'No.'
'Oh, it's like that, is it?'
'Yes.'
'Oh, well then, I'll give you a ring.'
'Please don't.'
'What's the matter? Wasn't it...'
'No, it wasn't.'
'I'm sorry.'
'Just go, that's all. Out of here. First the door, then the stairs,
down the hall...'
'Well, if you feel...'
'Yes, I do. That's how I feel.'
'But...'
'No... No!-No!'
'Was it something that I...'
'You speak Welsh, don't you? What's the Welsh for 'Piss off!''
It was the fact that he was a television announcer that had turned
him on for Moira. Say what you like, it was very kinky to be sitting
in front of the telly and looking at that face and hands and know-
ing... *knowing*! All that had been there from the beginning.
'I don't think you've met Moira? Moira, have you...'
'No, I haven't seen you on the box Goldilocks, never-ever!'
Moira wanted to say, but she said; 'How d'you do?' and watched

her p's and q's for an hour.

To be honest, at first, he didn't seem anything at all that special
except for his clothes, and the fact that when you were with him,
everybody was looking at him and you were aware of it everywhere
you went, the telly fame despite the fact that he only read the Welsh
news on the local station which they called the Telly Welly.

But the clothes were something, so impressive that Moira listed
them, one, the teddy bear overcoat with the velvet collar that
showed his tight little bum through the slit at the back; two, the
sports jacket with the most incredible soft blue wool with some kind
of special stone thread speckled in the weave, and then the button-
down collar of his monogrammed shirt, the heather-coloured tie
and the polished brogue shoes which gave him an altogether different air from the kind of people Moira met. He was so groomed, she
thought, with a suave elegance that knotted her insides and made
her want to ruffle his short wavy fair hair. When you put your hand
on that beautiful jacket, it was like touching a tapestry, and while
he must live in the dry cleaners and it was a laugh watching him
taking care where he put his elbows when he sat at a table, you had
to admit that the impression he gave was of another altogether
desirable and unflurried world. Later when he took her for a meal
in the restaurant down the road where, he said, all the Telly Welly
top brass went, he made such a business with the serviette, tucking
it in like a bib before he ate his soup, that she should have realized
then. In fact, it had taken ages to realize that he was terrified of the
slightest stain, and that should have told her all, but they weren't
alone then, there was the other one who was with him when they'd
clicked, and, of course, Eileen Feeley who had to say what Moira
always dreaded letting new men know.

'You'd better be careful with Moira,' Eileen said, rubbing her
contact lenses once they'd ordered.

'I hope I haven't been anything but careful to date!' he'd said,
preening himself with a flash of teeth, two gold crowns and a cap
— and the almost perfect lips that had never stopped smiling at her.

'Moira might nab you!'

'I wouldn't mind being nabbed by Moira at all.'

'Moira's in the Force.'

'The Force?'

Didn't they speak bloody English up at the Telly Welly?

'I'm a policewoman,' Moira said calmly but she could have
clawed Eileen Feeley who was supposed to be fixed up with the
other one, the fat one with the beard who was much more drunk

but kept recovering and jabbering in Welsh at intervals. He seemed to be more important, a producer, she thought somebody'd said, but her first thought that he was more Eileen's dap with the beard and the belly on him plus the pocketful of credit cards, including the red privilege card for the local taxi firm which had brought them.

'How intriguing!' Goldilocks said.
'But I don't like to talk about it,' Moira said, giving Eileen a look.
'Of course.'
'I'm very glad we didn't drive!' the Welshy one said through his beard.
'I wouldn't have let you.'
'Wise girl,' Goldilocks said.

That was for starters but very soon she'd felt his leg against hers under the table, all the time keeping up an insistent pressure and she knew that it was up to her then. As he said later, 'The woman always decides!' which was a very intelligent thing to say really but at the time she was all confusion and didn't quite know what to do until the meal ended. Eileen was stuck with Hanging Belly and Hanging Belly had suggested they go back to his house which was quite near.

'Oh, I think we'd better put it off tonight,' Goldilocks said.
'It is rather late.'

Then there was a bit of jabber-jabber in Welsh which might have meant, 'Wife's away with the children. There's nobody in. I know I'm pissed but a lot of people have seen us come here and if I order a taxi home in a loud voice, it'll make it look innocent, d'you know what I mean?'

Or so Moira imagined. Both she and Eileen, being Cardiff girls, did not understand Welsh and right until the end of the meal Moira didn't know what had been decided. First, they ate, and how they ate! Moira didn't understand French either, but as soon as he found out, he led her through the menu, his French spot on. They had leek, onion, and potato soup garnished with chives and a swirl of cream, then, resisting her first inclination to settle for a steak to avoid embarrassment and get it over with, she got herself talked into veal and there was a long argument with Hanging Belly as to whether it was a French or Italian dish, and then they had apple and cinnamon crêpes, flambéd at the table with the maximum bullshit. Eileen, who worked as a typist in Telly-Welly's sports department had fixed it up, an invitation to a public relations party given by some firm who were selling sports equipment and Moira had gone because she'd been into karate. At first, they'd thought half the Welsh rugby team would be there, but in the end as people drifted off, they'd found themselves with this pair who were obviously on the town. It had been quite unexpected and as it was, Moira was already getting used to going home alone, reconciled even to the thought of the empty flat and the silence at the end of the day, and worst of all, to sitting alone looking at a book whose pages she seldom turned. She'd now abandoned everything she'd ever done, she thought gloomily, swimming, life-saving, karate, and lately, married men. There were even times when she felt she was drifting in a way that she would not have thought possible five years ago, and now and again, a phrase of her mother's returned to haunt her: 'You should find something to take yourself out of yourself, my girl.'

Him, she'd thought that night. She really had.

When the meal was finished, the two couples had parted once they got outside on the pavement, Moira leading him away. They'd exchanged but two sentences.

'Do you live near?'

'We can walk.'

And that was it. He took her arm and as they moved at once around the corner, he tucked her arm into his, holding it firmly with his elbow and it was almost a married feeling as they walked up the street, the only sound their measured footsteps as they walked. There was a whole passage of complete contentment then and when they neared the trees and the park at the end of the street, she could just hear the wind ruffling the branches of the cherry trees which were a sight in the spring. She knew because she could see them from the flat. Thinking of them then, and listening to their regular footfalls in the deserted street, Moira felt almost as if she were in a film walking endlessly towards the trees. It was a very special feeling.

Then he spoke softly.

'If it's far, I can get my car.'

'Better not.'

'I haven't had that much to drink.'

'Enough.'

'You're very firm on that?'

She gave her real self away then.

'I don't want anybody to do anything they'll regret in the morning,' she said, feeling very lofty and cool.

He squeezed her arm as if the necessary caution had immediately put everything on a different and more substantial footing.

And so it remained like a film. Somehow, walking down that

empty street seemed to her like the most romantic thing in the world and she was very conscious of his tailored good looks, the regular, open features, the set of his short wavy hair, the soaped cleanliness of him. She liked uniformed men and it was as if he wore another uniform altogether and the street now was an avenue of escape, just the two of them walking towards the trees. It was very silly, but she felt it, all of it.

Her flat was on the second floor of an old Victorian house. He'd released her arm to allow her to find her key, and in the doorway, he made an effort not to be seen noticing her height.

'Yes, I am tall,' she said smiling.

Inside, she was very glad there was no waiting. It would have spoiled the walk. The knowledge that he couldn't wait either was as welcome, as welcome, as welcome as ... *'Oh, the flowers of spring!'* she said to herself. She never felt any need to be that serious about sex.

Afterwards, laying there, her uniform hanging up unremarked upon at the front of the wardrobe, she felt warm, protective, matter-of-fact even.

'You've been saving that up?' she said.

'Yes,' his grin was boyish.

It's going to be different, she thought. This time it's going to be different. Yes, it is. She wanted to say, 'Now, when I see you on the Box...' but she didn't. It was the same as her uniform. Their public selves were separate. They might have made a pact there and then.

But he couldn't keep his eyes off her.

'You've such lovely legs, d'you mind my mentioning that? Chauvinist, d'you think? What d'you think?'

'You're not so bad yourself.'

He even caressed her afterwards, running his hands softly over her thighs.

'You exercise a lot?'

'I used to.'

'I like long legs more than anything.'

She was very pleased. So did she!

Cherry trees! Cherry trees! Hi ho, cherry trees!

And he didn't want to go either! Later she'd slipped on a robe and walked round, provoking him very slowly.

'Oh, Moira!'

'Oh, you've remembered my name?'

'Yes!'

'Sh...' she said. 'Sh...'

Cherry trees! Cherry trees! Why did everything ever have to end?
Eventually, there had to be a speech.

'I suppose you're beginning to wonder? Well, you must know I'm
married, I mean, I have to be very careful now, don't I? In what I
say?'

'You don't have to say anything.'

'Not tonight, but later, I must.'

'Oh, later,' she said. Speech had broken the mood.

'Well, I hope so?' he looked at her anxiously.

He was the first man she enjoyed watching as he dressed. Somehow men always looked ridiculous as they stepped into their under-
pants. She had long had the habit of giving certain men private
nicknames that she never revealed to anyone else. Hence Goldilocks
and Hanging Belly. She began with nicknames, changed to real
names, then when the affairs faded, took up the nicknames again
and she was recently getting over the Canton Beast, a police
sergeant who took his name from the district he patrolled and she
couldn't help comparing the Canton Beast with Goldilocks. The
Beast wore boxer shorts which were so big, you could have fitted
them on a small rhino and he even balanced on his thick legs like a
zoo animal squatting at stool, but Goldilocks wore Y-fronts and was
as slim and neat as a dancer. Even when he sat down to pull on his
socks, he did so in an almost feminine way, leaning backwards
instead of forwards and drawing up his socks like stockings. It was
the same with his shirt, the way he knotted his tie, checked his collar.
He was a neat and fastidious man, and suddenly she wanted him
waiting for her outside the central police station, parking illegally
with his elbow on the edge of the window, the sun shining in his
hair, the little smile playing about his lips, the rueful look as when
she'd said playfully, 'You've been saving that up!'

But now he was suddenly solemn.

'I want to see you again, but it's a little difficult.'

She nodded.

He put his hand upon her shoulder.

'There'll be things to talk about. You'll have questions, but now,
all I want to say is, thank you.'

And that was that. No date, no telephone number, nothing.

She had a rest day the following day and Eileen did not go to work.
She rang and said she wanted to come over but Moira said no, she
was going to do her hair and have an early night.

'How did you get on?'

'Slob!'

'No good?'
'Out of his mind.'
'Did you go in the house?'
'I'll tell you when I see you. Are you sure you...'
'No, I'm going to have an early night.'

Eileen had one development to report. Hanging Belly had rung to say that there was a Telly-Welly production team going to California and then on to Patagonia for the umpteenth time to make some Welsh language programme and he might be able to swing it if she wanted to go.

'Is he serious?'

Eileen wasn't sure.

'Wouldn't they all be talking in Welsh all the time?'

'Not in California.'

'I'll keep my fingers crossed,' Moira said.

Well, at least HB had telephoned, Moira thought. She wished Eileen luck, then flopped suddenly. Moira used her rest days for cleaning the flat and doing her washing but all day she knew she was only waiting for the evening News. It was quite extraordinary because she was not normally the stage-struck sort. She knew enough about celebrities, both from her first hand experience and from what she picked up in her job. On her plain clothes detective attachment, she'd learnt enough to make her unshockable and there was a never-ending flow of information in the C.I.D. room about all kinds of public personalities that never saw the light of day. Nothing was as it seemed. And that was another trouble, she thought, her recent view of things. It was a dirty world and she'd been given a view of it from the inside and it was about time she switched on. Everybody knew you weren't encouraged to make friendships outside the Force and while it was not exactly written into the papers you signed, she'd already had enough of people like the Canton Beast to want to spread her wings. She'd leave the police eventually, she'd no doubt, she didn't really have a future in it and didn't want one either. She wasn't keen enough any more and you saw such terrible things. This was why, perhaps, she'd got to spending more and more time on her own, trying to read, day dreaming, trying to think what was the matter with her, why she wasn't the knock-out the Canton Beast said she was.

Remembering him — and his boxer shorts — she thought of the previous night as a kind of Hollywood idyll which made the absence of a telephone call even worse. Cherry trees, she thought again ruefully. Perhaps he'd made a mistake? Like she had with the Beast.

But what she'd liked about him was that he made her laugh. He wasn't a beast at all except in appearance but he had led her up the garden path all last year, talking about the divorce that would never come from the asthmatic wife he would never leave. Underneath his huge frame and those bonny red cheeks and voluminous moustaches and quite surprising soft brown eyes, there was a small, grubby, careful, streetwise urchin who wanted to have his cake and eat it. Coming across him, or rather the back of him, quite unexpectedly in the canteen one day she had heard him say, 'She's alright, Moira, doesn't make a fuss after, and you can take her anywhere!' Men, Moira thought, oh dear Lord, men! And they never gave up, for the Beast telephoned every week and was still hopeful.

When the News in Welsh came on, she'd all her chores finished and sat watching the screen with the volume turned down because she knew she wouldn't understand a single word. But she sat eagerly, her hands folded across her lap in complete silence as she watched him begin to read, his lips moving soundlessly, a dimple showing, a slight lift of an eyebrow, a small pursing of the lips, then almost a grin, and now a long serious frown that went on and on and then the face lightened again, his features adapting to whatever he was reading. The sight of him, the light grey suit, the maroon rugby club tie, his wrists with their fine downlike covering of hair showing beneath his shirt cuff made her catch her breath... 'Cherry trees! Cherry trees! Cherry trees!'

Oh, what was the matter with her? She was twenty-nine years of age!

It seemed a long News. She moved closer noting the hand-stitching on the lapels of his jacket, the wafer thin watch that she'd noticed on the previous evening. She was pleased to see he didn't wear a ring. Now she had her face so close to the box she was in danger of not being able to focus, so finally she stood up and moved back and watched him say 'Goodnight' with that rueful little smile again. She was glad there weren't two newscasters as there were on the networks, usually a man and a woman, as then he would have turned and smiled at the woman like they did when they very often said something that no one ever heard. She'd had some thoughts about that, about what actually was said, and now, if it had been like that, she was in such a mood that she'd have imagined some derogatory remark about herself, she was sure.

It was as if her mind was back in the C.I.D. room again, her particular nightmare. End of News, then the fade music, then the obligatory exchange of smiles and the unheard words: 'Did you get a bit last night? Copped lucky myself!'

She stiffened.

Oh, God, it had to stop! Her mind was on the skids, tainted by that bloody C.I.D. room. He wouldn't ring. Not him. It was what she'd thought it was, everything she feared, another one night stand. Of course, he wouldn't ring.

Then he did.

'Yes? Oh, hello, I didn't expect to hear from you? Well, not quite so soon. I didn't know you had my number? Oh, of course, you did? Did you really? Well, I didn't notice that. I must say. I don't normally drink as much as that but today was a rest day. Yes, we have rest days. Well, all the things normal people do, washing, cleaning, I was about to wash my hair. No, you're not interrupting... I was thinking about washing my hair but I hadn't actually taken steps. What? 'Proceedings?' No, we don't proceed any more and I certainly don't on my day off. No, it's just that, well, I expect you find it the same, people asking you about make-up, things like that. Yes, very boring. No, I didn't say *you* were boring. I meant, people have these things they always say and you have to get it over with, and then leave it alone. All right, it's left alone. Actually, it's very nice to hear you and I *am* glad you rang. Oh, and I watched you on the News too. I didn't understand it but I'm sure you made it a very nice News the way you read it! Yes! No, you said you would and you did. Oh, the weekend? The weekend... *This* weekend? Just a minute, I'll have to look in my diary. I'm not sure. Hold on a minute...'

But she did not move. *Count ten! Turn a page! Any page! The phonebook will do, just turn a page. Right! Ten counted, pages turned.*

It looks pretty clear at the moment. What do you have in mind?'

When she put the telephone down, she wondered if she'd laid it too much on the line. Well, if she had, she didn't care. 'Yes, David,' she'd said. Dafydd, the Welsh version of his name, was too much for her in the daylight. 'Yes, David. No, David. I'll be ready David.' Goldilocks was dead. The only problem now was keeping it from Eileen.

'What d'you mean I haven't been answering? I haven't moved all evening. When? What time? Oh, that was my mother, she goes on for ages. No, I can't tomorrow or Thursday and I'm on all this weekend. No, it'll have to be next week. I'll give you a bell, or maybe you'll be in California!'

Immediately, and in the days that followed there were things to be done, hair, manicure, a sauna, then hair again. There was also a

store detective she knew who let her use her own discount card for
occasional purchases. She must have something new. A country
hotel near Chepstow, he'd said. The room was already booked
before he'd even asked her. Somehow she knew that. Cheeky
bugger! Now she didn't have a second to herself and it took a week's
organising.

They went first for lunch in another gourmet place, tucking
themselves away in a country inn at a secluded table where there
were not too many people and she could see him looking countrified
in a roll neck cashmere sweater and a suede jacket that was so soft
you wanted to stroke it. And not a mark on that either! It was as if
she had been whisked away with the minimum of fuss and deposited
inside a delicious bubble. You wouldn't think that her uniform lay
gathering dust on the floor as she'd left it where it fell and there
were half a dozen uniformed men with sore telephone ears from the
pressure she'd put upon them, rearranging duty rosters.

'Well, cheers!' he said, all smiles.

'Cheers!'

'And thank you again.'

'You keep thanking me. I do what I want to do.'

'Thank you for wanting to.'

Let's get down to it, she thought; let's have the spiel. But it wasn't
too bad as it happened, his story, there were job problems, wife
problems, even body problems, a spot of cartilage trouble in his left
knee that interfered with his squash. He was also older than he
looked, and his wife, far from being a complaining lily, was a
veterinary surgeon, high up in some government department, their
marriage one of those struggles where each partner was ruthlessly
insistent on succeeding in a career, their movement almost a traffic
problem as they passed in the corridors of a house that was now
worth forty times what they'd paid for it. (Why did he have to tell
her that?) The way he described things, it was a status war, cold
clipped sentences, precise little notes on official notepaper, their
biggest rows over such matters as which car was going to be serviced
or taxed and when, or what afternoon they could jointly arrange to
meet their accountants. You got the impression that if there was
any fucking, it was by appointment, clean towels at hand, His and
Hers, and now Moira understood his choking little gasps at the high
moment. But the more he told her, the better she felt. She could
not have stood another crippled asthmatic in the background. What
she enjoyed most was the insider shop talk. He spoke of broadcasting as if she understood it as well as he did, at least as it affected

him. There was what the public saw, and what went on behind the scenes. (Like the Police, she thought.) He wanted to do more producing. He had been in the public eye long enough. He had a great interest in sport.

'Sport?' she said. Somehow she didn't associate him with any particular sport.

'I had a Welsh cap,' he said. 'But only hockey, alas. You swim, I should imagine?'

'Why should you imagine?'

'Thigh muscles,' his eyes were sparkling.

They'd got through the stuffed crab, the garnished sole, and were on the ginger syllabubs before he told her. There was a small snag about the weekend.

'I should have told you on the 'phone.'

'Told me?'

'But if I had, you wouldn't have come.'

'What?'

While he was talking, she'd kept comparing his expressions to those she'd seen throughout the week as he'd read the News and she'd categorised them in her mind even though she did not understand what he was saying. There was his warm *Crippled Child Walks Again* smile, with full mouth and crinkly eyes, the eyes creasing just as they had when he'd squeezed her arm in that married way; there was the *Colliery Closure* frown, the *Minister of State Opens Garden Centre — How very interesting!* po-face, his eyelids lowered and the slightest catch at the back of the throat as there was now when he looked at her.

'You're not going to like it.'

'Tell me!' Was his wife coming or something, or the children in little vet's costumes, whatever little vets wore?

'I told you this was a long-standing engagement!'

'What was?'

'This weekend. I couldn't have got away otherwise. I'm going to have to slip away for a couple of hours tonight.'

'A couple of hours?'

It was a long News. She was not the lead story, he was. It seemed he had been invited to speak at the local rugby club, some kind of annual dinner. They had booked the hotel room. He would have to trot off and be famous for a couple of hours. But it was all right, he wouldn't stay. He would leave as soon as he decently could. There would be no embarrassments.

Oh God, she thought, everything's slipping again, it's all on the slide. She'd listened so carefully, even refraining from putting her special oar in when he said that both he and his wife were so busy they never got around to the simplest things, like taxing the cars in time which normally would have prompted her to make one of her sensible, safety-first remarks. She'd just sat there and listened, looking — she was sure — as elegant as he did for she'd made some expensive purchases at the store, exhausting her friend's discount card. She'd chosen a thick cherry coloured taupé trouser suit with a tight-fitting and rather snazzy jacket and a black sweater whose sheen was sufficiently dazzling to make it suitable for evening wear. She kept seeing herself lounging elegantly in lingerie in languid mood. But now she felt as if her feelings, like petals, had been driven from her by one savage blow.

Then, manfully, she tried to see it from his point of view. What else could he do? If the room was booked, it was booked. And if he had mentioned the function on the telephone, she probably wouldn't have come. He was quite right. What upset her most though, was the conversation she now imagined, him ringing up some rugby club secretary to check that it would be all right, that the club would stand the bill. Somehow, he was such a careful man, she knew he'd done just that.

Now he looked at her anxiously and she thought: I should leave now. If there's to be any chance, I should leave now. That's what the vet would have done, she thought, and she had an image of a short determined woman in sensible heels walking firmly down a corridor, mouth like a purse, her white coat flapping. Yes, she should definitely leave now.

But he looked at her anxiously, his face concerned, his eyes grave and there was just the slightest tremor of his hand as it rested on the tablecloth. He was so slim, neat, precise and sensitive-looking, she thought, but for some reason her mind wandered to the face of the Canton Beast who had but two expressions, triumph and perplexity, 'You're nicked!' and 'Well, I'm buggered!' Yet there was a kind of overpowering honesty and warmth of feeling about that huge man that made him incapable of any real dishonesty save that necessary for the protection of a drab, tearful, and sick woman who couldn't cope. There was no doubt in her mind, Beastie was her kind of man for all his faults. This one was from another stable.

'Well?'

'Well, what?' She was aware she was sulking, her full face heavy.

'I was hoping you'd forgive me, that you'd understand?'

'Oh, were you?'

'Yes, it's not an easy situation.'

She hated people who used words like that. The trouble was, as Eileen once said, these telly people never dealt with anything fundamental like being broke, or hungry. They lived such protected lives and most of them did nothing but whine about things that never mattered to anyone else. They were also secluded, hiding in groups, seldom venturing out except to meet their own kind.

She should leave now, she thought again. Now Goldilocks looked forty-plus and he seemed to be ageing in front of her as he looked fixedly across the table. He hadn't said a word about her clothes. He hadn't even touched her, not a movement of the hand, not a kiss, oh no, not in public. She'd also bought new shoes, refusing to compromise with the heels. In a strange way, even though they were now both seated, he still looked so much shorter than her, shrunken somehow.

I'll give him the elbow, she thought. She could see herself saying it to Eileen. 'I gave him the elbow. It was only the telly bit that attracted me really. I just wanted to see his face!' *Under me*, she thought. That would knock Eileen out!

'Darling...' he said.

Oh Christ, now he was in his own cherry trees!

But now her own powers of observation led her to quite the wrong conclusion. After an almost interminable silence when he kept looking fixedly at her — as at a camera, she thought — he suddenly lowered his eyes and started going through his pockets one by one, desperately searching for something, clearly flapping and in a panic that completely surprised her. For a moment he offered no explanation. It couldn't be that he hadn't brought any money, she thought. Surely sitting there in front of half an antelope — that beautiful jacket — he wasn't going to land her with the bill?

Now it was her turn.

'What's the matter?'

'It's just occurred to me. I was looking forward to seeing you so much, I think I've forgotten my speech.'

'Your speech?'

'I have to make an after-dinner speech. It's all written out on cards. Oh, it's probably in my case. I just got into a panic.'

But he looked so worried, everything changed again. So she didn't leave as she should have done. The bland expression on his face had changed for a moment into a kind of abject terror as if he had at last revealed something of his real self. It was quite extraordinary. And she was suddenly curious.

Then they were off in a kind of showbiz whirl, his hand on her arm, the bill signed (not paid), the car creaming through country lanes, his face taut, shaking his head when she suggested she look in his suitcase, then a bit of advanced driving, precise rear observation and due consideration for other road users, and then they were there at the hotel and now it was the full V.I.P. treatment; Manager out to greet them, the receptionist head down and not a blink while he signed them in, even a hotel porter-cum-handyman appearing to take their bags. It was the porter who caught her attention. He was an old man in faded dungarees, his wheezing so pronounced as he struggled with the bags that she grew alarmed for him. But then he threw open the door and almost collapsed inside the room which was at the back of the hotel and she was immediately confronted by a huge four-poster bed, its curtains and draperies pulled aside so that it literally appeared to be gaping and she smothered a laugh. The old man took himself off tipless with a grumpy nod, and the moment the door closed, her recently acquired and falsely declared husband threw his suitcase on the floor and seemed to be having a nervous breakdown as he opened it in a frenzy.

'David, what's the matter?'

But he did not answer. Within seconds, he had rifled the pockets of the suitcase, hastily creating a mess of expensive possessions on the floor, pyjamas in a satin case, initials embroidered on the flap, evening shirt in cellophane, then his dinner jacket, the cleaner's label still attached. He looked like a disappointed little boy kneeling there with unwanted presents. But he found three postcards in one of the suitcase pockets and stayed kneeling on the floor looking at them disconsolately.

She leant over and saw that there were numbered paragraphs typed upon the cards in block capital letters. But there were only three. Half the speech, it seemed, was missing.

'I must have left them in Fishguard,' he said dolefully. 'I had a speaking engagement there last week.'

Big deal, she thought. She still didn't fully understand.

'Can't you make it up?'

'No, everything's in sequence, all worked out. I have it written for me.'

'Surely, you can remember bits of it?'

He shook his head.

'I'm terrible without a script.'

The misery on his face was real. For a moment, he did know what to do and would not speak. It must be serious, she thought. She was also at a complete loss. Still not speaking, they sat around looking very married like a stranded couple who had lost their passports. She lit the gas fire while he sat at a table and began to pencil some notes. He remained in a state of deep dismay, his face drawn, now and again making curious exhausted grunts like an athlete who had overstretched himself. Finally, he looked up to where she was sitting on the settee before the fireplace, her long slim legs crossed, her small breasts pert against the tightly drawn sweater, the frame of the four poster looming behind her. Although it was a large room, the huge bed dominated it, as indeed, she did the settee. She could never have looked more idle or glamorous, she thought. She stretched herself luxuriously.

But clearing his throat nervously, he said: 'Moira?'

'Yes.'

'Moira, you don't know any dirty jokes, do you?'

'Jokes?'

'For this kind of function, I mean?'

She stared at him. It said much for her good nature that she even considered his request but she immediately thought of the Canton Beast who was a joyous attender at functions, liked nothing more than to see flunkeys wheeling in a baron of beef, bagpiper in attendance, and was himself a popular organizer of those private police parties which the public knew nothing about. She'd attended several in his company, including a retirement party for which he'd organised a stripper. Making a presentation on that occasion, he'd said, 'I give you Inspector Idris Jenkins, the only man who ever went for a vasectomy and had to pay fifty pounds for a search fee!' Inspector Jenkins and everyone else had laughed themselves silly. Perhaps it would do?

Stony-faced, Moira repeated it.

'That's not bad. I haven't heard that before. Have you got any more?'

But she had not. And she had nothing further to give, she decided, not for a while at least. When he left, scrubbed and lotioned and clutching his reworked cards, she lay on the bed and must have fallen asleep because when she awoke the heat in the room was so overpowering she had to open the windows. Now she heard the sound of applause coming from the dining room downstairs and later a noisy scraping of chairs when the Gents lavatories must have been put under pressure because a number of burly dinner-jacketed men came out into the old stable yard below her and were soon seen urinating against a wall. In full view of the opened rear gate and the public highway, she noted automatically.

Pissing men, she thought. She'd half a mind to get out her warrant card, go down and book them, but of course, she didn't.

When at last, he came back, flushed and full of himself — her joke had gone down exceptionally well, he told her — she was already in bed, but now she stared at him as at a stranger.

'What is it, darling?'

Nothing, she thought. 'Nothing,' she said. Then she told him she had a headache and didn't fancy it, adding with a meaningful look at his left knee: 'I shouldn't try anything if I were you.'

And that was that.

'You didn't?' Eileen Feeley said, all agog when she at last confided. 'In the four-poster?'

'Bloody jokes, bloody men!' Moira said.

There was, as it happened, only one joke. Neither the Canton Beast nor Goldilocks gave up that easily and one night there was an altercation in the street outside her flat. It was all she could do not to intervene, but she did not, nor did she answer the door, or the telephone, and the information she later received was, as usual, delivered in an unmistakable way by an unmistakable voice.

'I noticed the tax disc first, then the tyres, then I got a niff of him.'

'You bastard!'

'Honest, Moira, I didn't know you was having it off with him. Look, there's no previous, I checked. We'll just do him for the tax and the tyres, I won't say nothing about...'

'Just leave me alone!'

'Moira, I wouldn't have been there if you'd only answer the telephone, girl?'

Of the whole affair, there was but one consolation, the expensive shawl which Eileen Feeley sent her back via the Film Unit from Patagonia. It would have been nice to know that someone was clicking somewhere, but there was also a complaining letter, Eileen hadn't copped lucky either. Putting it down, Moira gave her mind to a recently delivered brochure advertising new flats whose living rooms overlooked the cherry trees on the other side of the park.

She was alone again and silent, day dreaming once more, hazy images drifting lazily through her mind. First came the shawl which was of many colours and contained flecks of silver threaded through the weave, then the flats, the cherry trees in bloom, finally Eileen and herself, hand in hand like tiny child-like figures seen from a long way off, together at last.

The Former Miss Merthyr Tydfil

Nothing is more regrettable than the speeches we compose, and never make.

'Art be buggered!' Ivy Scuse Lewis would have liked to have said. 'Art, painting, and his bloody gouaches, or whatever he called them. It could take a long walk off a short pier — and the St John's Wood mob who went with it.'

Half of them were queer anyway, she was convinced. Never mind the condescending looks they gave her once they had heard her speak.

'Oh, for a man who simply put his hand up your dress!' she might have said. Well, you knew where you were with plain lust. There was something wholesome about it, like brown bread.

But she said none of these things, smiled her professional, full-lipped, front rostrum smile, and guiltily reflected instead. And more shame on her she thought, considering where she was from and everything.

The truth was that she felt herself threatened by Melville's painting, and also by the new people who had begun to call at their little flat in N.W.3 since his exhibition. The people were not of her world and defied her understanding. Half of them spoke to her as if she were the maid, she felt. *In service*, to use her mother's dreaded phrase. *Them and their Pouilly Fuissé!* They were English, of course, people he'd met on these courses of his, and at the gallery, but it wasn't a question of nationality, Ivy knew, it was the art-lark, prattle and paint, all excluding her and everything she stood for, meaning life, being yourself, having an identity of your own.

It was not that they didn't pay her compliments. One of them said she was beautiful. Said it straight out.

'Her dark Celtic good looks,' he emphasized knowledgeably through a mouthful of *paté*, standing there against the stereo, six foot of skin and bone in aubergine corduroy, his touched-up, greying sideburns needing a nightly rinse by the look of them.

How could she say she'd turned down the chance of being Miss Merthyr Tydfil years ago? She wasn't from there, but she had her visitor's qualification through her aunt who worked in Hoover's. Then as now, she knew she was fancied and she'd kept 38-38 at the operational ends, but it was such a wet thing to say, as if she wasn't a person in her own right at all. It seemed they had to pay tribute to her appearance, but that was where it ended. 'Open your legs and close your mouth!' she'd said to herself, her sense of humour always shocking in Melville's eyes. Not that he'd said a word, not so much as a wink coming from his taut little face. If the lights had fused, she wouldn't have been surprised to see them all holding hands in the dark. It was a problem, them, her, and Melville's newly acquired weekend gear, the Breton beret, fisherman's shirt, worn *espadrilles*, and the overall aroma of bare feet and *gauloises* which marked the retirement of the primary school teacher every Friday at four p.m. sharp.

But then again, this last she could have laughed at. It was a change from him sitting scowling over his marking. What was more disturbing, was the way he now had of looking through her with the pained expression of a man whose wife had become his burden. At thirty-six, she no longer understood what made him tick.

'Self-self — bloody-self!' her mother would have said, in no doubt whatsoever, but then her mother was a tartar who'd remained back home in Aberdarren, ginning up on the corner stool of the bar they called the Two-Foot-Six, making occasional trips to London to see them, and one thing husband and wife continued to have in common, was a sense of relief when Ma returned home. They were always glad to see the back of her. About her ravaged face, outrageous wink and festooned hats was the ever present whiff of a past that was best left buried. A war widow, she'd gone wild when the Black Yanks hit town; or so the story went. Gossip, riotous nights, slammed doors, vanishing lodgers, the weekly visit of the police court missionary and a long-departed brother who'd done time, all formed the backdrop of Ivy's crowded memories. She was fond of saying that the street had brought her up. She'd had hearths other than her own to comfort her, and was shrewd enough to discount a good deal of what her mother said. If she'd had any ambition, it was to create in her own life what had been so clearly lacking in her mother's: order, stability, and some fixity of purpose. It was why she'd married Melville, conscious always of the difference in their backgrounds and ever hopeful that things would be different.

But the melody lingered on, she thought bitterly. She lay now in her black apache outfit, white headband and skin-tight sleep suit on the G-plan divan which Melville had insisted on buying, an extravagance which they could ill afford at the time, but then, when they'd got married, Melville had been more houseproud than arty, and again, she had dutifully fallen in with his wishes. The fact was, she'd tried to be a good sort, and had exhausted herself in the attempt to find some kind of rapport with a man whose face was even more of a mask now than when she'd married him. By arrangement, they'd had no children, then when they'd changed their minds, they hadn't clicked and the lengthy process of adoption had yielded nothing except Ivy's embarrassment at the social worker's inquiries, and now Melville's painting seemed to dwarf her and everything else.

If she swore at the art-lark, it was as at a rival. His canvases represented his escape from her. Nightly, he was making a world of his own in which she had no part, and the last straw was that he had now adopted a permanent pretence that she was incapable of understanding anything he said.

Their recent row was a clincher and only went to show. It wasn't only the art-lark, it was something else. Although they had lived in London for the ten years of their married life, Melville maintained the Welsh connection in traditional ways. He was a member of the Exiles' groups, attended St David's Day dinners, and frequently spent his Saturdays at the London Welsh rugby ground in whose clubhouse he was inclined to spend a beery Saturday night in the company of like-minded fellows. They frequently had a skinful and Melville would come home hoarse from singing, an aspect of his life that was quite different from his activities with the new people in the art-lark. As it happened, she did not mind a traditional Saturday night in the least, even went with him on occasions. A man and his beer she could understand. She was no prude, but then again, it was not as simple as that since the very Welshness of the occasion tended to get up her nostrils. Melville spoke Welsh and she did not, and another sign of the times was the way even the London Welsh were quietly separating themselves up into groups so that she tended to be left out and often declined to accompany him as she had done recently. It was an absence she now regretted for it seemed that two worlds had collided when Melville met a prospective buyer who enthused about his painting. Melville had received, as he said, a certain invitation, but she'd bridled at the very phrase.

'A certain invitation?' she said. What a way for a husband to speak to a wife! His speech was so careful, it might have been carefully thought-out evidence given before a magistrate.

'If you must know, it's Clayton-Hayes.'

'Who?'

'Spencer Clayton-Hayes. He's a millionaire. From Treorchy originally.'

That took her breath away.

'Oh?' she said. If there was one reassuring thing about money, it was that, unlike politics or religion, it contained the possibility of change.

'And he wants me to call up at his flat tomorrow night.'

'Tomorrow night's Christmas Eve.'

'That's why he's so anxious for me to call. He's looking for something to surprise his wife and was delighted he ran into me. He wants me to bring as many things as I have framed.'

'He's heard of you then?'

'He's seen some paintings at the Walter-Thomases.'

'What about Ma? She's coming tomorrow night?'

'I can't possibly meet her now. You'd better get a taxi.'

'On Christmas Eve?'

'You can order it here and go with it to the station.'

'What if the train's late?'

'Then it's late,' Melville's pale green eyes stared at her intensely, his round little face slightly flushed by his irritation. 'I should have thought you'd have been glad for me. If he buys my work, it will be quite a break-through. He's a collector, a man of taste and discrimination.'

She bit her lip. That went home.

'Look,' he repeated; 'Don't you see? It's such a chance.'

She wouldn't have minded if she could somehow have accompanied him. What was wrong with a wife being an asset to a husband? A millionaire too. She had a vague feeling that money and sex went together. Why couldn't she be a help? She was short on one, but the other was lying fallow.

'Couldn't you fix another night?'

'It's out of the question. I can't dictate to him. Anyway, you'll have to meet your mother.'

They normally spent Christmas in Wales, sharing themselves out between her mother and his people, but this year her mother had expressed a wish to come to London and Melville wanted to use all his spare time for painting. The irony was that he'd completely changed his style since his exhibition. Now he painted Welsh industrial scenes exclusively and his little canvases were all expressions of some aspect of valley life. Pit wheels, ravaged coal tips, cameos of gaunt chapels and back-to-back houses now made neat little patterns whose colours somehow formed an idealised picture of a way of life that was gone. There was something immensely nostalgic about his work, however. It had a prettiness and charm and clearly evoked memories in which people still delighted. It was as if part of experience had been reduced and falsely crystallised into manageable proportions, and although she could not quite express it, Ivy was aware of a parallel with those glass baubles she'd seen as a child. When you shook them, they produced artificial snowstorms, snowflakes swirling down upon some miniature log-cabin and showing a little world enclosed with all the properties of a cosy dream.

'I'm going to ask fifty pounds for the larger framed,' Melville said. 'All the Treorchy pieces.'

Ivy was respectfully silent. Money was money.

But that night, she found it difficult to get to sleep. Her anger at her rejection had given way to melancholy. It was not often that she succumbed to self-examination, but when she did, it was usually at these lonely hours of the night, and she had a dismal conviction that, all her life, she had been surrounded by lies. Sex was a lie, marriage was a lie, art was a lie. Living itself was nothing like it was cracked up to be. There came a time in your life when all you could do was look back and then images floated into your mind without rhyme or reason, all combining to make everything that ever happened to you seem disconnected and meaningless. At these hours of the night, there seemed to be an overshadowing greyness to her powers of recall which affected everything like a blight. Take her marriage...

Melville's parents, who were ironmongers in a small way, very chapel and self-contained, had raised the earth when they knew who she was. She remembered all the phrases, 'as common as dirt', 'no background to speak of', 'no education', and the most damning of all 'worked in a factory'. She also 'went to no place of worship' and the very name of the street in which she lived filled them with horror.

Poor old bloody Ruby Street, she thought now. It was in the worst area of Aberdarren, over the tramlines near the canal. Originally, it had received its bad name from the immigrant Irish but the arrival of the Black Yanks had really clinched it. There was a famous incident when the local constable, Ikey Price, had been ordered by his Inspector to investigate Number 33 which was suspected of being used as a brothel. Ikey was told to cover the back entrance in anticipation of a raid on the front. Unfortunately, he had climbed over the wall too soon, and upon taking up his station at the lavatory out the back, was at some pains to remain undetected. Fearing discovery, he had crouched down in the lavatory with his cape over his head. ('A very smart disguise in the blackout when you came to

think of it!') But two Alabama Joes sauntered out and peed all over
him, the Inspector's master plot forcing him to be silent all the
while. Mind, it was done unwittingly, but in the subsequent raid
there were arrests made and Ruby Street was placed out of bounds
to U.S. Forces. The irony, as far as Ivy could remember from her
mother's account, was that half the blackies were Methodist anyway, and flooded the Sunday Schools with chewing gum and
goodies from the P.X. store. But the damage was done as far as
Ruby Street was concerned, and Ikey Price, far from being a hero
of the hour, told his story and became the laughing stock of the
district.

The Aberdarren wits came out like flowers after the rain:

'Turned out a bit damp again today, Ikey?'

What a thing to remember, Ivy thought. Her mind was like that.
She had an uncanny facility for remembering incidents of that kind
which made Melville's short body twist uneasily in his chair when
she revealed 'the fur coat and no knickers' side of her nature.

'God bless America!' Ivy always ended up saying when relating
the story. It was one up on the police, but Melville did not really
share the joke and, at the time of her wedding, his mother had
actually hinted that she fill in a false address on the registrar's book!
She'd been obliged to get married in Melville's chapel, and the few
pews which contained her side of the family were probably disin-
fected afterwards. The Scuse Lewises had taken care of everything.
He was, after all, their only boy and if ever there was a case of the
groom going to the slaughter, this was it, she thought.

But that was from the outside. She belittled herself when she
thought of it like that, taking what you might call the street view of
things. The chapel was no different from the street in that sense.
Neither affected your insides or your deepest needs. It was as if the
outside world coated your real self and blanketed your aspiration,
coarsening them in the process. The fact was she'd had a real sense
of Melville's needs and more than anything, his need to escape from
their cloying respectability and awful concern for appearances.

He'd told her once that he was eleven before he was allowed to
tie his own shoelaces and the stories of his mother waiting up to
smell drink on his breath would have kept Ruby Street agog if she'd
ever related them. The Welsh Mams in Ivy's book should have been
turned over to the S.S. and given to the Gestapo for training. They
ate their own young by all she'd heard.

She herself was not that kind of Welsh, but of the earth, earthy.
In the old days, they'd talked about it and, although they'd lived in

London for years, the old ties were still there, and recently Melville
had started to drift back to Welsh haunts. She had made new
friends, learned hairdressing and mixed with everyone, but recently
Melville's discovery of the Welsh streets in his imagination had set
his feet moving along ancient trails. There was not a terrace or pit
shaft that escaped him now, it seemed, and his best known study,
a group of lads playing dick-stones outside a blacksmith's shop with
a haulier and blackened colliers in attendance, had been bought by
a famous London Welshman who'd described it as 'indicative of
the true spirit of our people'. She'd been there when he said it, as
had Melville's mother, but what relation it had to anything Melville
had ever known about, Ivy could not imagine. If his mother had
seen Melville even talking to a collier in the old days she'd have
phoned the police! But there it was, these memories which were
now paying off a treat. Everybody was very complimentary, including his mother, whose attitude towards Ivy had softened over the
years. Now she spoke of Ivy as one who'd overcome tremendous
odds. You'd think she was from Biafra, not Ruby Street, but there,
they were all alike in their incapacity to see things as they were.

In Ivy's view. As it was, she could understand the snobbery bit,
not wanting your precious to *ychafi* himself, and she also understood
their reserve about Ruby Street; but now, in addition, there seemed
to be this other harassment, the Welshy bit whose lot had miraculously found the guts to get bolshie according to the paper, some of
them very nasty with it too. Educated people, mark you. But try as
she would, she could only see it as a new madness. Nothing
changed, it seemed. First the Revival, then the Band of Hope, now
everything in bloody Welsh! Well, fortunately, she was far away
now, except that Melville, after years of feathering his nest with the
L.C.C., seemed to have turned the full circle and returned to what
he had earlier rejected so conclusively.

'From over by there to by here,' Ivy thought, 'and getting bloody
nowhere!' It was the definitive Ruby Street sentence, and having
summed the matter up so succinctly, she promptly fell asleep.

But in the morning, there was a telegram which brought her
quivering up to the bedroom where Melville had determined on a
lie-in.

'It's from Ma. She can't come.'

Melville did not answer. Things had been strained lately and he
was inclined to brood over what was said.

'She's broken a bone in her arm: club outing.'

'Oh dear... Is there someone looking after her?'

'The people next door, I 'spect. She says she'll phone. She sounds all right. Wishes us all the best.'

'Perhaps we can go down after Christmas?'

She knew he was avoiding what precisely concerned her. The news meant that she was free to accompany him on his visit to the millionaire.

'Look, cock. You know very well what I'm on about. If you're going to see this fella...'

'No,' he said. He understood at once. He stretched out his hand and lit a *gauloise* nervously, his round little face tense with the pain of having to tell her. 'It's not what you think,' he began, his concern obvious. 'It's just that, well, with luck, I'll catch him in the right mood.'

'Catch him?' she caught her breath.

'I want him to study my work in, well, silence.'

'What do you think I'm going to do?'

'It's nothing to do with you,' he said gently by way of explanation.

'Oh, I bloody know that.'

'It's just him and his paintings.'

'Are you going to sit outside on the lav' or something?'

He frowned. He painted the streets but their directness had escaped him.

'It's selling, that's all.'

'Selling?'

'Yes. A certain mood has to be created.' He smiled, as if that were the end of the matter, picked up his reading glasses and put them on. Now the prospective headmaster seemed to look at her, pink-cheeked and reproving. 4C again, she thought; her mark.

She still stood awkwardly in the doorway.

'You won't say, will you?' she bit her lip.

'Look, he's an old man, and he's got memories.'

'Memories?'

'It would be better if there were just two of us.'

'You sod!'

Now he was aware of the intensity of her feelings, he could see, but she did not wait for him to speak.

'I shan't say anything. Honest. What d'you think I'm going to do? — talk my head off? Well, do you? D'you think I'm going to tell him about Ikey Price or something?'

'He'd probably like that.'

'Well, then?'

'I'd rather you didn't.'

'I'd rather you didn't!' she minced, but while there was still a chance, she kept her cool. 'All right. Look... Supposing I was to drop in after? Say I was on my way from shopping?'

'At six-thirty at night?'

'I'll leave it until late, then we can go and have a meal?'

'We can have a meal anyway,' he smiled.

But she wasn't having that.

'You know what I mean, don't you?' It was very simple. She wanted to see the millionaire! And he knew.

'But he's a perfectly ordinary chap.'

'From Treorchy?'

'Originally.'

'Then what's wrong with me calling in on a perfectly ordinary chap from Treorchy originally?' she said breathlessly. 'After you've done your bit of business?'

He took off his reading glasses once more. His eyes were hard and uncompromising and she felt she knew his answer before he spoke.

'You won't say what you mean, will you? I'll let you down, that's it, isn't it?'

'Nonsense.'

'It's not nonsense. Every time we mixes with your sort of people, I can see you wincing. You insult people, you do. Just by looking at them. Me, I mean. Yes, you do.'

'Ivy...'

'Look at you, you can't even get out of bed to have a decent row can you? All right, I'll tell you something else. I don't know why you married me, I don't. At all!'

With that, she flung herself out of the room. God, how she'd tried. Tried and tried. When he'd made no effort at all. From being a petty irritation, a squabble which she could handle in her own way, it now seemed to be much more, as if a match had been struck only to light up greater areas of unhappiness than ever she'd imagined.

In the other room, she heard him get out of bed and begin to dress. She knew that he would attempt an apology, but it made no difference. She'd answered her own question. She was sure that part of the reason why he'd married her was to get away from the dreadful clamminess of his upbringing, but the moment he'd done so and the initial pleasures of conquest had worn off, he'd begun to regret it, as if he, too, were searching for something and had not found it.

When he came into the room, his face was solemn and his tone of voice indicated that things had gone too far.

'I'm sorry, but it's not personal. It's nothing to do with you at all.

It's just that I see this as a chance and I don't want anything to go wrong. That's all.'

She did not reply, kept her thoughts to herself once more and served him breakfast in tight-lipped silence through force of habit. She felt weak and exhausted suddenly. He made her think too much. She did not want to think. She just wanted to be liked. Couldn't he understand that?

Apparently not, but when the time came to leave, he still affected concern.

'I don't like to leave you like this.'

'Why don't you just go?'

'Ivy...' he put his hand on her arm.

'Leave me alone.'

'Look...'

'It's very common to say "look" all the time. I wonder where you picked that up from?'

'Please...'

'Oh, why don't you just go?' she said again.

'Not like this.'

'Listen,' she was already tiring of it and just wanted to be on her own. 'I've got the turkey to stuff.'

And that did it. He was out of the room, off on the art-lark, his suitcase of canvases under his arm like a rep with a foot in the door.

Men, she thought. But she couldn't generalise. It was the Scuse Lewises and their offspring. But the extent of her feeling in the bedroom startled her. Was she right about her marriage? There were some doors that were frightening to open, but having opened them, you had to decide whether you wanted to follow your inclination and proceed further. So she hesitated. The curious thing was that, despite the intensity of her thoughts, she still felt there was something missing, a key to her understanding of her husband which still eluded her. Why was he like he was? Why did he behave in this way?

She poured herself a large bacardi and coke and put a Frank Sinatra on the stereo.

'Only the Lonely,' the record sleeve said.

'You wouldn't bloody nob it!' Ivy said to herself. But it was not like her to sulk for long and she was recovering continuously. To tell the truth, she did not have the energy for a prolonged row. There had been tears in her eyes, and only one thing was certain. Once you got past thirty, you couldn't cry without your eyes giving you away. She felt she looked like the victim of the dentist's apprentice, and for no reason she could think of, decided to get herself up, doing the best she could with her eye shadow and slipping into a sheath dress, her backless and breathless. She was thus dressed to kill when he returned.

'Well?' she asked. That mask of a face gave nothing away. But his voice was choking.

'Nothing,' he put down the suitcase and came blundering into the room, and she saw his lips quiver as he blinked at her.

'How d'you mean?'

'Nothing,' he said again. 'I didn't sell a picture.'

'Was he in?' She didn't understand.

'Yes, I had difficulty getting to him, but he was in. He... he told me to lay out all my canvases on the floor.'

'*The floor*?' she said incredulously.

'Then,' Melville nodded and his face became enraged; 'then he put out all the lights and examined each picture with a pencil torch. It took him twenty minutes. He said he didn't like my brushwork. I didn't get a drink — anything. Not even a cup of tea.'

'But I thought it was practically certain?'

So did Melville. But it was not.

Normally, she would have comforted him with a remark or two, but she was not in the mood. She watched him sit opposite her and loosen his collar, his face still numbed as he stared in front of him.

'It's the end of something,' he said melodramatically.

Lor' what was she going to say? 'What did he look like?' she asked in a low voice.

'Small, bald and mean. But I don't want it mentioned,' he turned his eyes to her.

She shook her head, biting her lip to hide her smile.

'I mean, I don't want anyone to know. Especially your mother.'

She nodded again. She understood that. They sat in an uneasy silence. She had a little picture of the millionaire scrabbling over the floor with the pencil torch and thought it rather a scream, but she did not dwell on it. Evidently, she was required to say as little as possible, but the mention of her mother caused her mind to stray back to Ruby Street once more, and again, she had a vision of the other crouching figure, the suffering uniformed Ikey Price, his peeved face glowering beneath his dampened cape, and then she had a flash of intuition which went to the heart of the matter. The trouble with Melville was that he'd never been peed on before. All his life, he'd been protected in one way or another, all his expectations were ministered to, and despite his attempts at escape, there remained a niceness of conventions, the confident expectation of a style of life and a sameness of manners and language which surrounded him like a comforting mist. She had thought it especially Welsh, this conditioning, but it was merely a dressing and in any case, did not affect her. Never been peed on, she thought again. That was it, the trouble with the lot of them, the art mob as well. Her intuition had divined a condition of life that existed irrespective of countries and national boundaries.

'A good job your mother's not coming,' Melville said.

She noticed that he was looking at her anxiously. She was not often silent and she had not stuffed the turkey.

'What have you got yourself done up for?'

She smiled, and for a moment, smelt his fear. Whatever she was, she was all he had.

'Nothing,' she said and went presently into the kitchen and put on an apron in preparation for her chore. But for the goodness of her heart, it would have been a right Ruby Street Christmas, she thought: poached egg, flagon and a fag! But that was another dog-end she'd better keep behind her ear for after. As it was, without even seeing the man of mystery, she felt in an awed way that they had both received a salutary lesson in what it took to be a millionaire.

There was a movement behind her in the kitchen doorway and although conscious of Melville's eyes upon her, she did not turn round. Now her strong deft fingers began slowly and confidently to tear the innards out of the turkey.

Hon. Sec. R.F.C.

Elgar Davies lived alone with his ancient widowed mother on the far side of town in one of those rare detached houses built in a brick festooned style known as Rhondda baronial. It was large, squat, grey, multi-chimneyed and ugly and much too big for the widow and her bachelor son. However, there were times when it seemed that it was not large enough for Elgar who, despite all the appearances of the dutiful son, escaped from his mother when he could.

He was helped in this by his long-standing position as Secretary of the Pontlast Rugby Football Club where he displayed a love of the game and his fellows that was deeply felt, so much so that when any disagreement occurred, say, between players and officials, he would return home and seat himself in his study and ponder on the matter with intense seriousness, shutting himself away from both his mother and the world, his small podgy bespectacled little frame, short legs and tiny feet, lost in the large hide armchair bequeathed to him by his father.

Elgar was the son and the grandson of local heroes, both much decorated veterans of the wars, whose distinction had overawed Elgar all his life. 'Your grandfather was one of the tunnellers of Messines,' his mother was wont to say, and a framed Distinguished Service Order with attendant decorations was proudly displayed in the hallway of the old house. Elgar had not known his grandfather, and had scarcely begun to know his father when he died of wounds sustained when the first batch of territorials went to France in the second war.

For years, Elgar had felt rather shame-faced at his own lack of distinction since he had escaped the battlefield, and indeed, he was soon made aware that he was not the man his father was. As a child, he had been puny, given to bronchitis and was much cosseted by his mother and a bevy of aunts who had lived with them, and later, in college, where he went — inevitably, it seemed — to become a primary school teacher, he was the quiet sort who has difficulty asserting himself. Things did not improve until later in life when he began to take an interest in the administrative side of sport where his quiet efficiency and adroit book-keeping skills were much valued, and when he began his secretaryship of the rugby club, he had at last found a position and status in life of which the menfolk in his family would have thoroughly approved.

By now, he had developed a love of the game of rugby football, and in his late forties, he spoke knowledgeably of past games and players, sometimes forgetting his own complete lack of prowess as a player. As Secretary, he was also a selector and a man of some influence, and it was in this role that he tangled with a young man known as Bashie Williams, who had recently been recruited to the club and who, while distinguishing himself on the field, had been heard in the showers to refer to Elgar as 'a bit of a pouf'. It was a vulgar and completely uncalled for remark, Elgar thought, and it cut him to the quick.

'Not meant, Elgar boy,' said Abe Beynon, the Chairman, as they walked from the changing rooms to the clubhouse itself. Abe, once praised as a forward — 'slow but dirty' — towered over Elgar's short figure and when he spoke, he could look down and see the full circular rim of Elgar's sporty pork-pie hat and a wide skirted riding mac swishing beneath it. 'You know what these lads are. No idea of what an effort it takes to run a club. Unappreciative is not the word.'

'I just happened to overhear it,' Elgar said. He stared at the path as he spoke, an intense stare as he scowled through rimless lenses.

'Overheard and overlooked, I trust?'

'He's not a very good forward and a lout into the bargain.'

'Oh, don't say that. He's built like a tank.'

'Robust, I give you.'

'Robust? He's got shoulders on him like a young bull. And what a worker!'

'He gives the appearance of working,' Elgar said pointedly, 'but if you ask me, there's nothing much else, certainly not upstairs.'

'Oh, come on, Elgar, it's not a dancing class we're running.'

'I didn't think it was.'

'Well, whatever he is off the field, he's a lion on it. If ever I've seen international potential, he's got it.'

'Really?' Elgar was surprised.

'Never been surer. You watch. He's one of those who'll rocket to the top. A bit of an animal around the house, I dare say, but he's not here to ice the cake.'

Elgar did not pursue arguments about the game if contradicted by so knowledgeable person as Abe Beynon, but he did not disguise his dislike for Bashie Williams. The boy was indeed built like a tank, standing six-foot-two and sixteen stone with the short neck and powerfully developed arms and shoulders which make for mastery of the front row trade. His face was moon-shaped and pock-marked, thick sensual lips constantly lolling open below a short cropped haircut which added to the ferocity of his appearance. In any other circumstances, Elgar would have described Bashie's forehead as Neanderthal for there was about his appearance more than a hint of things primitive. But what annoyed Elgar was the boy's truculent and disrespectful manner when in the presence of club officials. To break wind in the showers or coming off after a game was one thing, but to do it when Elgar was reminding players of the promise to wear black armbands on their jerseys to mourn the death of an old and trusted servant of the club, was another. It showed lack of respect, both for the dead and the living, and more, was no doubt a directly aimed insult, if aimed was the right word.

Then there was his insolent reply which Elgar could only term 'naturalistic'.

'I can't help it, Mr Davies, faggots it is. The old girl keeps a stall on the market.'

There had been a general titter since Bashie was the maker of statements which some found amusing, but as his coarse wit was generally at the expense of someone else, Elgar found it inexcusable. He had blushed scarlet in front of everyone, a childhood habit which he thought he had long conquered, and he could do little more than turn on his heel, thereby increasing the effectiveness of the slight and no doubt causing prolonged comment behind his back. How could he tell the others that he was no prude, and always liked a laugh with the boys? He could not, of course, and had no answer for these farmyard habits which distressed him more than he could say, so much so that he dwelt on it for weeks.

Putting it mildly, Bashie Williams was not the sort of person you liked to meet indoors anyway. He was somehow too big for rooms. When he was in them, things tended to get knocked over. Chairs creaked, sagged, split; doors slammed, shuddered and shook as if in protest at Bashie's potential for physical damage. Everywhere he went, his size created problems and everything about him was too much, Elgar felt. Bashie was a beyond-person, and big-mouthed with it. That he was a splendid forward into the bargain was a pity. They always had wilder spirits in the club. When Morlais Morgans and Dai Price had been arrested after an altercation in a Warwick-shire fish and chip shop, Elgar had gone personally to see the local police superintendent and taken a brace of stand tickets for the English international with him.

'You know what these lads are, sir,' he said in a man-to-man fashion, and later everybody had complimented him on the way he'd smoothed things over when the charge sheet was kept clean. Elgar was a fixer, people said, and there were innumerable occasions when a well-chosen word in the right ear had worked wonders. Elgar had a very nice manner. He knew enough was enough. He did not take advantage and he knew when to stop asking. Then he was very good at remembering the people who helped out the club, the grocer who supplied them with free tea, all the local tradesmen who helped out, and it was noticeable that the club's annual dance had progressed from a scruffy hop to a gala night with Elgar in charge and the police safely seen to in the back kitchen of the local hotel.

No one disputed his work and no one had ever publicly said a word against him, but ever since Bashie Williams had been recruited from a soccer team (and didn't that say it all really?), bringing his sixteen stone over the mountain from a foundry in neighbouring Aberdarren, Elgar had noticed a subtle change in his relationship with the boys, as they called the players. It was a change that began imperceptibly, altering little things, seeming in Elgar's eyes to spread out like rising damp from one central spot. And the core of infection was Bashie, Elgar knew it. It was not that anyone said anything specific, but that, in an extraordinary way, like the girl with body odour in the television commercial, Elgar now felt people to be moving away from him. There was one more very noticeable effect that gave him hours of regret, but again, he was slow to realize the cause.

For some weeks, Elgar noticed that his fellow committee-men tended to head him off when he made his way from the grand-stand to the dressing-room after a match. He had thought this interruption to be a coincidence at first. He was used to being spoken to constantly, often being asked to consider this problem or that at the most inconvenient of times. He usually acquiesced so that on several Saturdays running he was buttonholed at exactly the same time, at the very moment when the players were changing in the showers, but he had thought this to be a coincidence.

Then the same thing happened before the match when the players were changing in preparation for play. This occurred on several occasions. Now another committee-man would get hold of him and Elgar became aware that he was being held in conversation for the specific purpose of preventing his entering the players' changing rooms. He was not welcome there any more, before or after a match.

At first he could not believe it for there was no atmosphere he loved more, the players sprawling about half-dressed, stamping their feet into the metal studded boots, some rubbing themselves with embrocation — legend said Bashie Williams drank his the first time he saw it! — and one or two of the younger lads nervous if the opposition was to be feared. Hands were laid on shoulders and there was a great deal of frisky jollity, but best of all, Elgar loved the skipper Ikey Owen's pre-match instructions, and Elgar almost felt himself to be a member of the team then, standing in the background, blazered and gloved amongst the lads as Ikey spelt out the plan of the day, or enumerated the likely sins of well-observed sinners who had known criminal records.

'If that fella McCool starts anything, you bloody cool it, not him. Give him his head and leave him to me, I'll cobble him quiet.'

And Elgar would grip his gloved little hands fiercely and the downward curve of his thin lips might well be taken to mean that McCool would be well observed from the Committee box and had better watch it with him.

It was on these occasions that Elgar, perhaps more than at any time in his life, felt truly at one with the boys who were sprawled attentively on the benches before him. When they got to their feet, Ikey in the lead, he watched them go out into the tunnel, savouring the roar of the crowd as Ikey led the team on. Elgar always locked up after them, then hurried to his seat in the stand. If a player were carried off with a serious injury, Elgar would open up again, and had been witness of some special in-jokes. Once he had been Ikey Owens's companion when Ikey lay there groaning with a broken leg, muttering at the boos which floated in from the terraces as the play continued outside.

'I dunno,' said Ikey as the crowd continued their disapproval. 'This is the only club in the world that plays before a hostile crowd home and away!'

It had made a good story in Elgar's annual report at the dinner, and when a year later, the offending McCool had a little difficulty seeing out of one eye, Elgar was in the know in a way that few others were. Being in the know, being indispensable, being the man to whom people turned for the keys or the cash, mattered to Elgar, and better still, after a hard match when the warriors returned, boots scraping on the concrete floor, their bodies muddied and bloodied, Elgar had his factotum, Moss Thomas, get the shandies ready and he loved it then, the chatter and the final diagnosis.

'How was it, Morlais?'

'What a cow of a ref! Braille gave him up when he went for the test!'

Then there were the complaints.

'Look at this lump by here! Good Christ, I'm moulting.'

It was sweaty, masculine, of the earth, earthy, and when they started singing in the showers, the songs were often bawdy and delighted Elgar:

> Here we come full of rum,
> Looking for wimmin who'll peddle their bum,
> In Pontlast R.F.C.!

Certainly no prude, Elgar was in his oils on these occasions, standing near the showers long after the steam had clouded his spectacles, inventing excuses to linger on, sometimes strutting importantly with his little red cash book and gold propelling pencil, casting a blind eye upon those who were leaning heavily upon him with their expenses, and giving as good as he got when there was any backchat about money.

'*Iesu Grist*, Elgar, three shifts I lost?'

'Three kicks you missed too.'

'Oh come on, Elgar, I got two maintenance warrants owing?'

'Training night Monday, then. You'd better notify Securicor.'

It was such fun there in that hothouse atmosphere with the steam rising and the gorgeous smells of sweating flesh, linament and sodden gear, a kind of weekly male orgy which Elgar felt privileged to savour to the full. But ever since Bashie Williams had come, trailing his other soccer uncouthness, there had been a definite shading off in the approval in which Elgar felt himself to be regarded. After three Saturdays of pointed interruptions when on his way to the dressing room, he was more than sure of his exclusion, although Abe Beynon put it very delicately despite his fractured English.

'The boys want to be on their own, I dare say. There's been too many people getting in through the doors. Kids and that. You know what the language is like.'

'I don't mind a bit of language. Good Christ!' Elgar swore impressively.

'Get's a bit overcrowded in there.'

'But there's the expenses?'

'Ikey suggests Mondays. In the clubhouse.'

'Well, I usually lock up after?'

'Moss is doing it.'

'I wouldn't trust Moss with a packet of crisps.'

'The boys prefer it.'

'The boys?' Elgar caught his breath.

'You know how it is,' Abe Beynon's lantern-jawed undertaker's face was wet-lipped and evasive. He had a large polychromatic nose, more a badge of office than an organ, and he rubbed it embarassedly. 'They'd rather be on their own. Anyhow, be better if you opened up the club bar. They've got very slack there lately.'

Elgar, always glad of an opportunity to exercise his authority, saw the sense of this as there was a big-bosomed, sharp-tongued girl behind the bar who needed an eye keeping on her in more senses than one, being a bit of a drop-drawers, according to Abe. But since this conversation quite clearly referred to after-match procedures and there could possibly have been some doubt about Ikey's unstated objection, it came as a double shock to learn that another member of the committee thought it would be better if Elgar supervised the ticket collectors immediately before the match.

'Ticket collectors?'

'There's people creeping under hedges — everything.'

Elgar knew that this was patently untrue.

'What d'you want me to do?'

Well, me and the committee, like... well, perhaps, 'stead of going into the changing rooms while the boys is changing, we think that you could be very useful at the gate, like? That's the general idea.'

So there was no doubt. Elgar was being very definitely excluded from the dressing-room, he, the Secretary. At first, although he took care to show as little of his concern as possible in the presence of his cautioners, his inclination was to protest openly. He could have given a polite but very firm reminder of exactly how much he had done for the club, and just how very important he was at this precise moment since he was acting as guarantor for a much needed extension to the clubhouse proper, and without him, the bank manager would very probably have hesitated. But he checked himself. He had not survived for so long in this ultra-male world without acquiring skills and he knew that a moaner was never appreciated. Never a squealer be, they said in the collieries, and it was a code that was implanted in many others beside the colliers. Also, it would not do to protest openly since there was clearly an undercurrent of feeling that he did not fully understand.

On its face value, the objection to him, for he was sure that it must be personal, could not be that he was officious or disliked as an authority figure. He contradicted no one, certainly not the players. He never expressed an opinion before a game, and generally did not contradict those who held strong opinions afterwards. His habit was to listen attentively to all, then come down firmly in the middle.

When two of the boys had been sent off after a nasty business involving a well-known trouble-maker from a more famous West Wales club, he had taken the line that the referee was overawed by the occasion and had seen, not the original offences, but the retaliations. Elgar had a genuine sympathy for those punished and had made it his business to have a cheery but inoffensive word with them in the bar. Then, after a particularly violent fracas involving more than the odd punch, he might add a comment like, 'And they're sending missionaries to China!' which was a good enough crack in the aftermath of a particularly bloody afternoon, but he took care never to offend. As far as he could see, he had done nothing wrong. He had said nothing, certainly not to Ikey Owens with whom he was on the best of terms. What then was the reason for the change? And why was Abe Beynon being so tactful?

Elgar searched his mind for reasons, and he could come to only one conclusion. His enemy must be Bashie Williams.

It was at this time that Elgar began to return home earlier than usual, leaving others to lock up the clubhouse. His mother, now in her seventies, was a sportswoman herself and on Saturdays would invite her cronies into the house to play contract bridge. This group, a gaggle of women in their sixties and seventies, were sometimes referred to as The Last of the South Wales Posh for they were the widows of colliery managers or important officials, those who in the lean years had known such luxuries as maids, foreign travel, or clothes sent on approval from the leading Cardiff stores. They were women whose investments had prospered, part of a group whose wills were the subject of great local interest. Money had been made in the old days, even considerable sums, since the wisest had not invested in the coal industry but in the booming multi-purpose stores of England, but the women had lived longer than the men, and Mrs Blodwen Davies's bridge parties were the last occasions for the display of jewelled finery represented by lumpy garnet broaches and occasional Italianate cameos, the souvenirs of Mediterranean cruises of long ago.

Besides Mrs Davies, Elgar's mother, there were three other women known to Elgar by the nicknames he remembered as a child. Mrs Owsher-Bowsher, Mrs Eadie-Beadie Jones and Miss Caldi Caldicott-Evans, the sole spinster who seemed to have been a chain smoker all her life. They dressed inevitably in sombre clothes, drank the occasional port and lemon, leaving behind a mixed aroma of cigarette smoke, eau de Cologne and damp talcum powder in any room used.

When Elgar came home early from the club, it was a matter of politeness that he should put his head around the card room door, but since this was a Saturday night world of his mother's, and one in which he had no real interest, he usually did no more than utter a few pleasantries and soon excused himself. Elgar did not play cards and now and again sensed that his mother's cronies seemed to view him with a compassionate amusement that made him feel uncomfortable.

Mrs Owsher-Bowsher he privately referred to as That Disgusting Chocolate Person since her husband had made a small fortune in the manufacture of sweets and his widow was a splendid and visible sampler of sweetmeats all her life, while Mrs Eadie-Beadie had been born poor and retained the occasional crackling malice of one who did not quite belong amongst the corpulent hoi polloi of long ago. Miss Caldi Caldicott-Evans, known as The Caldi, a doctor's daughter who had been to Roedean, was wont to chivvy Eadie-Beadie in matters of grammar or decorum, and was the thinnest of the quartette, well-known for such eccentricities as entering the local shoe shop, saying, 'Have you shoes? I mean, have you *good* shoes?' when confronted with shelf upon shelf of proprietary brands.

When Elgar entered the room, all eyes turned to him except his mother's. Only The Caldi smiled, as she always did, her spinster's heart remaining the warmest.

Elgar had a stock joke for Eadie-Beadie who held the cards between her thick be-ringed fingers as if they were enemies who might get away.

'Everything all right? They're not taking you to the laundry, Eadie-Beadie?'

'Not with tram tickets,' said Eadie-Beadie scowling at her cards.

'You're home early?' said Elgar's mother with a sideways glance.

'Do with an early night.'

'Anything happened?' said Eadie-Beadie maliciously.

'We won six-nil.'

'I thought you'd be drinking when you didn't take the car,' Eadie-Beadie said.

'Always a bad sign,' said The Caldi with a fluttering, if crinkled, ageing débutante's wink.

'I walked,' said Elgar, returning her smile.

'You'll be walking if you call on a hand like that again,' said Mrs Davies menacingly to Miss Caldicott-Evans. 'If Ely Culbertson ever came down to this valley, he'd go back mental!'

The Caldi flushed while Mrs Owsher-Bowsher, replete in the majesty of her fourteen stone, said nothing and began painstakingly to count up points on the tips of her fingers.

The women, no less than the men, had the gift of repartee and while Elgar nodded pleasantly in the doorway, his mother's determination to get on with the game was quite usual. He was not going to be cross-examined. Elgar nodded at the back of his mother's head, smiled once more at Miss Caldicott-Evans who gave another coy wink, then excused himself. For years now, he and his mother had existed in a state of uneasy truce, each pursuing a separate life, coming together at meals and passing the time of day, but little else, unless either happened to be out of sorts when they would fuss over each other with habitual clucking solicitousness.

Elgar knew that she was disappointed in him, at his failure to marry or get a headship, but both subjects were now left alone by unspoken consent, and it was accepted that Elgar should live his own life between school and rugby club, with dutiful visits to chapel once on Sunday when he drove his mother to the one remaining chapel several miles away. That it was a bleak life in which the spirit was crushed by the aridity of long-established habits did not occur to him, although now and again he cast his eye on the images of the outside world as presented by the television screen, and sometimes heaved a sigh.

He had travelled little because he could not leave his mother who always left him with the idea that it was best for him to remain where he was well understood and where the family name (Davies D.S.O.s) still counted for something. He was also delicate and there was his weak chest and the old embarrassing loss of hair which had been miraculously arrested so that he was no longer a sufferer from alopecia, thanks to the prescriptions of the local general practitioner who had expectations under Mrs Davies's will.

Best for Elgar to stay put, both had long agreed, while Mrs Davies, it should be said, remained in remarkably good health, a big boned, strong woman, quite unlike Elgar in appearance, with a firm strong line of jaw and sharp piercing eyes which looked Eadie-Beadie firmly in the face when she answered Eadie-Beadie's piercing questions, stating categorically that Elgar had made his place with her and that was the end of the matter. It was a mistake to think that Elgar was deep. He was not deep, just liked the simple life at home, being a very good boy to his mother, and if she had any disappointment, it was that he was not musical as she had hoped when she first named him.

It was against this background that Elgar had found a way of life for himself which was manageable until that one word floated across to him from the sneering lips of Bashie Williams. It might have been the breach in the dam which caused the dyke to burst.

'Pouf' he repeated to himself as soon as he had left his mother and settled himself in his study chair. It was extraordinary that one word seemed to have done so much damage. What on earth did it mean? Why should it have such consequences? Why should he be singled out as untouchable when he was so companionable? If it meant effeminate, it was absurd since he was the most sporty of men and his entire wardrobe of blazers and ties proclaimed his attachment to this sporting group or that. In a curious way, it made him feel childlike to be so set apart and he had a renewed understanding of those children who were sometimes excluded by their fellows because of their appearance. It was a pariah word, no doubt about it. But what could he do?

With his legs tucked under him in his study chair, he came to a decision. There was only one thing he could do and that was soldier on, he said to himself, using a phrase of his mother's which must in turn have been passed on to her by his father.

'Soldier on, John Willy! Best foot forward!' Better still if he could manage not to give the slightest indication of his hurt. He had a number of favourite exhortations to the team when things seemed to be going against them, and now and again he applied them to himself when he tended to get down in the mouth. He stood up now and reached for his correspondence file with a typical rallying cry which he applied strictly to himself for once.

'Come on Pontlast — show your class!'

He knew he had to come back from behind, as the boys had done on many occasions, and immediately his good nature showed itself. There was something he could do for Bashie Williams as the club were about to make their annual tour of the West Country, and Elgar always made it his business to write personally to employers, seeking permission for the players to absent themselves from their places of employment. It was a formality since most of the local people accepted the penalty of employing rugby players, but it was one of those routine little tasks which Elgar did extremely well. He saw to it that the letters of application were followed by letters of thanks, and knew that the provision of international tickets was a useful lubricant when favours were required.

He decided that he would write first on Bashie Williams's behalf to the manager of the Aberdarren foundry and he settled the headed notepaper on his lap full of good intentions only to find that he could not remember Bashie Williams's christian name. Once again an immediate good intention was abruptly followed by an irritation, as it always was when that young man's name came up. He could not put, *re: Mr Bashie Williams* at the head of his letter. But the wretch must have a christian name. *B* was inserted in the programme and he was inevitably known as Bashie. But that would not do. Elgar decided to telephone the clubhouse which was still open.

'Abe?'

'Who is that?' Abe Beynon usually had a skinful on a Saturday night and his voice was thick and accusatory, as if a wife might have actually dared to intrude on his Saturday night privilege. 'What is it? Hurry up, if you please. It's nearly stop-tap.'

'It's Elgar. Small point. The Easter Tour. What's Bashie Williams's first name?'

There was a moment's hesitation at the other end. Elgar could imagine Abe's babyish pout at being drawn away from his bottle at the bar.

'Leave the bugger alone,' Abe said.

'Listen, I must know his name. I've got to write to his employer.'

'His employer?' Abe sounded alarmed.

'If he's going to miss three days' work, his employer will have to be notified. I do it every year.'

'Are you sure, Elgar?'

'What d'you mean, am I sure?' Elgar's annoyance increased.

'I mean,' Abe said carefully at the other end of the telephone — and Elgar could hear him sucking his teeth as he always did when suspicious — 'are you sure it's only leave of absence?'

'I'm not thinking of having him here to tea!'

Abe did not reply directly.

'Look, I've got to head the letter.'

'Basil,' Abe said finally, but clearly after deliberation. 'B for Basil.'

'And he's in the blacksmith's shop, I take it?'

'Yes.'

'Thank you. That's all I wanted to know.'

Once again there was a hesitation in Abe's manner, another note of reservation indicating an area of concern about something that was not directly mentioned, and Elgar did not understand it. Did Abe think he was going to socialise with the fellow? If not, what did he think? Could it be that Bashie Williams had done him further harm, and did Abe think he was going to retaliate in some way? The puzzle remained and Elgar had no answer. He sighed at this latest nuance, but soon dismissed it and gave his mind to his particular expertise. As his mother always said, Elgar wrote a very nice letter. He also had a very good hand.

Dear Mr Warbuoys, [he wrote]
     re: Mr Basil Williams (Blacksmith's)
     As you know the Club will be making its annual tour of the West Country prior to Easter Week, and I write to ask you if the above-named can be released from the foundry at 12 pm on Wednesday, the 15th. I am sure you will appreciate how important it is that the Club should be well represented against the English clubs. I would like to take this opportunity of thanking you for all your co-operation in the past. As usual, I have reserved two stand tickets for you and Mrs Warbuoys for the international encounter at Twickenham, and if there is anything else I can do, please do not hesitate to ask.
     Kind regards,

                                                  Yours sincerely,
                                                  Elgar J. Davies
                                                  Hon. Sec.
                                                  Pontlast R.F.C.

Elgar wrote a number of such letters and received expected replies, but in the case of Mr Basil (né Bashie) Williams, nothing was ordinary it seemed, and when the reply came, Elgar was furious.

     Dear Elgar,
          re: Mr Basil Williams
     Thank you for your letter concerning the above-named, and also for your offer of tickets which Mrs Warbuoys and myself will be only to pleased to take up. As you know, I have done everything I can to help the Club in the past, and indeed, will continue to do so in the future, as I quite agree that it is very important for us to be well represented in our annual battle with the English clubs. In the case of Mr Basil Williams, however, I cannot grant him leave of absence as you request, since he has already applied for seven days' leave of absence over the period in question in order that he should attend the funeral of his grandmother in Ireland.
     Regards to your mother.

                                                  Yours sincerely,
                                                  E.F. Warbuoys
                                                  Manager.

'Look at this — lying in his teeth!' Elgar said when he showed the offending letter to Abe Beynon. 'He's no conception of what I do to keep up good relations for the Club.'

But Abe exploded with laughter until the tears showed in his rheumy eyes.

'I pisses myself every time that Bashie opens his mouth,' Abe said hoarsely. 'That'll be another one for the dinner, Elgar boy.'

'The dinner?'

'Your speech, man. Grannie in Ireland... What a character!'

Wisely, Elgar did not comment. Clearly, others saw things which he did not and, as it happened, Bashie's status as a character had recently been increased by the fact that he had been returned comatose in a drunken condition to the clubhouse by an irate girlfriend, who exasperated at being kept waiting outside, had pushed him back in through the door, saying, 'You can have him back. I don't want him!' Once again, everybody thought this hilarious except Elgar, but Elgar kept his peace. If everybody thought Bashie Williams a character, then a character he must be.

Elgar soon busied himself finalising the details of the tour and in the weeks that followed, he nodded cheerfully enough to Bashie whenever he saw him, but Bashie did not speak, merely gave a caustic nod in reply, and there were times when Elgar would look down the corridor outside the committee room, hesitating to go down it unless accompanied, in case some further remark by a loitering Bashie would add to his discomfiture. Although busy, he had a sense of something building-up between Bashie and himself. It was uncanny, his apprehension, and he confided in no one, but it remained, and every time he saw Bashie lolling at the bar or playing darts with the boys, Elgar had a sixth sense of danger which sometimes caused his throat to dry and he was often the victim of intense nervousness. He took care not to stand near Bashie at the bar, and once when he passed him on the way to the Gents, was forced to dig his hands deeply in his trouser pockets to disguise their tremble. Of course, it was absurd since no one in the club would have allowed Bashie to offer him even the threat of physical violence, and there was no indication that Bashie was even considering it, yet his glances seemed to Elgar to be full of threat.

Bashie had let his hair grow longer so that his forehead was crowded by an untidy fringe and he appeared more uncouth and villainous than ever. In an odd way, Elgar felt that Bashie had found him out, and if he had no clear idea of exactly what Bashie had diagnosed, his huge aura of bustling masculinity seemed to contain an explosive charge when it passed Elgar's puny little frame. It was quite absurd, and yet it was quite real. The man's presence was like a taunt which was repeated whenever they met and yet there was not a further word spoken.

One night, Elgar dreamt about Bashie. The two of them were locked in a cage with people coming to visit them, and in his dream Elgar saw Abe Beynon standing complaining to other spectators outside the bars. The complaint was that it was not fair to put the two of them together and, as a spectacle, the fact that they were together was in some way a cheat on the public purse. No violence was offered even in the dream, and while Elgar would not have confided with a living soul about this extraordinary occurrence, his obsession caused him to resume the sleeping tablets which he had long abandoned. Indeed, he packed them when the time came to leave on the tour of the West Country and he was aware that he must have given something of himself away because his mother affected a rare concern for his welfare.

'Are you sure you're all right, Elgar?'

'Of course I'm all right, mother.'

'You look pale, and you're very restless in the nights.'

'Nonsense.'

'Yes, you are. You're up at the crack of dawn, and there can't be be any good in you drinking all that water.'

When under stress, Elgar drank water continuously. It was one of the giveaway signs of his tension.

'You're not doing too much are you, Elgar?'

'Probably.'

'Well, give yourself a bit of a holiday.'

'I will.'

'Eadie-Beadie can't come to Llandrindod Wells for the Bridge Convention.'

'Oh?'

'She reckons she'll be rooked. Mean, if you ask me.'

His mother's mind soon passed on to her own concerns and, when the time came, Elgar was relieved to see her off in the hired car which she shared with Owsher-Bowsher and The Caldi. Owsher-Bowsher, of necessity, sat in the front with the driver while his mother and The Caldi sat firmly apart, proudly demonstrating the room between themselves in the rear, the latter's lined and dotty face wreathed in cigarette smoke as they gave him a final scrutiny before the car pulled off to be driven at a prescribed speed along a prescribed route.

They went to one or other of the watering spas every Easter while

Elgar joined the boys, taking his seat at the rear of the Club coach, with Abe Beynon, flagons clanking in the outside pockets of his poacher's overcoat, his gay check trousers and co-respondent's shoes in strange contrast with the hoarse solemnity of his cracked voice as they sang their way up and out of the valley.

'Tonic solfa on the brain.' Abe would complain every year, but he underscored 'Sanctaidd' and the more maudlin of the Welsh revivalist hymns with the rest. They began with the hymns, careful to hit the right note under the caressing voices of the tenors, making their getaway like cliché-haunted actors in a television commercial, the repertoire changing to a cheerful obscenity at the first sight of the Severn Bridge and foreign England. Here, Abe and Elgar hooted wantonly with the rest, and with no more than an hour or two's separation in time from his mother's firm admonition to check that the sheets of his bed would be properly aired that night, Elgar, bright-eyed and pink-cheeked, would bawl in his high piping tenor with the others:

> 'I done her standing and I done her lying,
> If she'd have wings, I'd have done her flying!'

It was true abandon, one of the joys of Easter, and for Elgar, happy to be on the move once more, it should all have been normal. But why was it that even now, safely tucked up beside the faithful Abe, he imagined hostile glances were being cast in his direction? Bashie, seated far down the coach at the front, was constantly visible since by some bizarre coincidence his face appeared in the interior driving mirror, and as if that were not enough, Bashie actually turned from time to time and peered down the length of the coach. His eyes seemed to seek out Elgar and rested scornfully upon him so that Elgar looked away, at the same time crossing and uncrossing his neatly trousered legs and smoothing their creases with a nervous gesture. Throughout the trip, Abe Beynon gave him puzzled side-ways glances, and even when they trooped into the hotel which was persuaded each year to accept them, Abe continued to watch Elgar with a genuine concern that added to Elgar's embarrassment.

It, said Elgar to himself, whatever *it* was, was beginning to show.

Immediately, they had other problems. There had been flooding in the area, the hotel could not accommodate them all and the party had to be split up. The hotelier had made alternative arrangements. Would Elgar care to inspect the rooms in the adjoining boarding house, and would he also decide which members of the party would use them? At first, Elgar suggested that the committee be separated from the players.

'Oh, hell, no,' said Abe reproachfully. 'There's got to be someone responsible in each place.'

Elgar had a sudden terror of being in close proximity to Bashie Williams.

'Perhaps you and I could go with a few of the youngsters?'

Abe was anxious to remove his shoes since his feet swelled on long journeys.

'You go, Elgar.'

'But...'

'Just nip down, have a dekko.'

The whole party now stood in the foyer of the hotel and the baggage was being unloaded on the road outside. A decision was needed at once.

'Quick, Elgar. 'Fore they gets the gear off the bus.'

But Elgar could not decide. Through the doorway, Abe saw the last bag come out of the boot of the coach.

'Here,' said Abe. 'Mog, Dai, Mush, and you, Bashie, get hold of your gear and nip down the road with Elgar. What's it called, this place?'

'Harbour Rest,' said the manager.

'That'll be changed,' Abe said knowledgeably. 'Go on, Elgar, I'll sign us in by here.'

So Elgar found himself leading the party through the streets of the little Cornish town, Bashie bringing up the rear, the toothbrush which he described as his luggage sticking out offensively from his top pocket. The Harbour Rest was a tall Victorian boarding house set in a terrace and the landlady believed in making space go round since normal bedrooms were partitioned into two, with single beds jammed up against each partition. If Abe had intended that Elgar should inspect each room, he had not reckoned with Elgar's apprehension for no sooner had the party entered the building than the players began to deposit their luggage, and it was all Elgar could do to ensure that he had a room of his own on the ground floor. The players were anxious to rejoin the main party, so there was no inspection and Elgar began to unpack his suitcase with a continued sense of his own inadequacy. Once again, the presence of Bashie Williams had disturbed his sense of equilibrium. He simply must pull himself together.

'Where the hell you bin?' said Abe when he returned eventually to the others.

'Perhaps he's got a bit of stuff there already?' Bashie said loudly.

Elgar was silent. Normally, his practice when confronted with suggestive remarks of this kind was to give a sly wink and mysteriously imply that the jester was closer to the truth than he realized, but with Bashie, he had no such confidence. What might the fellow say next? Bashie, as it happened, was distracted by the arrival of a pint, and Abe drew Elgar to one side.

'I didn't mean you to stay down there yourself.'

'I could do with an early night.'

'Yes, you're looking a bit peaky.'

That night, Elgar dosed himself with tablets and awoke in a drugged stupor which had the effect of lessening his unease. Surely his fear must be a grotesque product of his imagination? What was needed was a return of his old confidence. If only he could find some remark which would cut Bashie down to size. He remembered his silence on the previous night in the face of Bashie's snide remark and tried to rehearse replies which he might have made.

'Perhaps he's got a bit of stuff there already?'

'Not under the same roof as you!'

That was better than silence. How he envied those like Abe to whom remarks of this kind came as second nature.

'You are,' Abe once said in a famous reply to an offender, 'about as much bloody use as a chocolate fireplace!'

If only he could sharpen his tongue and learn to defend himself. He would do well to learn from Abe, but then Abe had a street corner facility for repartee. Perhaps the best he could do was to continue to make himself indispensable to the club and seek whatever shelter he could beside Abe who knew very well how much he did for them all.

'There are some,' Abe said on one occasion, 'who could talk the robin off a packet of starch, but our Elgar is a worker; I say no more.'

Such praise as this, proclaimed when the committee was in full session, Elgar with his head modestly bowed beside his chairman, was for the Hon. Sec. the ultimate in acclaim, and the memory of it after a night of assisted sleep marked a return of confidence which was immediately bolstered by an odd occurrence at the breakfast table. Bashie, as might be expected, was late getting to breakfast. When he did arrive, bleary-eyed and unshaven, he sat at the end of the table in his shirt sleeves, blinking at the remainder of the party who were already beginning to eat the bacon and eggs which formed the main course.

The landlady approached Bashie with some diffidence and held a menu card in front of him. Elgar feared that he might come out with some uncouth remark, but as he studied Bashie's scowling face, he saw his lips move unfamiliarly as if trying to form the shape of a letter. Out of politeness, the landlady, thinking perhaps her handwriting was causing the difficulty, read the menu aloud.

'Would you like cornflakes, cereal, fruit juice or grapefruit?'

Bashie glowered once more at the menu, then at her, then cast a resentful glance up the table where several rashers remained on other plates.

'Wassamatter?' said Bashie aggrievedly. 'Can't I have bacon and eggs like the other boys?'

Elgar gave a little gasp. Bashie's thick lips bending themselves about the letters on the menu card was an oddly familiar gesture and Elgar suddenly realized that Bashie could not read. He was probably totally illiterate for Elgar now remembered his attempts to evade making his signature on the accounts book on several occasions, and when he did, he made a hasty scrawl, one foot in the door as if anxious to escape. So that was it. Elgar's own isolation from his fellows had given him a certain understanding of the problems faced by others, and it now occurred to him that Bashie's belligerence was explained by this inferiority. Would you expect him to be anything else but hostile to a schoolmaster? Perhaps the whole thing was an educational matter.

When the opportunity arose, Elgar dropped the news casually to Abe.

'Can't read?'

'No, he couldn't even manage the menu.'

'You didn't say anything, did you?'

'Of course not.'

'All I hope is, it don't put him off his game.'

Abe had other worries and their first game did not go well. Bloodied by visits from other Welsh clubs, the local side had made preparations and the first half was fiercely fought, a ball-denying contest with many abrasive confrontations up front, frequent whistling up by the referee whose nervousness far exceeded that of the players. It was not a game for the connoisseur, maul succeeding maul, scrimmage following scrimmage, and kicking up field predominated so that the ball-to-hand agility of such stalwarts as Ikey Owens, who in the past had displayed a thief-in-the-night quality when outwitting opposing outside halves — he had previously been named Ali Baba — was not obvious. It was grey football on a grey day, and Abe Beynon complained and complained and complained.

'I wish I'd never got out of bed.'

'Come on Pontlast — show your class!' entreated Elgar coura-
geously from the side of an opposing committee-man half his size.

'Boneless,' said Abe, all loyalty vanishing. 'If they was dogs, I
wouldn't give 'em house room.'

'Up and under Pontlast!' shrilled Elgar. 'Vary it a bit.'

'Vary it?' said Abe. '*Vary it?* Vary what? With what?'

'There's still time.'

But Abe grunted. He was inclined to take the game with religious
seriousness and when it passed below minimal expectations, would
brood in a sullen sog of memory, images of better days flowing
through his mind while his face took on the saturnine appearance
of a man confronting total and expected disaster of Asiatic proportions. In the vintage years, when there had been violent arguments
over the respective merits of two world-famous Welsh centres
known to him as Bleddyn and Dr Jack, he had quarrelled with his
brother-in-law and not spoken one word to him for two whole years,
thereby putting his undertaker's business in jeopardy since his
brother-in-law had county council connections and was instrumen-
tal in passing over the bodies of paupers and mental defectives at
two-pounds-ten the single journey. It had cost Abe dear, this
passion for Bleddyn, and when a game went wrong as it did now,
Elgar often felt that Abe was grieving, seeing not the present but the
past, though Abe still maintained his capacity for cutting everyone
down to size.

Elgar tried a new shout.

'Feet and take!' he yelled squeakily. 'Feet and take!'

Abe's eyes swivelled from under his cap.

'They're planting rice,' he said. 'Didn't you know?'

Elgar concentrated on the game. Now the play seemed to be
cemented under the Pontlast posts which rose like two sombre
headstones above the steaming packs of forwards. Ikey Owens,
hands on hips, stood with his back to his own line, but the bodies
in front of him might have been digging their own mass grave and
as the forwards slithered about, ball lost and never seeming likely
to emerge, Elgar saw Bashie's face break open as he gazed blankly
before him. On this occasion, he packed on the blind side, the side
nearest the touchline, but his appearance for once was devoid of
threat. All promise of a game had vanished. Even the rough stuff
was carried on in slow motion as if by men suffering from influenza
and Bashie's gaze resembled that of a foraging cow. Elgar saw him
detach himself from the maul and wander forward, passing the centre
line in his search for the ball, still moving forward while the ball was

dextrously held by the opponents and kept invisible, and now both Elgar and Abe saw the trick coming, one of the oldest in the book.

'Oh, look at him! Look at him! What's he waiting for? Milking time?'

They watched helpless as Bashie wandered offside and kept their silence as the referee blew and the inevitable penalty was awarded and kicked. Now ragged cheers from the few remaining supporters rent the air. Pontlast had lost, penalty goal to nothing.

Abe shifted his false teeth a notch, readjusted them, then sucked his breath as if rationing saliva for the remark that would immediately come.

'I always said he didn't have much upstairs,' Elgar said as they walked over to the dressing rooms.

Abe made no reply.

'Of course, he's big enough, but, well... is he worth the trouble?'

Abe continued to make no reply.

'I mean, of course, it was a pisscutter of a day,' said Elgar using a graphic phrase of Abe's. 'But I mean, the oldest trick in the book?'

Abe walked on bitterly, hands ground into his overcoat pockets. Flecks of mud splashed against his sporty check trousers, but again he held his tongue.

'A bad start to the tour,' Elgar said gravely. 'And needless. I mean, a draw would have suited us fine?'

Abe seemed inconsolable, did not return an opposing committee-man's cheery 'Well done!' and Elgar followed him into the visitors' dressing room where the exhausted players lay in various attitudes of despair about the benches. Bashie, as it happened, was standing examining various marks about his body and displaying certain scratches, the consequences of binding, as if these wounds were in any way an expiation of his cardinal ignorance. Offside under the posts... Was there any worse crime?

Bashie saw Abe enter, Elgar beside him, shark and pilot fish together.

'Oh, don't you bloody start,' Bashie said defensively to Elgar but the fact that he had picked on Elgar first was itself an indication of weakness.

'I've nothing to say at all,' said Elgar. But it was untrue. He felt decidedly perky. Now Bashie Williams positively looked as if he couldn't read. 'In fact, you're not even on the menu,' Elgar said sharply.

Bashie made no reply and Abe, overcoat open and thumbs to his braces, leant forward to look into Bashie's face, his eyes narrowing and lip curling, creating another Pontlast legend as he delivered the *coup de grâce.*

'Basil,' said he, using the name which young Bashie must have dreaded in street-corner confrontations as a child. 'Basil, my son, blind side don't mean shut your bloody eyes, you know!'

Bashie flushed, then turned away sheepishly. They would all change their views, of course, since the rugby world would come to know Bashie Williams, from the high veldt to the packed stadiums of the Pyrenees, as there were honours, both amateur and professional, awaiting him, and Abe's initial judgement was right, but now the lizard-like stare of Abe did not leave its prey, and Elgar, taking courage, capped Abe's remark with a pearler of his own making.

'Yes,' said he, also going for the throat. 'On reflection, it would have been better if you had attended your grandmother's funeral in Ireland.'

If ever there was a Pax Britannica, it did not extend to Pontlast R.F.C. at home or away, and the event marked a temporary decline in the career of Bashie Williams, for that night a chapter of accidents occurred that were not believed afterwards. Fifteen pints down, Bashie blundered by mistake into the landlady's bedroom, an occurrence that was made worse by his entire sixteen stone being in the nude. The landlady summoned the police. The police would not come. Then she roused Elgar and Elgar summoned Abe. At three o'clock in the morning a committee of investigation was set up.

'What was you doing in the altogether?'

'I thought it was the lav.'

'But she says you got hold of her?'

'Yes.'

'Well, then?'

'I thought she was the light.'

'Thought she was the light!' said Abe disgruntled. 'You're not in the foundry now, you know? How much had you had?'

'Fifteen.'

'Pints?'

'Yes.'

'And shorts?'

'No shorts.'

'Thank God for small mercies, anyhow.'

'Leave it to me,' said Elgar.

'Entirely in the altogether,' said Abe disgustedly. 'I mean he's got a stalk on him like a cauliflower even in the cold showers. What was the poor woman to think?'

'I'll have a word with her,' said Elgar blushing.

'After that penalty, this is the last straw,' said Abe.

'Please,' said Elgar.

'No, no, no,' Abe said. 'One thing leads to another, and as for that penalty...'

'As it happens, I've got a box of Mintoes in my case,' said Elgar helpfully, 'and we passed a flower shop on the way here. I've got my Barclaycard and...'

Now Bashie Williams looked more humble than Elgar had thought possible for he eyed the floor between the investigators like an abashed lout outside the headmaster's study.

'Well, what have you got to say to Mr Davies by here? Where have he got to now and on whose behalf, if I may ask?' fulminated Abe in his vintage county council English. 'Well, *Basil*? Say something, or have your tongue got mixed up with your what-d'you-call?'

'Sorry, Mr Davies.'

'I should bloody think so too. What a start to a tour! Go on, Elgar! Tell her he was born in the workhouse, didn't use a knife and fork until he was ten. Tell her he's an animal and we'll chain him to the coach for the rest of the tour. Tell her what you like. I'll leave it to you. I mean, Good God, it's not as if he'd met her before, is it? Never mind, go to it, Elgar. Bleddyn or no Bleddyn, all I hope is that Cardiff try to book in here next week.'

Elgar went to work and it was one of those occasions and one of those feats for which the Hon. Sec. was justly praised.

'What he done at the material time,' said Abe when the full committee were assembled, 'was to take charge at once. No messin', no adgin'. Without him, we'd have had a rape case on our hands more'n like, very unsavoury and not at all for the good of the game.'

A vote of thanks was in order and a vote of thanks was given.

'Well, did you enjoy the tour?' said Mrs Blodwen Davies when her son returned.

'Drew one, lost one, won three,' said Elgar. And that was all.

'D'you know, I think he's put on weight?' said The Caldi from behind her inevitable Benson and Hedges. 'Look at his little cheeks!'

'Nonsense!' said Eadie-Beadie.

'Yes, he has, he's positively glowing,' said The Caldi, coughing continuously.

'I have found out certain things about that woman,' said Mrs

Davies darkly when her visitors had gone. 'Public school indeed! She is the sort of woman who needs a recipe for toast.'

Elgar paid no attention. Remarks, remarks, remarks, he thought. They were surrounded by remarks which cut about their ears like knives, but remembering his own improved performance, he smiled. Not bad, that one about the funeral of Bashie's grandmother in Ireland. He had turned that to his own advantage, and it would keep. Then he might also dig up something about a box of Mintoes being as essential on tour as Mush's embrocation. Having learned to bite, there was suddenly no end to the number of points he might make in his speech at the annual dinner.

The reinstatement of the Hon. Sec. was complete.

Off the Record

Bunny Leyshon had two protruding front teeth which earned him the nickname which people were to remember him by all his life. They also gave him a certain undistinguished air which was much liked by old Aberdarren boys and by those who never left. His face, round and rabbity, made him seem always approachable and he was never without a certain open-mouthed concern for whatever went on around him. Although a busy man with a successful law practice, which included a hefty proportion of the miners' compensation cases which formed the bread and butter of his income, he was also much involved with conveyancing which added to the jam and amply supported his comfortable family. He was prosperous, he was happily married, he knew everyone there was to know and people liked him.

'Bunny Leyshon has done all right,' they said.

But it was said without envy. Bunny Leyshon had not only done all right, he *was* all right. He had no side, and what was more, he had a sense of humour. With his face, he once said, wryly pulling at a large pink ear, he took care never to eat salads in public. It was a joke which although well-known was much quoted in Aberdarren, and people also said that Aberdarren would not be Aberdarren without Bunny and they meant that also.

When you went into his office, you saw below that peculiar grey-tufted head with its unfortunate lower jaw, a short, dumpy little man with small fat hands and small fat legs, but this ample covering on so short a frame was somehow not unhealthy, since his smallness was a matter of height, rather than width and he was quite well made. He also displayed enormous energy on occasions, was peppery on the tennis courts where he played with some agility well into his fifties and could move with surprising speed when the occasion demanded. Sometimes, he had to stand on tiptoe to make his full presence felt in court, but he could be peppery there too. But even then his cheerful smile seldom left his face and he was a man incapable of scowling. Most important in a lawyer, he was also discreet and, since he was so well known and had somehow always been well known, he sent part of himself away with those who had left and whenever people met up and got to talking about old times, sooner or later, Bunny's name would come up. It was this capacity of his for being favourably remembered which brought the Hubert

Prices into his life, and with them, what might have been the Aberdarren scandal of the century.

It began with a telephone call at an unusual time.

'Hubert Price telephoned,' his wife told him one evening. Normally Bunny liked to be by himself as soon as he came in from the office, and he had a set routine of calling an endearment to his wife as soon as he entered the front door, pausing to pick up the evening paper where it was left for him on the hall stand, then vanishing into the front room where he seated himself in a large armchair and put his feet up on an adjoining stool. It was a practice which he had adopted to compose his digestive juices, he said, but his wife knew well enough that he wanted a respite from the noises of the children so he normally had what was called in the house Father's Half Hour, all to himself.

But now, as soon as he entered the front door, his wife came straight into the passage with the news.

'Did you say Hubert Price called?'

'He sounded hoarse, and said not to ring him at home.'

'Did he say what it was?'

'Only that he wanted to see you as soon as possible. He said he'd be here at seven, and please not to ring his wife.'

'Hubert Price said that?'

'Yes.'

Bunny raised his eyebrows, picked up the evening paper and went into the front room as usual, but when he had seated himself in his chair, his legs not quite touching the floor, he found he could not concentrate on the evening paper. Like most lawyers, he was used to urgent telephone calls and when they were from his contemporaries, he knew that the urgency of the call usually related to the caller and not himself. Nowadays he had very little to do with criminal practice but there had been times when his advice had been sought at all hours of the night, although nothing he could think of in that direction could possibly be associated with Hubert Price who, as headmaster of the town's second largest comprehensive school, was usually thought of as beyond reproach, one of those pillars of Aberdarren society in whose presence Bunny had now and again to discipline his yawns. This was hardly fair, however, since Hubert, a conscientious and much respected man, could not help the fact that he was somehow impregnated with education in Bunny's view. Hubert was a positive memory man as far as every act and statute dealing with education was concerned and he had actually caught Bunny out on a number of unimportant technical points when the two had been concerned in a recent matter.

Moreover, Hubert, although unchallengeable in his educational expertise, was the son of a railwayman who had been very good with his hands, passing on to his son further skills and, whenever Bunny thought of Hubert, he also thought of Hubert's do-it-yourself handyman's shed, on the ceiling of which one-hundred-and-thirty-seven screw top jars, containing one-hundred-and-thirty-seven varieties of nuts, bolts, screws and nails were carefully fastened for their owner's convenience. Hubert threw nothing away, and his knowledge of woodwork and building had once been the cause of threatened litigation as Hubert refused to accept a contractor's workmanship when an extension was built to the school. Hubert, of course, was in the right, but his stance as the man in the right had not endeared him to anyone, least of all Bunny, and, at first, when he thought about this urgent telephone call, he could only assume that it must refer to some builder's malpractice for which Hubert needed his advice.

But the more he thought about it, the more puzzling it became, since the idea of Hubert not wanting his wife to know that he had telephoned was itself extraordinary. Bunny assumed that there was nothing which Dorothea did not know about Hubert, and vice versa, since the two of them, from the outside at any rate, were as alike as two peas. She herself had taught for many years, only giving up when Hubert had become a headmaster and although childless, she now busied herself in good works about the town. They were both in their early fifties, a year or two younger than Bunny, but Bunny would not have said that he knew them well since he seldom saw them, and they kept themselves very much to themselves. Dorothea was a daughter of the manse, a history graduate like her husband, a large grand woman very much given to large grand hats. She was invariably polite, if a little proper, and whenever he saw her, Bunny invariably nodded and raised his hat to her across the street, but dallied no longer if he could help it. She was a trifle forbidding and Hubert himself was also so proper that Bunny could not for the life of him imagine what Hubert would want to conceal from her.

The question bothered him since he could find no easy answer for it. He knew they lived in a new detached bungalow at the edge of town but as far as he could remember they were not in an area where there were likely to be problems from neighbours and since it was a detached bungalow on a new estate, they were unlikely to have their ancient rights intruded upon. Savage dogs did not lurk

in the neighbourhood and, as far as he knew, their life together was
one of cosy contentment and indeed, whenever he saw them, they
invariably had a virtuous air of people about the common good.

If he had a reservation in his mind it was because he himself had
sprung from old chapel stock like them and he knew that the simple
puritanical codes of their forefathers had led to untold miseries in
people's lives, of which he was sometimes professional witness. But
misery was not a word which you associated with the Hubert Prices
either. They were too proper, too self-contained, perhaps even too
ambitious for any fall which might lead to such disappointment.
Think of them, and you put them automatically in what Bunny
termed the No-no-no category which description he reserved for
the town's ultra respectables. These were old Aberdarren stock but
Aberdarren had for years been eroded by the influx of immigrants,
first to build the canal, then the railways, then to be fed to the pits
when the pits were booming and, in the battle between the new
immigrants and the older farming and chapel people, the new
arrivals had won.

'You can't stop the world, nasty as it is,' was the general delighted
conclusion at this lessening of Aberdarren's ancient Welsh ties, but
the only conclusion which Bunny could come to was that Hubert's
difficulty must concern a building matter. 'Pound to a penny,' he
thought. The block floors had probably started to rise in the new
assembly hall and Hubert wanted his pound of flesh. Knowing him
as Bunny did, it was the most natural of conclusions.

But his wife kept Hubert waiting in the hall before she announced
his arrival. She came into the room and shut the door firmly behind
her.

'It's Hubert. He looks dreadful.'

'Hubert Price?'

'I can't believe it. He hasn't shaved and he's reeking of drink. He's
got a look in his eyes. I don't think I like to leave you with him.'

'*Hubert Price?*'

'If you don't keep your voice down, he'll hear you.'

'You'd better show him in.'

She did so and Bunny was careful to keep the surprise from his
face. She was right. Hubert was short and slight with pale weak eyes
masked by thick horn-rimmed spectacles and he covered his balding
pate by gathering lank fronds of hair across his forehead parallel to
his eyebrows, a practice which normally increased his harassed
monk's appearance, but now the strands had unwound and he
could not have looked more unlike himself.

'Hello, Hubert,' said Bunny. 'What can I do for you?'

The visit was not in any way to be social. Hubert did not speak for a moment, swayed mutely on the spot.

'My dear fellow,' Bunny said, 'it must be serious. Sit down.'

Hubert did so, passing a hand wearily over his forehead, avoiding Bunny's eye.

'Would you like a drink?'

Hubert shook his head.

'I've had enough.'

'One more won't hurt.'

Hubert sniffed, then fixed his eyes on Bunny. 'I take it that anything said in this room is absolutely confidential?'

'Of course.'

'Your wife?'

'She doesn't need to know anything.'

'Are you sure?'

'Of course.'

'She must have seen me.'

'She said you weren't well.'

'I'm not. My God, I'm not.'

'What is it, Hubert?' said Bunny. 'For goodness sake, man, I've never seen you look so rotten.'

Hubert sighed as if this remark was so inadequate as to be ridiculous.

'It's Dottie,' he said desperately.

'Dottie?'

'Dorothea. She's gone to her mother's. I mean, she's left me.'

'Left you?'

'Yes. She says she wants a divorce.'

It was on the tip of Bunny's tongue to come out with some mild blandishment, a chiding reproval of Hubert's hasty conclusion after a domestic quarrel which had grown out of all proportion, but he checked himself. He had seen Hubert niggle away at a carelessly worded contract and knew him to be a determined man who did not come to conclusions lightly. At the same time, he pulled embarrassedly at his ear and reminded himself of Hubert's age. If there was an age for indiscretion, Bunny supposed, then the fifties were as good as any. But Hubert was so staid normally that he could not for the life of him imagine Hubert committing any indiscretion.

Then Bunny remembered the one-hundred-and-thirty-seven brass screws in the oak beam. They must represent something he thought; every screw and every turn of the wrist needed to secure

them. Who else would have taken such care? And what thoroughness! He could see the line of them stretching with mathematical
precision in his mind's eye and wondered what it was that drove
Hubert to such exact lengths and to such precision. He had not
known Hubert well as a younger man, and now wished that he had
done so, for over the years he had formed a general conclusion in
this life that might be pertinent. If a man went off the rails it was
some woman's fault. It was a cliché but in his experience life was
full of clichés, repetitive patterns that occurred again and again.

'You'd better have a drink,' Bunny said. 'And you'd better start
at the beginning.'

The story Hubert told was quite extraordinary but the way in
which he began to relate it was even more odd. History was his
passion.

'You know of course, that I was born and brought up in Morgan
Street?'

'Morgan Street?'

'At the back of Ruby Street, by the canal. It wasn't quite as bad,
but you must know the area. I dare say a good deal of your criminal
practice originates from there. Half the truants in school come from
there still.'

Bunny again concealed his surprise and as Hubert went on, jerkily
telling the story of his life, Bunny who knew better than to interrupt,
began to see Hubert in a different light. The man he knew with a
fetish for filing cabinets and a positive lust for order and precision,
had begun life as the only son of a railwayman handicapped by an
ailing wife who, like Hubert, had a weak chest. The strains in the
little household must have been considerable, but not more, Bunny
thought, than in many houses in the thirties when the railwayman
like the postman, being continuously employed, was a minor aris-
tocrat in an age of strike and lock-out in the coalfield. Hubert was
also the only son, whereas others had large families to feed on
pittances, so that it was hardly accurate of Hubert to claim for
himself an impoverished background when there were so many who
were clearly much worse off.

But as he listened, he gathered that it was Hubert's mother who
was the bone of contention. Things, Hubert said heavily, had to be
just so, and it was imperative that Hubert should lose no chance to
get on and improve himself. She had the Welsh veneration for
education. The road out of the pit led through a school book.
Everything must be subjected to that end, and since she herself was
a woman of little education, having been in service since the age of

fourteen, it was the appearance of things that mattered. She seemed the sort of woman whose hands were never free of a duster, and Hubert's school books were inspected nightly. A fingermark would be commented upon. The correct margin on the side of a page was inspected as if it were a thing of beauty in itself. An answer was not an answer unless it was doubly underlined, often with the abbreviation *Ans* written alongside it.

Piece by piece, Bunny began to put together a picture of a childhood of straight lines, dominated by pencil boxes, penwipers and rulers, with school reports carefully filed on the mantelpiece and taken out to show admiring relatives and neighbours on high days and holidays. It was a world of timetables and allocated hours for this and that task, a routine which Hubert's father, far from helping him to escape, actually helped to maintain. In order to conserve his eyesight, Hubert was instructed to seek relief in wood-work, and there again a rigid order prevailed. Bunny had a sudden comic vision of Hubert in school cap and blazer sardined between his parents, an academic prune in the making, but then he chided himself. The trouble was, it was so difficult to be sorry for Hubert. The perfect boy had become the epitome of his mother's dreams but somehow you could not feel sympathy since he had so obviously acquiesced in everything she had desired.

'Home, school and chapel,' Hubert said bitterly. 'I did everything she wanted.'

Perhaps the fact that he had been drinking before this visit accounted for his outburst, Bunny thought. He had listened to a good many men whose feelings caused such cathartic outbursts. What he could not understand was the bitterness which now accompanied Hubert's recollection. He was positively lisping with resentment.

'D'you know, Bunny, I never went out with a girl until I went to University?'

'Never once?'

'Never. I never even made an assignation.'

Bunny had never heard the word pronounced before. Assignation, he thought. Only Hubert would have used it in conversation.

'You mean a date?'

'My mother wouldn't let me. She wouldn't even let me go to street parties and every time the Sunday School treat came up, she declined on my behalf. She said I got sick on the bus.'

'Did you?'

'I did, but I always got over it, and I always wanted to go.'

'And your father?'

'She ruled him. If I wanted to do anything, she always brought up the subject of my weak chest.'

'But didn't your father protest?'

'Not as long as I was allowed to help in the shed, and the allotment of course.'

'But you must have enjoyed some things, Hubert?'

'Some things, yes.'

'And school.'

'Yes, I enjoyed coming top. It was all I could do really.'

'And you still enjoy school? I've never heard anyone say anything that isn't entirely creditable about you. There are few disciplinarians left,' Bunny said with a smile. 'Surely, all this has meant something to you?'

'I'm beginning to wonder,' Hubert said hoarsely. 'What's it all for?'

For some reason, Hubert had declined to remove his raincoat and now sat facing Bunny, his eyes staring in front of him, mouth hanging limply open, his whole being revealing a man who had reached the end of something in his life. There was now a definitely seedy look to him, the points of his collar had twisted upwards, his tie was askew and behind his thick lenses, Bunny could see that his eyes were reddened by crying. It was an occasion for some commonplace remark to restore normality but Bunny could not find it.

'What's it all for?' Bunny repeated. 'You're asking me questions I can't answer, Hubert.'

'I know,' Hubert said. 'I can't either. But I thought I could, you see.'

Bunny wished that Hubert would come to the point. He must have called with a specific purpose in view, he thought, but then he realized that Hubert would not have indulged in this long preamble about his childhood if he were not seeking to explain some action as yet unrevealed. He decided it would be best to listen, knowing that Hubert was like many relatively innocent men whose lives had been led along prescribed paths, and the slightest lapse often took on consequences out of all proportion. There never was more remorse, he thought, than among the newly guilty. He decided to try and steer Hubert around to the subject of his wife since he had no doubt that it was to the person of Dorothea that his own attentions would be finally directed.

He rose, took up a bottle of Scotch and poured a drink for them both. Perhaps it was typical of him that he thought at the same time of the freshly filleted lemon sole which his wife was keeping for supper. Perhaps he should also invite Hubert, he thought. But he decided against it, knowing that Hubert would not want to confess even a fraction of his misfortunes to a third party. As it was, he must have been desperate to have come to him at all.

'Well, all I can say, Hubert,' he said warmly, 'is that whatever happened, you've been married, you've been successful. You've got twenty-five or so exemplary years to look back upon.'

Hubert smiled wanly and something of his old self returned with the smile which Bunny had seen before. It was the same thin-lipped smile which he had encountered when Hubert pointed out a penalty clause in a contract between the education authority and a firm of contractors for whom Bunny was acting. Sums of money were to be withheld if completion was not made on a certain date and the contractor had quite reasonably asked for them to be waived in view of unexpected and quite atrocious bad weather, but Hubert could not lend himself to this view. It was unfortunate for them, but they should have thought of it at the time, he'd told Bunny with the same smile.

'Twenty-five years,' Hubert repeated.

'Exemplary years.' Bunny said. 'Surely?'

'I'm afraid not,' Hubert said with a sharp little gasp of breath. 'I don't like to use the phrase, it's so novelettish; but I can think of no other. I'm afraid there's been another woman.'

Bunny controlled his surprise.

'And Dorothea has found out?'

'More than that. There are telephone calls all the time. She... she won't give me up.'

'I shall have to know her name, Hubert — this other party. And I shall also need to know what it is exactly that you want me to do?'

'I want you to see her. It's got to end. You could put the case formally. Or perhaps a letter.'

'I'll certainly do what I can,' Bunny smiled gently; then, sensing Hubert's embarrassment, became comfortably formal. 'But to whom should I address myself?'

Hubert delayed, but although his distress remained, Bunny was sure there was a trace of the old look of superiority on Hubert's face, a pursing of the lips that was not quite a smirk, yet left you in no doubt that Hubert was about to score a point.

'This is in absolute confidence?'

'Of course.'

'It's Nancy Smalls.'

Bunny swallowed, such a flood of information coming to his head that he could not prevent his mouth dropping open.

'She's married now, but in the old days you probably knew her as Howie Beynon's girl,' Hubert went on. 'Oh, I know everything about her, don't worry. I knew at the time, about Colley Peters, all of them, that set. Dorothea said that if Aberdarren ever had a Red Lady, she was it. She said it made her humiliation complete.'

It was Bunny's astonishment that was complete. Now he understood Hubert's smirk. Although they were all now in middle age, there'd been a time when Nancy Smalls had been worshipped from afar by a good many. She had film star characteristics, the cool disengaged look of a celebrity even at an early age. There was about her an air of difference, a variety of attractions, most of them physical and Bunny had in his mind's eye a picture of her riding pillion on a motor cycle, her long black hair flowing behind her, skirt awry, and his own envy of the somewhat racy men who escorted her. He had not seen her for years. After a chequered life, she'd married a newcomer to the district and lived out of town. Trust Hubert, Bunny thought, even his foolishness had somehow led him to the top of the class. She was such a cracker, he remembered. But what on earth could Nancy Smalls have seen in him?

Bunny cleared his throat.

'Is the er... relationship long-standing, Hubert?'

'I'm afraid so.'

'You've been very discreet.'

'I met her through Colley Peters. I went there to coach his son.'

'It must have been years ago, then?' Bunny remembered Colley Peters' death which was itself spectacular.

'Five years ago. She's married since, but that's another story. Her husband's quite indifferent.'

'And now you want me to put an end to the relationship?'

'Yes. Oh, yes. She'd got to stop ringing me up.'

'More than that surely?'

'It must end. Dorothea's put her foot down.'

'How long has she known about it?'

'I'm not sure. Unfortunately, however, she's taken the precaution of withdrawing all our securities from the bank. A good deal of the money is in her name. She says she's going to take enough and a lot more besides if I don't put a stop to it at once.'

So that was the squeeze, Bunny thought. One thing puzzled him, however.

'You were very anxious that she shouldn't know you called here tonight. But if she knows...'

'I'm afraid I told her I saw you some time ago.'

'And?'

'That you'd acted on my behalf previously, and the matter was ended.'

'When, Hubert?'

'Two years ago.'

'But it hadn't?'

'No.'

'Did she believe you?'

'Oh, yes. She has every confidence in you. She knows I wouldn't dream of consulting you unless it was final.'

Bunny grinned. 'Well,' he said, 'let's hope I'm successful a second time.'

There was more said and when Hubert left, Bunny's wife did not come into the hall and as Bunny opened the door for Hubert, there was an awkward silence between them as if the exit from the study was a step into an outer world where there could be no more confessions. Now action was required and it was clearly up to Bunny to do his stuff.

'Well,' Bunny's wife said when he got to the dinner table, 'don't tell me it's school buildings this time?'

He shook his head and the frown on his face indicated that he did not want to discuss the matter further. But the more he thought about it, the more his astonishment grew. He could understand Dorothea's reaction, he could understand Hubert's predicament, what he could not fathom was the behaviour of the third party and he had an uneasy suspicion that his lack of understanding was rooted in the fact that almost all the information he had ever received about Nancy Smalls was second hand and was, to put it bluntly, gossip.

From the very first time he'd seen her — it was at the end of the war — in clothes which defeated the idea of rationing, and riding in cars in the company of Howie Beynon, a bookmaker and one of the boxing fraternity, he'd associated her with a twilight world that he very seldom contacted. Howie Beynon had died of a perforated ulcer after a fight in a shop doorway when poaching Cardiff bookmakers had invaded his territory. It was the era of illegal street corner betting and Howie, a handsome man, wore his girls as flamboyantly as his clothes. But there was nothing at all odd about Nancy being *his* girl. It was a way out of Ruby Street, Bunny supposed.

Years after Howie's death, his memory next put Nancy in the company of old Doc Colley, and here he could not resist a grin for you didn't think of Colley these days without thinking of his end. Colley had ended his professional life as he began it, on horseback. Breathalysed at seventy-four, rumour said he had the British record for the amount of alcohol identified in the bloodstream. It was also said that the moment he put the police bag to his lips the crystals inside it had coagulated into something resembling minute beetroot. He'd lost his licence and made the national press by insisting on using one of his niece's horses on his rounds, but the manner of his death was even more spectacular, for Colley had expired after a fall while attempting to mount a parked car outside the Conservative Club at three o'clock in the morning.

That was Colley Peters for you. Some men went through life breaking all the rules. They seemed to have too much of everything, too much spirit, too much life if that were possible, whereas poor Hubert seemed to have no sap at all. His dampness never left him.

And yet... Bunny thought, chewing his lip. And yet indeed! He was forced now to think of Hubert as successor to men in whose company he would himself in some ways have felt inferior. And it was clearly no affair of the moment. She just would not let him go, he'd said. Bunny's last thought that night was of Hubert's purposeful application in his garden shed. Again, he remembered the screw top jars and smiled. There was a good deal he could not possibly know but it pleased him to think that Hubert as a lover might very well have the same meticulous thoroughness. He had once seen Hubert taking P.T. in the school yard and now the words of command came back to him with Hubert's precise enunciation: 'Open — stretch — bend!' and he chuckled to himself.

The next day, he determined that he would write to Nancy Smalls, but then it struck him that the affair might have been carried on unknown to her husband and he did not want to add complications, so he discreetly found out when she was likely to be alone, and telephoned her instead.

Somehow or other, he could tell by the promptness with which the telephone was answered that Nancy was in bed.

'Yes?'

'Leyshon and Leyshon. Bunny Leyshon speaking. I don't think we've actually met.'

'I know who you are.' The voice was cool at the other end.

'It's a rather delicate matter.'

'Hubert's told me.'

'I was wondering if I could have a chat with you at some time convenient to yourself?'

'It'll make no difference.'

'If you like.'

There was a moment's pause and Bunny heard a rustling of paper, and felt sure a shopping list was being consulted.

She was having her hair done on Wednesday. She could probably fit him in.

He shook his head ruefully. Some people...

Her appearance when she came was something of a let-down. It was ridiculous of him to have expected the old Nancy Smalls. She was certainly in her mid-forties and it was natural that she should wear a hat. Dorothea too was a hat person, he remembered. Hubert seemed to encourage them. What was more surprising was her complete composure. She looked at him shrewdly, a small neat woman in a check tailored suit, the formality of her white gloves, and the faint odour of an expensive perfume reminding him that his memories were unlikely to be of help. As it was, he could not help but notice that her lips, set in her perfectly composed face, were pursed with amusement and he felt distinctly conscious of his own unfortunate mouth. She remained a cracker and, despite her casualness, had evidently got herself up for the occasion. Good legs too, he noted, sighed, then began in his breezy confidential tones.

'I'm very glad you came to see me. Hubert as you know is in some distress and it must be very upsetting for everybody. I'm sure you'll appreciate that Hubert's an old friend and I'm really speaking to you as an old friend.'

She did not reply. Around her neck she wore the slightest of neckerchiefs, a blue polka-dotted scarf as fragile as a tissue, the only colour in her ensemble, and as he looked at it, he was reminded of Howie Beynon whose gipsy swarthiness often lent itself to gay handkerchiefs. But he cast away the image. Lucky man!

'And I hope too, that you'll regard me as a friend.'

Her lower lip quivered contemptuously in reply and he sensed something beginning to build up inside her.

'And really, what I want to say is, whatever has happened in the past, surely at your...' he corrected himself hastily, 'at Hubert's age, wiser counsels must prevail?'

She said one word. There was something very common about her voice, he noted, but perhaps it was that she came directly to the point.

'Yours?'

He gulped, but continued automatically.

'I'm sure I'm right in saying that Hubert has a great deal of affection for you, but he simply can't go on seeing you. There's Dorothea, there's his age, his position...'

She snorted at this, crossed her legs impatiently, fixed her eyes upon his own once more, a steely indifference to him obvious.

He was about to go on to say that all things come to an end, but he was becoming increasingly aware of the ineptitude of his remarks. Normally, he had a gift for the mundane expression which would cover up an awkward silence. He could find a truism for every situation, and in the most uneasy of social occasions his gift for lubrication had made him into a person that most people wanted to see. But for the first time in years, it occurred to him that a silent woman seemed to be making a complete fool of him, despite the fact that he had conducted a score of such interviews in the past, but then they were usually people who were intimidated by his position and status. Now, very much aware of the cold green eyes still fixed upon him, he felt an uncomfortable dryness at the back of his throat. It was very upsetting.

He hesitated, was about to continue when, prompted by that hostile stare, his mind went right back to his early years when he had scored a considerable success in breaking down a female witness. He had forgotten her name, but she too had seemed to look into him in the same way, as if exposing a quality of smugness and silently contradicting the rightness of a stance that he knew in his heart to be false. He was on the verge of moralizing again when he remembered those other eyes smarting at his attack.

'*Were any familiarities used towards you?*' (It was at a time when the formalities of the courts made the law even more of an ass than it was now.)

No answer.

'*Did he get the better of you?*'

No answer.

'*Come... He had connection with you, did he not?*'

No answer.

'*I must put it to you that you had connection with him on a number of occasions?*'

The foolishness of the phrase stuck in his mind. He had not used it since, but now, confronted by a similar hostility, it returned, and with it, a second dampening thought. He might laugh at Hubert, but now it occurred to him that there was a whole aspect of life in which his only connection — that word again — was that of voyeur.

A happy marriage, like an immense double bed, had swallowed him up, he thought. He was the prune, not Hubert.

He gulped, and changed his tune entirely.

'Well, what's to be done?' he said despairingly.

He did not like the way his mind was working.

Nancy Small rose to her feet. Her breast heaved. She had removed one glove and now she held it tightly in her hand like a weapon and beat it against her thigh. Again her eyes seemed to bore into him, hating him, and again he remembered his youthful aggression on that previous occasion.

'And after you had connection, it occurred to you that you might use the situation to your own advantage, did it not? Yes, or no?'

'You,' said Nancy Smalls in a small choked voice, 'you get him in here, and get him to tell me that he doesn't want to see me. Just get him in here.'

Bunny stared at her.

'And tell him, I'll have him whether he's on his arse or not. He doesn't need to bring a ha'penny with him. I'll find for us both. Oh, yes, I've more put by than you think.'

And with that she left abruptly, and Bunny immediately realized that he was witness of what he could only describe as a grand passion. Indeed, such was the violence of her feeling that he'd himself felt a thrill of excitement as he listened to her. It was extraordinary to think so, but there was a tempestuousness to the affair which was already communicating itself. Romance and devil take the consequences, Bunny thought. There was no doubt of it and feeling himself caught up with the destinies of these unlucky lovers, he at once telephoned Hubert only to receive a second brush-off.

Now it was his own excitement which was dashed and, within a day or so, he was made to realize that a door had been opened to him, but then very promptly closed in his face. Not only would Hubert not speak to him on the telephone, but he wrote him a dismissive note that was a complete about-turn.

'... in the circumstances, I'm sure you'll understand that the very act of talking to you was an indiscretion on my part and I would very much appreciate it if you would consider the matter closed. Dorothea joins me in thanking you.'

In short, Hubert regretted his confession, which was not surprising, but now it seemed that Bunny was to be kept completely in the dark and there was a considerable interlude of time when he heard no more. Hubert, as it happened, did not leave his wife and whatever passed between them remained private. In public, when seen, they nodded politely to Bunny, exchanged a few pleasantries and soon moved on. Of Nancy Smalls he heard not a word until one night, nearly a year later, when he was awakened by his wife at three o'clock in the morning.

'What is it?'

'It's Nancy Smalls.'

'Who?'

His wife handed him the telephone.

Now her voice was contrite. She hardly knew him. Did he remember her?

'Of course.'

'It's Hubert.'

'What is it?'

'He's dead. He just died. Just now...'

Bunny felt his own heartbeats.

'Where are you?'

'In the school. His room.'

'Then you'd better call the police.'

'I can't.'

'You can't?'

'He hasn't got a stitch on and I can't dress him myself. The caretaker's here, but he won't help unless somebody in authority's called and we don't want him to be found like this.'

Bunny did not hesitate.

'I'll come at once.'

The caretaker, an ex-collier and a local character, waited for him outside the school, a sweater, oilskin and gumboots over his pyjamas. He was a small ugly man and, for reasons best known to himself, held a storm lantern half hidden beneath the flap of his oilskin. Bunny noticed there were no lights turned on in the school.

'I told him and told him it would come to no bloody good, Mr Leyshon.'

'You knew?'

'Every Thursday. He even told me to turn the central heating up.'

Bunny swallowed, but said nothing.

'You'd better put your car lights out.'

'We shall have to call the police.'

'Let's get the poor bugger dressed first.'

'You could have dressed him?'

'More than my job's worth. She was going to call her husband, but I said anybody in authority would do.'

Nancy waited in the darkened corridor outside the headmaster's study. It was evident that she'd dressed hastily. Her hair was awry and in the lantern light Bunny could see that her eyes were animated. She closed them thankfully when she saw him but again she said very little, extended a hand and gently squeezed his arm.

'I knew you'd come,' she said warmly. 'He always thought of you as a friend.'

As before, he was at a loss for something to say, but the caretaker was a man of parts, Aberdarren to the core.

'We'll have to chop-chop,' the caretaker said, 'otherwise he'll be stiff as a board.'

Hubert's naked body lay face upwards on a leather couch which was normally used for medical examinations. His eyes were closed and the expression on his face was one of utter calm, with even — or was it Bunny's imagination? — the suggestion of the old scholar's triumphant, top-of-the-class smirk upon it. It was obvious that connection had taken place and upon Hubert's skinny shoulder the imprint of Nancy Smalls was left in a small circular bitemark. *Q.E.D.*, Bunny thought: *Ans.*

The caretaker held up the lantern and began to assemble Hubert's clothes which were strewn haphazardly over the floor.

'First his little socks,' the caretaker said and Bunny was very grateful for his colliery presence since the task was somewhat gruesome for so fastidious a man at this hour of the morning.

'Oh, yes, I told him and told him,' the caretaker said. 'Known him for years, but it's the old story. You can always tell a college boy, but you can't tell him nothing! Smart piece, mind, I give him that.'

They worked swiftly and silently and now Bunny gave his mind to his own position. He decided that the only thing he could do was to tell the absolute truth to as few people as possible. He would call his own general practitioner and then a police superintendent of his acquaintance and throw himself upon their mercy. He realized he was letting himself in for obvious reproofs, and it was he who would have to tell Dorothea part of the story and, in fact, the entire tidying-up operation would be under his direction.

'There,' said the caretaker when they had finished. He gave Hubert's tie an ironic twist. There was all Aberdarren in his crooked grin as he winked at Bunny. 'I never seen him look better even on Speech Day.'

Bunny went into the corridor again, but Nancy Smalls had gone. No doubt she would have some explaining to do. It did not bear thinking about, and now Bunny had to busy himself once more. There was Dorothea to be contacted, and all those phone calls to make, and now his depression set in and he began to regret his immediate response to the call for help.

It was only after Hubert had been buried with due propriety that Bunny came to any kind of conclusion, and by this time he was heartily sick of the whole affair. It was the first time he had ever compromised himself, he'd had a good deal of explaining to do, there'd been words with the police, some very unpleasant unofficial cross-examination and it was only his good name which had kept the matter relatively quiet. But finally a thank-you note came from Nancy Smalls which he opened in the presence of his wife who by this time, of course, knew everything. It was short and to the point and ended with a polite invitation to call in any time he was passing, and Bunny gave a little chuckle.

'You're not going to go?' his wife said.

Her momentary concern was a shot in the arm.

'I might.'

'*What?*'

First Howie Beynon, then Colley Peters and now Hubert, he thought. *Femme fatale* was not in it. And he knew no more about her than he'd ever done. Still... he made a little joke with himself. Perhaps there was only the one connection.

His eyes twinkled as he looked at the comfortable spread of his wife's full cheeks.

'In that corridor — in the lantern light — she looked about thirty,' he said teasingly. 'And her make-up had come off, of course. I mean, I don't know how she does it. Diet, d'you think?'

'The bigger the whore, the bigger the luck,' his wife said.

But he doubted that.

Jehoidah's Gents

M urder at the back of it!'
'Get away?'
'Murder, plain, unadulterated murder!'
'Jehoidah?'
'Not him, of course, not actually involved himself.'
'You do mean Jehoidah Wetter?'
'The same.'

The name was unfortunate but somehow right, and among generations of Aberdarren schoolboys who knew Jehoidah Wetter as the keeper of the oldest Gents in town, there must have been some who grew to manhood and power, for Jehoidah's Gents survived even the planners when the new ring road carved up the mainstreet. They pulled down the revivalist chapels, relodged the dead from their crumbling graves, gutted the old arcade, took away the hitching steps from which tipsy horsemen had once mounted in lofty gratitude and even decimated a solitary elm which had stood fungus-free for a hundred years, but Jehoidah's Gents remained.

True, it was subterranean, roofed by myriad lead-framed panes of frosted green glass, and true, it contained such luxuries as solid brass taps, boot-scraper and six of the best of those giant, man-dwarfing, china urinals with two-toned bull's eye targets to assist the aim of users both regular and casual, but where the planners had profaned the living and the dead, it was unlikely that they would pay heed to Jehoidah's beloved china. Neither he, nor his long suffering assistant at the time, the gaily peroxided Vida Hodge who had responsibility for the adjoining Ladies, could be said to be persons of influence. That they did not get on was well known, that weeks could go by without them speaking was normal, but none of these things could have been known to the planners. More likely, Jehoidah's Gents survived like a buried china temple perched above the river beside an ancient one-span bridge, simply because it was virtually out of sight.

But on the other hand, someone not knowing Jehoidah's Gents might not have heard of Jehoidah's habits and wished with a quirk of anarchic mirth to preserve them. For Jehoidah, dark and brooding with things on his mind, had begun a stealthy practice of giving the Ladies a thorough weekly clean, and then immediately locking it to guard against any possibility of use. This was in the absence of

Vida Hodge, but to Jehoidah, it was as if the Ladies with its extra
portion of post-war terrazza flooring was lovely as it was, acquiring
by his action a new virginity not to be despoiled by the slightest
shadow of a female footprint. Of course, Vida's absences contributed to the general deprivation and they were much reported, but
to no avail. Bursting women had been known on market days to
rattle locks and chains on the separate Ladies' gate, some evenings
crossing to shout down the Gents' iron stairway opposite where
Jehoidah lurked safely out of sight in his tiny office.

'I say... Attendant! Excuse me, is there anybody down there?'

But Jehoidah, a small, hunchbacked, beetle-browed figure ever
conscious of his deformity and with the grey pallor of his trade,
would smile secretly to himself, reach over his brooms, brushes,
scuttles of sand and cans of disinfectant and score another *A* for
absent on the time sheet of Vida Hodge. If a male customer were
present and just happened to overhear while he was about his toilet
and drew Jehoidah's attention to the desperation of the caller above,
Jehoidah would shake a hand fussily as if to say, 'I can't be
everywhere'. He would take care to make no sound however, and
usually the caller would walk stiff-legged away.

Once, the wife of the Chairman of the Urban District Council, a
reforming busybody known as Mrs Ivy Price Bevan, finding herself
caught short and receiving the silent treatment, had actually come
tottering down the hallowed steps of the Gents to confront Jehoidah
who had his feet up on a makeshift desk in his little caboodle.

'Mr Wetter, I've called and called.'

Identified, he sprang blinking to his feet like a startled mole, took
his peaked blue uniform cap from the hook beside him, and immediately
ushered the good woman back up the steps with a sympathetic
tut-tutting.

'Goodness gracious me, I *am* sorry, Mrs Price Bevan. It's that
woman Hodge.'

With much rattling of his silver key chain, he emerged into the
daylight to find a WVS coach party recently returned from a salmon
tea in Tintern Abbey and now bulging across the pavement in a
huddled group. All looked intently at him, but he immediately
assumed a pose of obvious deference, continued tut-tutting to
demonstrate that he was sympathetically disposed, flourished his
keys once more, plunged the appropriate key into the lock, and
rapidly slid open the metal gates of the Ladies, at the same time
extending a welcome palm to indicate that those who were desperate could enter without further ado. With his other hand, little

master of the trade that he was, he displayed a pocketful of chosen coins, indicating that they may be taken up as they passed, a thoughtful gesture that was not appreciated by Mrs Price Bevan who remained standing haughtily to one side, in control of herself as ever.

'Surely the convenience should be kept open until ten-thirty?'

'Quite right, Mrs Price Bevan. But I can't be everywhere. I got a stop cock giving trouble as it is.'

'Where is Mrs Hodge?'

'You may well ask, madam.'

'But surely she should be here?'

Now Jehoidah was silent, shook his head gravely, followed this movement of the head with a disparaging lift of the palms, managing at the same time to give the impression that he was well aware of the gravity of the situation but for reasons of professional loyalty was compelled to say no more.

Yet when pressed, his reserve leaked away.

'I do the best I can, Mrs Price Bevan. I've put in for reliefs. I've been down the Sanitary and up the Council Offices times without mention.'

Mrs Price Bevan frowned.

It was clear that this was no casual absence and that she had uncovered a nest of tangled resentments and feelings, but her strong investigatory will was now under pressure for she dallied no longer and made a swift movement to pass him. With great daring, Jehoidah also moved a pace, partially blocking her way and they descended a step together in unison.

'If there's anything extra I can get you personally, Mrs Price Bevan? I'm sure you'll find everything's spotless.'

Purpling, she turned, crossed one leg over the other.

'There's no need for you to come down, Mr Wetter.'

'I was just going to tell you to mind your high heels there on that bit of lead flashing. And if there's anything you require, just give a knock on the pipe. The Ladies connects with the Gents, d'you see?'

Mrs Price Bevan, despite the pressures evidently at work upon her, paused to look at him carefully for the slightest trace of insolence but his thin little lips were gravely downturned, his green eyes discreetly lowered and his bent hunchback's frame in its blue uniform conveyed such an overwhelming air of official concern that she was partly mollified.

But again he held her in conversation.

'I'd rather have it happen to anybody but you, Mrs Price Bevan.

And the same goes for your good ladies. I mean, I can see by them that they'll leave everything as they find it.'

She had not the will not the physique to reply, nodded with what dignity she could muster, then hurtled down the steps while Jehoidah adjusted his cap, passed his key chain behind his back and stood officially on duty above the frosted green glass roof, maintaining one of his rare above ground public appearances, while below him, the ladies at last relieved themselves. Despite his deformity and small stature, there was something of the prison warder about his stance as he awaited their reappearance with proprietorial interest, and indeed, he gave the impression of counting the party as they returned up the steps, making a little business of his extra duty. Mrs Price Bevan emerged last of all, evidently considerably relieved for she now moved with a more glamorous languor, adjusting the large purple hat which she wore as she looked down upon Jehoidah with an agreeable condescension.

'Thank you, Mr Wetter, I'm sorry you've been troubled.'

'My pleasure, Mrs Price Bevan.' Sensing her better humour, he lowered his voice to inform: 'And if you or your husband can do anything about that Vida Hodge, I'm at my wits' end here on market days, I don't mind telling you.'

Mrs Price Bevan nodded, shook her several chins, but now the severity seemed to have left her ample features and he caught a whiff of port and lemon as she passed. Sadly, he realized that once her urgency had gone, so too had her animosity. Vida Hodge was safe again. He sighed, then bade the party farewell with a slow deliberate lifting of the cap, muttering a few sociable words as the lightened coach sped off into the night.

'Any time, ladies!' he called with obsequious gallantry but as he returned below to his cubbyhole, his depression returned. He'd never get The Vida sacked unless the powers were compelled to act at bursting point in the full throes of their deprivation. He seated himself behind his plank once more, scowled, and in his mind began to assemble the facts of this latest breach of duties on the enemy's part, fitting them together in the workmanlike manner of Central Cleansing, that council department which allegedly kept a log of the inadequacies of its servants.

'*Vida Hodge,*' his mind ran; '*absent throughout day. No notice given. Compelled to open up. Party of twenty. Mrs Ivy Price Bevan among. Duly reported. Gents left unattended 5 min.*'

As everybody at Central Cleansing knew, he could have gone on all day about The Vida (his pet name for her). For years he'd had single control over both the Ladies and the Gents and when supervising the former, he'd been mindful of the peculiarities of the other sex and had always taken care to place the chain upon the gate above. He did not want some little pretty to come stumbling down upon him out of station so to speak, and he had always behaved with the utmost propriety, but the time came when Central Cleansing, doubtless with the approval of Sanitary (its controlling body), had insisted upon a partner.

'You're going to have a little dickeybird down there with you.' (They were a jocose lot in Central Cleansing.)

'Another attendant?'

'That's right.'

'A woman?'

'That's him. You got it.'

'But I've managed on my own for years?'

'Well, not any more. It's a council minute. You're all having them.'

'General distribution?'

'That's him.'

He was relieved that he had not been suspected of anything untoward, one of the distinct risks of the trade. But there was more information of a disquieting nature.

'Who is she then? Mine?'

'Vida-something. Hodge, I think it is. A widow, it says here.'

She was a widow with a difference however, for she had returned to Aberdarren after a long absence, and rumour had it that she had been dramatically deprived. It seemed that her husband was an acrobatic motorcylist who had plunged in flames to the ground while doing a high altitude turn in a side-show known as The Wall of Death.

'Wall of Death?'

'You know, one of them fairs.'

'Get away.'

'That's what I heard. The Council was in tears when they gave her the job.'

That was Central Cleansing for you, and Jehoidah did not believe it. They would say anything, but when she came, his first thought was that they were playing some grotesque joke upon him, for Vida Hodge was so small with such short fat legs and squat dumpy body that his reaction was graphic: out of a circus!

'This is Mr Wetter.'

He attempted a limp smile.

'Pleased to meet you,' she said flatly. From her tiny face, as brown and wrinkled as a walnut, her cupid's bow of a mouth gave a miniature smile, but her pale eyes looked up at him with a flicker of resentment. He noticed that pale stare at the outset, something not quite right about her, a gap between what she thought and what her face said.

'Mr Wetter, Mrs Hodge.'

'How d'you do?'

'Middling, thank you.'

'She'll be starting Monday,' the duty foreman said. He leaned forward over the counter, towering down above both of them.

'Very convenient,' Jehoidah said.

But even as he spoke, she took a step away from him. Her lips were frankly disparaging.

'Anything you want, don't hesitate to ask Mr Wetter. Been at the game all his life,' the foreman winked.

Jehoidah did not like the way the foreman seemed to exclude him with that wink. Trouble already, he thought. People on her side, not his. Game, indeed! He drew himself up as much as he could and folded his arms gravely.

'Monday will be quite convenient,' he said again. 'Nine *sharp*,' he emphasized. Start as you mean to finish, he said to himself.

She made a small distasteful pout with her mouth, then accompanied it with a disrespectful snicker at the back of her throat before nodding finally with sneering condescension. As she scuttled away he noted that she carried a handbag as big as her head.

The duty foreman sighed. Clearly, it was going to be no romance.

'All right for brushes down there, are you?' said the foreman, but Jehoidah did not reply. His instinct had divined an oddity about The Vida in the first moment of meeting. There was definitely something not quite right about her, a something that spelt a lack of feeling evidenced by her automatic smile and the cruelty of that snicker. Her contempt was her true self, he felt. Just who did she think she was?

On the Monday she presented herself with her flagrantly peroxided hair and listened to his instructions in complete silence as if she had not previously believed her fate and now the reality had dawned upon her. They stood uneasily on the green glass sward separating the two offices, and he held his chain with its jangling keys importantly behind his back.

'Of course, we clocks in, d'you understand? Clocks in and clocks out.'

'Is there a clock here?'

'A manner o' speaking. I keep the time sheets. Very important, them.'

'Is there one for me?'

'There is, but I fill it in. Then there's Indents.'

'Who?'

'Indentations. When drawing from Central Cleansing, you indents. On a form. But I do that.'

'I thought...'

'Pardon?'

'I 'spected you did.'

'But anything you want, let me know.'

'Ta,' she said. Just that. 'Ta.'

'They go in every week. But in good time. Thursday is too late for Friday if you understand me?'

She said nothing; the lizard eyes flickered over his hump, then looked lazily away.

'In twenty years,' he elaborated proudly, 'I've never failed to get what I want from Central Cleansing.'

She was unimpressed, pouted once more.

'Is there keys?'

He produced them. 'Here,' he said. But he'd open up. And close. He did not say so but he slept with his chain under his pillow. 'All right?' he said. 'I think that's everything. Have you got that?'

'What if you're not here?'

He gave a small superior smile.

'I'm always here.'

'If you're on the sick or something?'

'Never been sick,' he said. 'Never once. Haven't missed a day in twenty years.'

'It suits you, I can see,' she said. 'It's your cup of tea all right.' She moved a step to one side, half-turned, then looked back at him. 'Gawd, there's nothing else is there?'

He had nothing else to say but he could not keep silent.

'Breakages,' he said. 'If you break anything, keep the bits. They're very fussy down in Central. A brush, anything like that.'

'Charmin',' she said. Again she moved to one side of him, looking down at the river with that small secretive smile.

'What did you say?'

'I wonder you don't take it home with you at night.'

He flushed. 'It's Central,' he said, inventing an enemy. 'They're on top of you in this job, the slightest thing.'

It was the longest conversation they were ever to have, and through it she kept fidgeting, looking this way and that, only looking directly at him to scrutinize his hump, it seemed. It dawned on him that she did not want to be seen talking to him above the ground and in public view. Even as he addressed her, she seemed to be moving this way and that as if contriving to give the impression that she was not actually with him and this impression was to be confirmed. In the weeks that followed, he might be standing at his gate or loitering with a brush at her entrance, and whenever he appeared, she'd be gone again in a flash, scuttling down the steps, purposely placing the railing in between them, or hurrying across the road where there was a café kept by Italians which Jehoidah did not frequent. She was a woman on the scuttle, he soon saw, for she simply would not stand still and her little legs would shoot out from her body as she jerked away from him with startled irritable movements, and always that deadpan, ignoring face.

'Good morning,' he might say.

No reply.

'Off now, are you?'

The snicker was her answer. She never passed the time of day and whenever he spoke, his voice was like a repellent wind turning her face in the opposite direction.

He soon formed the habit of talking to her under his breath. 'Scuttle you, my girl,' he would say. 'Yes, go on you, turn away. There you go again, crabby. One of these days you'll be running out of something.'

When she was gone, he immediately went down to the Ladies to check. If there was so much as a layer of rime on the wash basins, or a brush out of place, he reckoned to himself that he would have her back, stand over her while she scrubbed out, but as it happened, he had little cause to complain. She could not reach as high as he could, nor had she mastered the double-jointed brushes, and of course usage was not particularly heavy since the Ladies, being placed like the Gents immediately over the river was somewhat dank and draughty in its approach. It was not as popular amongst the pretties as was the Gents amongst the lads and only those in dire need ever went there, but all in all, he had to admit she did her job well enough for her size and if he had been asked to report he would have pencilled in *adequate*, with reservations. 'Well, for someone her size anyhow,' he thought. Naturally, if she was avoiding him all day, she had to do something down there, so he could not really fault her on that score.

But after a month in virtual solitude with both of them resting haughtily apart in their separate offices, he found that she was attempting to leave early, so all one forenoon he rehearsed his employer's speech.

'Don't you come that with me, my pretty. Oho, no. We've been too long at the game this end. Think I started yesterday, did you? Now then, just stand up if you please, and *stand still, gel!* This Authority is not made of money, you know.'

But as it happened, he had to bolt up the steps to catch her. He only knew she was leaving because of the rusty hinge of the Ladies' gate which he purposely did not oil since it acted as a useful give-away sign of her comings and goings. He nearly tripped over with the effort of confronting her, then extended a forefinger in front of him in an ancient school-masterly gesture.

'Excuse me, Mrs Hodge, you're not thinking of leaving, are you?'

It was their half day, and as he recovered himself, he drew out his watch pointedly. 'Unless I am mistaken, there's still ten minutes to go?'

Her mouth formed a sulky parabola, but still her eyes avoided his. She seemed to speak to the passing traffic.

'Travellin',' she said.

'Travelling?'

'Travellin' time. I'm off down Central Cleansing.'

Trust her to put him in an agony of indecision! Whether or not she was in the right was a debatable question. He would himself have left early to visit headquarters, there was no doubt about that, and if she had asked — if only she had asked! — his reply would have been magnanimous.

'Certainly, it's a tidy step down there.'

But she had not asked. Even now she did not look at him, and her gaze flittered this way and that. She would not keep her eyes still in case they fell upon him.

'Is there anything I can do?' Again, he attempted a benevolent condescension.

Her answer was to snicker again, arching her little eyebrows, and creasing up her snub nose. Her lips were frankly parted, as if to say, 'And what d'you think you're capable of?' Once more she looked pointedly at his hump.

He blushed hopelessly. 'In that case, no doubt they can wait ten minutes,' he said cuttingly. It was all he could manage.

He would have stared her out, blush or no blush, but in a flash she was gone, her short fussy walk darting her across the road, a ridiculous umbrella picking at the ground, her whole body heaving with contempt. Even her small sack-like rear spoke volumes of unpleasantness, he thought, and now his authority was totally flouted. And what is more, it was not a matter for which he could report her in Central Cleansing. The short-arsed little minx!

He knew his blushing had given him away, and now he covered up. Very well, he thought; all right, my beauty, softlee softlee catchee monkey. If that was the way she wanted it, he would keep his distance and bide his time. But one slip, he said to himself; just one slip, she'd be out on her neck... if anybody could play a waiting game, he could.

But he couldn't. Despite himself, he experienced a change of feelings and he now began to take her home with him like a growth rooting in his mind, home to his solitary bed in the solitary room above a flower shop where the scent of dead flowers from the bins behind the shop was forever in his nostrils.

Those born with deformities learn at an early age to cope with the buffets of fate, the unkind looks, the hostile glances, even the shivers of repulsion which come their way, but it had been years since Jehoidah had been so affected by a rejection from the opposite sex. Of course, he had taken part as a child when certain matters were talked about at the street corner and listened wet-lipped when the street boys talked about this girl or that, but he had always known that such affairs were not for him. If girls were nasty, women were much the same — look at the way Ivy Price Bevan looked all the way down her nose at him! — and if he had any wish, it was for a bit of company.

'My old woman,' the foreman raged in Central Cleansing. 'My old woman this, my old woman that...' The foreman liked his few jars and after a good Sunday wet, he would smack his lips appreciatively and boastfully inform the boys that he was always last to leave the Club, and no one dare say a word when he got home. The boys said his dinner was always fried to a crisp and he was only allowed out on condition he washed every dish in the house the moment he arrived back, but it made no difference. It was such an 'old woman' that Jehoidah wished for, someone to complain about, a name to drop, even disparagingly, in the company of like-minded fellows.

'What d'you think my old woman put in my box today? Jam sandwiches! I'll give her what for!'

Such talk was the meat and drink of idle mornings in Central Cleansing and how Jehoidah would have loved to have joined in with the men, elbow on the counter, cap flat-a-back with yet another tale of 'the one I got'.

And from the first, The Vida had seemed at times — he had to admit it — eminently suitable for this role. Like himself, she never seemed to have been young. You could not imagine her in a pretty dress or tripping the light fantastic and, like Jehoidah, she seemed to be permanently middle-aged. He was discounting that cold remote part of herself for the moment, but whatever was the truth of her story of her husband as a fearless rider on The Wall of Death, he could not imagine her wringing her hands while the machines roared above her. Instead, she was more likely to be placed in the ticket office, that repellent gaze keeping people away. All that, he could imagine, and indeed cope with. Who better? Even the gaze was manageable.

'I can take most things, boys, but the way my old woman looks at me on a Friday...'

He might, he might not, use the words, 'old tart'.

'My old tart may be small, a little *twt*, but by God, she's got a tongue on her!'

All roads led to this image in his mind; a bit of company, even if it were only someone to complain about. And it did not seem far-fetched once he had retired to his bed and propped his hump against its special cushion and folded his hands unevenly behind his neck to gaze as usual at the shadeless bulb. It was not at all far-fetched, not in any sense of the word. If he had thought of kissing The Vida, to say nothing of other unmentionable things which he had long ago forbidden himself, it would have been ridiculous, but he had no such thoughts. He merely wanted her to be sociable. And she wouldn't even look at him! Wouldn't even stand still while he talked to her!

It was a problem. He had not felt so wretched since the time when all the street boys seemed to acquire roller skates on the very same day and how he remembered that, pretending he did not care while the whirring steel-shod feet struck sparks around him, and he, like The Vida, looked anywhere but at the source of his discomfort. It wasn't as if she herself were normal, he thought aggrievedly. No great catch, he decided, just as he was no great catch. And that manner of hers, the deadpan snicker and the strange absence of any feeling which only he had divined. Of course, it would lead to trouble, big trouble, but that was a piece of foresight he was to remember later. Now he thought about it with compassion. Could it be the result of her tragedy? Perhaps she really had been widowed in tragic circumstances. There was such a thing as The Wall of

Death. There were riders who risked their necks for other people's entertainment. Perhaps he had been wrong to ridicule it. Somehow or other, he had found out that her husband's name was Arthur and he tried to visualize the crash. Again he saw her in the ticket office, the roaring machines audible behind her — and the more he thought about it, the more perfectly at home she seemed amongst all those ne'er-do-wells who followed the fairs. And he could just hear the dreadful crash, the stunned reaction on the fateful day. Perhaps machines had collided. He could just see the witless Arthur dragging others to their deaths with him while the spectators screamed and covered their faces. Before long, he saw himself there as he broke through the curtain at the rear of of the ticket box.

'What's up?'
'Your Arthur.'
'What's happened this time?'
'Drink again. Either that or plugs.'
'I'll give him a roasting when he gets home.'
'Didn't you hear them screaming?'
'Oh my Gawd, I knew it would happen one day.'
And he could just see himself relating it in Central Cleansing.

'From the moment we met, me and my old girl, there was tragedy behind us. Of course, she gave up the shows the moment she married me. I put my foot down. I told her straight...'

But how could he tell her anything when he could not get within spitting distance of her? No matter how he dreamed, and he dreamed more and more and spent half the day talking about her to himself — she remained slippery and her slipperiness, her very silence, was the cause of his fantasy.

'Think I can't ride a motorbike? Yes, I can, I got a licence. Ride one easy. Don't you talk to me like that, you wait until you been down here one whole winter. There's sights to be seen and not very pretty either. We are above the river, you know. Yes. Yes, well don't come screaming to me when the rats starts. They bark some of 'em do, and there's one here, an albino with pink, pink furry little eyes that cries like a baby.'

He had long ago discounted the unpleasantness of his job and he had not the capacity to see it as others saw it. Now The Vida's increasing silence drove him further and further into himself.

To begin with, there were patches of reality when he attempted to cover up.

'How're you getting on with her?' they said in Central Cleansing.
'The place is clean enough.'

'What's the matter then?'

How could he tell them? He could not confess his need for company, let alone his wild imaginings.

'Keeps herself to herself,' he said at first. But it changed: 'Never on time.'

'What?'

'Brought up in the fields for all the attention she pays to the clock.'

'Get away.'

'I can't do a thing with her.'

'What is there to do then?'

He did not bother to explain and the final insult came when she began to ignore him completely. She formed the habit of arriving after him and leaving ahead of him, and whole days might pass without their seeing each other, although from the scufflings he heard next door as she tripped about in her slattern's slippers, he knew well enough that she was there and ignoring him. The insult was definitely personal, and her behaviour was neither sociable nor proper, not with him in charge and on the top rate. When the wages van came on a Friday, her money, properly docketed, was paid to him first and he had the immense satisfaction of handing it over.

'Mrs Hodge? Just a minute if you please. I think you'll find that's correct.'

But then, with the low cunning of her sex, she formed the diabolical habit of timing the arrival of the wages clerk, slipping up topside to meet him so that the precious envelope was put directly into her own hands, thus cutting him out of the transaction alto-gether. For several weeks, there followed a comedy of exits when they would both rush up their separate stairways so as to be the first to confront the wages clerk, she beating him by a head and again making him conscious of his deformity. The third week it rained and Jehoidah, despite his oilskins, got himself soaked as he hung around above ground, only to find that she had left her place of duty and sought out the wages van from the better vantage point of the café over the road. She got to the clerk first yet again, and stood parading herself under her umbrella, addressing the clerk with a familiarity that was sickening.

'There you are! I was thinking you'd took off!'

Beaten again, Jehoidah watched her with the rain soaking the collar of his good shirt, positively glowering as she twirled the umbrella with coquettish triumph, but again she did not speak to him directly.

'He won't want his,' she said. 'Not him. He does it for love.'

Another giggle and she was gone.

And Central Cleansing could not resist one of its poorest jokes.

'What are you doing up here in the pissing rain? I should have thought you had enough down below?'

'Hand over!' Jehoidah said to the wages clerk. 'Just hand over!'

Autumn came, leaves, floods, footprints; the river rose and they could hear it rippling ominously below them, but to cap it all, Jehoidah formed the impression that she was now entertaining next door, since an old biddy who might or might not have been her mother, began to call daily and he could hear her voice rising and falling as they quarrelled. The old biddy, a bedraggled woman not much taller than the Vida with wrinkled lisle stockings and the worn exhausted look of the poor, also paid no attention to Jehoidah, except to give him a queer look as she hurried past. She went down below daily, often carrying a parcel which contained sandwiches. On several occasions, she was accompanied by another woman of much the same age, two old bodies in black who stayed hours and now he noted *Friends* with acute jealousy.

The Vida's caboodle was much the same as his, had an electric point, and when they began to brew up in there next door he heard the rattle of teacups, a sign of domestic sociability which he felt to be quite improper. He was sure they were talking about him, and as they cackled together his fury increased. That sort of thing would encourage the rats, he was sure, and she'd better take care that she left no scraps about. As usual, he inspected the Ladies nightly after she had gone, and the height of his loneliness was reached when he began to take cakes of her soap away at night. On another occasion, he hid a brush in a hiding place known only to himself. All he wanted was that she should speak to him. Still, he imagined fruitful conversations.

'Mornin' Jed, a little low on soap this morning.'

'I'll drop a case down right away.'

But no, crafty devil that she was, she did not mention anything to him directly, but addressed him through wages clerk, letting everybody go without until Friday, depriving the general public and turning the tables on him without the slightest loss of face.

'I don't know what he does with the soap. I'm right out.'

'Jed?'

'There's soap here in plenty. All she's got to do is ask.'

'Then there's brushes. I got one here that walks.'

'Jed?'

'Brushes cannot walk.'

'I got one that does.'

As usual he came off worst, the only thing he could do was to get himself in his best uniform and present a face to the world, as he strutted immaculately in his council blues, only to meet the worst that central Cleansing could do.

'Hey Jed, you're all done up today? You haven't got a competition going on down there, have you?'

Her laughter and the appreciative smirk of the wages clerk sent him down below for the day, and when the old biddy came he could swear she was repeating the story and for weeks, he addressed the wall in his fury.

'Vida Hodge, I have suffered in my life and I am not going to suffer further. Let me tell you, I have spent my life in the service of this authority...'

Once when two scrubbed colliers had called in on their way home from the club and were steamily installed, he blurted aloud: 'It's got to stop!'

The colliers exchanged glances, adjusted their dress and left, carefully picking up their booted feet with eyes averted, the grim expression implanted on their faces that of men well used to harrowing sights. There were also times when he would aim the nozzle of the hose at the partition wall like a man dealing out a jet of lethal insecticide, but quite oblivious of the fact that The Vida was long gone. By now, his obsession was total. He had even begun to lose weight, his cheeks were hollow and now the fantasy began to run riot, but still for the most part following the lines of his real experience. Like the time when he had gone to work on a grey November morning and his beloved Gents loomed out of a mist which was so thick that parts of the swirling river below were quite obscured.

'Don't go in there!' She approached him from a vantage point beside a telephone kiosk.

'What's the matter?'

'There's something happened. Look, beside the bridge. Some-body's broken the windows.'

Behind the Gents and connecting with the Ladies, there ran a boardwalk used by maintenance men. It hung over the river and from time to time, hooligans had to be prevented from swinging along it. It had been wired over to prevent urchins from looking into the Ladies, but the wire was often disturbed. Now several panes of glass had been smashed, and the Gents bore all the signs of forced entry.

'I've been over and listened, but there's not a sound,' she said.

A tramp, he thought. He had encountered tramps before. They took one look at his hump and accepted him as one of themselves before moving on without the slightest sign of hostility, and, in the same way, meths drinkers or drunken men of violence held no fear for him, and for the downtrodden and the beaten he had a curious cajoling gentleness. On another occasion a savage dog had intruded, but for this contingency he kept a small bottle of ammonia on the wise advice of a park-keeper, and there was no occasion or eventuality with which he felt himself unable to cope. He gave the trembling Vida a superior smile. Be spiders next, he thought.

'I honestly don't think you should go down there alone, Mr Wetter.'

'Nonsense,' he removed his key chain of office from his belt with a flourish.

'Please...'

'Got to open up.'

'Call the police.'

'The police?'

'You never know. It's been broken into. Please...'

He stared at her. There was no mistaking her alarm. Behind the usual pancake of make-up, her face was pale and as he looked down at her, that enlarged cupid's bow of a mouth trembled. The hostility which normally greeted him was totally absent. With this expression she must have watched the whirling riders on The Wall of Death, he thought. Her concern was a delight.

She even confided: 'I know we've had our differences, but I'm frightened.'

'Nothing to be frightened of.'

'There is this morning. Call someone.'

'Nonsense,' he said. 'Can't. I'm in charge.'

Once he had inserted his key in the padlock and thrown the chain aside, he pulled open the iron gate, unlocked that, then stared down the steps. There was yet another door at the bottom which was locked. Anticipating a crime, he pushed back his uniform cap and checked the steps for footprints. But there were none.

'There's not a sign of anybody here.'

'Be careful.'

She stood behind him, peering down.

He descended further, inserted the second key in the wooden door, paused, and looked at her again. Despite her fear, she followed him down the steps.

'Please call someone.'

'I'm in charge,' he said again.

He opened the door slowly and, at first, nothing untoward was visible. He switched on the light, looked first at his caboodle, but his brushes and pans stood in apple pie order, and he saw immediately that nothing had been disturbed. Immediately in front of him, six clean stalls glistened in the dim light, and to his left, the hand basins with their brass taps were equally spotless. He was glad she had followed him and now had the opportunity to see how things should be. Her eyes followed his and he gave a little self-congratulatory smile.

But next his gaze passed to the cabins opposite and before he could say anything, she screamed, jumped towards him and hid her face in his shoulder. He started back, one arm supporting her, the other stretching out for a broom ready to defend himself against any intruder. But the first thing he saw was the bend in the main inflow water pipe which ran above the cabins below the glass roof. It had been partially wrenched from its fittings and below the raised door of one cabin, a booted foot was visible raised above the floor. He darted forward and threw open the door which had already been forced and came face to face with the garrotted neck of the intruder who had hung himself, making the fatal jump from the lavatory seat and leaving himself only three inches to spare, for his weight had caused the pipe to bend. The face was not a pleasant sight.

'Don't look,' he shouted, shielding her at once.

'I couldn't help seeing...'

'Then forget it.' He shielded her face in his arm.

'I'll never...'

'Yes, you will. This is my fifth.'

'Fifth?'

'They generally pick the Gents. It's a bigger drop. Now, then, if you'll just put the kettle on...'

But she never put the kettle on, not even in his dreams, and for the first time in his life, he began to mind the coarse lavatorial jokes, the wit of Central Cleansing, all made intolerable by the maddening silence of the woman without a heart. He had come to the end, he felt. He had coped with everything. Now everything was getting him down. And still she did not change, continued to ignore his very existence.

Temporary relief came one day when the old biddy arrived the worse for drink. A bottle slipped from her handbag and broke above the ground on their joint territory. It was a bleak November afternoon and he came up to see The Vida arguing with the woman at the top of the steps.

'You've had enough.'

'Where's my money?'

'You've had enough.'

'But there's nothing in the house, you're bleeding me, you are.'

It was very embarrassing to be witness of another's discomfiture and while he might very well have got on his high horse, he could see that the old woman was well gone in drink, and his immediate concern was to be helpful. Now he thought of The Vida as a colleague and he had an inbred sense of loyalty to a workmate.

'You'd better get a taxi, Mrs Hodge.'

'Taxi? Who's going to pay?'

He gulped. His chance. 'I will! Please. She's in no condition.'

But The Vida turned again to the old woman who now lolled helplessly against the railings.

'You always falls on your feet.'

Jehoidah could see the resemblance between them, the same mouth, also too large for the face. It was clearly her mother and he sensed the antipathy between them.

'I'll go at once. You'd better put her down below.'

There was a garage nearby. The taxi came without fuss, the driver lent a hand and between them they got the old lady into a taxi.

'You'd better go with her,' he told The Vida.

'I'll have to.'

'There'll be nothing said.'

The Vida made no reply and even when he thrust a coin into the driver's hand, he saw her eyes resting coldly upon him and he shivered. That odd fishlike stare again. When he thought of the two of them together, her and the old biddy, it gave him the creeps.

Now began the period of her intermittent absences and the day came when he was left with her wage packet. Instead of returning it to the driver, he conceived the idea of delivering it himself, and again an old sociability reasserted itself. It was nearly Christmas, there was even snow on the ground, a white edging on the roadside which turned grey as the day wore on. He would call and see her, taking the wage packet and he would buy her something, make a clean start perhaps. He thought about it all the morning, and eventually decided on a plant and when they wrapped it up in the shop, he made his way to the bus stop with the gay Christmassy parcel under his arm and the wage packet pinned to the inside of his overcoat.

It was a strange errand for him and as he made his way to the house where she lodged, his wish for a bit of company returned. Perhaps he should have realized that others might not have his dedication? Perhaps he had been too overbearing and expected too much? As for her not wanting to be seen talking to him, well, he remembered his first reaction to her: out of a circus. Between them, they must look a sight. Her small stature with that mask of a face and those darting eyes amounted to a near deformity and no doubt she was very conscious of it. Perhaps her little trouble now, whatever it was, would help her come to the realization that in this life you had to make the best of everything. Best foot forward, he had always said. No good crying in the beer. Things wouldn't change, you just had to manage. If only he could get her to see that.

But when he turned the corner of a gully leading off the street to reach the house, he stopped short. At the end of the gully there was a police car parked, its blue light flashing, and across the road, the neighbours were assembled in little groups, all casting glances over the road and talking together in low voices, and he knew at once that she would be the focal point of their concern. It just had to be her. There was something about that woman somehow. And that background. Off the shows. He knew all right. He had a nose for disaster, a degree in it.

His heart gave a beat of excitement as he approached the house and he hugged the plant with increasing self importance. Finally, he faced the doorway with its distinguishing letter, 43A. The police car remained unattended and he could hear the monotonous bleep of the radio from within. Before he could press the bell, a woman spoke from the shadows.

'I shouldn't go in there if I was you.'

He did not answer.

'House of trouble right now.'

He jerked his head haughtily, a man about a man's business, then pressed the bell firmly.

The door was immediately answered by a police officer who stared at him as if expecting someone else. Behind him, in the hallway, Jehoidah saw another officer framed in the kitchen door-way, but at the foot of the stairs there was the unmistakable shape of a body beneath a cotton sheet. From one end of the sheet, a shoe was visible.

'Yes?'

'Mrs Hodge.'

'Who wants her?'

'I do.'

'Who are you then?'

'From the council.'

It was a magic formula.

'You'd better come in.'

Now Jehoidah drew himself up importantly as he entered. The constable eyed the plant while Jehoidah gave an almost professional look at the body. It was not The Vida but above the shoe he could see a lisle clad ankle like her mother's.

The constable eyed the parcel.

'What you got there then?'

'Parcel.'

'I can see that. Who is it for?'

'Mrs Hodge.'

'You'd better give it to me.'

The constable was insistent. Jehoidah handed it over. Then the Sergeant called him into the kitchen. he stepped carefully over the body and entered blinking.

The Vida, clad in a man's red dressing-gown and clearly under the influence, was seated in a chair beside the fire. She'd had her hair dyed again but the rain had soaked it. Her features remained deadpan until they saw him, then that mouth of hers cracked open as she gave a hoarse laugh.

'That's all I need,' she said.

'Who are you then?' the Sergeant said.

It was out before Jehoidah could stop himself.

'She's on my staff.'

'I'm not!' she shouted wildly.

'Well,' he said. He cleared his throat without embarrassment. 'She hasn't been in work and I've brought her wage packet and a little present.'

The Vida stared.

'Present? You brought me a present?'

The Vida suddenly began to cry, but it was laughing-crying he recognized, a note of hysteria in it, and she shook her head from side to side, looking even more doll-like in her distress. A pink wedge of thigh showed through her dressing-gown and Jehoidah looked away hastily. As usual, it was his desire to be helpful.

'I think I know who that is outside. Her mother. She used to visit her.'

'Where?'

Jehoidah did not like to say, 'My Gents'. 'At our place of employment.'

The Sergeant looked at him keenly.

'Of course,' he said. 'I knew I'd seen you somewhere.'

'She hasn't been with me long,' Jehoidah said.

'And she won't be with you again.'

The Vida erupted.

'Get him out of here, for God's sake. I can't stand him near me.'

It was the precise definition of their relationship, but it was not without profit. The Vida had pushed her mother downstairs, rifled her purse and been called back from a public house by the neighbours. Her denial of all knowledge had led them to call the police and the police were just getting to the bottom of it when Jehoidah blundered in. It was murder, plain unadulterated murder, and it sent a ripple of excitement through Central Cleansing.

'I told you,' Jehoidah said. 'I told you at the time. Yes I did, I bloody told you.'

Clerks came out of the interior offices to listen to his account.

'You didn't say...'

'Yes, I did, I told you here and I told them up in Sanitary. I even mentioned it to that woman Price Bevan.'

'Not Mrs Councillor... Not Mrs Ivy Price Bevan?'

'She caught me with my feet up when a load of 'em come back from Tintern Abbey. Party of twenty. Bursting, they was. I said, she was never there.'

'Who's never there?'

'The one you put with me. That beauty,' he said, and as one or two began to laugh, he held up a warning forefinger. 'It's all very well for you down here,' he said. *In the warm,* he added, emphasizing the age old complaint against Central Cleansing by the out-stations. 'But it could have been me lying at the bottom of the stairs. Or in the river.'

They looked at him, at his hump and at his indignant face, in respectful silence, and that was how he eventually saw it, another of the risks to which he was exposed.

'Good morning, Mrs Price Bevan. Good morning, ladies. Yes indeed, we have had a bit of unpleasantness. She tried to get off with manslaughter, did you hear? But they wouldn't have that, and I could have told them, I could.'

He could too. Then there was the plant. For some unaccountable reason the police would not let him take it away.

'I don't know what she cost me all.'

'Cost you?'

'Little items here and there. And then I couldn't sleep at night.

my nerves went quite to pieces. She hated her mother, you know. *Hated her.* I had her rolling drunk here one day. Frightening to watch, it was, the expression on her face. Her husband died in very mysterious circumstances too. Yes... oh, right you are, Mrs Price Bevan. I'm sure you'll find everything as it should be down below.

It became his story, and in the telling of it, he came at last into his own.

'Vida Hodge, yes. I knew from the beginning. And, of course, I reported it. But you know what they are down in Central. *Thick* is not the word, Mrs Price Bevan. As two planks, yes.'

Groceries

1

Whenever Huw Pugh Davies thought of his wife of late, it was with the sure knowledge that everything about her was blameless. In a curious way, she also looked blameless, belonging as she did to that rare group of women whose sensible habits and stern attention to diet, together with the regular inhalation of the exactly appropriate amount of fresh air, gave them that healthy colouring and perennial freshness associated with those who live perfectly balanced lives. Where he was plump, red-complexioned, with a thick thatch of cropped grey hair, and addicted to heavy tweed suits so that he often looked like a farmer come to mart, Rhiannon, whom he called Nanw, was the neatest of persons, a little woman who took care that women admired what she wore. She could still wear her daughter Beth's clothes and remained small, dark and neat, with a small mouth, small features and the tiniest ears from which two single pearl ear-rings now glistened as they sat opposite each other in the comfortable living room of their home in one of the northern counties of the Principality.

Nanw was reading a letter from their daughter, who had recently moved south to complete a course in social administration at university, and as the mail usually came after Huw Pugh had left to pursue his duties as Medical Officer of Health, it was her practice to gather the letters together and place them beside his chair so that he should have them conveniently to hand when he returned home in the evening. When a letter came from their daughter, she would usually read it a second time, often quoting from it, and he, sitting opposite her with the top button of his trouser fly undone for comfort, would nod appreciatively and ask the questions that seemed appropriate.

On this occasion, although he had long entered the house and they had taken a meal together, he had an uncanny feeling that there was something rather strange about her manner. At first, he thought that she might have decided to go out, but this was not so. They had conversed as usual. She had spoken of day-to-day matters without a trace of excitement, but when the time came for him to make his customary waddle into the living-room, he fancied that she was actually hovering behind him, willing him to sit down.

He did so without comment and then gave his correspondence a cursory glance. There seemed to be nothing of any importance save for a glossy package from one of the motoring organizations. It contained a magazine and a handsome road atlas which gave him much pleasure, but as soon as he opened the package and glanced at the book, the realization came to him that his wife was waiting for him to put it down. He'd noticed a letter from their daughter beside her chair, but he made no comment about it, knowing that she would refer to it in good time. Now, however, as he fingered the road atlas and she took up the letter, he fancied her fingers were trembling. There was definitely something different about her manner, and for the moment, he held the atlas firmly in front of him, perusing a map of East Anglia with a show of interest he did not feel.

His apprehension was quite extraordinary but there was no denying it and out of the corner of his eye he noticed the sharpness of his wife's stare. There were those who thought her an unnerving person but this was when she was pursuing her role of public woman, much involved with various charitable and political groups as well as the Women's Institute. She was the daughter of a university administrator and, as might be expected, precise and efficient.

In a way, as Huw Pugh well knew, she managed him as she managed the house, putting up with his untidiness and organizing him with good humoured efficiency. It had been years since a cross word had passed between them. Indeed, the last time Huw Pugh had raised his voice was when he couldn't find his golf shoes, and the only time he had been on the receiving end of that stare recently was when he had succumbed to the chance of a bargain and purchased a perfectly balanced pair of Churchill shotguns at a price which could have provided their daughter with a second hand Mini. Of course, this was also at a time when politically minded friends of theirs were going to jail rather than pay television licences to the English government, and Huw Pugh had also made certain disappointing statements about that. He did not mind striking a blow for the Welsh language, but he was not going to bleed for it. She was dismayed by his attitude there, he knew, but all in all, they were a couple who had reached the end of any disagreements they once had, and there were even times when Huw Pugh thought of his wife in much the same way as the council workman who had once made an apt remark in his presence.

'A good gel, my old gel,' the workman had said, and Huw Pugh agreed with the sentiment. Despite the stiffness of her manner, he had nothing to complain of in his wife. They suited each other, and if sometimes he looked back with an uncomfortable nostalgia, well, that was his fault and not hers.

But that letter. She still held it in her two fingers and still waited for some relaxation of his attention, he was sure, and the odd thing was that he now felt impelled to concentrate even harder on the contours of blameless East Anglia. Whatever had caught her attention must concern their daughter and here he was not without uneasiness.

Earlier in the year he had been persuaded to address a group at the local university and had got himself trapped into a discussion on sexual mores — in front of his daughter, mind you — and without knowing how it happened, he'd found himself airing opinions he scarcely knew he held, opinions which needless to say were later reported in the press. He had been more explicit than he cared to be normally, and although he'd said nothing improper — rather the reverse — it was a subject that on the whole he preferred to avoid.

But there he'd been, standing up on the rostrum, declaring the fact that he challenged the idea of universal promiscuity amongst the young, and students in particular. One thing had led to another and he'd gone on to say that he was sure that there were a majority of students who were virgins when they entered university and remained in the same condition when they left it. And if that were not all — and he had no evidence whatsoever — next he had loudly proclaimed, perhaps with his wife's views unconsciously in mind, that where Welsh values were strongest, the incidence of promiscuity might be shown to be less also. Of course, he said — having started, he did not seem to be able to stop — the more sophisticated girl who came up to university from a strict upbringing had the Pill to cope with, and he had never been in favour of its free availability, but girls, he was able to assure his audience with complete confidence, were as capable of saying 'No' now as in the past.

This had made the responsible authorities give vigorous approving nods and this part of his speech had been quoted in full, but in retrospect he was slightly stunned by his performance. How he had got himself to say all he'd said, he would never know. Normally, he was more wary and although his wife approved, he fancied his daughter had given him an old-fashioned look later; although, she, being closer to her mother than to him, said nothing. It was a situation that had arisen quite by chance and he hoped it would soon be forgotten. Soon after, the time had come for his daughter to apply to another university to complete her training as a social worker and she had decided without recourse to him to move South; and again, perhaps with the things he had not said in the lecture in mind, he had an apprehension which did his intelligence no credit. To tell the truth, he did not realize the nature of the morass into which his wife's opinions had led him. You drifted on through this life in a haze without quite knowing what you believed unless challenged. And he didn't want his daughter to go South.

'In a way, I'd prefer it if she were going to London,' he'd told his wife.

'What's wrong with Cardiff?'

It was difficult to explain (and he did not try) but it occurred to him that if Beth had gone to London where she'd probably have made Welsh friends, she would have known she was in a totally foreign place. The problem with Cardiff was that she might be lulled into a feeling of security falsely induced by the fact that she was not leaving Wales at all. She'd also be more likely to meet the worst of her own kind there, he thought uneasily. One middle class is much like the other and he was troubled now by his very success in life. Perhaps, by doing the best they could for their daughter, they had brought her up in comfortable circumstances in the most sheltered environment possible. For all his attachment to his native land, he was well aware that there was something about the indefinable Welsh way of life which cloaked its adherents, not only with the exclusivity of the language, but a subculture of chapel mores and approved societies that had the effect of ensuring that like always met like, and where there was argument, it was always on approved lines. At times it seemed to him that where Welsh Wales was strongest, it was also a more totally encapsulated society and if he were not careful, he would end up believing that there was such a thing as a Welsh germ! Their daughter, through school, neighbourhood and college, was very much a part of this mileu, and although he had given it his approval, the moment she was at risk he had second thoughts. In every sense, he thought, he had reached the age of doubt. But he confined his reservations to a single sentence.

'Cardiff is not Aberystwyth,' he said.

'Rubbish!' Nanw said. 'She's twenty-three years of age.'

'It's just a thought.'

'But you're always defending young people against these accusations of promiscuity?' Nanw seemed to know the precise area of his concern.

He wasn't always doing it, as it happened. He'd been pushed into doing it, and when he'd got to his feet beside that rostrum, his tongue had run away with him on lines which she might very well have prescribed herself. In a bizarre way it was almost her speaking! But he remained silent.

'What is it then?' Nanw asked.

He scratched his ear thoughtfully and decided to wriggle out of it.

'Age, I suppose. But I still think it's different down there.'

She made no reply to that and if her smile was a trifle superior, well, there were whole areas of his life that she did not know about since he was nearly thirty when they married and they never saw any of the people he knew then. And of course, with her intelligence she would rapidly have demonstrated the illogicality of his apprehension. It was a prejudice that simply would not stand the light of day.

But he knew in his bones that he was right.

Presently, he could stare at the atlas no longer, and sure enough, the moment he put it down, his wife spoke at once like an actress coming in on cue, and again, her fingers trembled as she held the letter.

'She *has* got news!' Nanw's thin, precise lips found an expression of wry amusement with some difficulty. 'She says she's met one of your Exes!'

'My *what*?' He affected surprise but his heart gave a curious beat.

'This boy's mother.'

'What boy?'

'The current boy,' she screwed up her eyes. 'Cassie, is it? Her writing's got so terrible, I can hardly read it. Somebody Preece-Jones. D'you know them?'

Huw Pugh lit a cigarette and slowly extinguished the match with his forefinger and thumb, feeling the momentary burn with a sense of peculiar pleasure. It was bearable pain.

'Preece-who?'

'Jones. She says his mother knew you when you were a houseman.' Huw Pugh shook his head matter-of-factly and wrinkled his stubby moustache. You could not spend your life in the service of a local authority without learning a trick or two, and the expression on his face now implied that some obscure clerk had asked a question relating to the distribution of paper clips throughout the country.

He cleared his throat. 'There were the usual multiplicity of

Joneses,' he said, running his tongue calmly over an upper molar. But there was a forced casualness to his voice that his wife must have recognized since there was no mistaking the tartness of her reply.

'Well, whatever the case, she says you must be a dark horse since this boy's mother told her you were actually engaged. She also says she never gave the ring back and still has it. Beth's seen it. You never mentioned anything to me about being engaged?'

Huw Pugh could not control a moment's irritation.

'Oh, for goodness-sake, I got the ring in a Christmas cracker.'

'They must have been very expensive crackers.'

'Why d'you say that?'

'You know what a passion Beth has for detail. She says it's a sapphire and much nicer than mine.'

Huw Pugh had an absurd desire to whistle. A part of his mind began to comment: 'To which the defendant made no reply'.

'That's just mischief,' he said. Of his daughter, he thought: the little bitch!

'At any rate, she sends you her regards.'

'I can hardly remember her.'

'Beth seems to be seeing a good deal of this boy.'

'Which one is this?'

'David. She's mentioned him before.'

'I can't keep up with them.'

'There's only one.'

'Wasn't the one that came here a David?'

'Dafydd.'

'Ah.'

'She's only just met this one in Cardiff.'

'Of course.'

Nanw closed the letter, folded it over in its creases with precise deliberation. She had never looked more like a committee woman.

'Is there something you don't want me to know?'

'Of course there's nothing I don't want you to know. What on earth are you accusing me of?'

Now Nanw sat upright in her chair and smoothed the folds of her skirt, at the same time casting a glance at the plain band of her engagement ring with its solitary garnet stone. It was inexpensive but he'd hoped she'd like the simple shape as much as he did.

'There's no need to get into a state, *cariad*.'

'I am not in a state.'

'Your face is quite flushed.'

In reply, Huw Pugh said an extraordinary thing.

'It would serve you right if you'd married a soak.'

She stared at him. 'I merely quoted from your daughter's letter.'

'I think we'd better leave it there.'

'But why?'

'In view of your remarks.'

'What remarks?'

'Perhaps you'd let me see the letter?'

'Don't you believe me?'

'I am not here in a judicial capacity. All I want to see is my daughter's letter.'

'Here.'

'Thank you.'

'And perhaps in your own time, you might see fit to give me an explanation.'

It had been so long ago since they'd had a row that both were somewhat at a loss and their remarks took on a curious kind of formality. Neither uttered a sentence which would have sounded out of place in a committee room.

He did not answer her request and Nanw soon busied herself with some duty in the kitchen while Huw Pugh stared at the offending letter. He did not re-open it and pulled up the flap of a little manoeuvrable side table which formed a neat desk top over his chair and then busied himself by filling in a questionnaire from the motoring organization. When Nanw returned to the room, she looked at him and at the untouched letter.

'Aren't you coming to bed?'

'One or two things have come up.' He gave a gesture to indicate the other correspondence.

'I can well understand,' Nanw said, and with that, she turned sharply on her heel and shut the door behind her with the slow deliberation of a warder.

The Medical Officer of Health did a very unusual thing. He swore.

'Oh, shit!' he said to himself.

But his thoughts were not confined to the letter or its revelation. In an odd way, he felt that the disturbance seemed to originate from that lecture which he had been cajoled into giving and the foolishness of his remarks then had now come home to roost. It was one thing to be talking in general terms about somebody else's virginity; it was another to be called to account for your own.

2

Upstairs, Nanw began to undress with the sinking feeling of one who feels her whole life to have been called into question. First, she sat before her dressing table mirror and examined her face. She wore very little make-up, just a trace of lipstick and her complexion now was much the same as it had been as a girl. She was forty-three, had been a total innocent when she married, and for all Huw Pugh's protestations of affection, there was a remote part of herself that held aloof and did not quite believe them. Her own naïvety as a young woman had been accompanied by a realization which she kept strictly to herself.

She wouldn't admit it to anyone but there had been periods in her life, in adolescence and beyond, when she'd despaired of ever getting married, and she had long known that there was something rather off-putting about her as far as men were concerned. Perhaps it was her formidable intelligence, her serious nature, perhaps it was her consciousness of the family's standing in the county. When Huw Pugh had begun to pay attention to her, she could never quite rid herself of the feeling that theirs would be too good a match to be true. Her father, her father's friends and connections, were exactly what Huw Pugh needed at the time since he was applying for a higher post in the county and Huw Pugh was an expert at paying them the lip service they required. Then again, there was another fact which had haunted her at the time, her uncle's money. This was a considerable sum which had come her way from properties leased to the university and later bought outright.

Her uncle had started life as an ironmonger, and had, in the Welsh tradition of the time, sought the approval of the Deity by clearing the debts of the chapel before he died, and she had a memory of him on his deathbed, a hunched and emaciated figure in a disgusting flannel night-shirt drooling as he fingered some financial statement with the glowing satisfaction of one who had made his peace in the end. Had he been a traditional English capitalist, she might have made some pointed remark, but the old man had always shown such total approval of her that she did not. Ever since she could remember, she had been taken to see him at regular intervals and had learned even as a little girl to express delighted surprise at the florin which he pressed into her fingers. Of course, she quite realized now that her father had taken good care to see that she made the visits, but she still could not bring herself to dislike the old man. His largesse had made her independent at an early age, and if there was one thing she thought she was sure of before she'd married, it was that Huw Pugh was unimpressed. True, she soon found out that he had expensive habits, and he was also rather anglicized by her standards, but his career progressed like a copy-book plan and she had every reason to feel satisfied with herself.

But now she realized with a sinking heart that these were external matters, and despite their importance, superficial compared to the violation of the true bond which she felt necessarily sacrosanct between husband and wife. What really counted was the security which she should be feeling in the core of her being. She had all along felt that there was something unexplained about Huw Pugh's past and she knew she would not rest until she got it out of him. The letter then, would provide the focal point for her attentions in the coming days and some of the old ironmonger's cunning remained in her for she decided that she would put him at his ease by not mentioning the matter immediately.

Finally, as she slipped into her night-gown, her hair braided for the morning, she experienced a slight uplift in morale. There was no doubt as to which side their daughter was on and she was sure he would have some very awkward questions to answer.

3

Seated in his chair — he had moved twice, once to pour himself a Scotch, a second time to bring the bottle closer so that he would not have to move at all — Huw Pugh stared at the four glowing bars of the electric fire which they sometimes switched on in the evenings. He'd kicked the switch on the side of the fire to illuminate the second pair, two bars being thought adequate, but now the room was uncomfortably warm and he had the pleasant feeling of causing waste, something which he had denied himself of late. Perhaps he should not blame his daughter for the tactless way she'd written of her discovery. What right had you to expect your children to be allies anyway?

But she should have known what a disturbance her letter would cause, and she probably saw him as he was inclined to see himself in low moments — as his wife's creation. The problem had always been that his wife did everything so well that he was almost required to do nothing, and, as far as their daughter was concerned, he always seemed to have been produced as an aide on required occasions, then put back in the box to live his own separate life.

Away from the office, and without a gun or a fishing rod in his hand, he was as good as kennelled. It was a sad thought, come like a mist on an October evening, and it was followed by another, equally dampening. Age thickened you. It made nothing clearer, only increased your dependence on comfort. You organized your life away and a sense of thrill was gone. There were dimensions of sounds and smells which went missing, casualties of certainty and order. Even his lecture — that lecture! — was a comfort. What could anyone with the slightest perception have thought? Yet they'd all applauded.

But now his mind had been given a savage jog at the mention of Cassie's name. What if he had spoken his mind? Told them exactly!

'Listen!' he should have said. 'Whenever she came into the room, she was always wet, d'you see? Wet from walking in the rain. So it followed, got it? She had to take her stockings off. Absolute compulsion. Ladies and gentlemen, the weather was on my side!'

But that was wrong. The joke was wrong and the confidence was wrong, and anyway, there were things about your youth which you didn't want to share, not with anyone. Like Cassie. Like the fact that she made such a business of removing her stockings, so much so that he'd been compelled to turn his back on her in the little room which they'd borrowed to get out of the rain, and he could still hear, coming back to him after all these years, the unmistakable slithering sound of nylon against bare flesh. That was memory for you, as was the soon-to-vanish impress of his teeth upon her bare shoulder, a mark he had seen between the coarse strands of her hair and which he could even now see before him as clearly as if it were yesterday. He stirred uneasily. She'd been a nurse with a reputation, he recalled, and in an ominous way, he remembered more facts about her father than about her.

Her problem was that she'd had an illegitimate child, he remembered. The child had died but the wound remained. She was from one of those valley towns where everyone knew everyone else. Her father, a widower, was a trade union official, a Marxist, a cut above the others, he'd been led to believe, and she'd been brought up in that hothouse atmosphere, challenging everything. Her father was himself a rebel against the old chapel mores, both of them hating the narrowness of it, the kind of life which Huw Pugh had again come to support in a nominal kind of way. If anybody could understand her, he could, he'd told her at the time.

'Why?'

'Because I want to.'

'And why should you want to?'

'Because I do.'

'So you say.'

'No, I mean it, I really mean it.'

'And a little bit of the other thrown in on the side?'

'Why d'you keep harping on that?'

'A little bit of this and that,' she said. 'Men and their groceries!'

He would not reply when she taunted him, although when she taunted him, she was all the more desirable.

'Now then, Huw Pugh, you go home and be a good boy to your mother.'

Finally, perhaps worn down by his persistence, she took him home. He was aware that her experience had hurt her, but he had no idea how much it had hurt her. He himself, like so many of the country Welsh middle class, had never suffered any major wounds. They hadn't as a class, and they tended not to as individuals, perhaps because they were so self contained and unchallenged. Almost everybody he knew lived off the country and the town, all with a little bit put by, and, perhaps because of his sheltered upbringing, he thought that he would never forget the street where she lived. It took its shape from the contour of the bare mountain behind it, and below there was a succession of other streets like chevrons on a sleeve, dropping dramatically down to the colliery, a leaden river and the road out. They had walked high above it and stood watching the smoke curl up from the chimneys.

'I hate it,' she said. 'It's so bloody small.'

'You mean small-minded?'

'Like a nut. Little layers under a shell.'

Perhaps she was thinking of her own life, her own mistake.

The place was witness of it, she told him. Everybody knew. Everybody talked. She'd come home to have the baby and lain in bed thinking of them talking outside the house. Of course there were friends, loyal neighbours. But not many, not outside their own immediate circle. Couldn't he understand what went on in a small town?

He did not understand. There was so much that he did not understand, but he was not unattractive, and when she finally yielded, it was because he had given her a sense of security, but he did not remember that, he remembered her scorn at his country ways and more than anything else, the sharp physical intimacy of that little room, the days, nights, weeks of anticipation when what there was between them seemed to be rustling in the air in a way

that never happened afterwards. It was as if sex had a smell all of
its own, and now, a new thought came to him. One of the saddest
things of age, and marriage for that matter, was the dwindling of
the intensity of desire where there was no uncertainty as to its
outcome. Certainly he had never felt again as he had in that little
room whose sights and sounds were as vivid now as any of his life.

He gave a rueful grin as he picked up the letter once more.
Poor Cassie, he thought. But apparently everything had turned
out well. She'd had her son. But then he thought of the look his
daughter'd given him after that wretched lecture, and he stirred
uneasily in his chair and reached once more for the bottle. He
remembered Cassie's scornful phrase, 'Groceries... Men and their
groceries'. He was glad he'd never married her anyway. She was too
direct, and he had no doubt that it could all be easily explained away
to Nanw when the time came. A South Walian, he would say. He
was sure it would be enough. There was even an old Welsh proverb
of her uncle's which he might quote: 'Tell me where you come from
and I'll tell you what you are'. He had a conviction that everything
boiled down to sociology eventually. That dreadful place, her
father, those wretched streets, that leaden river, the voluble, argu-
mentative, non-deferential, valley Welsh, *Shonihoi's*, he thought,
slipping into the idiom. It said everything. He took yet another drink
from the bottle and left the letter unread.

4

He woke up in the same chair in the morning with a fine rime of
mucus around his lips from smoking and a dryness at the back of
his throat, the effects of excessive heat caused by the electric fire.
He also had a hangover, and just above his eyebrows he felt a
pressure like a layer of wire pushing insistently against his temples.
As he uncurled himself stiffly from the chair, he heard the movements of the daily woman in the kitchen. He imagined her comment,
'Doctor on the tiles!' and scowled. On the table beside him, the
cover of one of the motoring magazines showed a palm-fringed
Caribbean shore fronted by a cover girl. The girl was tanned and
nubile with a deep assisted cleavage. He ran his eye down the
cleavage to her tight cotton slacks which were fastened with a large
belt and a triangular brass buckle, the apex of which extended to
her crotch, seemingly directing his glance to the precise spot.

On offer, he thought; but now he was the Medical Officer of Health again and added: totally exploited and disgusting.

When his wife entered, she made no reference to the previous night, nor to the unusual position in which she found him.

'I forgot to tell you,' she said. Her smile was gently reassuring. 'Your foulard ties came back from the cleaners. They were dreadfully stained but they made quite a good job of them.'

It seemed the matter was closed.

5

Nothing further was said that night, nor the next night, and on the Friday he left for a long-standing fishing engagement with some cronies on the coast. It was an expedition planned with his wife's approval weeks before, but as it happened an easterly wind blew all the weekend, held there by the Equinox, and the fishermen spent the mornings getting over the night before, so that when he returned direct to the office on the Monday, it was with the feeling that he needed a holiday to get over a holiday. He kept a suitcase with a clean shirt and accessories for just such an occasion and, fortunately, nothing occurred which taxed him unduly. He had, however, neglected to telephone his wife over the weekend, and at the back of his mind there was a smarting sense of ill defined injustice that extended both to her and to his daughter. They had disturbed his equilibrium and, as far as they were concerned, he felt like a man aggrieved. Since the fishing trip had also proved abortive, he also felt the weight of that, he decided. One damn thing after another.

Thus he was in an irritable mood when his secretary told him that his wife was on the telephone. She did not ring him at the office as a rule. She wasn't the sort to forget any item of shopping and ask him to pick it up on the way home, and she well understood that he didn't like to be disturbed.

He pulled down his shirt cuffs and picked up the telephone with one hand, tapping his blotter impatiently with the other, immediately assuming the pose of an extremely busy man.

'Yes?'

'Huw Pugh?'

'Speaking.' It was quite unlike him to behave as he was doing. In fact, whenever he rang home unexpectedly, it was she who put on her committee voice so there was an element of tit for tat now.

'I've been trying to get you all the week-end,' her voice was tremulous and urgent. Somehow he knew at once that she'd been crying and he felt a pang of guilt. He should have rung. He'd always done so in the past. In twenty years, he'd always made contact with her, even on the occasion when he'd gone on a medical convention to the Soviet Union and getting through on the telephone from there would have taxed the patience of Job unless you tipped lavishly, which he had not.

But he was in a mood and determined to stay in one.

'You knew very well where I was.'

'I rang and rang and didn't get through until you'd left.'

In his mind, he could see the telephone kiosk in the busy corridor of the public house where they stayed. It was always answered but whether anybody was called to it depended on the goodwill of whoever picked up the receiver. And now he remembered they'd purposely avoided drinking in the pub for the express purpose of avoiding the telephone. 'Let smallpox rage!' he'd said. But he couldn't explain that.

'The lines must have been down,' he said.

'*No*, they weren't. I rang Faults. Oh, Huw Pugh...' she paused and he screwed up his face because there was no mistaking the anxiety in her voice. But surely, it couldn't be on his account?

She spoke again: 'Is there any possibility of us being overheard?'

'Certainly not.'

'Listen, you must come home. At once.'

'But what is it?'

'I can't explain over the telephone.'

'Oh, for goodness' sake... a weekend's fishing?'

'It's nothing to do with you.'

He might have guessed that.

'It's Beth. She's come home. And she's brought him with her.'

'Brought who with her?'

'This boy.'

'Who?'

'This boy. Please... please come home at once.'

It was on his mind to offer some objection but she sounded so abject that he did not have the heart. Then he gave his mind to his daughter.

'She er... she's all right, is she?'

'Please come home.'

'But...'

'I'll tell you then.'

By now, his mood had left him. Whatever had happened did not involve him, that was clear. What was new was his wife's anxiety, her need for him. There was no mistaking the urgency in her voice. There was even a note of helplessness in it. At last she had met with a situation with which she could not cope alone, and his response was immediate. He picked up his hat and weekend bag and went at once to his car. Of course, he had an idea of what had happened, but could not get over the urgency of his wife's appeal.

6

He noticed the motor cycle parked in the drive with new alarm. It was Japanese, electric blue in colour, low and rakish with a profusion of gleaming chrome mirrors, crash bars and a veritable vine of multi-coloured stretch elastics wound round the rear carrier. It leant over on its side stand, an alien and evil thing, he thought. At first, he suspected some dreadful accident, but the machine seemed undamaged and, as he passed it, he could not help looking at the speedometer which registered a possible speed of one hundred and twenty miles per hour. Now he thought of his selfishness in purchasing the pair of sporting guns, but that was not really the cause of his daughter not having the Mini she'd wanted. The idea was that she should wait until she'd found somewhere suitable to garage a car. Then if his wife had really insisted, she could have afforded the purchase herself, and he hadn't definitely put his foot down. They couldn't get at him on that score.

The sight of the motor cycle upset him, he had to admit, but when he got into the house, the cleaning woman came from the kitchen and she was another bone of contention, another one in his wife's pocket, a South Walian with the habit of ungrammatical speech which irritated him intensely. As she approached him, he fancied that her small, round wizened berry of a face with its deliberately grave lips controlled an ironic amusement.

'She's in bed. She haven't got up all day.'

He knew better than to ask more, removed his hat and went on up the stairs aware that the woman was watching him. It was on the tip of his tongue to ask after the ownership of the motor cycle but he checked himself. He made his way to the bedroom with a sense of calamity, opened the door with a final glance down the stairs where the woman remained with the same expression on her face. He gritted his teeth, entered the bedroom and closed the door firmly behind him.

Over her night-dress, his wife wore a pink quilted bedjacket that he hadn't seen for years. It definitely spelt invalid. She'd done her hair but her eyes were red from crying and the tip of her nose was also red. She looked wan and feverish and he felt a sinking feeling that was more than guilt. You took everybody for granted, he thought; everybody and everything. He had always felt her good health to be oppressive but perhaps it was the care with which she looked after herself that irritated him. Now, whatever had happened, she'd been laid flat.

'I thought you'd never come.'

'I came as soon as you called.'

'I tried ringing all the weekend.'

'We'll have to stay in another place.'

'First you — I thought something dreadful had happened.'

'Well, it hasn't. To me,' he added. He did not quite know what to say next, but he thought he might as well start with the obvious. 'Whose machine is that outside?'

She looked at him long and hard but there was nothing accusing in her eyes, he was glad to notice. She was looking at him to see how he would take the news.

'It's hers. Beth's.'

'*What?*'

'She's bought it.'

'She couldn't afford it. It's...it's...' but he had no idea of the exact cost of the machine. 'It must be two — three hundred pounds.'

'Five hundred. She's overdrawn.'

'But those things are lethal. She's no experience. She...'

'She can't drive it yet. She bought it for him. This boy. They came on Saturday morning. Oh, Huw Pugh, I can't begin to tell you...'

He sat down beside the bed. His first thought was of that glistening machine, the absurdity of it as far as his daughter was concerned. And as for buying it for someone else... It was wanton extravagance. Certainly not a thing to buy anyone. It was improper for a girl to buy a boy an article costing that amount. All his fears seemed to have been realized. She must be obsessed. She'd been so sheltered and then the first time she'd really left home... He suddenly saw his daughter's face as he had last seen it, a flat immobile stare with just the slightest suspicion of a raised eyebrow and he had an inkling that he had heard nothing yet.

'He's filthy.'

'Pardon?'

'This boy... Filthy. His appearance, it's disgusting.'

Hair, he thought.

'His fingernails,' she said. 'His clothes. His talk.'

Sociology, he thought again. He was not that unfamiliar with the sight of the young at a distance and his disapproval was, if anything, more severe than his wife's. But in his case it was functional. You couldn't fish or shoot with hair like that. You simply couldn't. Every time you bent your head down it got in your eyes, and anyway, the sight of some of them made him want to scratch. There were young men in his office whom he couldn't bear to be near. He hadn't actually said anything, but they soon got the message. He could well imagine his wife's dismay and for once he was completely on her side. Of course, they'd had it in London for years, they'd had it locally, even in the office, but in your own home, well, it went down his spine. But then he had a very charitable thought.

'Of course, they may have been dirty after the ride?'

His wife had moved up on her elbows in a sitting position when he entered the room, and now she shook her head.

'It's not only the way they look.'

'They?'

'She's as bad. She won't wear a bra.'

He swallowed.

'She can't have changed that much in six months?'

'There's no doubt she spent last night in bed with him.'

'In this house?'

His wife nodded. Now there was an air of ashen solemnity about her. An illusion had crumpled. She did not know how to face the world. But he had a very human thought himself. Bit of a bloody cheek, he thought. In his home. All of the trophies of childhood remained in his daughter's bedroom, her dolls, pandas, teddy bears, and he had a lunatic vision of them as witnesses of the event.

'I told him to get out,' Nanw said through tight lips.

He was startled. 'You told him to...'

'Of course. They made it absolutely clear what they were doing.'

He thought of his daughter's actions as a double-pronged attack. First at him, then her mother. Hard faced wasn't the word.

'What did he say?'

'They're absolutely without shame. His language... She didn't say anything, but he said... He...'

'I'll deal with him,' Huw Pugh said.

'Yes?'

'He said...'

'He said she was pissed off with the two of us. She didn't

contradict him. I can't tell you the way she looked at me.'

The young couple had apparently gone for a walk and before the confrontation which he knew would come, Huw Pugh determined that he would take a bath. If they came in while he was in the bath, he would make them wait, and he hoped the waiting would not be pleasant for them. He was sure they would know that he was in perfect accord with his wife. There certainly couldn't be any doubt about that in his daughter's eyes he was sure. In *his* house, he thought again. That amazed him more than anything. And to be so brazen about it. As he predicted, he thought; but curiously, the news set him off on a quite unexpected tack for he now began to imagine himself in roles he might have adopted if his daughter had made the slightest appeal to his good nature. She should have said something he could take. 'We lost control,' he thought; a standby from his youth, that one. Then again she might have sought his help in soliciting her mother's approval for a boy who was not quite up to scratch. He'd have been delighted to be her ally. It would have given him the chance he'd long awaited. But instead of setting him up in any of the benevolent father-roles he might have played with distinction, it seemed she'd come home with the deliberate intention of outraging them. And with that damned Japanese Thunderbird to prove it!

The motor cycle was definitely the worm in the apple as far as he was concerned. If it were not for the motor cycle, he might have taken the boy on one side and had a man-to-man talk with him over a drink. 'No need to upset the old girl like that. What the eye doesn't see, etc.' But now having accepted the gift of the motor cycle, what else might he want?

Huw Pugh stripped and got wearily into the bath, lying back to soak as he gave his mind to the problem. He left the water running so the bathroom began to fill with steam, but even in the comfortable, familiar fug his unease remained. His wife was quite bowled over, he could see. She wasn't going to get up for dinner and he did not blame her. He hadn't seen her cry for years. Something seemed to have snapped in her.

He stretched his thick legs out to their fullest extremity and now the level of water reached his chin. With one toe, he practised his special skill of gently turning off the hot water tap and then rested his head on the plastic head pillow which was fastened by suckers to the bath, a provision that ensured his head was well below the level of any possible draught. He was already beginning to doze when the door opened and into the steamy room there came a

strange apparition in the person of his daughter who was kitted up
in black leather hides and wore a crash helmet that reminded you
of some space fiction odyssey. She just stood looking at him for a
moment — an infuriating invasion of privacy — and the sight was
so bizarre that he was momentarily speechless.

But not for long.

'Now look here...'

'We're going,' she said, raising her voice as if he were deaf.

He sat up in protest in the bath with a great commotion of water.

'We've waited all day, but Dave says the roads will be terrible if
we wait any longer.'

His position was ridiculous and he did not forgive her for barging
in unannounced. That was another thing like the motor cycle.
There were things you simply did not do.

'You're running away,' he said.

'No, the lights are shorting. There's something wrong with the
wiring and the indicators are on the blink. It's my fault, we'll come
again and give you warning.'

It was a put-up business, of course. For all her matter-of-factness,
she was frightened really, and had even gone to the extent of
masking her face. Then she must have timed her entrance when he
was firmly ensconced in the bath.

'Wait downstairs until I'm dressed,' he ordered.

'We can't.'

'Why can't you?'

'The lights are on the blink.'

'You'll do exactly as I tell you.'

'We'll give you a buzz next time. The week after next.'

And with that, she was gone. She hesitated a moment, grinned,
then turned on her booted heel and he heard her clatter down the
stairs as he still squatted in the bath in a state of shock. The helmet
had the effect of removing any trace of femininity from her face,
emphasizing her square chin and the full purposeful mouth of his
wife's family. The concealment of her forehead made another
contribution and for the first time he saw the marked resemblance
to the old ironmonger whom he had last seen in bed wearing a night
cap. They were unmistakably of the same stock.

He heaved himself out of the bath and shouted at the door.

'Have you seen the state your mother's in?'

But there was no reply. And he had not even set eyes on the boy!
He looked frantically for his bathrobe, then realized that it was in
his weekend case. Undaunted, he swathed a towel around himself,

and that not quite fitting around his waist, another, but the slight delay was enough to make him even more impotent, for now he heard the motor cycle engine crackle to life and there was a sizzle of shifting gravel in the drive, and by the time he had got to the window at the top of the stairs, the two of them were off. The last thing he saw was his daughter crouched on the pillion seat, a small, squat, alien figure clutching at the barely visible boy in front of her. A dribble of blue smoke came from the twin exhausts as the machine went past the paddock, sweeping on to the road without the pause he always gave. Although it was a country road and they had leant on the planning authorities not to allow any other development, you never knew who or what might be coming. But he could see her no longer, and he could hear the engine revving, two-three-four-five and up through the gears, soon reaching the screaming whine which marked its optimum performance, and then it, and they, were gone.

It was so utterly humiliating. She'd no guts either, even though she must have had that boy in her pocket. *He* wouldn't have run away like that.

There was complete silence in the house, then he heard the noise of saucepans being shifted in the kitchen. With the cleaning woman as a witness, his discomfort was complete. He went wearily back to the bathroom and towelled himself vigorously. He thought of what his wife had repeated. 'Pissed off with them'. Well, it was mutual.

His wife could not be persuaded to come down to dinner and he ate alone in a forbidding silence, daring the cleaning woman, who had remained to wash up, to say anything at all. They would keep their eyes open for someone else and dismiss her in due course. She was unsatisfactory anyway. Well, they might, they might not. It would depend on her behaviour.

But that was the last of his strictures, even to himself. When the time came for him to retire, he mounted the stairs with a strange eagerness, carrying a glass three-quarters full of cold milk as he had been requested. He entered the bedroom and put it dutifully beside his wife's bed and then crossed over to his own side of the bed and got in, humping himself up into a sitting position while he waited for her to drink the milk. The shock was so complete that there was nothing more to be said, not one word. It was a complete disillusionment of all their hopes, hers in particular, and he had never felt more for his wife than he did now. When he came to think of it, he didn't worry about his daughter one jot. She was too clever to get herself pregnant, no doubt. What she needed was a good jolt and he'd no doubt she'd get that with the motor cycling fraternity. Let her come home then, when the world had rubbed off on her a little more. All the platitudes began to rise in his mind. When she had to provide a home for herself, she'd learn to appreciate her own.

His indignation had given him new energy and he turned impatiently on to his side and snuggled closer to his wife. Then of an impulse, he did a surprising thing. He ran his palm slowly and purposefully up the length of her thigh until his knuckle rested finally at the high point.

'How long are you going to be with that milk?' he said.

Dream Girl

Will remembered her living in the corner house of the terrace. She wore her hair bobbed then, sometimes a neat, page-boy style which rose and fell when she ran, but still remained neat, despite her mother's shouted insistence that young ladies did not run. Neat was the word for her, always neat, always a little different even as a leggy schoolgirl in long black stockings and gymslip. Her mother insisted she wore a uniform despite the fact that like Will she had failed the eleven-plus and, as if to make up for it, her mother made her concentrate on her appearance, and there was always a sheen coming off her, her peachy cheeks, milky complexion, that groomed, ash-blonde hair especially. The *Shampoo Girl*, somebody called her, Queen of the Dan y Graig Hairbrushers, but she was too serious for that, Dorothea Lemon.

'Dottie Lemon...' (the street kids sang then).
'Figure like a film star.'
'Face from a bottle...'

She was groomed, manicured, poised, somehow untouchable even in adolescence. From an early age, and especially after the dreadful disappointment at eleven, she was schooled in the art of keeping herself to herself, a young lady of destiny and a manufactured cut above the Dan y Graig crowd from the tips of her elegant toes to the assisted curves of her arched eyebrows. Like Will she had grown up in wartime austerity, rationing and shortage, but it was also the age of the screen star, ten foot close-ups in the Workmen's Hall, lights glistening in enlarged eyes, held poses and glam' above all. 'It', was around, written in large letters, an indefinable quality that some girls had, others didn't.

'Daft,' Will thought, ruefully recalling her name and the pertinent facts about her. With the picture of the schoolgirl and the imposed adult glamour of her appearance, Will also recalled her mother's voice. It was shrill and carping, often a complaint and a warning in it, in marked contrast to the honeyed tones of the heroines of *Screen Secrets*. Anybody'd think the world of the terraces was poison.

'You be careful who you speak to, and come home straight, mind.'

Then there was a specific reference to himself.

'Will Willis will never get anywhere. He's too half-soaked.'

If Dottie had protested, and she probably had not, the reply was duly reported, cutting him down to size.

'He's got plumber written all over him.'

His attentions were thus discouraged, but he had not pursued them with any ardour. Perhaps the old scrag was right? He was always easy going, and since he was then apprenticed to the trade, it was no great feat to assume he would serve out his time. But what Mrs Lemon could never have imagined was the urgency of the note he received nearly thirty years later.

> I expect you remember me. I saw your name over the shop and made a note of the phone number, but then lost it which is why I am writing. Could you please call personally at the above address? I really am desperate and have no one else I can ask. I've been living away and have returned. Always in after lunch.
> Sincerely yours,
> Dorothea.

There was only one way he could describe her handwriting and that was scatty. Great extravagant loops, curls and flourishes proclaimed her indifference to straight lines. She dashed things off, he remembered, and as he considered her request at the back of his shop which bore his name, he sucked a tooth, freeing a blackberry seed which had embedded itself in a cavity. He now went home to lunch, as did most of the local businessmen, and for years nobody had dared call him by his nickname to his face. Not that he would have much minded. Nicknames were going anyway. Will Pipes, Jones the Bricks, and their local untransferable bobby, Dai-Book-and-Pencil, were names which were part of a past that was changing anyway. The fact was that Will now had his own business and employed men, seldom laying a hand on the tools himself. Since Dottie Lemon's day when they had all been kids together, he had prospered. He was married with two boys, and if his wife, Vi, had become even more easy going with prosperity, so had he. No phrase described them better than when people spoke of them as being comfortably off. Although he wouldn't admit it, he'd made a small bomb out of sub-contracting for the council house building which had mushroomed since the war, and they now had an office with an accounts staff of two in addition to the shop, a general foreman and the plumbing squad. But that was the ceiling. Full-stop, as Will said. Cautious always, he didn't want to get too big, nor have to borrow too much. In the building trade, he'd seen enough high flyers come off the tools, only to get milked in the solicitors' offices. But not him, and if, as one solicitor had added, he probably always

kept a pair of dungarees in the wardrobe, just in case, he merely
smiled. Didn't it go to show that he had no side?

Of course, there'd been high days and holidays. Once, the opportunity had arisen to merge with a large competitor who had landed
public service contracts and was floating a public company. There
was big money to be made and talk of directorships. But Will had
drawn back. He was told he would have been a valuable man. It
was explained how many founders' shares he could have. There was
a pool of building land that made the mind boggle. Stock was
explained to him. The floating capital ran into hundreds of thousands.

But he shook his head. With one hand, he wiped away the quiff
of hair that frequently fell down over his forehead and grinned
apologetically. They'd taken him out for a lavish expense account
meal, table flowers, olives, crushed ice and gleaming silver, but
he might have been in the Sergeants' Mess, and he remained
unimpressed. As far as he was concerned, he still got a kick out of
wearing a suit to work! He was very grateful for the compliment,
but enough was enough. Fortunately, Vi wasn't greedy or pushing.
They had enough to run a Jag. on the business as it was.

'You do what you want, Will,' she said.

He had done, all his life, and what is more, parted on good terms
with his competitor who promised sub-contracting work on the
side. There were no ill feelings, and when, some years later, bad
weather, the current credit squeeze and mal-administration put the
new company in a very rocky situation, people who knew said, 'By
God, that Will Pipes has got a head on him!' But they were wrong.
It was simply as he said, there were things he fancied, and things he
didn't, and being his own man was important. If anything, his main
preoccupation nowadays was that he had almost worked himself
out of work! A morning on the telephone and he could employ his
men for weeks ahead. He was so successful in his own small way,
and every job he handled was so perfectly within his compass, that
it ran like clockwork and left him with time on his hands. It meant
he had time to think, something he regarded himself as ill prepared
for, and when the note came from Dottie Lemon, he gave the
morning to it.

'What's up with the Boss?' the workmen said, looking at the
closed office door.

'Thinking,' the general foreman said.

It was somehow disturbing.

Will thought first of Dottie's mother, a harridan if ever there was one; and posh with it. Upbringing on the brain, that woman had. He lit a pipe and cast his mind back, slowly realizing that but for one incident involving Dottie, his whole life might have been changed. It might sound a bit far fetched, but few people realized how soft he had been all those years ago. Love, he thought. Romance, he thought. And the pictures, the bloody pictures... he meant the cinema and the degree of their thrice weekly involvement on those blackout nights. In his daydreams, there had been times when Chicago seemed more real than Dan y Graig itself.

But there were more immediate images which excited his recall, the crow beak of that woman Lemon for a start. Crowbeak, scrag-neck, down-curved lips, hennaed hair, the perpetual reek of powder and paint. Madam Make-Up they called her, Madam Make-Up, Nancy-posh.

Dottie's mother was a shrewish widow with a small pension who had inherited a house, but from an early age, Dottie's life had been moulded with a single intention, getting out of Dan y Graig Street. With this end in mind, the personality seemed to have been screwed out of Dottie and she had been stamped and moulded in the shape of the available templates of the times, Shirley Temple to start, then moving up the Hollywood ladder. To be fair, she must have realized that there was a chance of Dottie being a beauty and beauty had to be cultivated. Indeed, it could not be left alone, so dancing classes followed elocution classes ('speakin' nice'. Will called that), and then there were winters on the accordion which put a stop to roller skating, loafing about the Bracci's cafés, or ruining the complexion in the mountain winds and the unladylike stains of whinberries which might play havoc with the lips. Dottie had a career ever in front of her, and although it took no very clear shape for years — the war interrupted a good many things — the first steps were taken when she packed her accordion and went off with a gipsy band, to a great halloo of front page glamour in the local newspaper. There was also a cheesecake photograph and a black star inset beside the headline, an afterthought by a sentimental compositor which drew a relaxed smile from Mrs Lemon's pursed lips. From such humble beginnings, stars were truly born. If only Dottie's voice had a little more volume, but then, perhaps that would come; anyway the microphone was God's gift to the whispering tenor, no less than the budding soubrette.

Will remembered it all, the sparkling sequins on the tight-fitting dance costume, the metal bars on the tap-dancing shoes, the gipsy blouse with its pretty crochet work and pink drawstring, most of all

Dottie's performing smile, her lips carefully parted and the precisely calculated glance which was so levelled so as to include everyone 'out front'. Dottie did not only have *It*, she had that show business bazaaz, the illusion of life and energy when performing, that reached out over the front rows even of the Workmen's Hall.

There were also other moods, equally phoney.

'*Please...*' she sang, her head on one side, her pale little oval face straining with that smile, eyes blinking until she got used to the lights, always projecting an unrealized and as yet, anonymous self; '*Say you're not intending to tease...*'

Sweet, she was; a good turn, fair play. Winsome was the word, as neat as a top. She'll go far... Oh! Listen now...

> 'Your eyes reveal,
> That you have the soul of,
> An angel white as snow...'

From 'Animal crackers in my soup', she had progressed and unwittingly acquired something of the borrowed image of the girl next door, the captive blonde who never washed a dish however, but whose hair brushed your cheek when you kissed her in the moonlight, Glen Miller smooching in the background. 'And you never thought of knickers,' Will said to himself now. They were all strangely puritancial, the wartime teenagers, uneasily poised below the general disturbance. Perhaps that explained the one afternoon he had spent with her when she was free of her mother and Dan y Graig Street, one hour which stood out in his mind, perhaps the one note of reality in his whole recollection.

'Always in after lunch,' she'd written. Would he go and see her? He had certain reservations. He looked again at the note. 'I really am desperate.' That was another poser. He was not a careful man for nothing so her rang Vi, to ask her advice, but it so happened that Vi was out. He remembered it was her day for golf lessons which she'd begun to take. She'd be out all day. He could nip home and change without a word said if he wanted to! But steady. He checked himself. It wasn't as if Dot was a what-you-call, he said to himself, an old flame, did they call it? Rather the reverse. He'd never, in fact, been out with her except for that once. It was true he'd wanted to, but her mother'd put the block on it, and he was not the pushing sort. He didn't really know her at all, she was one of those girls who were always on the other side of the street really, somehow aloof and beyond him. A face, she was, and somehow as remote as a face

on a poster. Except for that one day. But there was no mistaking
the directness of the note. Personal, did they call it?

'Always in after lunch,' he repeated to himself, then added a
thought that scandalized; 'Knock twice and ask for Mamie!'

His general foreman entered, staring at him. 'What the hell are
you doing, boss?'

He had done nothing all the morning except stare at that note and
now he put it away guiltily. The effort of answering the question
caused him to make the decision at once.

'I'm taking the afternoon off.'

'Oh aye?' the foreman, who liked a predictable employer, was
frankly curious.

But Will nodded curtly and went off without explaining himself
— straight home to change, and since one decision involved others,
he now began to take some pains with his appearance, selecting a
recently bought charcoal suit, an expensive blue Dior tie, a mess of
intricate blurred whorls, the gift of a soft-soaping brick salesman.
With his grey, button-collar shirt and sporty tweed hat, it was his
best outfit, and as he looked at his short stocky frame wth its friendly
big-boned, blue-jowled, all-weather face, he could not resist a grin.

'Will Pipes coming out,' he said drily to himself.

He was about to realize that he had a sense of himself now, a sense
of himself as a human being, but he had not always been so lucky,
nor so sure of himself, and as he went out of the house and began
the drive to the address which she had given him, he remembered
another self almost lost now, an unsure bewildered boy without the
comfort of nicknames, plain Will.

He'd met her once by accident outside the Tech where he was
uneasily pursuing the theoretical side of his apprenticeship, but he
was glad because he was not wearing his working clothes. They were
both seventeen. She'd been to her music teacher's only to find that
the teacher was ill. She was never his girl really, he'd just hung about
with her in the last year at school, and briefly walked her home from
the youth club before her mother'd found out the youth club was
occasionally frequented by American serviceman. They'd walked
straight into one another as they came around the corner of a
subway.

'Will!' she pronounced his name with a smile, an exclamation.

He hadn't mentioned her name, just smiled. The thick-shoul-
dered man had been the awkward stocky boy, and he actually had
books under arm, and she a mandolin case. Her mother spent the
earth on music lessons and while Dottie would vamp several

instruments by ear, reading music was a chore to her.

'My day at the Tech',' he said sheepishly.

It was a sharp winter's day, bare trees standing behind them, a nip in the air that gave her a high colour. She wore a scarlet coat with a high cape collar. He said a very silly thing. 'Little Red Riding Hood.'

They never seemed to say anything sensible. He could reason in his own slow way, and he was gentle with everybody, a quiet docile boy from a chapel home. But when she wouldn't speak to him on her mother's instruction, he had been hurt. Not being good enough was a slur and unjustified. He knew it wasn't her fault, but he wished she'd more spirit. There was nothing wrong with him then except who he was and what he was going to be, just Will. He was a nice boy whom girls took for granted, quite safe to be with, never a suspicion of going too far, but useable — useable and discardable. He didn't generate any heat and it worried him then.

Standing there that day, he was quite tongue-tied for a moment. He noticed the mandolin case was slung over her shoulders and her two hands were clasped together inside a little red muff made by her mother from the same material as the coat. She always had on a complete outfit, and liked matching things.

He should have guessed by her smile that she was glad to see him, but he just stood there silently, a half smile on his lips, a couple of tongue-tied kids.

'My lesson's been cancelled,' she said. She wore a scarf over her head and had it tied under her chin, something she rarely did because her mother said it was common and made her look like the factory girls. Perhaps it was the wind that made her relax that rule.

Finally, he asked her. 'You doing anything?'

She shook her head.

He had enough money for one coffee only and cursed himself, fingering a threepenny-bit in his pocket. She did not seem to want to leave.

'I don't have to go back,' he said, referring to his employer.

He wished he could think of something smart and snappy to say, something American. 'What's wrong with jingle bells, baby?' Humphrey Bogart had said that very week in the Workmen's Hall. But all he could manage was, 'This wind would blow you away.'

'Mum's working,' she replied. Although she was as serious as her mother in her ambitions, she managed now and then to convey a hint that she saw some of the folly of it, he remembered. At least, it seemed so that day under the subway.

'D'you fancy a walk?' he said. They were quite near a mountain slope which marked the end of the valleys and slid down gradually to the sea and to the coastal plain before it. 'There's some nice walks about here.'

Before he knew quite what was happening, he had slung the mandolin over his shoulder and they were making their way behind the technical college where there was a kissing gate that led to the mountain path. She still did not say much, just nodded as he made some awkward remarks about his course and the trade he was pursuing. But they both entered the kissing gate together, pausing at the same time. Perhaps he should have stood back to let her through first, but he did not. He had not thought of kissing her but she was obviously in a mood to be kissed. Standing there, he knew it by the way she looked at him, a real smile on her lips for a change, her oval face pale beneath the scarf, the tilt of her chin and that perfect mouth poised and ready.

So he kissed her and she put one red sleeved arm lingeringly on his shoulder. He kissed her again and they stood there with both her arms around his neck. She was in no hurry to move, he remembered, and still she said nothing. They were innocent. There was no come-on about it. He did not feel any of the desire that was to trouble him with other girls later. He had told her once that she was the marrying sort, an extraordinary thing for a boy of seventeen to say, but she was that serious, and there was always that air about her. Despite the frivolity of her ambition and the constant aura of the tinsel costumes, she herself was often grave and silent. Perhaps it was that her mother had worn her out with instructions and constant surveillance. It couldn't be that she was just vacant? Or could it? A dumb blonde. A bit thick. How did he know? A kiss was important he remembered. The next question was, would she go with him? But he did not like to ask it. Instead, he said something that made her laugh.

'That was nice,' he said. He wiped his lips with the back of his hand, and grinned. 'I could do with half a dozen of those.'

They walked on, following the mountain path and winding their way above the opening of the valley, climbing all the time until they could see the haze of the smaller townships on the plain before them. One of the joys of living where they did, was that they could always look down on things, a pleasure that had remained with him.

But he couldn't understand the girl, couldn't get a grip on her. She seemed to have no kind of reality. She was just there, demure in red, clutching that muff, smiling at him, perfect to look at in the magazine sense.

'I didn't expect to see you.'

'Nor me.'

'You're always on your own?'

'Busy,' she said.

'The dancing, and that?'

'Everything.'

'You like it?'

'Mostly.'

'But sometimes...'

'It's hard work,' she said. 'It really is. Really.'

Her ambition...

'I know your mother doesn't like me,' he began to say.

'It's not you personally.'

'Personally? What does that mean?'

'She's had a hard life,' she said. Her eyes were a very light blue, normally expressionless, but there was a frown on her face at the mention of her mother that changed her whole expression.

'Slave driver, if you ask me,' he tried to help.

'She wants me to get on.'

'But you haven't got any friends?' he said, stating the obvious. She didn't hang around with any crowd.

She did not reply.

'I always thought you was nice,' he added. 'I called around, but your mother...'

'It would interfere,' she said.

'But the pictures? Surely, you can go to the pictures when you want?'

'I go with my mother.'

That was another thing. They went everywhere together, and once, two Americans tried to pick them up. Officers, of course, as Mrs Lemon had related to somebody he knew. They would have had to be officers even to have entertained the thought. Texas Rangers for all he knew. Class again.

'Well, I dunno,' he said. 'You're a mystery, you are.'

'D'you think so?'

He fumbled for words, standing there glowering like a farmer's boy in a Sunday suit. 'I'd like to go with you steady, Dot. I would. Honest.'

But her mother wouldn't have that, he knew, and kiss or not, she wouldn't rebel. It was unnatural, but he understood it well enough. In a curious way, she'd never been a child at all. Even in school, he had never seen her in the least bit upset. She never lost that composure, the silent perfect girl in the corner who never asked questions, never answered one if she could help it. It was uncanny.

He tried a joke. 'If only you was a bit more common. Like me!'

'I couldn't,' she said. He was sure she gave a little shiver.

'*What?*'

'It wouldn't be nice,' she said.

'What wouldn't be nice?'

'You're not all that common,' she evaded the question. 'Not uncouth anyway.'

'Your mother thinks so.'

Again she didn't reply.

The mysteries of human beings! She was silent for a while until they reached the topmost point of the hill but as they walked he gave his mind to her furiously. Whatever kids did nowadays, then it was almost impossible to find words to give full extent to your feelings.

'I could go overboard for you,' he wanted to say. He really went a bundle on her, but he couldn't say that either. She was such a smasher, the identical replica of all those girls who stood on lonely tarmacs watching pilots fly off to their doom or moved with lips sealed through the plush furniture of foreign consulates, monocled German spies in attendance. He didn't think that at the time, he thought she was beautiful, but it was a beauty curiously unrelated to anything sexual. She would have made a perfect Snow White, always trapped in a daydream.

'Why don't you answer?' he said.

'I'm going away,' she told him.

'Ah, the band,' he'd heard about that. 'What will your mother do when you're gone?'

'That's just it,' she said. Her face was suddenly hard and pouting. 'Suffer, I expect.'

'Oh, go on . . .'

'She's had a hard life,' she said again.

He made a note to inquire of his sister who helped on the bread round and could give you a potted biography of everyone in the town. But that didn't help him at the moment.

When they reached the top of the hill, there was an old shed called Dai's barn which was quite often frequented by courting couples. The doors were locked but it could be lifted off the hinge on the side. He suggested they went in there to get out of the wind, but she looked at him curiously.

'Out of the wind, like?' he said.

'I'd better not.'

'Your cheeks are blue. I'm freezing myself.'

'You'll have to break in.' She hesitated, implying what? The law, retribution, punishment? He did not know.

'You just lift the door off the hinge.'

He demonstrated.

'You've been here before?'

'I'm not in any band, am I?'

It was perhaps the sharpest thing he had ever said to her.

As he lifted one door off the hinge to allow her to enter, she looked at him strangely.

'I'll leave the mandolin outside,' she said.

Did she think he was going to play it?

Inside, she shocked him by taking out a cigarette. He had never seen her smoke.

'My mother doesn't know,' she said. 'But it calms my nerves.'

'You got no need to be nervy with me, Dot?'

'I know,' she said. She smiled. 'I like you, Will.'

Thinking back, he knew he had one desire on that afternoon, and that was to be pals. As simple as that. He could not get close to her and he could not explain her attraction for him, unless it was that she was so well mannered. He always liked a certain kind of conformity.

There were some empty grain sacks in the corner of the shed and she sat on one, brushing it down, so that her coat would not get dirty.

'When are you going away then?' he asked.

'As soon as it's fixed.'

'Far?'

'On tour to start.'

'All over then?'

'Forces mostly.' She flicked the ash off the cigarette and raised an eyebrow to condescend to him. 'Playing to the Forces.'

It sounded glamorous then. He had seen films of troop concerts, cigarette smoke drifting through beams of arc lights, the wolf whistles of sex-starved men ogling in the dark.

He sat down uneasily beside her. It was extraordinary that they had so little to say to each other, but then they had very little in common. She did not take much interest in the street but he mentioned the name of a boy they knew who had been shot down over Bremen.

'Sad,' she said, and that was all. It did not touch her.

There was also a girl nearby who had married an air-gunner who was posted missing. She'd waited six months, then married again, only to receive the news that her first husband was reported alive, a prisoner.

'Hell of a thing,' Will said, referring to it, but he did not fully understand the situation. He had heard his sister talk accusingly of the girl as a fly-by-night. Seven boys had been killed from the fifteen houses at the end of their street alone and mourning was at a premium.

But Dottie didn't seem to take it in. She was completely uninvolved in things that did not immediately concern her.

'Are you going to be air crew, Will?'

'Army, I suppose,' he grinned. He had a vague idea you had to have County School maths to be air crew and had fixed his mind on the engineers. 'Keep your nose clean, they might let you do your trade,' his father'd said. 'Better that than cutting the barrack lawn with nail scissors.' Real Dan y Graig, his father'd soldiered in the First War, had seen the folly of it, was inclined to let Hitler vent his spleen on London before he took a view of this war. First London, then Cardiff; he'd start to worry when the street copped it.

'Haven't you any ambitions then, Will?'

He grinned again. He had not. But for some reason, she persisted.

'You're no trouble, are you?' she sulked.

He didn't understand.

'How d'you mean?'

'You don't want anything much, Will?'

'I dunno,' he said.

She finished her cigarette, sighed, tapped it out on a brick.

'Half-soaked's right then.'

He was hurt. Other people said that and he did not fully understand what they meant, except that it wasn't complimentary.

'But never mind, you're nice,' she added, madam that she was. She stood up and went towards the window of the hut, looked out, then turned alluringly towards him. One foot posed before the other. Charm was on parade again, and more than that, as ever, she was sounding her g's very carefully.

But his mind was still on the half-soaked thing. What did it mean? That he didn't rush things? That he was careful? That he did things at his own pace? Well, he had always done that. Like his old man, he wanted to be a sticker. She was still looking at him, that teasing smile playing about her lips. She opened the top buttons of her coat, continued to pose. He still couldn't understand the interference. Half-soaked, it stuck in his mind like an unpleasant note of music. 'Room for improvement... Must make more effort... Concentrates, but not enough...' His school reports ran with monotonous regularity. But she wasn't brainy. Then another thought occurred to him and he flushed. Did she mean that he was slow?

'What you got on your mind then?' he said in his low monotonous voice. 'Coming in here?'

She did not say anything.

'You're not up to anything, are you?'

She gave a little gasp of impatience.

'Will Thick,' she said.

That did it. He was on his feet in an instant. He saw it as an attack on his status and it hurt him more than anything she could have done.

'I don't know who you think you are,' he said. 'But if you got anything in mind, you can forget it. Or are you just doin' your bit of actin', havin' me on?'

For answer, she did up the button of her coat and marched towards the door. Whatever there had been between them, was over. Two kisses by the lych gate and nothing else.

Remembering, he chuckled. There were still parts of him that were as sentimental as they come, and as far as women were concerned, it was years before he looked at them as human beings. Upbringing, he thought ruefully. He'd known nothing about girls at all. His sisters were much older than him, motherly figures at that, and he'd been virtually brought up as an only child. What a fool he'd been! She'd gone out of the hut before him, made her way alone, cross with him as he'd followed in a sullen silence. It was such a problem and they were so preoccupied with it, that they'd committed a real sin by leaving the mandolin behind, and he'd had to walk all the way up the mountain to get it, and only then had she smiled as he assumed the normal and predictable helpmate's role. She went away soon after, and although he'd caught a glimpse of her across the street, they'd never really spoken since.

'Thirty years ago', he said to himself, easing down his cuff-links as he drove towards her now. What kids they were. But still he couldn't seem to recall her as a human being somehow. It was as if she had a gift for remaining unrealized as a flesh-and-blood person. Or perhaps it was just his memory. Of course, when he came to think of it now — and he'd learned a few good things since — the whole thing was an attempt at protest, he supposed. Everything in her life up to then had been directed at the one ambition, getting out of Dan y Graig Street and doing everything her mother said. She was not only the *Shampoo-Girl*, but the *Yes-Girl*, and for one afternoon, she must have had thoughts of rebellion, picking him as patsy.

He found her flat and parked the car a little away from the kerb so that it would be in full vision from the house. When he pressed the bell, he could not suppress a quiver of excitement. It was a drab old world, and there was only one Dottie Lemon. Whatever you had, never altered what you had been.

Presently, footsteps shuffled towards him inside. Must be in her slippers. As the door inched open, he smelt the odour of stale curry lingering about the interior of the hallway, then, as she spoke, he recognized her voice at once.

'Yes?'

She had not switched on the interior light and he could barely see her. She was wearing some kind of flowered kimono and dark glasses. Her hair was near enough the same, but piled above her head. Was it blue? A rinse, did they call it? And there was a lot more of her, bulging behind that slatternly dressing gown.

'Will,' he said sheepishly. He nearly said, Will Pipes.

She took a second to recognize him. Behind the dark glasses, the lower half of her face had become exactly like her mother's, deep drawn lines pulling down the corners of her mouth, the sallowness of her thin neck all indicating the wear of age and giving her — her of all people! — the pinched, worn look of bitter experience which he associated with those exhausted women who'd populated the terrace before the war. The exception was her hair which remained a set piece as if it were someone else's property. Scrag had bred scrag, he thought. The flat, the face, the down-at-heel slippers spelt penury and dismay. That career... Those dreams... He knew the obvious in a second. She had failed at everything.

'Oh, hell,' he thought. 'Poor Dot...' He was not used to dismay and felt upset to see her so. She'd really fattened too, in all the wrong places. Well, whatever he could do...

''Lo, Dot,' he said. There was a catch in his voice. 'How is it, kid?'

She had not spoken, and indeed, seemed determined to remain a creature of disguises because she did not remove the sunglasses.

'I knew you'd come,' she said flatly. She opened the door fully.

He wished he hadn't left that expensive car in so obvious a position. Show-off him.

'Of course, I came...'

'You remembered me?'

''Course,' he said again. ''Course, Dot...'

'Well, you'd better come in.'

Desperate, he thought. Things on her mind, no doubt, but her abruptness now was in marked contrast to the urgency of her note.

He took off his sporty hat and followed her into the gloomy hallway. If it were not for the sunglasses which remained a barrier, he would not have been surprised if she had collapsed into his arms the moment the front door was closed. It was such an emotional moment. Had she done so, he would have said, 'There...There...'

But she did nothing of the kind. She led him past the open door of the bedsitter to a makeshift hardboard partition beneath the stairway. She couldn't be living there...

'Come here.'

He followed, his hat in his hands. If only she would take off those dark glasses.

She stood outside the partition and pointed in.

'Look at this!'

He looked instead at her face, peering into the lenses but seeing only his own reflection there.

But she waved her outstretched forefinger downward like a schoolmistress.

'Look at it!'

He did so. Inside the partition was an ancient lavatory, the pan of which had been smashed into two halves, and water trickled over the grubby linoleum on the floor.

'Look at it!' she hissed again. At last she took off the sunglasses, but there was an expression of such fury in her eyes that he blinked.

He fingered his Dior tie. Did nothing ever happen to him that was not obvious?

'Vandals,' he said tiredly.

'Tenants,' she said. 'Students.'

'You're running this place?'

'I share it.'

'Share it?'

'The toilet!' Preoccupied, she did not take her eyes from the wrecked pan.

He swallowed. Had she nothing more to say to him? Apparently not. But what could he do? Stuck for something to say himself, he pulled a small notebook from his pocket, and began to measure up.

She stepped back into the hallway.

'Be sure you get it right,' she snapped. 'The measurements —

everything.'

'I'll send a man.'

'Can't you come yourself?'

'Well...'

'It's been like that for a week, and I can't keep on trailing up and down the stairs.'

She did look uncomfortable.

'I'll see to it right away,' he said briskly. 'I quite understand.' Part of his success as a small time jobber had been the confidential air of concern he assumed when dealing with lavatorial matters, a facet he'd observed in undertakers, and automatically the consoling note returned to his voice as he communicated his understanding of the urgency of the problem.

'Very awkward indeed.'

'As soon as you can. I shall stay in until you come.'

'Very good,' he said, controlling a sigh. What a fool he was. He'd put his good suit on for Myrna Loy, only to have his face rubbed in the pan once more. But surely, they'd have a bit of a chat? What happened to her mother? Who had she married? What happened to the showbiz?

'How've you been then?' he said when they went back into the hall.

She did not appear to have heard him.

'Perhaps you can put in a coloured suite?' she said over her shoulder. 'There's room there for a basin. I expect you've got seconds lying about the shop?'

He stared at her back.

'Seconds?' She wanted a cheap job. 'Well, yes.'

She turned and looked at him haughtily.

'And if the water's switched off, I must have notice.'

'Of course, Dot.'

It was as if he did not exist as a human being at all. Had he ever in her eyes? But then, who was she? She'd begun to doubt him again.

'You always were very slow,' she said as he put the notebook away.

Half-soaked again, he thought.

She did not show him out, but sidled into her bedsitter. Not before he had sneaked a glance into the room, however. He just had time to see a hand of cards laid out on a green baize table, and behind it, an elaborate sandalwood chest on raised legs. The lid of the chest was open, and in the centre, beside compartments containing racks of playing cards, there was a large crystal ball protected by raised felt. Dottie Lemon had become a palmist.

He gasped as if the sudden peep into that room had given him total knowledge. 'Dottie Lemon really on her arse,' he thought.

He felt a wave of sadness overwhelm him so that his throat became dry and he could not speak. But she had never really been part of his life, and would now vanish from it unknown. As it was, he soon reverted to normal.

'Toilet and suite, Number Thirty-One A, Telelkebir Gardens, ground-floor bedsitter,' he said briskly to his general foreman. 'And no plastic pipes. Use a bit of that scrap we got in the yard. Don't book it, charge it to me.'

'Will-Robin-Hood-Pipes still careful,' he thought finally, reverting to his workday self. Give her a lav, anyhow. Even in her retirement, it was a pity to think of Snow White being caught short.

Fly Half

Your drinking!' she said. 'My God...'
'Oh, for goodness' sake, I just met some people.'
'Have you seen what you look like this morning? Your eyes? Well, you should have seen yourself when you came in last night? A man your age. You weren't just squiffy, you were paralytic. Simply dreadful. It took the Under-Manager and a porter to carry you up the stairs.'

'It didn't?' He was small and chubby, run to fat now, pear-shaped and pink, and his sharp, pale little eyes narrowed with concern as he looked at her, immaculate in white shorts and tennis shirt, her rather severe face and pointed features browned by the sun, her hair still thick and lustrous, her shape good, still youthful, that detached, untouchable air of the well-groomed woman remaining with her even in the casual clothes which she wore on holiday. She remained a Miss Muffet in appearance even though they had been married for seven years. There was still something pristine about her, and trying to alter her had exhausted him. If it could have been done at all, it should have been a younger man, he thought. The seven years between them was too much. And now she was getting waspish. It wouldn't be long until she did it before other people like the other one. Neither of his marriages had quite worked out as he'd hoped, but perhaps that was because he hadn't enough to give them. He wasn't blaming anyone and he wasn't complaining. The fact was, he'd had his moment and his time, and he'd doubted if she'd understand either. He never spoke about it anymore. He'd have to say something though, if she went on in that vein. Her voice... God save him from ageing head prefects.

But in the event, he controlled himself.

'Steady... Play it close to the chest now, boys. Keep it tight first half.' What a hell of a night it had been though! *Sospan Fach* in Portuguese... What about that?

'They had to carry you up the stairs,' she continued. 'The lift wasn't working and they had to manhandle you. Where were you? You weren't in that place again? Not with that disgusting lecher, the dirty joke person? Not him? Not in that bar?'

'It came on to rain,' he said. He didn't seem to have the energy to make up good excuses anymore.

'Can't you understand that they're just hangers-on in that bar?

I'll bet you paid for every drink.'

'I didn't, I... ' but he'd really filled his boots, he remembered, and now a pain like a marble seemed to roll down his intestine.

'Every drink! Only you haven't got the sense to see it. I'm sure they laugh at you behind your back anyway. They take one look at what's coming, and just know they're on a good thing. Well, be your age. There are fifty-two weeks in the year and we're just over here for two.'

'They're rugby men.'

'Rugby men?' That again, she thought. 'They're any kind of men you want them to be, provided you're paying.'

'Where's the Alka-Seltzer?'

'By your bed.'

'Have you got a spoon?'

'Can't you do anything for yourself?'

'There's no need to be like that,' he said.

But there was every need, she thought. It was more than just another night out with the boys this time, it was their annual holiday, and she hadn't come abroad just to have a repetition of what went on at home, his finding exactly the same kind of places and people as those with whom he normally cavorted on his night out. It was absurd to think of having a night out on your own when you were on holiday with your wife anyway. What was wrong with wives as part of the human species? But to be fair, it hadn't begun like that this time. She'd wanted to see some pottery in a display they were putting on in the hotel, and then she'd taken coffee with some women who were staying there and he'd said he was going to take a stroll down to the village. But the stroll meant another visit to a tavern and a session, and he was on the tiles again, her husband.

That was how it started, a little thing like that, but the trouble was, as she well knew, she was the second wife, and being the second wife, she had to cope with the impossible as far as she was concerned, his memory of the first wife who as the years had slipped by had become a hallowed figure in his mind, she was sure. He had that capacity for romanticizing the past and although he checked himself from actually mentioning her name now, in his private thoughts it was still Lil this, Lil that, Esme was sure. Even the difference between their two names was chalk and cheese. Lil was valleys and Esme was Cardiff, a Tory Lord Mayor's daughter and that again was part of the problem, one of the many things which stood between them. The other was that she had not known him in his heyday, for he was something very special then, she was given to understand, and indeed, people who had known him, men now in their late forties, spoke of him as a special being whose darting heels and will-of-the-wisp figure had made him the idol of the crowds. For he was that rarest of beings, a much capped Welsh fly half, one of the greatest according to journalists who kept bringing up his name in their columns, a man to be put amongst the immortals, Trew, Willie Davies, the two Cliffs, and head and shoulders above the recent crop, even 'King' John who did other things better, but could not beat a man off either foot and shirked a physical game. He sneaked through anyway like a thief in the night, but her husband could beat a man openly and make him look a fool. It was this beating a man off either foot which was apparently important. In thirty years only two men could do that, one was Bleddyn, and the other was her husband and that was something according to the connoisseur. He had an eye for an opening, and more important than anything else, absolute confidence, a wicked acceleration over twenty yards, and a wonderful pair of hands. He had once sold a dummy which deceived even the referee who blew up for a forward pass and could not then reverse the decision, or so the legend ran.

People who knew went on for hours and hours in this vein, and at first, she was not adverse to listening. She had played games at school herself, and she thought physical excellence an excellent thing in itself. But that was in school. She did not think it reasonable that a prowess at games should haunt you all your life, but rugby was not a game where they lived, it was a religion, and a Calvinist religion at that. She went with him occasionally to internationals, and listening to the roar at the Arms Park and watching the seething faces beside her, she had felt rather sorry for the All Blacks until they started a little bit of this and that, to use the phrase, but that only made them more like the others, in her book. But for their jerseys they were indistinguishable from the Welsh side as human beings, and if people looked at her as if she had committed treason when she said things like that, she did not care. It was no longer a joke and it had got past the point of irritation. The game, the past, his continual wallowing in it, aided and abetted by everybody he seemed to meet even here in Portugal, added up to a kind of cancer which she wished she could exorcize.

But she couldn't. And she couldn't remove his first wife from his mind either, it seemed. The famous Lil. This going out on his own when they were on holiday had to be stamped on, however. That was one thing she could do.

But she hesitated for a moment, opening the shuttered door which led out from their bedroom to the balcony, and crossed out into the early morning sunlight. It was a beautiful day again, the wind from Spain which blew nobody any good as the legend said, had died down and she felt pleasantly warm. Down below her, past the hotel swimming pool and the terra cotta roofs of the houses, she could see the sea in the distance and a picturesque line of sardine boats chugging their way homewards into the little harbour. It was a perfect little spot. It was relatively undiscovered. The food was splendid, the service superb. In the nights you could hear that savage *fado* singing drifting up from a club nearby and last year, he had liked it as much as she had. That was the thing. They did enjoy things together. She was right to have married him. He had some splendid qualities. He was generous and kind and quite successful at what he did, even though her father had helped him considerably, putting business his way, and one thing and another, but then that was what fathers were for.

Esme's husband was an estate agent by profession, in as much as men who gave as much time to football as he did, could be said to have a profession, but they were quite comfortably off with what he earned and what her father had left her, and there shouldn't have been a care in the world, unless it was not having children. She was in her thirties when she got married, he was forty-three, and they hadn't really expected to start a family, and he hadn't any children by his previous marriage either, so he couldn't blame her on that score. But he would drink, would go off into this male world of his, and even when she took him away from it, he recreated it with total strangers. At first, she said, well, good for him, he was a man's man, small, but one of the boys, jovial, jokey, clubbable, something tweedy about him that made you think of cheese and beer, mellow tobacco and the smell of old leather. Wearing his sporty cloth cap, he looked like a prosperous pork butcher, she often said, but it was said good humouredly. Before she married him, she did not think of going to bed with him, he was not the sort. He was someone you saw doing accounts, dealing with workmen, telling off the gardener, or giving the vicar a glass of punch and an elbow-jogging story as a bonus, and she did not mind that either.

After forty, if you wanted anything in a man, it was comfort. She'd had the other sort. She supposed he suspected but he'd never said anything, although at one time, there were quite a few stories going around about her because she'd been just a little unstable after her mother'd died and her father married again, but that was old, old stuff now. She looked pristine but she wasn't pristine, and she'd never married previously because, after her earlier playing around — hole in the corner stuff in borrowed flats — she felt an aversion to men her own age, preferring the company of women. Not that she didn't know they could be bitches and dreadfully possessive at that, like the County Club and that dreadful Bridge League which had swallowed up her mother. But nothing was simple, nothing was clear before her marriage, although she hadn't worried about it, busying herself with business interests, charity and political committees, only to meet him in the Squash Club in one of his vain attempts to get fit again.

And then it was so unlike her! It was extraordinary that they had a single word to say to each other. She knew he thought her rather a toff, which she was by his standards, but he also thought her more attractive than she did herself. She was very honest about that, and believed she had a capacity for objectivity. The truth was that apart from her father's money, she was rather unattractive, she knew. By the norm, that is. Her features were too severe, her nose too large, and unless she was very careful with what she wore, she could be thought angular since she had a long body and short legs. She compensated by being immaculately turned out always, paid special attention to her weight and complexion, but all this she could cope with. She had settled for what she was, and she could even accept him as he was, apart from the football thing, the bar-bonhomie syndrome, and of course, the famous Lil. It always got back to that.

The cardinal fact was, Esme had now decided, that in his two marriages, her husband had done two opposite things, just the sort of things a man would do who was unsure of himself with women. He had married above him — that was her, and he'd married beneath him — that was Lil, and being the sentimentalist he was, now all his affections extended glueily like chewing gum to the past, and his old stamping ground in the Welsh valleys where he'd met Lil, probably wearing jersey and boots in bed, for all Esme knew. He had once confessed that Lil was the daughter of a fish-and-chip proprietor who made a habit of bathing three times a day in order to remove the cloying odour of the product. It was apparently something that seriously worried her, kept her awake at night, and as an adolescent, she'd even had to take sedatives because she got quite hysterical about it, refused to work in the shop and actually stopped eating until her father had been persuaded to leave the flat above it. He'd told Esme that, but shaking his head affectionately on recall as if it was some precious detail and part of the mythology

which surrounded a person who later became distinguished, rising
above rather squalid circumstances.

Hence the 'famous' Lil. She'd once asked him outright what she was
really like. (The other information had come in bits and pieces.) 'Oh,
she was just a Ponty girl,' he said dismissively, as if that said anything.

Well, what was Esme supposed to do about it? Fish and chips,
typical of the valleys, she thought. But the information she had
received upon the subject in roundabout ways was considerable. Lil
made grammatical mistakes, couldn't count, was terrified of thun-
derstorms when she hid under the stairs, wouldn't answer the door
in a pinafore, always made tart for Sundays and let it stand overnight on a cold stone, gave money to gipsies, loved male voice
choirs, actually cried when they sang unpronounceable songs, and
once threatened to run on the field brandishing an umbrella when
he was being trampled in the Neath match. It was difficult enough
to compete with any kind of first wife, but when the first wife was
common as dirt, a kind of rugby adjunct who probably vaselined
her ears and wore shinguards before divesting herself of her chapel
black! — well, Esme's private sarcasm knew no bounds.

It was laughable to think about it all. And yet, in moments of
uncertainty, it preyed on her mind. There was only one consolation.
From what she could gather from other people, the impression he
gave of Lil was markedly different from theirs. Mother Earth in
embryo on the one hand, was an insignificant and rather sickly little
mouse of a thing on the other. Not that Esme was going to say
anything about the eventual illness which was tragic, but if a man
is not a complete man, then it is some woman's fault. That's what
her mother would have said, and the thing was, to make a diagnosis
about their marriage now, and then do the necessary. It was no good
dwelling on the past. No good at all. Absolutely not.

What then, was the diagnosis?

His lack of physical fitness for a start, she thought, beginning to
itemize the details. If he was a pound overweight, he was three stone.
You looked at photographs of him in the old days and you saw
features, actual features, like cheekbones and a chin which had long
vanished. He had to diet then, rigorously, that was the first thing.
He took no exercise, had not for the last three years, and although
he still went to clubs, golf clubs, squash clubs, the Athletic, it was
only to bend his elbow. His golf things had mildew on them and he
didn't possess a pair of shorts he could step into.

Well, she could do something in that direction. They might go to
Champneys, that health clinic in Tring, as her mother and father

had. Hertfordshire would be a relief after Cardiff and its grubby hinterland. Sitz baths and massage, she thought. Not altogether unpleasant. But what else?

His drinking. That was another conundrum and something which she felt to be a criticism of her. Before they were married, she did not realize just how much he drank. It was very difficult to know at the time, and while he pretended an interest in the things which amused her and they went to the theatre, concerts and all the gymkhanas and point to points which particularly interested her, he never seemed to drink excessively. Of course, he liked his glass, but never gave any indication of serious drinking or even drunkenness. What she hadn't realized was that the moment he left her, raising his cap like a jockey after doing his bit of middle aged courting, he must have gone straight home to his bottle. When they were actually married, it wasn't long before she noticed his nightly tipple. He had a very large way of dismissing all he'd drunk before dinner, including what he'd had all the afternoon in the Spanish Club or the Exchange, by insisting that it could be discounted by what he'd just managed to get into his mouth while they ate. Ironically, they'd inherited a cellar from her father and he'd soon side-stepped his way through that like a will o' the wisp all right. To be fair, he wasn't an alcoholic, there weren't sinister overtones, he didn't normally make scenes or smash things, but what he did do was fall asleep more often than he should. He was an Olympic sleeper, she'd once remarked. Nothing disturbed him. Like a bat, he could practically sleep upside down. Then he could sleep in trains, on aircraft, in boats, at the dinner table, even squatting at stool on the lavatory pan. It would have been rather amusing if it had been somebody else's husband, and that was another thing, he did look rather amusing, a jolly little man. And he was normally jolly, she was forced to admit.

When he wasn't asleep, when he wasn't escaping her with his fellows, when he wasn't being himself, in short.

So what was she to do? She knew she was the kind of woman who always made decisions, made them, and stuck to them, and there were three short vertical lines above her nose giving her face a frowning intensity when she was not relaxed. But there was precious little chance of relaxation when he carried on as he did, without paying the slightest attention to what she called her inner needs. Very well then, she would bring matters to a head. But should she? Was it dangerous? Questions, questions, she said to herself and continued to frown.

She had gone out on to the balcony to think, but now she returned to the bedroom. He remained in bed, in exactly the same position as when she had left him, but he condescended to open first one eye, then the other. As usual, every inactivity on his part set her off. She forgot her doubts for the moment.

He said, 'The thing was...'

'I don't want to know.'

'Some of the people we met last year...'

'I said, "I don't want to know".'

'... were there, and we had a bit of a... well, a sing song actually.'

She sat calmly and deliberately in the chair facing him. Must not shriek. Must be objective.

But she said, 'Have you ever thought what it's like to grow up?'

'Just a bit of a sing song. What's the harm in that?'

'You said you were going for a stroll?'

'It er... came on to rain.'

'You could have got a taxi?'

'I didn't think. I thought you were on your pottery lark.'

'The truth is, you'd rather be with them than me?'

'Not at all.'

'It's true.'

'Really, no. You're making an issue out of it.'

'Don't you understand, it's a pattern, your leaving me, always for men, always your grubby acquaintances.'

'Oh, come on. I haven't got any grubby acquaintances. Not here anyway.'

He was making it good humoured, a domestic argument, but she was not going to have that.

'I never realized you were such a soak.'

'Soak? Steady on.' He raised his thick little eyebrows and pursed his lips as if a mild protest was justifiable at that remark, but for her sake, he wasn't going to make it.

'I know what you are, you see? I've read about it.'

'Read about it?' he looked puzzled.

'You're a problematic heavy drinker,' she said. She had actually read that, and it fitted, but she felt foolish saying it. And she was keeping none of her resolutions. She not only sounded like a shrew, but a dreadful blue stocking shrew. She bit her lip.

He was silent, looking away reprovingly. Again his face indicated he was saying nothing for her sake. He had no idea of the seriousness of the problem. Try again.

'I'll tell you — you can lie there, you can do nothing — you can say nothing, but the way you live, your life is dribbling away. Can't you understand? You're making yourself less than a human being.'

'Oh, come...'

'Yes!' she said.

'I admit I had a bit too much.'

'You were incapable.'

'Indigestion. Olives,' he said regretfully. ' I like them, they don't like me.'

Nothing she said seemed to get through to him. His one-dimensional conversation. He still had the quilt pulled up around his neck and there was something almost comic about him lying there like a dazed little pig tucked up in an expensive pram.

'I wonder sometimes what you want of me. Why you ever married me at all. I don't know what you think — ever. You never discuss anything. I don't even know what you think at any given moment. On any topic.'

'Listen,' he said. 'I haven't got any complaints.'

'What do you want then?'

'To do? Now?'

'No!' she said, but paused. He didn't understand. Or if he did understand, he was saying nothing. And his refusal to come to terms with her was an act of stubbornness for she knew he was basically a shrewd man. Nobody took him for a fool except her, and it was only on this domestic level that he put up a front. His mind was like wool when he wanted it to be, and that had come as a shock to her, because she came from a quite outspoken family. They weren't as Welsh as he was though, and they certainly weren't valley Welsh, who could, in her experience, be like Africans saying only what they thought you wanted to hear. They had that capacity for living life on two levels, public and private, and it was this private self of his which she wanted to penetrate. Not that it was a Welsh problem, the two of them were so different as people, she quite realized.

But she would have to do something, she knew. Immediately! She would have to get through to him. But how?

He continued in his sog like a long-term hospital patient, not even looking at her when she had finished speaking. That was Welsh again. If you ignored a thing, it went away. But she must be reasonable. 'Cool head!' she repeated to herself. But now his eyes closed again and she could have screamed. It was all she could do to stand up and return to the balcony where she continued to probe. She knew she had to be careful. She could go too far. But if only she could answer that one question. Why had he married her? And what had changed since he had? She meant from his point of view. Therein lay the crux of the matter she was sure.

She determined to make one last attempt. She'd dealt with his obesity, his drinking and the famous Lil. The only thing that remained reflected more on her. It couldn't be that he'd married her for her money. Vulgar as it sounded, one of the problems earlier in her life was just this, and of the three men who'd actively pursued her, two had their eye on the main chance, she was sure. If only parents realized what harm their money did, she thought. She remembered the casual inquiries about the number of cars they ran at home with a shudder. But she couldn't say that about him. One of the endearing things about him was that he'd done rather well, like almost everybody who'd been in property since the war. And Welsh or not, like most Estate Agents, he was a frightful snob when it came to the women he had working for him. The girls in the front office always had to come from a good school. Diamond Lil would have been no good to him dealing with the county families, the Butes or the Lord Lieutenant, she thought maliciously, and she knew well enough that he always took care to have her with him when he did his country-house prospecting in the Vale. So that was one relief, she was sure. She was everything he wanted socially. It followed without saying, but it was reassuring to say it. Of course, he'd once said that nobody would see a Welsh outside half in the gutter, but that was a joke. It had to be, or where was her father's toryism then?

She sighed. If only she could have shared jokes like this with him. It was so sad, his retreat from her. But she musn't digress. It was marriage-mending day, she said to herself with an attempt at gaiety. There remained only one avenue which she had not explored — herself. Supposing she were lying in there, seeing things from his point of view, but looking out at herself? Perhaps that was the crucial thing. There was no point in keeping up with things or being well informed unless you were prepared to turn your mind inwards, spotlighting your own deficiencies, and of course, as she well knew, she was not perfect. Not by any means. But if there was one thing she would have liked people to say about her, it was that she had character and was honest. Very well... What was the picture of her which could be seen from outside? It was a rather intelligent question to ask when she came to think of it, but having asked it, her jealousy returned once more like a sharp stabbing pain.

It was the old problem, the other one again, and no matter how furiously her mind worked, laying one idea on top of another like slices of crispbread, she always reached the same point, the moment when she hesitated and there came, floating into her consciousness like a sail around a headland, that face from the discarded wedding photograph, Lil, Lil, Lil. It was small and whimsical, chin tilted as she looked trustingly up at him, the soft parted lips, that clinging hand, the adoring eyes, that dated, page-boy hairstyle that must have been thought so *chic* in some backstreet hairdresser's. There was a dependent helplessness about it that Esme had never possessed and it was always in the same pose, always striking the same unobtainable note. She was the sort of *little* girl that men felt guilty about leaving, whereas Esme knew that she was the sort who was punished, and at times, she felt there was no escape from the role which her personality had cast for her.

Despairingly, Esme stuck to her train of thought, however. If she had any quality, it was grit, and while it was absurd to be sitting here in Portugal worrying about some trollop from a fish-and-chip shop in Dan y Graig street, or wherever it was, if there was something which she could learn, she would learn it. And perhpas she was on the right track after all. There was one quality which she did not lack and which was manifestly apparent in that photograph. She was never clinging, Esme realized, never openly dependent. Worse — and she had trouble with this before — she was very often thought too clever by far. People went off you when you were always right. They found it so formidable. Cleversticks, she thought. She did feel guilty because she had taken pains to disguise it during their courtship, but no doubt, like his drinking, it must have showed afterwards. She was just as much to blame then, in this one respect. Well, if she had to come all the way to Portugal to find this out, it was worth it. Now she knew what to do. It was her business, her very feminine business to be the flyer half. She was jolly lucky she'd given her mind so ruthlessly to the situation in time.

Right! Decision — action!

She went back inside the room. Of course, he was pretending to be asleep now. He lay back on the pillows, his eyes closed, looking strangely boyish in his sleep. His hair, once fair, was grey, but still curly and she was delighted he still kept it short. Say what you like, he was a rugger man, a famous rugger man, and that was something, she supposed. She really was proud to believe that he was the best of them all. Her thoughts had turned the full circle. That was what insight did for you. And she did care for him. Now that her father was dead, he was really all she had.

'Darling,' she said. 'I've got a confession to make. Really... I want to apologize.' She put one hand on his shoulder.

He opened his eyes and blinked. The Alka-Seltzer had done some of its work. He scrambled up on one elbow and leant against the bed-head.

'I want to talk to you,' she said in a much gentler voice. 'Really talk to you.'

'Of course.'

'I've been thinking...'

'Just let me get dressed. I'll take you out to lunch.'

'Will you?'

'Yes. And I'm very sorry about last night. Will have to cut down.'

'That's just what I was going to suggest.'

'Good then,' he gave her a friendly grin.

'And if I'm a bit bossy,' she said shyly, 'Sorry, I sounded like a shrew just now.'

'Not at all.' His famous hand seemed lost for something to do, but he patted her affectionately.

'We have to make adjustments all through life,' she said. She suddenly felt rather grand. 'Especially at our age.' It was very nice of her to include her age with his, she thought.

'Of course, dear,' he manoeuvred himself out of bed slyly, first an arm, then a leg, then both legs. It was a controlled slide, edging discreetly away from her. 'But I don't want to hear another word. My fault entirely.'

There, she thought, It had worked. Just like that.

But in the bathroom, he stuck his tongue out at the mirror, his mind returning immediately to an argument of the previous night that had driven him to apoplexy. Neither husband, nor estate agent, nor clubman was recognizable.

'Barry John,' he said to himself. 'Barry-bloody-John!' Dear God, under the old rules he wouldn't have lasted until they got the oranges out! And as for this All Black lot, why didn't they strip 'em to the waist, give 'em knives and have done with it! He'd thought he was going to have a coronary every game they played — and won. God blast them, and damn them all to hell! Thank God for Llanelli anyway.

'Scarlets forever!' he said, and later: 'Now then, darling, where would you like to go?'

Actors

There were few porters at the station and no one recognised them except the chauffeur of the hire car who stood just outside the ticket collector's gate. The chauffeur who was local and mostly used for funerals, wore a dark suit with a black tie and a stiff starched collar which was too small for him and had already caused an angry red weal along one side of his neck. He did not salute but removed his peaked cap, revealing a startlingly bald, egg-white head impregnated with tiny blue marks as if made haphazardly with an indelible pencil. He was smiling at first because he thought there was no luggage but then he saw the porter trundling a loaded trolley behind them as they came towards the barrier, both bulky in new fawn sheepskin coats, both wearing fur hats, the woman a pair of high tan boots whose steel-tipped heels made a loud authoritative tapping noise that seemed to fill the entrance hall of the station. The woman carried a vanity case and swung it to and fro, a precise almost military movement that continued while her husband handed over the tickets, staring at them curiously as if he had not performed such a simple operation for a long time. He seemed surprised when the ticket collector handed them back and then crushed them into his pocket as if he had no idea what they were worth. Either that, or he was putting on another of his acts, the chauffeur thought.

'Good evening, sir,' the chauffeur said. 'Mr. Brayley, er... Madam.'

'Hello, Norman,' Ben Brayley said.

'The car's just outside, sir. I'll get you settled and then get the luggage.'

But the porter was already following them with the trolley, its wheels skidding against the uncleared slush on the pavement. The chauffeur saw to the woman first, opening the rear door, eyes discretely lowered as she made a leggy business of getting herself, the bulky coat, the hat, the vanity case, and finally the boots into the car. He had to wait until she removed the coat, revealing a wide leather belt which she wore over a cashmere sweater, the large silver buckle of the belt a creation of gleaming volcanic stones mounted in a web of silver. Despite their subdued colours the stones glinted like eyes and they were so unusual he could not take his own eyes from them, but then she moved across the seat, and Brayley pressed

a five pound note into his hand and nodded at the porter who still
had to be prevented from transferring one of the expensive pigskin
suitcases on to the wet pavement. The luggage stowed, the porter
took the tip with a grin and peered inside the rear window.

'Isn't that?...' he began to say but the chauffeur had already gone
round to the driving seat and the car drove off leaving the porter
standing there. He wasn't sure, but if it was who he thought it was,
he wished he'd been quicker and got him to sign the note or
something. He had a daughter who collected autographs, and a son
who was always threatening to sell his sister's collection. But the
porter was too late. The car was gone.

'You'll want to go straight to the house, sir?'

'Yes, Norman. We're staying the night.'

'In the house?'

'Yes.'

'I just wondered, the last time you came I took you to the hotel?'

'No, I spoke to my brother. There's room in the house.'

'And tomorrow night, after the funeral?'

'We'll let you know, Norman. But have the tank full, just in case.'

'Yes, sir.'

They joined the mainstream traffic but the chauffeur seemed to
have a compulsion to crane his neck, the collar biting into it,
deepening the red weal which became even more visible.

'I don't know if the lady'd like me to point anything out. We're
just passing the Cardiff Arms Park, then we'll be going up Cathedral
Road past the Welsh TV Studios, and then the cathedral with the
Epstein. There was an American forces camp there in the war, I
think.'

'It's all right, Norman. It was my second wife who was American.'

'Well, just let me know if there is anything, sir, if you want to stop
or...'

'No, we'll go straight there.'

Brayley lent forward and slid the glass partion shut.

'Did you see his head when he took his cap off?' the woman said.
'All those blue marks?'

'Pit blast,' Brayley said. 'They're coal scars. The coal dust con-
geals under the skin when it's broken.'

'It's revolting. Why doesn't he wear a wig?'

'You'd better watch what you say.'

'He can't hear us.'

'You don't know.'

'How long will it take us to get there?'

'About an hour.'

'Who'll be there exactly?'

'I told you, my brothers, sisters, people. I shouldn't think there'll be anybody there but family tonight. Tomorrow'll be another story, the world and his wife.'

'Who?'

'Everybody'll know we're coming.'

'That's what you wanted, isn't it?'

'Not exactly, but we had to come.'

'Will it all be in Welsh?'

'No, a mixture, I expect.'

'There'll be singing though?'

'It's a funeral, not an entertainment.'

Oh, it's going to be like that, the woman thought but she said: 'You'd better tell me the names of the people again. I'm simply dreadful on names.'

'My eldest brother's name is Lloyd.'

'He's the unmarried one who lives there?'

'That's right. And Elsie lived next door.'

'Didn't they ever think of getting married?'

'They must have thought about it but I don't suppose he ever got around to it. He's very shy.'

'Reserved, you mean?'

'No, just a very simple man.'

'Didn't Elsie have any feeling for him?'

'She'd been married. Her husband was killed underground. She practically brought the youngest children up when my mother died.'

'Lloyd's much older than you?'

'Twenty years, yes.'

'How old was your mother when you were born?'

'Forty.'

'Forty! Gosh! I thought that went out with Queen Victoria. I still don't understand. Why didn't your brother marry Elsie?'

'I don't suppose he asked her. They lived next door for forty years. He didn't need to. She did everything for him anyway.'

'It was Lloyd who got you to come, wasn't it?'

'Yes. But I wanted to come... I didn't come over for my father's funeral.'

'Tax?'

'Yes.'

'I don't blame you. Did *she* come?'

'She? You mean Cora? No, she came once and never again. She

didn't like it down here. They didn't like her and she didn't like them. They called her The Californian Bitch if you want to know!'

Her face was dead pan. She let this pass. Of course she wanted to know!

'What about your other brothers? Will they be there? And surely you had girlfriends?'

'No.'

'What?'

'I never had any girlfriends close to home although I went out with Ivor's wife once. A few years ago, she sent me a Christmas card. "I always knew you'd end up in horror films", she said.'

'You've only done one.'

'Three actually.'

'What's her name?'

'Iris.'

'What?'

'Iris, like the flower. They also call her The Mouth.'

'Iris. I'll look out for her.'

Now the third Mrs Bayley began to look fixedly at the chauffeur's neck. When he was staring ahead at the road, the weal was not so red and they were certainly doing him a favour by keeping the partition closed. Now she could see small hills bordering the motorway which was grey and regular like any other but she just got a glimpse of a fairy castle, all turrets and spires visible for a moment in a belt of trees and then it was gone and very soon there were further hills ahead but it was growing dark now and little necklaces of lights appeared above and beside the motorway. She noticed small isolated terraces of houses on the hillsides, then woods and a railway line and very soon factories and a concrete landscape of box-like structures that might have been anything, with electricity pylons reaching up beyond them, their outlines stark against the snow which stood everywhere on the high ground. It was not as bad as she expected.

Probably the snow made it look better than it really was, she thought, but she did not say anything, just wondered idly what she might do if she were the chauffeur's wife, watching him come home with a neck and a head like that. They'd have to tell him to wear an open-necked shirt if he drove them again, she thought. There was no sense in avoidable pain.

'Oh, there was a castle back there,' her husband said — too late. 'I saw it.'

'They made *Prisoner of Zenda* there, I think, or at least, the telly version.'

'Is that so?'

'Totally phoney, of course. It was copied from those castles on the Rhine. It doesn't belong here.'

Belonging was the crucial question, she thought. Did he any more?

'When we get there, I expect you'll find it very small, but it's just for the one night. I expect it'll be very different from everything you're used to.'

The chauffeur half-turned then and she could swear she could see specks of blood above his collar. Somebody ought to say something to that poor man, she thought again. Suddenly, everything was painful.

'I don't believe you never had any girlfriends here?' she said lightly, for something to say. 'Didn't any of them make something of themselves? They didn't just disappear?'

'Well, there was Eileen. She was my first, I suppose. She hung around for a long time.'

'Not very bright?'

'No. Finally, she married a dentist. I didn't see her for years and when I did she had a black eye, a real shiner. Like a fool, I said, "How are things going, Eileen?" And she burst out crying and said, "He's knocking me about".'

'The dentist?'

'Yes. I saw her again a few years later. She came back stage with her daughter. "How are you?" I said, and she said, "He's stopped knocking me about since I became a magistrate".'

'Well, good for her!'

'Yes, I expect she'll be there, in the funeral anyway. Maybe they'll both be there.'

Now it was quite dark and suddenly they turned off the motorway and moved into congested streets where she became aware of people looking in at them through the windows, their faces vaguely hostile. The streets were so narrow, they moved at a snail's pace for an age and then began to climb after following a river where there were terraces of houses whose doors opened directly into the streets and now and then she got a glimpse of narrow side streets, so steep that you would think it impossible to walk up them, but there were children playing there in front of brightly painted doors whose colours seemed garish in the artificial light. Here the snow stood on the streets and made everything seem unreal. Like her being there at all, she thought.

She thought of the dentist's wife, the black eye, the daughter and the two of them hanging around the stage door and then entering the dressing room, savouring the story for their friends at home. The fools, she thought. He would speak of things like that but she had long noticed that he never spoke about the first wife or his son who must be in his twenties now, but that was an old wound. It was the present that really concerned her, in particular, his insistence that she should be here now when it wasn't strictly family, just the woman next door who had died, although of course, there were apparently complications and a layer of the past yet to be uncovered. She went over the names in her mind, Lloyd, Ivor, Iris who had the mouth, Elsie, the one who'd died, and then there was somebody else, she was sure, a somebody who didn't like the idea and who could be expected to give trouble, but maybe she'd imagined this. They'd been in London when Lloyd had called, they'd no intention of coming here at all but her husband had answered the telephone himself, there was a long painful conversation and that was that. She hoped she'd get the names right and she tried to imagine the complicated and mostly untold story of his growing up in this remote Welsh valley. He'd told her very little, bits and pieces, and it was like trying to remember a book you'd read without giving it too much attention. Little things kept on escaping her, but one thing was clear. At fifty her husband was long gone from here, and most of his famous actor friends were long gone from this world, so mercifully, there would be no painful hours of reminiscence, that special kind of punishment that did nobody any good at all.

Finally the car made a detour off the main road and stopped on top of a hill where there were two modest sized houses built back to back, their sloping roofs standing starkly above a high wall against the grey wintery sky. Through an open gate she could see a large yard and a number of out-buildings. It was like a small farm, she thought, except for the wall. When she wound the window down, there was a distinct smell of farm manure and their arrival had started a dog yapping somewhere and now it began to bark continuously, a thin whelping noise accompanied by the sound of a chain rattling. Without quite knowing why, she was sure that the dog hadn't been fed, there was that kind of helpless resigned note in its barking.

The chauffeur slid back the partition.

'I'm sorry, Mr. Brayley, I can't get this car in through the gate.'

'That's all right, Norman.'

'The path is quite clear but a bit slippery.'

'We'll manage.'

'Would the lady like me to take the handbag?'

'No, thank you.'

When they got out of the car, a light came on below them at the end of the path leading to the front porch. There were two houses joined together and the porch was communal, covering the two front doors. Several cars and a tradesman's van stood in the yard and there did not seem to be any division between the two houses which were stone built with iron downpipes, all in need of a coat of paint, the whole sombre like a small, squat Victorian institution. One of the front doors opened and a heavily built man came out wearing an old fawn cardigan and an open necked shirt. He was grey and stooped with a high forehead and a cadaverous face, his eyes tired and confused as he stared up at them. He raised his hand to shield his eyes, a hesitant wavering movement so that he seemed for a moment like some biblical character. But then she saw his jutting chin which was a family trademark.

'That's Lloyd?'

'Yes.'

They went down the path, her heels clicking again. When they got near, Lloyd gave a tired smile and she could sense that her husband had suddenly become tense.

'Lloyd, this is Mildred.'

'How d'you do?'

His hand was quite soft and she could feel him trembling. He pumped her hand, his eyes moist, peering at her, then at Ben.

'Thank you, Ben.'

'Who's here?' Ben asked.

'Only Ivor and Iris tonight. And Nantlais has come.'

'Nantlais?'

'The Minister. He's waiting to see you.'

'See me?'

Lloyd didn't reply because the clergyman came out of the door, a fussy, tiny little man, emerging like a bird from its perch with both hands held out in welcome, bright green eyes surveying them with a peculiar intensity.

'Benjamin!' he said in an unexpectedly deep voice.

'Oh, hello, Mr. Williams. Er... The Reverend Nantlais Williams, my wife, Mildred.'

'Mrs. Brayley!' the Minister said. It was a pronouncement.

They heard the chauffeur come down the path behind them with the luggage, then Lloyd took her inside the door into the hallway

where there was a stuffed fox's head mounted on a shield which
Lloyd had to duck to avoid. He must have done that every day of
his life, she thought.

'If you want to go upstairs?'

'Upstairs?'

'There's only one, I'm afraid, but you'll be sleeping next door to it.'

She thought she would. She gave him her sheepskin coat and the
fur hat, the bulk of the coat filling the little passageway and went
on up the stairs to the bathroom. When she was seated, she felt the
cold and shivered and then she heard someone come out of the
bedroom next door and a woman said, 'I didn't have time to hoover
under the bed,' but no one answered and it was as if the woman
was speaking to herself because then she said, 'Well, I can't do every
bloody thing, can I?'

The voice was strong and throaty and when she got downstairs
she identified it when a heavy woman of her own age came down
the passage from the kitchen and surveyed her. She filled the space,
massive breasts straining against a taut silk blouse whose sleeves
were rolled to the elbow. Her double chins shook as she smiled and
brushed a strand of dyed blonde hair from her face, lipstick visible,
staining her teeth.

'You found it then?'

'You must be Iris?'

'That's right. Warned you, did he?'

'I'm Mildred.'

Iris surveyed her, her eyes drawn to the handsome silver clasp of
the belt.

'They should have told you, the lavatory door don't shut properly,
and that bedroom's like ice.'

'It's only for one night.'

Iris's eyes flickered behind her to the wall where the three suitcases
were now piled one on top of the other, almost reaching up to the
fox's head.

'We'll have a cup of something in a minute,' Iris said, smiled and
went back into the kitchen.

The men were in the little front room opposite, and Mildred was
suddenly at a loss as to where she should go. She entered the room
tentatively. The Minister was in full flight, holding the floor, Lloyd
and her husband standing before him and a third man seated in the
corner with a whiskey bottle and a half-full glass beside him, his
head averted as he stared into the blazing coal fire in the grate. The
Minister seemed unaware of him and talked continuously. No one

seemed to notice her.

'Right, I think that's everything, but I'll just run over it again. The cortège will start at eleven-thirty, an hour in the chapel and at the Crematorium by two, and back here, is that right?'

'Yes, just the family here,' Lloyd said. 'I'm hoping it'll be a simple service.'

'*Bread of Heaven* to start, I thought, then a few words, *Rock of Ages* and *Lead Kindly Light* as a finale. Give it a bit of lift if you know what I mean?'

'Just the same service as Elsie's husband had,' Lloyd said. He seemed to be pleading.

'Of course, but in the Crematorium, I think we can be entirely traditional there?'

'As long as we keep it simple.'

'Leave it to me, Lloyd. Now then, there just remains the little problem next door.'

There was a pause and suddenly she felt all eyes upon her. Without quite knowing why, she sat down and for the first time, the seated man in the corner looked across at her. His eyes were bleary, and from the heaviness of his jaw, she recognised Ivor, the third brother, but he did not say anything.

'It's very embarrassing,' the Minister said. 'Elsie's son, Walter, is being difficult.'

'Walter?' Ben said sharply.

'He's insisting that the funeral will be family only.'

'Well, it is, isn't it?'

The Minister put his hands together and cracked his knuckles, then put them behind his back as if they had given offence. Now he addressed Ben directly.

'Walter is being unreasonable. Your brother explained that you happened to be in London and that you wanted to pay your respects.'

'No, I asked him to come,' Lloyd said. 'He's never come home for a funeral before.'

'That's what I explained to Walter. I said the family would be together at last.'

'I don't know why you're worrying,' Ivor said from the corner. 'He's in no shape. He might not be able to make it at all.'

'What's going on?' Ben said. There was a catch in his voice, a strain evident that she had never heard before. For a moment it amounted to a barely concealed hysteria. 'Is there something I don't know?'

Now she could feel the tension in the room. There was an ancient photograph of the family with the boys and girls as children on the mantelpiece and as her eyes passed over it, ten pairs of eyes seemed to be looking back at her. It was absurd, but the heat from the coal fire, the men in their black suits and the awkward silence gave her the feeling that she had slipped a century and might have been sitting there awaiting the result of their deliberations like some guilty domestic. And they left her in no doubt that her presence was an intrusion.

No one said anything when she got to her feet but the relief on their faces was obvious.

'I'll leave you boys together,' she said foolishly and went out, closing the door behind her, immediately aware of the sudden burst of talk once she had left.

In the kitchen, Iris had rolled her sleeves up even further and was rummaging at the back of an ancient refrigerator.

'Look at this,' Iris said. 'Nobody's opened it for a week, and there's things living in it, I swear! Why I have to do everything when there's two sisters, I don't know. D'you want a cup of tea, or a drink?'

'A drink.'

'I thought you would. Ivor's got the whiskey in there and that'll be the last of that, but there's some gin in here. Why don't you sit over there? No, not there, at the table. I've just wiped it.'

'I don't think I should have come,' Mildred said.

'They give you that impression, don't they?'

'What's going on?'

'What's going on?' Iris repeated sardonically but her grin was cheerful. 'I'll tell you, thirty years of bloody misery, that's what's going on! And it's not going to end tonight either.'

It took a long time for Mildred to understand what Iris meant, and as they sat in the little kitchen, Iris talking continuously and Mildred listening, with just the occasional raised voice barely audible from the little room at the end of the passage, Mildred's mind began to wander, and finally switched off entirely. She'd been married twice herself, widowed once and had known her own private despair, but she was different from most she supposed, in that she'd always had her own business to occupy her. She designed costume jewellery, had her own workshop and her own selected retail outlets and very soon she was about to branch out in another direction again. What nobody there knew, and must not be told, was that she and her husband had just bought a very large coaching house and hotel and would soon be established in it. It was a plan that had occupied them almost continuously since they'd met three years ago and this was the first occasion when she was completely at a loose end, hanging on to his coat tails in a sense. It was a role she was unused to.

Iris talked and talked and went on talking but soon Mildred sensed that she was coming to some crucial point and began to concentrate once more.

'So you see,' Iris said. 'Elsie brought him up, and the younger children, they all did well, but her own child suffered.'

'That's Walter?'

'That's right. And now Elsie's dead, both the houses belong to Walter and the first thing he'll do is get rid of Lloyd.'

'Lloyd didn't think of buying the house even?'

'No, he had a chance, but he never got round to it. But it's not Lloyd, Walter's after, it's your Ben.'

'Ben?'

'Yes. Ben's the star, you see. So I hope he's brought his cheque book,' Iris said with a grin.

The conference in the little front room seemed to be going on interminably so Mildred thought she would excuse herself and go to bed. She would have liked a bath but she had already found that sounds travelled in an extraordinary way in the little house, and she had determined to be as quiet as possible. As it was, she was quickly in and out of the bathroom and finally settled herself in the inside of the large double bed nearest to the wall. She'd already decided that she'd have as little to do with them as possible, except as politeness demanded. From the number of things which Iris had told her, the early circumstances of her husband's life were beyond description and squalid in the extreme, and she did not want to think about them. It was not the poverty that she minded — she herself was the daughter of a florist in an English market town and her father had begun life as a greenhouse boy on a large estate — but there was something worse than poverty, and that was an atmosphere of defeat which she found very difficult to describe.

She had wanted to ask Iris about the other wives, in particular her own husband's first wife, the mother of his son who had long departed to New York, but Iris talked so much that one question would have set her off for an hour. Iris did not give you snippits but full biographies and Mildred had the feeling that once you got involved, you could never escape and she was glad she had restrained her curiousity and come to bed when she did. The sooner they were both away the better.

But an hour went by and she found she could not get to sleep. There was no sign of Ben and although various pairs of feet trailed up and down the stairs to the bathroom, and the noise of the water closet reverberated through the whole house, there was no indication of anyone leaving either. Soon there was the sound of food being prepared in the little kitchen and once someone left the house and could be heard tapping on the front door of the adjoining house, then ringing the bell and returning. It was clear that the man next door was not receiving visitors.

There was a carafe of water on the sideboard and she poured herself a drink, then returned to bed, stretching herself out and flattenting the pillow so that her body was almost prone. Her first husband had been killed in a car smash and she had been with him when he died, suffering undiagnosed damage to her neck which she had only cured by years of exercises which involved her lying flat, an exercise in discipline that had eventually paid off for the pain never returned. Now, slipping into her familiar posture, she pushed her head higher and higher until she touched the head board and then relaxed completely, but she still could not get to sleep. Having tried and failed on her right side, she now turned over on her left, arching her back against the wall, stiffening and relaxing again. It was in this position that she heard the low but unmistakeable sounds of sobbing coming through the wall from the bedroom next door. The sobbing was low and continuous, punctuated by intakes of breath, then a frail cry at intervals followed by a word that she could not at first distinguish. Without quite knowing why, she pressed her ear to the wall and then there was no doubt. There was a man lying in the bed very close to her and separated by the wall which was evidently very thin and the man was saying one word at intervals, 'Mammy... Mammy...' Then there would be a sharp intake of breath, almost an involuntary sound, then the sobs, then the word again, 'Mammy, Oh, Mammy...'

What was so chilling was that this was the first expression of grief she had heard all week. It must be Elsie's son, Walter, she thought, and guessed that the bedroom next door must have been his mother's room and Walter had taken himself in there and lay there now, pressed against the wall on the bed where his mother had lain.

It was eerie and Mildred tried to visualise Walter's face. He was, she knew, the same age as her husband, and to think of a man of fifty crying for his mother was unbelievable. She had never seen him, nor any photograph save for a solitary snapshot of him as a twelve year old when taken on some rare visit to the seaside. Beside the Brayley children, he'd looked a complete nondescript, a thin unkempt urchin with a scared grin. She'd only half-listened to Iris downstairs but she must have taken in more than she realised for Iris had been trying to explain this recent animosity on Walter's part and although she put it simply, you did not need much imagination to see that Walter had always had the thin end of it as a child. He was weak. He was frail. He suffered from earache. He couldn't do things; Ben could, and so, after a fashion, could his other rival, Iris's own husband Ivor who had been a footballer. It wasn't difficult to imagine how Walter had been in the Brayley shadow as a child and stayed in their shadow even when they left home. It seemed he had succeeded at very little and spent his life as an appendage in some back street business, having married a girl from another valley, a girl who had always pointedly refused to come to the house. There was so much veiled information of this kind. Walter's mother, Elsie, had also had a special problem with the man next door, Iris implied.

'Poor Elsie,' Iris said. 'She didn't see what everybody else could see, that nobody dared tell her. Lloyd would never marry anybody.'

It was the final pronoucement.

The sobbing must have stopped before Mildred drifted into sleep. She did not hear the cars leave, not her husband's unsteady footsteps up the stairs, but in the morning, she looked over his inert body to see his clothes crumpled on the floor. He had not brought his suitcase upstairs, had slept in his underclothes and was still asleep. He must have been very drunk, she thought, for he was the most fastidious of men, and indeed, what had attracted her most about him was that like the parts he played so often, he invariably demonstrated that English reserve and a self-control that made his every reaction predictable. It was the sort of steadiness that you associated with stereotypes of naval officers under fire but now, having listened to Iris and the rest of them, Mildred could not for the life of her think where it came from, or how he had acquired this persona. It was very unsettling.

Now she had to scramble out of bed, climbing over him like a schoolgirl and she soon felt the cold. She was about to go to the bathroom when he awoke suddenly stretching out his arm to find her, then not finding her, opening his eyes with a grunt. She crossed to the bed.

'Mildred?'

'I'm here.'

There was a rime along his lips and his eyes were bloodshot.

'Listen...' he sat up in bed, frowning immediately, opening his eyes, rubbing them and scowling. There was an urgency in his voice, a strain that was quite new. Suddenly he sounded like somebody else. 'There's been a bit of a cuffuffle. I don't want to go into it, it... it's awful, but, well, the general feeling is, it would be better if you didn't go to the funeral.'

She stared at him.

'Not go? Are you going?'

'Yes, I'm going, but... Well, it's Walter, you see. I think he's blown his lid or something. He wants family there, strictly family. No outsiders. Look, it'll be over by teatime and we'll get the hell out of here.'

'What am I going to do all morning?'

'I don't know, that's another problem.'

'Has Walter got it in for me personally?'

'No, no, nothing like that. Oh, there's a whole shooting match that I don't want to go into, not at all. It's well, awful, that's all. Awful, awful, awful!'

'What happened last night?'

'I don't want to go into it, not one little bit of it.'

'Iris had quite a few things to say.'

'Oh, I'm sure. Bloody sure!' He sounded quite Welsh now, another man entirely.

'She said that Ivor...'

'Whatever she said, can we just drop it? Please, darling...'

But there were one or two points she wanted tidying up.

'She asked if you'd brought your cheque book, more or less implied that they expected you to...'

'Please...'

She hesitated.

'All right, but remember, we're very heavily committed at the moment and if there's to be any substantial expenditure, I think you ought to...'

'Whatever it is, it's peanuts. Peanuts!'

'Well, I think you ought to tell me, that's all, before you promise them anything.'

'I will, but not now, not this morning. Let's just get it over with, and get away from here. Please, Milly?' He was pleading, his blue eyes fixed on hers, his face almost boyish under his tousled hair.

Someone had once said he looked like a Spanish grandee and there was often a mystery about his swarthy features. On the screen, his face, with its pronounced highcheekbones and brooding deep-set eyes, seemed to maximise every feeling, enlarging it, holding it so that you were compelled to look. But now it seemed haunted, pinched even, as if he had become physically smaller.

'All right,' Mildred said after an interval. 'I must say it's not like you to drink. Would you like me to go downstairs and make a cup of tea? Perhaps there's some Alka-Seltzer?'

'There won't be.'

'I've got some in my bag. I don't know why but I put it in just in case. Shall I make some tea?'

'Anything. And look, all we've got to get through is the morning.'

And somehow or other they did. After she had made the tea and brought it upstairs, they took their time about dressing, all in a gloomy silence, Ben moving like an automaton, his hangover settling upon him like an affliction so that all his movements were slower. He buttoned his shirt with difficulty, his fingers trembling. When he stooped to lace his shoes, he had difficulty with the simplest knot. Eventually, when he was dressed he stood in the window brooding. She'd had to go back to bed, not quite knowing what to do with herself. There was no space for her to dress at the same time, and as she watched him, she remembered the agony of that poor wretch's sobbing on the previous night. She knew better than to mention it. In front of the houses earlier, she had noticed a monkey tree, its curiously shaped branches and stunted limbs forming a convoluted mass of strange shapes that looked all the more tortured under their light covering of snow. Her designer's eye had noted its twisted shapes, and in the same way, she thought, she could imagine his feelings now in turmoil, and she knew from the strain in his voice, how upset he was. Watching him standing limply at the window, she felt nothing but sympathy. He remained a very handsome man.

But he said, 'I can't wear a sheepskin jacket.'

'But you'll freeze?'

'I should have brought the Crombie.'

'It's blue,' she said.

'I haven't even got a pullover to put on over my shirt.'

The way he said it implied a criticism of her.

'People are not so formal these days.'

'They are here.'

'Couldn't you borrow something?'

'No, I'll just have to get pneumonia, that's all.'

There was now a petulance to his voice that was again quite unusual and she did not quite know what to do. She had brought a black suit, a black coat with a high cape collar, a black headscarf with a concealed thermal lining and a silver ring with a black opal which she had designed herself and she did not see why she should not put it all on. But now she was at a loss. He seemed reluctant to leave the bedroom but presently, there was the noise of cars arriving and she heard female voices that indicated that the sisters had arrived.

He looked at her blearily, as at a stranger.

'I shall have to go downstairs. But there's no need for you to hurry. Take as much time as you like.'

'If I'm not going to the funeral, can't I help with the food, or something? There must be plenty to do.'

He didn't know. All he wanted to do was run, she could see. So much for the Grandee!

'Anything, anything,' he said wildly. 'Just be ready to leave the moment I get back.'

And then he was out of the room, still glowering, his footsteps heavy on the stairs, clearing his throat noisily as if preparing himself in the wings before an appearance on stage.

When finally she began to dress, peering into the mirror in the poor light and applying her eye shadow with especial care, she wondered how the American wife had managed, but then she remembered that the chauffeur had said they'd stayed in an hotel then. The Californian Bitch had been a television actress, not quite a star, another one of those whose face you knew but could never quite put a name to, and, she too had been into property development with a much married father who controlled some kind of catering organisation with franchises inside baseball grounds. This was a detail she did know and now she thought it strange how her husband always seemed to have an eye for activities outside his main profession. It was the first time she'd thought of it, but she envied the American wife only one thing. She'd arrived and left like a star without having to test the plumbing.

When she got downstairs, the house was full. There were at least half a dozen people crowded into the little front room, several black-suited teenage boys in the middle room and Iris was busy in the kitchen serving breakfast to Lloyd and Ivor who were seated at the breakfast table. Once again, there seemed no place for her to go.

'You'd better go and meet the girls,' Iris said. 'I'll deal with you second shift!'

Iris wore a pinafore over her black costume and her sleeves were rolled up once again. The two brothers grinned approvingly, their breakfast plates loaded, bacon still sizzling in the frying pan on the gas stove. In the crowded front room, she had another surprise. She'd thought the two sisters were younger than her husband, but somehow she'd got it wrong, or they'd aged considerably, for she was soon introduced to two plump little matrons with silver hair and bright button eyes on whom the unmistakeable family jaw sat uneasily. As she shook their gloved hands politely, she had the claustrophobic feeling that she was about to be prodded and squeezed. Behind the sisters, their husbands, two small, merry-eyed little men as alike as two polished Gurhkas put out their hands simultaneously but then the telephone rang and they all moved away from it, leaving Ben to answer it, standing in the cleared space as if he had suddenly resumed a leading role.

'Yes?' Ben said authoritatively. 'Benjamin Brayley.' It was the clergyman and apparently he had an urgent enquiry.

'I think Lloyd had better deal with that,' she heard her husband say. 'I mean, I haven't set eyes on Walter for years. It might be a further shock? No, I think Lloyd... All right, I'll ask Ivor. Just a minute.'

He put the receiver on the edge of a chair and went out while they waited in silence until Ivor came in with the unpeturbed look of a police officer used to disturbances.

'Yes, Mr Williams?' he said patiently. 'Yes, yes. Well, one thing is clear, if he won't open the door, we won't get the coffin out!' he nodded vigorously, and added determinedly. 'I'll go straight in there now.'

Then he put the phone down, surveyed the room and grinned apologetically.

'Problems!' he said but it was said in the tone of a man who would deal with them immediately.

When he went out, one of the sisters turned to Mildred and said, 'Ivor's the one. Ivor will deal with it'. And then somebody else said, 'It's exceptionally cold for this time of the year,' and there was general agreement that the snow was standing around waiting for more to come. All this time, Mildred noticed, Iris was still busy in the kitchen and when she went in there, it was to see Ben sitting down to breakfast. No one had thought of calling her and suddenly, she had a flash of insight into the entire household. There was always one who coped, she thought. Elsie must have been just like Iris, always coping, caring, always busy, an ever reliable automaton whom they all took for granted. Now Mildred felt as if she had uncovered an anthropological fact, as if after careful observation, she had at last uncovered the key to behaviour in the Brayley tribe. They only killed people off one at a time!

'I'll do your breakfast in a minute,' Iris said.

'I'll do my own. If I'm not going to the funeral, at least I can help with the meal?'

'All done,' Iris said.

It seemed that the sisters had brought an immense amount of food which was spread out on the table in the middle room, together with their own china and cutlery. There was nothing for Mildred to do, except do as she was told, she reflected ruefully. She had another bizarre thought. Perhaps Walter had felt the same, the need to become invisible. Somehow she could not get him out of her mind.

There was suddenly a burst of activity. The hearse arrived together with the funeral cars and a posse of black suited bearers led by the undertaker. Inside the house, there was a sudden rush for the bathroom and now a further conversation in lowered voices in the hallway as first Lloyd, then Ivor, and eventually Ben were all involved. Then Ben returned, now resigned it seemed, for everything that was to follow.

'It's Walter,' he said. 'He's refused to come.'

'To his own mother's funeral?' she was incredulous.

'I don't think he's himself,' Ben said carefully, his face a mask. He suddenly seemed to have aged in front of her and his eyes were now blank. She had a bizarre and cruel thought. Perhaps the horror films really did mark the beginning of the end of his career, the moment when he'd realized he was exhausted, that there was nothing more he could invent.

Behind them, Iris removed her pinafore, rolled down the sleeves of her blouse, then removed the jacket of her costume from a hanger at the back of the door and slipped it on, finally removing a brown paper parcel from a carrier bag and taking out a small black pillbox hat which she put on carefully, tilting it on one side, mushing her lips together as she surveyed herself in the mirror. She said nothing but suddenly she seemed like a caricature of herself and twice her normal size as she marched determinedly through the doorway.

'What d'you want me to do?' Mildred said.

Ben closed his eyes.

'Just be ready to leave the moment we get back.'

And then he, and they, were gone. When the front door was finally closed, Mildred went upstairs to the landing where there was a tiny window looking over the front yard. She was just in time to see the black coated bearers making their way through the gate with the coffin. There were six of them and they carried it upon their shoulders, their movements as precise as guardsmen and the family followed behind, Ben, Lloyd, Ivor, Ben leading, then the women and the other mourners with the two young boys following. There was a solemnity and dignity to the procession that quite belied the last frenzied moments in the house, as if, once in the open air, the true purpose of their being there was at last realized. She could not see much above the wall, only the top of the hearse and the cars, and one by one she heard them draw away until finally they were all gone. Then she went downstairs and, feeling the need for some fresh air, found her coat and went out into the yard, going around the house towards the fields behind. But when she turned a corner, she stopped at once. There was a man there feeding the dog, his head bent as he poured meal into a bowl. He did not hear her approach and seemed to be talking to himself but the dog stiffened and then looked up and the man swayed slightly, his eyes boring into her. He was pale and haggard, his eyes blotched and swollen and as he looked at her, he began to tremble as if riven by a terrible rage. His mouth opened and closed and he struggled to find words, one hand fumbling with a deaf aid, a lock of greying hair shaking.

'You're trespassing!' he shrieked. 'D'you understand, trespassing? They have that in America, don't they?'

It must be Walter, she thought in a panic, and half-demented with a lifetime's jealousy to avenge! She was suddenly terrified and backed against the wall, her hand going to her throat. He stood up and came forward unsteadily, and she felt the calves of her legs trembling. They were quite alone. If she wanted to, she couldn't get past him to the telephone. She swallowed and tried to compose herself.

'I think you're mistaken, I'm not American.'

He stared at her.

'They said he'd brought his wife...'

'That was his second wife. I'm the third, Mildred.'

His eyes passed over her face as if checking her features, his incomprehension suddenly reassuring. 'Three wives... three...'

'Yes, I'm afraid so,' she said. 'You must be Walter. I'm Mildred. How d'you do?'

She held out her hand, and, completely taken aback, as if such a common civility was rare, he took it shyly, and all threat vanished. She was even aware of the dog wagging its tail.

Walter attempted to explain.

'I wouldn't speak to her. She was very rude.'

'I don't think I quite understand?'

'The American.'

'Cora?'

'She was rude to everybody. Him as well. Know what she called him? *In public?*'

Mildred shook her head.

'A horse's arse,' Walter said. 'Everybody heard about that. Well, I wasn't having it at my mother's funeral.'

Mildred bit her lip. Afterwards, she thought ruefully, it might be funny, but it's what I've come to hear! Later, she could never satisfactorily explain what led her to instigate the procession of events that now followed. Perhaps she got the idea from the dog's plate, perhaps it was the simple fact that Walter seemed not to have eaten for days, or the sight of that groaning table in the middle room where the sisters had laid out the china, or perhaps it was some irreverent wish to score off the Brayleys, she did not know. But within seconds, ignoring Walter's mumbled objections, she led him into the house, sat him down and bullied him into eating something, taking charge of him, finally confronting him with the finality of what he appeared to have decided. It appeared he'd broken down at the last minute but, she told him firmly, he would have the rest of his life to regret his absence at the funeral. They had missed the service in the chapel, but if they hurried, there was still time to get to the Crematorium. He had clearly had a breakdown of some kind, she could see that, but he was over it now, surely? She made the suggestion with a confident smile. She would see to everything. Leave it to her!

He ran his hand over his beard, examined his shabby clothes.

'I'd have to change.'

'Why?'

'I'm in no state to drive.'

'I'll drive.'

'There's only the van.'

'I'll drive the van.'

In the end, almost as an afterthought, and because it was cold, she bundled him into her husband's sheepskin jacket and wound her own black headscarf around his neck, organizing him as she might a friendly but recalcitrant child, even running into his house to get the van keys. In seconds, it had become an adventure, and later she would recall that she only kept the collie dog out of the van with difficulty. The van was ancient, smelling of vegetables, with a hand gear change that she muffed repeatedly, but Walter sat beside her mutely, giving the occasional direction which included a short cut so they got to the crematorium before the cortège, arriving just as another funeral party was leaving. They were first there, seated themselves in the front pew and kept their heads bowed as the other mourners arrived. Immediately, however, the air was charged and Mildred felt as if the hostility behind her was real, as real as a wall or a pulsating electric current, and quite extraordinary. Presently, after some murmuring, her husband joined her, his face flushed with anger but nothing was said. She willed him not to speak and they sat in a stiff silence until the little Minister began the service, running his eyes over all of them, the hunched figure of Walter bulky in the sheepskin coat, herself hatless, Ben shivering, then the solid press of Brayleys, Iris in her pillbox hat, and a sizeable crowd behind them all too soon to be heard in thunderous voice as the opening hymn began.

Afterwards, Mildred could remember nothing of the service but all the time she was aware of the stiffness of her husband's body, the animosity which beamed across at her from him and the entire family behind. She could sense it in their averted eyes, in the sheer volume of their voices as they sang, Lloyd's voice singular and querulous as he lingered on certain notes. Finally, when the last hymn was sung and the coffin began to slide noiselessly away from them, she was again aware of Walter's body trembling and without thinking, she took his hand and held it firmly, almost as if she were supporting him and keeping him from crying out, another reaction which caused a further stiffening in her husband's body so that he actually moved an inch away from her. But then the coffin slid away and the funeral was over.

She turned to Walter.

'There,' she added. 'We made it.'

He nodded tearfully. He did not look at Ben. She released his hand and took her husband's arm, looked up demurely into his glowering face. 'We decided at the last minute and I'm very glad we did.'

He did not reply.

Outside there were a throng of people waiting to greet him but she turned away to Iris who was watching with a broad grin.

'Can somebody drive Walter home?' Mildred said in a loud authoritative voice. 'I don't think he should drive himself.'

Now Walter stood like a child waiting to be apportioned to some responsible authority.

'Ivor!' Iris summoned.

Walter nodded his thanks.

There was such a throng about her husband that Mildred had to push her way through it to get to him. A mouse-like little woman with a black toque hat obstructed her continuously, her apoplectic partner, a thin moustachioed man with thick horn-rimmed spectacles, turning an inflamed cheek to glare his hostility as Mildred insisted on making her way forward.

'We know him personally,' the man said angrily.

'I don't think you've met my wife,' Ben said eventually. 'Mildred, this is Eileen, and er... your husband?'

'Maurice,' the violent little man said.

It was the wife-beating dentist and the first girlfriend.

'We knew you'd come home for Elsie,' Eileen said. 'We were quite sure.'

There was more of the same but the presence of so many other people prohibited any conversation there, or in the car, and it was not until they were back in the yard, finally preparing to go, that Lloyd shook her husband's hand, his eyes tearful, his old man's head nodding as if with a nervous tic.

'She would have been very glad,' Lloyd said soulfully.

Mildred could have screamed for without knowing why she was quite sure Lloyd had got every penny he'd wanted out of her husband. His problems were solved, she was sure.

There was no sign of Walter who had disappeared into the house but Ivor brought the sheepskin coat and her headscarf which were taken by the chauffeur who had reappeared, his injured neck covered by a white silk scarf she was pleased to see. There were apparently no convenient trains and the chauffeur had been instructed to drive them straight to London.

Her husband closed the partition as soon as they left, a phalanx of Brayleys waving from the yard. She noted that the sheepskin coat had been savagely thrust into the boot with the luggage. Now at last they were alone but it was fully a minute before her husband spoke, composing himself as he looked intently out of the window. She knew exactly what was on his mind.

'What was that all about?' he said matter-of-factly enough.

She had an answer prepared.

'It wasn't about anything. I saw Walter in the yard when you'd all left. He was absolutely wretched and when I saw he regretted not going, I brought him.'

'Just like that?'

'Yes. It was on the spur of the moment. And I'm very glad I did.'

He eased down his shirt cuff absently and looked away once more, a deliberately casual gesture that she suddenly saw to be quite false. But somehow she knew that he was not going to say anything else and that despite the rage which she had felt in the Crematorium and the absolute hostility which seemed to be coming from every pore of his being, now it had all subsided. There would be no scenes, no repercussions; now he was fully in control again. She'd had one glimpse of a hungry, determined, disliked, and sulky little boy, and that was all.

'I had problems with that van' she said lightly. 'It had a hand gear change. It must be very ancient.'

'Yes.'

'I take it you helped Lloyd solve his problem?'

'Yes.'

'Well?'

'All in all it'll be about fifteen thousand if Walter agrees to sell, and he probably will now. It won't affect us. I've some money in a Swiss account.'

'You didn't tell me?'

'It's not a lot. Just something I kept for emergencies. It won't affect us in any way.'

And that was that.

'If you don't mind I'm going to try and sleep? I still feel dreadful.'

'No, you go ahead.'

But first he gave her a rueful glance, the kind of quizzical look that people associated with his relaxed, matter-of-fact, English style of acting with just a suggestion of that insouciant, devil-may-care, hang-the-consequences bravado that an earlier generation of actors had used to play fighter pilots or tank commanders. He wrinkled his nose.

'Awful, wasn't it?'

'Yes.'

He settled back. Now she knew he would erase it from his mind. There would be no more coming home. The final debt had been repaid. From an undisclosed source, she noted. She would remember that and enquire about it further when the time was ripe. She wondered if there was much else to be disclosed, but she doubted it. What she had discovered was nothing to do with money, although money meant things, and things he had always been without which explained the store he set on them now. No, it was more costly than money, it was the sense she'd had of the beginning of a relentless struggle to be someone else, to acquire a new personality, another self, the energy involved in creating an entirely new fabric that was rooted in imitation, even a way of speaking and feeling, all to be strived for and learnt, eventually acquired to the exclusion of everything else. It also meant he did not — could not — like himself.

It was over an hour before he awoke and now the terrain had changed completely as they approached a richer pasture land with more gently undulating slopes visible from the motorway. He blinked and looked about him.

'D'you know, I don't think I saw one coal mine,' Mildred said.

'No, I believe they've closed them all down.'

'Did you have a good sleep?'

'Still a bit headachey.'

'I've got some aspirins.'

'Have you really? You think of everything!' his smile was broad. He was relaxed again. 'We'll have a bite somewhere later. We've heaps of time.'

And that was that. There were no further embarrassments except a momentary glimpse of the chauffeur's bald head with its encrustations of tiny blue coal scars when he took off his cap to scratch it, but he soon put it back on again and she was very relieved that at last he'd had the sense to wear something more suitable around his neck. The only casualty was the sheepskin coat, she thought. Remembering the way her husband had so savagely bundled it into the boot of the car, she knew that he would never wear it again. Like the previous wives, the son, the past that had so resolutely refused to enhance the present, it was soiled and no longer part of the actor's calling.

Frilly Lips, and the Son of the Manse

They met in a light opera at the tail end of the War. He was eighteen and she was nineteen, tall, willowy and dark with a stunning physical elegance that was immediately displayed by the tight-fitting clothes she wore and a way of moving which was quite unlike the girls he knew who remained in school. She had poise, money to spend which was a puzzle, a predeliction for black and something extra which was very special to the times. 'It', they called it then, the superficial appearance of a glamorous detatchment, a quite beautiful girl who seemed altogether unobtainable to people like him. There were girls you made friends with, others you chatted to or had grown up with, but she was the one you turned around to look at, a raver whose high forehead, long black hair, large pouting lips and sinuous carriage added up to what the boys called an absolute knock-out. There was also something sad about her, a note of regret, the suspicion that a part of her mind was absent and elsewhere in a strange way, but this was a feature of herself that she revealed much later. At first sight, she was immediately distinguishable by those looks, that carriage, the haughty, curving lips, her natural leonine grace, and all his life he would remember the impression he had of her walking towards him in the hallway of the Workmen's Institute where the local amateur operatic society was meeting for rehearsals. A small beginning to a major transformation.

In the first place, being present at all was rather a joke to him. The shortage of men due to the war had caused the music master at the local county school to send a dozen senior boys down to rehearse as the group were short in the chorus. He was doing Higher School Certificate then, had been working too hard, and his mother thought it would be good for him.

'You ought to mix more, Selwyn. You take far too little time off. Musically, of course, they're not up to much, but it will be something different for you.'

Selwyn was a son of the manse, dutiful and obedient, and it was typical of him that he should arrive at the rehearsal room with twenty minutes to spare. He wore his school blazer and sat in the hallway just inside the main doorway. It was the first time he had ever been inside the building of which his mother had disapproved since it also contained a bar for the sale of intoxicating liquor which was open all the week, including Sundays. It was also used for political meetings and was associated with the miners, a group for which his mother also had no special liking, being country born and bred, some distance away from the Welsh mining valleys. Selwyn himself had gone to school with the boys who were now down the pit, but the break with boys of this kind had come at eleven, and there was all the difference in the world between Selwyn and these boys now. They were boys no longer and when he passed them as he sometimes did on his way home from school, they were booted and pit black, one or two of them openly sneering at the school uniform which he was obliged to wear. Now they spat and swore, and there was about them that pit-bred empathy of the working world. Years later, Selwyn would meet wealthy socialists, who had made fortunes out of the manipulation of Welsh television licences, who would insist of the classlessness of the Welsh towns, producing neat arguments about the narrowness of the wage differential then, but they were bolstering up myths that were useful to themselves. There was all the difference in the world between people, and his own self-consciousness bore witness to it all his life.

Not with her though. She came in out of the rain wearing one of those see-through plastic macs, shaking her hair loose from under a headscarf. He could see her breasts made all the more prominent by a tightly clinging black sweater. He did not know then that girls who dressed like that did so in full consciousness of themselves.

'Gosh!' she said. 'Gosh! S'raining cats and dogs.'

She looked across at him. He must have seemed a lemon sitting there, pale and bespectacled, that manse aura all over him, a tall, thin, lank-haired, stooping boy with this preoccupied student's look increased by the heavy, horn-rimmed spectacles he wore. At home, there were daily conversations over what he should do with his life. He did not feel that call to Christ as his father had, but he went religiously to chapel, had never failed an examination, and his sixth form essays were often returned with such comments as, 'Thoughtful. I can see you have given your mind to this.' But he gave his mind now to her as she removed the plastic mac. She wore nylons, he noted, a sign of affluence or connections in a time of war shortages. Her legs were long and slim and there was something about the way she stood which was at once provocative, one leg moving consciously in front of the other so that the leg muscles were better displayed. When she moved, even the slightest movement was noticeable. She was that striking. It was something of a relief to hear that when she spoke, her accent was much the same as his own.

She came straight towards him, and in an uncomfortable way, he felt her breasts were coming first.

'Is this for the rehearsal?'

'Yes,' he said. He did not stand up. Public schoolboys stood up in front of girls. County schoolboys did not.

'The opera, is it?'

'That's right.'

'Are you waiting then?'

'Yes, there are twelve of us from school.'

'I know. The Pirates,' she said with an amused smile. The operetta was more a musical and the male chorus were to be dressed as pirates.

She had already attended previous rehearsals but they had changed the rehearsal room and this was a new meeting place. In three weeks, they were to be on stage in the Town Hall. The boys had already learnt the songs in school and Selwyn remembered a chorus.

> Give me some men who are stout hearted men,
> Who will fight for the rights they adore.

The sentiments were somehow in keeping with the war effort, and except for those who were already committed to going to University, most of the boys of Selwyn's age had already expressed a preference for one of the armed forces. Selwyn had not and his mother was worried lest he be called up. She felt the Services to be dreadfully coarsening, and although the European war was drawing to a close, there were still the Japs. If Selwyn could not positively decide on a university course, then he had better go in for the Ministry, she advised. Either the Ministry or Agriculture, since both led to deferred occupations free of the universal obligation of military service. As it happened Selwyn did not like the thought of either profession, and since he had only one science subject, it would need all the family pull to keep him out of the Forces, but he was not sure he wanted that either. He was at that stage of his life when he had begun to look at his parents' life and marriage with some alarm, and any involvement free of chapel and school and the ordered life he had known was welcome. In the present case, it might only be light opera in the most amateurish circumstances, but it was different. It was out of the house and away from the classroom.

But he was not prepared for her.

'What's your name then?' she asked, sitting down beside him suddenly with a quick, decisive movement.

He felt the closeness of her thigh against his and gave a limp smile. Her lips were parted, a full cupid's bow made larger by the amount of make-up which she wore. She held her head on one side scrutinizing him and he immediately diagnosed she was what his mother would have called fast.

'Selwyn Lewis.'

'I'm Teg. Tegwen Hughes.'

'Ti siarad Cymraeg?' he asked. Did she speak Welsh?

'Oh hell no. We've got enough at home without that.'

He liked her at once. She had that warm, slightly self-depreciating frankness which valley girls had, a way of turning down the corner of her mouth when she smiled, as if to say, take me as you find me. His mother, his mother's sister, and the Welsh-speaking girls in chapel were more careful and reserved. Of course, as a minister's son, he supposed there was a certain aura about him. As a family, they were the epitome of respectability in the Welsh sense, and a good deal of this concern for appearances had passed on to him. He was aware of being protected. Because of the family, there was a difference in the way masters at school spoke to him, and since he was always quiet and conscientious, he had slipped thr0ugh school almost unnoticed, and he had never given trouble or been difficult as had so many of the wilder spirits in a trying time. The war was always omnipresent and a number of boys he knew had been killed. In Dan y Graig Street alone, six boys had died by drowning in six different ships in the first two years of the war. Each tragedy had made him think, and he did not really see how he could ever seek a reserved occupation in such circumstances. It wasn't so much that he believed in killing as that he couldn't bear to go on being unlike everybody else. But he had confided in no one, and when he came to think of it, there was no one he knew who could really appreciate quite what it was like to see this girl make a bee-line for him. He was very much a loner.

She had no self-consciousness in speaking to him.

'You haven't got a fag, have you?'

'I don't smoke.'

'Would you do us a favour then?'

'Certainly.'

'Nip into the bar and get me a packet. There's the money.'

There was another problem. He had never been in a bar before, and he did not venture now either, because no sooner had she made her request, than she noticed his County School blazer.

'Oh, hell no, you'd better not.'

'I don't mind.'

'There's an awful lot gets in here. I know, my father's a club steward.'

'Awful?'

'Awful chopsy lot. Making remarks and that. They got no feelings, some of 'em. Brutes, they are.'

He was surprised at her concern for him, and although he hated to admit it, the occasional grammatical mistake in her speech made him feel superior. She was the sort of person who, in his mother's eyes, always 'gave herself away the moment she opened her mouth'. They were quite a family for such sayings. Whenever someone went away, there was often an injunction delivered over such a simple thing as taking an extra clean shirt. 'You don't want everybody to know where you're from.' It was part of the chapel people's shame at the industrial turbulence which had gone on as the century advanced, giving really rooted local people 'a bad name'. Only one of the family had 'marched with the men', in the strike period, and was much disapproved of. All these things lay at the back of Selwyn's mind, a host of warnings, stereotypes, muttered precautions, and they would remain with him until he himself cast them off one by one as so much dross.

But what struck him as so extraordinary now was that she, Tegwen, was so open and considerate of him. She was not warning him, but protecting him instinctively within seconds of meeting. She chattered casually about the opera, but always with an eye on him, occasionally tossing her hair back. She made quite a business of that.

'I don't know what it's going to be like. There's no men about at all, hardly. We won't even know about the orchestra until the last minute.'

'You've been in plays before?'

'*Desert Song*. Well it's something to do with everybody away. Where are you from then, Selwyn?'

He told her. Then, without quite knowing why, he added that his father was a Minister.

'Oh, you're chapel. I had a auntie who was chapel once.'

'What are you?' he asked simply.

'Nothing,' she said. 'Not now; I used to be, but I'm not now. Sundays, I wash my hair.'

She was a harum scarum then. No religion whatsoever. He could not imagine what it was like not to have a religion. What else could you do on a Sunday? If his father was not preaching at home, they

often had another Minister to stay which meant a host of little
disciplines like leaving a clean spare towel untouched in the bathroom, lighting a roaring fire in the front room for his after-lunch
sermon preparations, and such little instructions as, not asking for
a second helping of tart, and generally minding his p's and q's which
were ordinarily impeccable anyway. By tradition, they took no
Sunday newspapers and did not even listen to the radio except for
the news bulletins. Sunday was a scrubbed, holy day of sombre
silence, and it was not until he was fifteen that he was even allowed
to do homework on a day of rest, and then he had to fit it in between
three chapel services. If he had dared suggest anything else, it would
have brought a frown to his mother's face, and while he suspected
that his father would not have minded some relaxation, it had been
impressed upon him that it was wrong to upset people, his mother
in particular. The idea that he was being brought up to suit her
convenience had not occurred to him, and despite the fact that they
received extra rations illegally from tradesmen who were members
of the congregation, his mother also contrived to implant the idea
that she 'took food from her plate' to enable him to continue his
education. It was quite untrue, but she believed it to be true, and
he had not the heart to question it, fitting in with her image, her
goal, 'a good boy to his mother, never a minute's trouble'. It was a
classic Welsh manse situation and it bred spiders in some people's
view, but of course, he was ignorant of that.

'Well, I mean, good Gawd, look what's happenening everywhere?' Tegwen said indignantly.

'Pardon?'

'Religion, where is it? Where does it get you?' Now she was angry,
and he saw her eyebrows twitch.

It was in his mind to use one of his father's phrases and speak out
of a personal salvation, but he could not bring himself to do so. But
it was she who controlled herself. There was a moment of sadness
then, causing an edge to her voice, but it disappeared as quickly as
it came. She seemed to have sensed his alarm. She was all smiles in
a second.

'Oh, I'm sorry. I didn't mean to upset you.'

'You haven't upset me,'

'Haven't I?'

'Certainly not.'

'D'you always say, "certainly"?'

'You haven't upset me.'

'Good then, isn't it?' she said with a shrewd smile, tossing her hair again. 'Well done, Selwyn.'

They were left alone for the briefest of moments because a whole crowd of people soon entered, the musical director, Mr Elias, other members of the cast, and the remainder of the schoolboys who were at once put to one side to rehearse the musical scores which were already familiar to them. While they were waiting, Selwyn's eye sought out Tegwen, and he watched her whenever he could. He noticed that she was extremely popular. The men in the cast were forever at her side. Arms were linked with hers; she was petted and cosseted. She had a small part but the male lead sang a duet with her. Selwyn noticed that she had a sweet voice which went up a few octaves from her normal speaking voice and when she was isolated on the stage, her glamour was even more apparent. She was taller than most of the other girls and that air of difference remained. They all went through their paces at the rehearsal, and when it was over, light refreshments were provided and the society broke up into little groups about the hall.

Selwyn was not the only one of the schoolboys to notice Tegwen.

'Who is she then? The dark piece over there? The Lana Turner one — Look!'

He did not say anything but she called him by name when tea was poured. This was at once noticed.

'Hey, Sel? You're a dark horse, you are!'

He blushed.

'Here you are, Selwyn. How many sugars?'

'Three,' he said. He did not know why he said it. He never took three. He merely wanted to make her say something.

'Three? Aren't you sweet enough?'

For that, he had no reply again.

'Biscuit?'

'Thank you.'

'Catch the act, did you?'

'The act?'

'My number?' she was an ardent film fan and had all the jargon.

'You were very good.'

'Is that all? You wait 'til you see the costume.'

'I can see enough now,' another boy said, muscling in.

'Well, you can see more than you can have.'

'Is that a bet?'

'Go on. There's a law against baby snatching.'

Selwyn stood silent while all this was going on and to show that she appreciated his silence, she seemed to stand closer to him. Later, he was to enumerate the special preferences which he thought he had been shown. She had sought him out while the tea was being poured, she had excused him the embarrassment of going into the men's bar, and what is more, when the time came to say goodnight, she lingered in his company.

'Well, I'll be seeing you then? Friday, is it?'

'Yes.'

'We generally go for a coffee after.'

'Good,' he said.

'What's that supposed to mean?'

'I mean, I'll see you.'

'All right then. G'night, Sel.'

He made his way homewards thoughtfully. One thing was certain. She did not appear to think there was anything wrong with him.

'What was it like?' his mother said when he got in. She always contrived to be on her feet and busy whenever he entered the living-room, as if idleness was a sin and never to be detected. She had a large round bespectacled face with his own serious regular features and greying hair drawn into a severe bun behind her neck.

'Much what you'd expect,' he said matter-of-factly, 'amateurish.'

She nodded, replacing a spoon in a Mazawatte tea container. She knew some of the leaders of the group and asked after them one by one. He said as little as he could, but when he went to bed, he had difficulty sleeping. *She* was so beautiful, he thought, it made him uncomfortable. He gave no thought to the fact that she might have singled him out for attention, and there was no doubt about the fact that she was quite unlike anyone he had ever met. 'Tegwen Hughes,' he said to himself, *'Teg'*. There was a warming casualness about the abbreviation. He said it over and over again to himself.

There is no girl like the first in a young man's life and he thought about her every day until the next meeting came, and although that passed innocently enough, he made it plain that he wanted to take her out. Would she come out with him?

'Where're we going to go then?' He was not aware that she was teasing him.

'Where you like. Pictures, or...' he did not know an alternative.

'Or what?'

'Whatever you like.'

'Walk, is it?'

'Yes,' he said. He knew at once that he had to contrive a meeting at the other side of town, away from his father's parish, but if you had asked him why, he couldn't have explained it, other than that he did not want to cause his parents worry, not even a moment's hesitation about him. He knew she was 'not his sort!', the family were very probably 'not their kind of people'. But see her he had to, and see her he did.

One, two, then three weeks went by. On the night of the first performance in the Town Hall, there was an atmosphere of tension which affected all the cast. They were to run for a week, but the first night was the most exciting occasion. It was a small amateurish affair by any standards, but their nerves were no different from anybody else's. Until the last minute, they were not certain that they would be able to muster a full orchestra, there was delay with the costumes, a leading tenor contracted a bout of tonsilitis and there were the usual anxieties, but finally the last few seconds came before the curtain went up and now Selwyn stood close to Tegwen. In the darkness beside a large scenery flat, his hand was firmly entwined in hers. It was not just their nervousness, or the camaraderie that comes to performers who face a common foe, by now he was obsessed with her. They could not stop touching each other and sometimes his grip was so fierce, it hurt her. He seemed always to be close to her, watching her protectively when he was not holding her in some dark corner. Now she opened her mouth when he kissed her, placed her arms behind his neck, ruffling his hair, and once, actually put *her* hands in *his* trouser pockets when she was cold. She seemed to set him on fire and he had experienced nothing like it. Indeed, he was experiencing all the male discomforts more often than not, and even in their pre-performance stance, he felt a full consciousness of sexual awareness which had come suddenly and violently and which occupied his mind to the exclusion of all else.

Now she wore a soubrette's costume, and in the last seconds before the curtain went up, he felt her trembling beside him. Her involvement with the production was total and he was aware that she believed in the songs that were sung and the trite sentiments they expressed, but it did not make a scrap of difference to him. He was made aware for the first time in his life that it was not just an idea which was important, but what cloaked it. He found difficulty in disagreeing with anything she said.

'You'll be great,' he muttered breathlessly. His own part in the performance was hidden amongst others in group movements and he had no real nervousness.

She turned her face to him to be kissed finally and he only withdrew his lips from hers as the curtain was actually rising. It was extraordinary to think that only that tatty piece of faded velvet substitute separated him from his mother and father whom he knew were sitting in the front stalls.

'Be sure to take deep breaths and gargle regularly,' his mother had instructed, a *Gymanfa* soloist herself.

He followed her advice, but with or without it, the opening night went well. All the clichés were perambulated. 'A bad dress rehearsal, a good first night.' There was prolonged applause at the finale. They had made a brave show and generally there is no more rewarding feeling than recognizing your much disguised butcher carousing romantically in the arms of Jones Weights and Measures' wife. There was no doubt that the society gave almost as much pleasure to others as they did to themselves.

But for Selwyn it was the beginning of something else. He had already walked Tegwen home before, and they had been to the cinema on one occasion, but he also knew that her parents could not be present on the opening night as they had suddenly been called away to a dying relative. It meant that the steward's flat on the other side of town would be empty. He had not met her parents as she preferred him to leave her at the corner of the street, and then ran home, a strange gesture that took him quite by surprise. But now as they hurried homewards after the performance, both were conscious of the difference of the occasion. The applause had delighted them. He was glad for her. She took a second bow and there was an extra ripple of appreciation which was quite recognizable. She was a success.

They did not stay for the celebrations which went on back stage and their absence was noted, but they did not care.

'I wanted to get away,' he said.

'It was great, wasn't it?' The universal adjective.

'You were.' He'd felt his throat dry as he watched her alone under a spotlight in a pool of light. 'And everybody knew it. I'm surprised you're coming home with me.'

'Are you?' she questioned, but she looked ahead into the darkened street.

'Yes,' he said. There had been others nosing about, but she left them in no doubt. She was his girl.

'You're funny, you are, Selwyn.'

'Funny?' He did not like that.

'Tense, you are, aren't you?'

'What does that mean?'

'Oh, it's all right, I know.'

'What d'you know?'

'Don't be so soft, mun. 'Course I know.'

He did not know what to say in reply to questions like that, but clasped her hand even firmer, warming to the reciprocal squeeze.

'Lotta boys is nasty,' she'd said once, 'but you're not nasty, are you?'

He never knew what to say in reply to questions like that either. He was becoming aware that she was a creature of moods.

'I dunno. I just dunno what to make of you. You don't half look at me, do you? You're a looker, you are, Selwyn boy. You watches people, things, don't you? Quiet you are, but I like you quiet, not saying much.'

Then there were her comments in general. She had a way of slanting her lips scornfully.

'The people there are in this town, the minds on 'em! Sieves, they are. Oh, you don't have to tell me, I know.'

He did not tell her. He did not know. There was such a contrast between her appearance and the things she said. One night, she'd remarked about complaints made against her in the shop where she worked selling shoes. She talked too much, they said, and the delivery boy had given her a nickname. What was it? She did not like to tell him, but when he insisted, she did.

'Frilly Lips,' she said, suppressing a giggle. 'Frilly-bloody-Lips. Meaning they were never closed. The mouthy little bugger.'

For his own part, he thought it was wrong that she should have a nickname at all and said so. In a curious way, he thought, it made her less than she was and took away from the total effect of her appearance, but he could not explain it. It was as if he did not want any part of her real self to obscure or lessen the total effect made upon him by her physical presence. Perhaps, buried within him, there was a deep and little understood predisposition to prefer myth to reality, the tribal hallmark of a long-defeated people. He was that Welsh.

But at night, walking along the silent street, her arm and hand tucked into his, he stole glances at her profile and marvelled again. There was no angle of regard that took away from her and he enjoyed the rapport of her silence as much as anything else. The feel of her close to him was enough. One other aspect of her which remained unexplained was the sadness he had earlier noted and continued to detect, a part of her nature that seemed alien. He did not speak about it, nor did he encourage her to, but it was something else, a way she had of looking past him at leaves blowing by in the

gutter, or at trees in the distance as if there was some reminder there
of things she could not express. She did not like the sound of wind,
he knew, a strange thing that, a mystery that added to her attractions
and made her all the more tantalizing. But for this, she might have
been thought to be scatterbrained, but she was certainly not that.
If anything, she was wise in the ways of relationships, an expert at
putting him at his ease. He was awkward, gauche, and shy, but she
did not make him feel so, although he did not count her special gift
as being a feminine trait. How could he, in the light of all those
admonitions and pleas which had surrounded him at home?

When they got to the end of the street where she lived, she did
not leave him and he had a sense of occasion as he watched her take
a key from her handbag. They had not spoken for minutes but now
she grinned at him.

'You'll have a cup of something then?'

'If you like.'

'Well! There's keen!'

'Yes, please,' he gritted his teeth.

'Temper?' she said. 'We haven't seen that yet.'

She could annoy him too, but since they were usually in the
presence of others, and the omnipresence of others had always been
impressed upon him, he had never really given vent to his annoyance. Now he was conscious of the empty flat upstairs, that knowledge and the accompanying thickening of his blood. They would
be alone together. There was no doubt in his mind as to what he
had come to do and although he had a sense of profound wrong,
he knew he could not help himself. From the moment they left the
company of others, it had been on his mind, but for all his mind
and the hesitations of his mind, there were other, more powerful
urgencies, the whole strain of being with her when every part of her
body caused him to want to protest, including a violence in him that
was right out of character.

The moment the front door was closed, he seized her roughly,
burying his lips on to hers, continuing to hold her and turning her
back against the door so that she was forced to free an arm to protect
herself. But the other arm remained around his neck and she had a
typical admonition of her own, the moment she could free her lips.

'What do you think you're doing?' she said in the darkness,
'playing against me?' her face was wicked, her eyes amused. It was
a rugby country after all, and careful is as careful does, it was she
who looked after his spectacles.

But he was serious.

'Come on. Let's go upstairs.'

'There is only upstairs. It's the top flat.'

'Let's go there then.'

'Wait boy... wait!' His mother might have said that, but that was all she might have said.

What he could never understand afterwards, (and which was really most obvious) was that there was an inevitability to the occasion. Of course, she was leading him on, all the way. 'As common as dirt', his mother was to say and the repercussions were mammoth, but that was later. At the precise time, he felt rather as if he were in a maze, pusing blindly at doors which sometimes opened, sometimes did not. There was so much he did not understand. Young people these days, he was to say years later, were far more sophisticated, better informed, and no doubt their instincts led them to their own pleasure and pains, but then, on that night, he was simply driven blindly by his instinct, and by his desire to be close to her, to have all that she was for himself, his need. More than anything he wanted to cease being himself, to be part of her, that close; the final and only closeness, he was to think for a long time. He wanted release too, an end to all those grubby, forbidden practices of the bedroom, but that was to take away from the total experience, to destroy what she gave to him, that knowing acceptance of his inexperience and her ultimate kindness as he lay there sobbing when the guilt came.

She had both her hands behind his head looking up at him wonderingly on a utility divan, one leg of which was broken.

'You old silly...'

'I couldn't... I couldn't help it.'

He hardly knew her as a person. Closeted in one world, he was blind to others, totally blind. He knew three facts about her, actual facts. Her father was a club steward, she worked in a shoe shop, she had a pleasing voice and was much sought after. That, and she liked him, had singled him out. But then, later, she watched him dress with a wry smile and took him by the hand into her bedroom. He had not been able to wait even for that scrap of comfort. Now he followed her wonderingly. The bedroom was incredibly small, moulded by the sloping roof and her bed was tucked under an eave. The bedspread was a cheap patterned quilt such as were sold by riff-raff in the market and her possessions were meagre. There was not a book in the room, he noted, in marked contrast to his own. But on the dressing table, there was a framed photograph prominently displayed of a young man a little older than himself with a wide cheeky grin. She picked the frame up pensively, then her sadness came on her again.

'What it it?' Now he felt embarrassed, an intruder.

She hesitated, suddenly seeming younger, even sisterly, a different person altogether. She made a regretful move of her lips.

'My husand,' she said in a small voice.

'*What?*' he stared at her frantically. He felt remorse come upon him in a wave, settling even in his stomach, like bile.

'It's all right, he's dead.' Again, she thought of him, his feelings.

'Dead?'

'"Missing presumed," at first, but then it was for keeps.'

For keeps... that was what he eventually took home with him, the finality of that. There were other details, a whirlwind courtship, the difficulty of obtaining her father's permission, the brief trip to the Registry Office, a weekend's honeymoon at a boarding house on the coast.

'Well, it wasn't actually a boarding house, it was rooms with attendance, they call it.'

He was a rear gunner. She'd met him once or twice, another one who couldn't bear to leave her alone. One or two people knew about it, but she collected her pension elsewhere and she kept it secret for a reason which Selwyn couldn't fully understand. The family didn't approve. She was too young. it would have been better to have waited. They'd had enough trouble with the elder sister when the Yanks were billeted locally. Please God they didn't have another one like her. But Tegwen's will had prevailed.

'So there!' she said. 'There... Now I've told you. So now you know, don't you? Me, see?'

If anything it frightened him. It was too much to hear and as soon as she told him, he knew she regretted it. His blinking schoolboy's face gave away the enormity of it, her experience and his ignorance in the face of it. Perhaps her parents were right in wanting to keep it quiet after all. Too much can happen to you, too much in too many places and perhaps her father knew that, had a sense of the world's ills and the smallness of people who could not face up to them. There was such a thing as a propensity for bad luck, and he did not want people to know that she was starting off her life with that behind her.

Selwyn swallowed, the tears in his eyes.

'Poor Teg,' he said. He was truly close to her then.

Her smile was brave, accepting, womanly. It was her secret and she wanted him to know. Then it was his first time and there could be no other, that she understood best of all.

But it was not long before he looked at his watch and it was two o'clock in the morning before he got home. His father had gone to bed but his mother waited up, her eyes reddened with concern. Fortunately he had declined a drink and his breath was virginal in that respect.

'Where've you been? For goodness' sake, it's hours past midnight?'

His mind was overburdened by thought, but he was not going to change overnight. He took off his glasses and polished them, blinking solemnly.

'Oh, they had a lot of difficulties with band parts. A good deal has to be changed.'

'The band parts?'

'I had to take a whole set of new scores to Mr Elias, and then we got talking, and one thing and another.'

He was to develop an expertise in the casual additional details he invented to embellish the most commonplace lies. He would be found out, of course. Things would be 'all over town', and his mother's concern for him, and 'everything she had done for him' was ultimately no more than a subject of dismay for him. The world inside the manse could be just as cruel as the world outside. His parents had prepared him for nothing. His whole life was cocooned by their wants and wishes, more than anything by their fear of the world and their inability to change it, even clinging stubbornly to their ancient language so as to separate themselves from the mainstream of the human experience. He was on the point of seeing them as small and frightened, and that worried him too, so for their sakes he began to hide his thoughts, his new self, his secret.

He lay in bed listening to his mother double-locking the back door but he did not think about her further. He had other things on his mind. Who would think that you could taste hair, taste it, and feel it and when it came down over your shoulders, it was like another world in there, the coarse, scented smell and feel of it, the touching — the touching, the little pains and discomforts and finally, actual sweat falling upon you and teeth glistening in the darkness and the final awful marvellous unthinkable release that was to be his again now; so that in a month or two when his exams had gone by the board and there was khaki looming and tears at home, he could even have his leg pulled.

'You County Schoolboys are all the same. Oh, all right then. What? You're a case, you are. Get away, I knew as soon as I seen you. Never had it, and'll never want it again.'

But she was wrong about that, of course, Tegwen Hughes, child-bride, widow, wit, goddess, saviour and sage, Frilly Lips.

Dai-logue

1

'In audience-terms, of course, the thirty minute slot isn't going to set the Thames on fire,' Dexter Tustian said, hooking one lemon-coloured suède bootee onto the bar rail in the BBC Club. 'Neither the Thames, not the Wirral,' he added with a genial smile and fingered his fourth vodka-and-tonic. It was Friday afternoon, he had one remaining appointment with an unknown compatriot, one Cyril Evans who had written what Tustian considered 'a felt piece' about coal mining for a northern literary magazine. Evans was waiting for him in Reception at this moment, but Tustian had cornered a Guardian journalist and didn't want to lose the opportunity of boosting himself and the slot. Awful, of course, having to do it at all, but if anything had changed in television, it was the attention paid to the press by the power people upstairs.

'We look upon it really as a show-piece for the young writers. I don't want to use the word "experimental" — God forbid! — but it's a try-out slot, and we can afford to make mistakes. Feeling, is what we're after, feeling for a character, nuances of language if we can't get to them. We're not stuck with having to get *obscene* ratings which is a help. D'you know what I mean?'

Dexter smiled, pushed up his thick black spectacles with a nail-bitten finger, then ruffled a thinning mane of lank grey hair. The journalist was in a hurry to move, he noticed. Even as he spoke, the man was edging away, casting well-known, Club-style glances over his shoulder to see who else might be around. He was so young too, young and cold, pretty little nose uncluttered by the cyanosed veins which marked the onset of television's industrial disease, Dexter observed, controlling a wince.

He'd a run of talking to people anxious to get away from him lately. He was the oldest script editor in Drama, if you excluded Series, and his achievements were slipping into the past. He'd written two romantic novels, an unsuccessful play, and a host of episodes for a popular series. Once, he'd had a certain cachet, there was an air about him that might be taken to mean promise, but now he was pushing his late forties and all his stories about wild nights in the drinking clubs of the Fifties fell on deaf ears. Only the angries had made any money while Dexter still lusted for liquid lunches and the *Caves de France.*

In one way, it was all a matter of sociology, he supposed. This was the fourth vodka theory. The trouble was, he'd come into the Corp too late, and had free-lanced for too long when he should have been inside, feathering his nest like the Oxbridge nig-nogs who started making it much younger these days. Series had done him in, sausage-machine writing, putting your guts into things you didn't believe in; series, his ex-wives — fifth vodka theory — his own failure as a writer, the distant Welsh thing, his capacity for bar-room talk, his lack of application, the frittering away of his talent, everything that ever happened to anybody who stayed too long in televsion or films. The problem was that he was aware of it all, which explained the vodkas, the nail-bitten fingers, the enforced lunchtime bonhomie. There was also the fact that he was working for yet another queer, the fifth on the low ratings corridor.

But there was a rider on this also. The queer producers, bless their happy little chuff boxes, were probably the only ones who'd have him, their pouffy goodwill being far more accomodating than those single-minded young gentlemen of determinate sex. So lay off the Aunt Fans, at least they weren't crucifying anybody for the sake of the career.

Ah, the career, he thought. He sometimes gave himself little lunchtime lectures in a jokey voice. If only mummy hadn't kept a shop in Dan y Graig Street... If only he could be suddenly reborn again as a Jew, a homosexual and an old Etonian simultaneously... And with that unbeatable combination, he might have gone into commercial television to outsmart the working-class lefties who'd been profitably angry at the right time. Somehow, he'd missed the mark in his Fifties and his mind had stuck there. But it was not without its funny side. There was probably no one else in the Corp who'd ever been interviewed by *Woman's Own* for his wholly fictitious knowledge of gipsy recipes. Come out of it rather well, he'd thought at the time. Not put a foot wrong and conjured up a hedgehog stew that might even have been tried. Ah, he had his droll side. If only the young appreciated him rather more.

'Mr Dexter Tustian,' the loudspeaker announced. He was wanted in Reception.

He leant his elbow dreamily against the bar and watched the journalist move away to join another group. He had originally gone to the bar in search of a production assistant called Amanda Smiley who'd given him the eye as well as an eyeful of suède mini, thigh-length boots, the whole pulsating breasty six-foot of her sending out unmistakable signals when he met her yesterday in the lift. Amanda had a large brown mole under one eye and it was rumoured that she slept around, gave wild parties which involved a motor racing crowd who sometimes scooted down to Brighton when the mood took them. Rumour also made Amanda rather Waughish, and she had a deep gurgling laugh, a habit of snorting, wrinkling her large nostrils and screwing up her wide-set eyes which like everything about her were also large. She was frightfully-frightfully, but a drinker with something foreign lurking at the back of all that lisping upper-class Englishness that interested Dexter immensely. Buenos Aires, perhaps, he'd thought at the time. She'd been brought up in the Argentine and he could quite see her on a horse, laying about the gauchos with a bolas. The thought cheered him up. Another vodka, he might sell the character to the Troubleshooters people?

But he couldn't see her in the Club. He looked around blearily and saw only the mid-day crush, all talking their heads off. Damn the *Guardian*, he thought. He'd wasted time selling the slot when he should have been thinking about his John Willy.

'Dexter, they're calling you from Reception!'

Dexter blinked, focusing his eyes on his dwarf-like secretary, an earnest and tiny Geordie with fantastic typing speeds. Her face was so small, she sometimes reminded him of a Gurkha bride. She was invariably concerned for him. There was that Northern niceness about her.

'Little Geordie mother,' he said sadly.

She lowered her voice: 'You're pissed'.

'Not at all. Melancholic, there's a subtle difference.'

'Mr Evans has been waiting for twenty minutes.'

'Ring up that place in Shepherd's Bush and order onion soup.'

'You left his short story on the desk.'

'We'll talk about it over lunch.'

'You won't get a table now.'

'Say it's for me?' he said hopefully.

'I said that last time.'

'Say it's Head of Religious Programmes then?'

'It's not funny. People are moving away from you again.'

Hell was not other people, Dexter thought vaguely, it was oneself, and the worst thing about being any kind of writer, was the insights one had into that self. He had been seven when he left Wales, could barely remember it, a jerseyed boy clutching a Sunday School medal as the family hot-footed it to Slough, bigger and better groceries and an eagerly sought, middle-class respectability. But he was always conscious of something left behind, a different self perhaps, and having seen the Dan y Graig Street address on Evans's manuscript, it set him off, he supposed. It was quite a notion, this meeting with the past, perhaps containing inklings of what he might have been. Like all the Welsh he knew, he had an immense pleasure in reading romantic lies about the Principality. What was that story about Lloyd George gasping when first hearing Bevan speak? The ghost of his youth, the old goat had said. Interesting... But would it make a Wednesday Play?

'Order a taxi at once,' he said decisively. 'I must get out of this place.'

Jenny went away to the telephone recess near the doorway while he went outside to wash. Slough, he thought. That was another undoing, Slough, *Series*, novels about gipsy feuds, *Woman's Own* and the *Guardian*.

'I have not been helped in this life,' he said sombrely to the washroom mirror and struck a new pose. He must be careful not to condescend. Everybody in Wood Lane condescended to the Welsh which was why he'd always taken such pains with his English accent.

Jenny waited for him outside. 'You'll have to apologize.'

He gave a merciless smile. 'Waiting's good for provincial writers. It brings them to the boil.'

But as he made his way alone to Reception, he walked straight into Amanda Smiley who came out of the lift, swinging a stop-watch on a tape. Yesterday, she'd smiled as soon as she saw him.

'What a good idea!' he said glassily, nodding at the stop-watch. 'You're timing yourself now?'

'Oh, hello!' She did not seem anxious to talk, was snort-free.

'I looked for you in the bar.'

'Why?' She was taller than him and her nostrils seemed huge as she looked down upon him. Her expression was infinitely haughty. One of the engineers might have stepped in perhaps?

'Drinkies,' he said lamely. The other day in the lift, she'd positively leant against him, lowering those giant eyelids and wrinkling that nose with unmistakable neighing friendliness. Now she wore a long black Maxi skirt and one powerful leg emerged from the slit as she tapped a toe impatiently. She suddenly seemed more athletic than seductress. Must be the engineers.

'I don't *live* in the bar, Dexter.' She gave him a smile of dismissal but he barred her way.

'Dinner, I thought?' he ogled.

She stood back and surveyed him coldly. 'You're leching, Dexter, I declare. And you're pissed!'

That word... Girls in the BBC used it with an inaccuracy that offended him. They ought to bring another Reith back, a Welsh Reith perhaps. Dexter blinked and suddenly saw himself in the role of Staff Morality Officer, card-index to hand as he peered down from the top of the tower. 'Gentlemen, a number of things have got to stop...'

But he nodded sombrely.

'Everything's got its funny side, Amanda.' Why had he thought he had a chance? Where did the gossip come from?

'I've got to go,' she said impatiently.

'Don't!'

'What?'

'Go... Come and have lunch? I'm interviewing a Welsh writer.'

'Christ!' Amanda said. 'The poor man.'

'Listen,' he swayed unsteadily. If people thought you were drunk, they made you drunk. 'I'm going to be persistent about dinner.'

'I'd have to feed you,' she said. But she grinned, suddenly seemed a good sort. 'Haven't you got a secretary, or something?'

He stared at her. He had, and at that moment, Jenny came hurrying down the corridor after him. Beside Amanda, she looked smaller than ever. The two of them stood together staring at him like spectators of a street accident.

'I've ordered the taxi, but...' Jenny hesitated.

'Did you get a table?'

'I didn't bother.'

'For Christ's sake...'

'Must be off,' Amanda said.

'But dinner?'

'Don't be such a fart!' Amanda winked at Jenny, who frowned, then went striding away up the corridor, the stop-watch swinging at the end of the tape.

Dexter leant against the wall, feeling the tears come to his eyes. For years, all his failures had led him into the arms of women, and that was another comfort which was slipping away.

'I honestly don't think you should see anybody,' Jenny said gravely. 'Shall I go and say you're ill?'

'No,' he blinked away the tears. 'Floreat Dan y Graig!'

'Well, don't comission anything until you get a synopsis.'

Nineteen, he thought. She would make somebody a marvellous mother. It was the most charitable thought he'd had all day, but immediately it was coupled with the knowledge that somebody in Admin had shuffled her into his office, knowing his reputation. Perhaps there was a file somewhere which said: *does not molest the tiny.*

He drew himself up. He was still immaculately dressed, still had a presence of sorts. Laundered shirts, he thought: his secret.

'Jennifer, you're fussing,' he said gravely, staring into her troubled currant bun of a face. He wanted to hug her suddenly, as a father would do. He should have had children. And then, he wanted to be gay. Gay and fey, he thought. His favourite sentence in the English language was the one uttered by the débutante in one of Waugh's novels: 'Can't come now, Daddy's gone to see the King!' Nobody understood anybody really, but at least they ought to remain ignorant with a certain style.

He winked, smiled, put his hand on Jenny's shoulder.

'Be all right on the night!'

Then he turned sharply and made his way to the lift with perfect aplomb, pressed the button and bowed to her as she remained standing in the corridor. The lift doors opened, he got in, then watched the lift doors close over her face. Her expression did not change. She might have been a trawlerman's daughter standing concerned on the jetty. Black ice, he thought. He was in a fertile mood today. What part of the world were the troubleshooters carving up now? Props could really have a field day with black ice.

But in the lift, he turned his mind to the waiting Evans whom he had never met. Supposing the chap had real talent? Should he be the one to channel it into all the murky corners where his own path had led him? But that was nonsense. He was filling slots. Either he got a half hour out of the fellow, or he did not. And what anybody did with his talent, was a private affair. Nobody corrupted you. You corrupted yourself.

'Floreat Dan y Graig,' he said again, pleased with the phrase. It would be refreshing to meet a good writer, exciting to pinpoint a new talent. The story he'd read had come burning off the page. Life, juice, vitality, he thought; what nearly everybody lacked in the building. It was also a little anti-Welsh too which was unfortunate. Wouldn't go down in England unless it was a new kind of thing that immediately invited articles and comment-pieces. One of the mistakes which he'd made himself was that he hadn't realized there was still money in singing miners. Art and Literature, he thought finally with a hiccup that came from nowhere. He thought of them as two large balloons sailing endlessly above him, and unfortunately out of

reach. Art and Literature... If he'd never moved from Dan y Graig
Street, he might have feathered his nest with the Arts Council,
become one of the leaders of the Anglo-Welsh? All in all, it was a
fruitful morning for the dreams!

2

'Jesus, Mary and Joseph!' Cyril Evans thought as Dexter came
hurrying towards him, hand outstretched, 'another bloody Home
Counties pouf.' He'd come over from ATV after an unsuccesful
interview with the people there. Unknown to Dexter, the one short
story which he'd had published had excited several inquiries. He
was pleased but puzzled. The story related his feelings after his
father had been brought home injured from the pit. What had
annoyed him most, was that his eldest sister who had charge of the
house, had bundled him into the front room where he was not
allowed to help or watch, and the story had been written from the
point of view of the little boy closeted in that front room. It was the
best room of the house, the furniture was precious and the cluttered
ornaments were milestones in the life of his parents. While his father
groaned on the kitchen table, he had sat alone examining the
ornaments, dinner plates from his grandmother's farm, an ostrich
egg in a genuine Swansea china bowl, a cheap little imitation
lighthouse from Polperro, a sad honeymoon purchase. The gifts
seemed like so much débris to the little boy who had seen the
chalk-white pallor of his father's face. It was a sensitive and unsen-
timental little piece, they'd said in ATV, but there was very little
dialogue. Could he write dialogue? He'd made a mistake answering
that, shrugging his shoulders truculently. If it came, it came. He'd
been embarrassed talking about a real experience, and he'd covered
up his feelings with an unbecoming gruffness. In a curious way, he
had a local indifference to getting on in the world. To hell with the
lot of them. So no commission.
    'Look here,' said Dexter beaming. 'I've been absolutely tied up
all the morning. The best thing we can do is get away from here.
What d'you think?'
    Evans suppressed a desire to shrug away the welcoming arm
which Dexter had placed on his shoulder. But he'd better watch his
p's and q's. In ATV, there'd been long silences and they'd sighed
with relief as he went out of the room.
    'Right you are then,' he managed dourly. If you weren't a windy

boy and a bit, spilling over the bars, the real rooted Welsh were distinctly unsaleable.

'Marvellous! Taxi's lined up, I hope. This way, old chap.'

The trouble with these people, Evans diagnosed, BBC types, telly people, smoothies on the art lark — was that they gushed. Evans did not gush. He was a sign-writer by profession, a technical college boy, evening classes and regular slog. Early unhappiness and the proximity of the public library had made him into a reader. From reading, he'd moved to writing. He'd tried his hand at short stories for years without success, but he was persistent and had learnt to chip away at a paragraph until he got it right. He'd taken a course at a correspondence college and although he hadn't got much from it, they'd brushed up his English and taught him to lay out a manuscript. Finally, after years of plodding, he'd dug something out of himself that was part of himself, and he recognized that as cardinal. He had a simple desire to tell simple stories to simple people, people like himself, and so he shut himself away from his family with a piece of paper in much the same way as his father had done with his pigeons. It did a man no harm to have a private part of himself. The sign-writing had paid off. It would be nice to make a bit on the short stories.

'I can see, of course, that you *enjoy* writing,' Dexter said when they were seated in the taxi. 'It comes off the page.'

'Aye, aye,' Evans said non-committally, not understanding. He had his father's low forehead, uncompromising spade of a face, and a good deal of the collier's truculence which made itself plain in the deliberate limitation of facial expressions. Short and stocky, with powerful arms and thick wrists, he had the glowering look of an aggressive Second Fifteen scrum-half about to have himself a hard afternoon. 'Have it any way you want,' he seemed to be saying,'you want the boot, boot it is, my old handsome!'

'When you lose your enjoyment, you lose everything, I mean?' Dexter said, breathing hard over him.

Was he a pouf? You could never tell in London. He couldn't be tight, not in the BBC.

'Eggsactlee,' Evans said. He struggled to find something to say but it was such an effort. 'You got to get a bit of a lift into it.' Would that do?

But in order to discourage further conversation at this closeness — Dexter had lurched against him — Evans looked moodily out of the window of the taxi, disapproving of the dated 600 Group sign on the building opposite. Was the problem with these people that they talked about things which normal folk kept to themselves? He was not used to expressing himself at any length. He did not have conversations that mattered to him, and like many artisans, a poor facility for small talk. If a man wanted a sign done over his shop, you showed him examples from the catalogues. There was a set price and set materials. It was a straight trade. But how did you sell a play when you had never written one? And what was a play anyway?

Evans had very little to go on, and did not quite know why they had sent for him. Must be short of stuff, he supposed. Take what you saw on the box. For his own part, he couldn't get involved with most of it. With one or two exceptions, it wasn't about anything or anybody he might have known. For a long time now, he'd thought that so much of it was so pat and tailored. There weren't any loose ends. It was tidy, whereas life was untidy. What was it then? Pictures, cartoons, caricatures... But there was money in it. If only he could fit in somewhere.

Dexter didn't seem to mind his silence, had taken the weight off one shoulder, and moved against the opposite window. He seemed to be thinking, had one hand to his brow in the attitude of a thinker. 'Brilliant man,' Evans could imagine people saying; 'you can see by him.' But he ran his eye over the gently flared trousers of Dexter's smart suit and his lemon bootees, the colour of soiled nappies. A bloody sugar daddy. Eyes glazed too. He wouldn't be surprised if there wasn't a syringe in his back pocket. Stabbers and jabbers, the lot of them. Christ, what part of these islands did they come from!

'What we're looking for really, is a feeling of character,' Dexter said suddenly out of the blue. The fixed smile returned to his face.

'Oh, yes?' Evans nodded earnestly. Christ, what about you! He composed a little rhyme: 'Looked like a pouf; was a pouf.' Imagine walking down Dan y Graig Street with that one bright Saturday. Thank God they never came to see you when you were with your mates.

Presently, the taxi drew up outside a small Italian restaurant, and Dexter got out, stumbling as he reached into his back pocket and drew out a wad of notes.

'What's the damage, Cabbie?'

Evans suppressed a desire to grab hold of the taxi driver and drag him into the restaurant with them for real company, but he checked himself. He gave a curt nod, then followed Dexter into the restaurant which was divided into small booths in a style reminiscent of the restaurants in Chicago gangster films. The waitress seemed to know

Dexter and immediately placed them at the rear.

'We'll be undisturbed here. What about a vodka and tonic?'

Evans would have preferred a pint, but he nodded.

'Large,' Dexter said to the waitress.

There was an embarrassment when they ordered as Evans had no idea what to eat, but Dexter took charge with an understanding nod.

'Canelloni to start, I think. D'you like asparagus?'

'Anything you like,' Evans said miserably, 'I'm not a big eater.'

He could not put down the thought that all this had happened because his father'd been brought home with a bump from the pit all those years ago. That, and his sister doing her little mother act. Where was the sense of it? This type of pouf, this type of food, this type of talk? And now he couldn't find anything to say, and sat there bulging behind the pretty little chequered tablecloth and the decorative candle in the Chianti bottle, like a spare tool in a wedding. And he ought to be making the running! He knew that. Go on, gush you bastard, he urged himself. But nothing came to his mind that altered his unease, and as he struggled, Dexter just sat there opposite, looking at him, and not looking at him, then looking dreamily around the restaurant and breaking up bits of long thin biscuit and scattering crumbs over the table, munching away like a lap dog. Perhaps he was drugged? Bloodshot eyes like a stuck pig behind the business lenses that was for sure. Oh Christ, he must think of something to say. His wife, Evie, had her eye on a washing machine. 'You can bet your bottom dollar they haven't sent for you for nothing! First class fare an' all!'

Evans began to sweat. He fingered his collar uneasily, then leant forward across the table and laid it on the line. He had to make an effort.

'I know there's not much dai-logue in that magazine piece,' he said hoarsely. 'But I could do you a coupla pages. A dummy-run, like-see?'

Dexter blinked. 'Like-see?'

'Pardon?'

'Like-see... I'd forgotten the expression.'

Evans did not understand. Jesus, he thought. It was going to be like that correspondence course all over again, grammar, syntax, Fowler and Fowler up your arse every time you put pen to paper. He always felt his lack of formal education. He had buried himself in books because books never corrected him, didn't answer back, weren't sarcastic about his deficiencies. But here it was again, he supposed, bloody grammar. Why did he bother to put pen to paper at all?

When the canelloni came, he looked at it suspiciously. The way his mind was working, everything that happened to him, seemed like part of a London plot in which the Welsh were always suckers. Unless of course, they could become Englishmen of the visiting cards and scent type. Take the wog food. Faggots and peas would have done him, faggots and peas, a pint, and bollux to Fowler and Fowler, and walking bags of pus like the wild-eyed old English drip. Pound to a penny he was on something, tablets, if not the needle, or the smokes, another charming London export to the provinces. But worse than that, he was so beat-up and that was the sad thing. One of those beat-up people with nothing to show except what they'd done to themselves.

He could smell dismay, could Evans. It has a scent and a look about it, a look you could see sometimes on the faces of dust-ridden colliers whose lungs had ceased to function. After a time, their sucked-in cheeks became putty-coloured and their mouths were drawn down at the corners as their movements grew slower and slower like men carrying a great unseen weight. They got so that they couldn't easily look you in the face, and if they did they appeared to look through you and beyond you into some unfathomable distance. That was one kind of dismay, the slow clutch of an invisible death which crept upon you while you were still alive, but this man Dexter Tustian — it sounded like a stage name — had the dismay of disintegration. He was a scraper, Evans concluded, done in by the fag of saying the right things. That was visible on the surface, and if he did not know exactly what went on inside the man, then he smelt it, the confusion, the lack of purpose. Evans did not know Dexter had been a writer, and if he had known, he would not have cared. Hard knock, Evans.

'The important thing to remember, is character in action,' Dexter said suddenly. He seemed to have been struggling for phrases. 'Description's out, must see conflict, conflict, character in action, and a pay-off if you'll forgive an Americanism.'

'Eggsactlee,' Evans said uneasily. He did not understand. Did he mean a punch-up?

'Take your little story...'

Now it was little.

'Marvellous feeling, but it will have to be recreated in speech?'

'Dai-logue,' Evans nodded.

'Threaded together like beads on a string, if you know what I mean?'

Evans put on a weary smile and watched while Dexter helped himself liberally to a carafe of wine which the waitress had put on the table. Dexter's hands were trembling and a sixth sense told Evans that he would have to hurry if he wanted to clinch anything.

'I think,' he began haltingly, 'it would be a help, like, if you were to commission me. I could do the same story, but start it with the boy and his sister quarrelling. Then the old man comes home and the boy is put in the front room.'

Dexter swallowed the wine at a gulp and leant forward knowingly. 'Aha, but who is the boy going to talk to?'

'Himself.'

'No, no, voice-over's out.'

'Voice-over who?'

'Voice-over picture. Dreadfully over-done. Chekhov never used voice-over.'

Bloody Russians now, Evans thought. He gave up.

'Still,' Dexter said. 'Still...' But he suddenly put one hand to his forehead and leant his other elbow on the table. A great sleepiness seemed to come over him, and for a moment, his eyelids seemed to be fighting the rest of his body. Then the weight of his head became too much for one hand. He brought the other hand up slowly, his elbow pushing the plate in front of him. Now he paused, nodding sagely as if in some cinematic close-up.

'I drink a bit.'

'Look here, watch your suit. There's grease and stuff on the elbow.'

But Dexter was gone, and now lowered his head gracefully on the table, his eyes closing as he began to breathe, a slow and relaxed passing out that took place so gracefully that it might have been rehearsed.

Washing machine — kaput, Evans thought. He raised his eyes angrily from the bald patch which became visible as Dexter's hair now curtained his face and looked uneasily around the restaurant. People were looking at them.

'Mr Tustian?'

Dexter began to snore.

Evans gritted his teeth. If they found out about this at the BBC, Dexter'd be bound to get the chop. He'd heard the place was stiff with North Walians and you couldn't reveal your real self for a minute. But his second thought was protective, as if he were covering up for a workmate.

A waitress came up to the table, a mischevious Italian face with

Mickey Mouse eyebrows. She did not seem unduly alarmed.

'Headache,' Evans said automatically. 'If you could manage a cup of coffee?'

The waitress giggled.

Evans flushed, deeply embarrassed. It was a public place. What was he to do? Bloody London, he swore to himself. Then he remembered the secretary who'd come down to Reception to apologize for Dexter's lateness. Geordie, he thought. She'd keep her mouth shut. Despite his dislike of Tustian, he did not want to shop him. It was an imagined thing, his protectiveness. A drunken man became one of us, us against them, and that war was always on. Nothing, it seemed, could change it. Besides, somebody had to pay for the meal, and he wasn't going to part with a brass farthing. He looked once more at Dexter's untidy head. Character in action, he thought.

He found a telephone at the rear of the restaurant.

'Mr Tustian's office?'

'Mr Tustian is not available.'

'I know he's not available, who is that?'

'I beg your pardon?'

'Look here, where's the Geordie girl, his seccy?'

Presently, he heard the voice he wanted.

'Er... Mr Tustian's had a little accident.'

'Has he passed out?'

'Not exactly,' he said carefully. 'But he's having a bit of a rest like.'

'Where are you? Oh, I know. Stay there.'

He put down the telephone, took a coin from his pocket and placed it beside the reciever, then returned to the table. Dexter had not moved and continued to snore quietly. The waitress brought the bill.

'It'll have to wait. The governor's paying by here.'

He took out the makings from his pocket and began to roll a cigarette. Carve-up, he thought; proper carve-up. Everything English made him feel ridiculous, then angry. Why had no one ever written about that? The jolly boys hadn't done it, and apart from the comic cuts side of it, there were worse, deeper, more awful areas of incomprehension. Like that Royal dolly bird sending toys for the remaining kids in Aberfan. Well meant, of course, you had to be fair; good intentioned. But awful too, there being no bread, to have some cake for your heartbreak. It had stuck in his craw that, but then it was only the distance there was between everybody, and he saw it from the bottom, he supposed. There were seams of life, running this way and that, like strata. Sometimes they crossed, mostly they didn't, and on the whole, it paid to ignore it, this separateness between people. He remembered his old man telling him about Royalty coming down before the war. Pits shut, trucks in the sidings, and a Prince saying, 'Something must be done...' And they cheered him! Perhaps it was because they preferred dreams to logic, good intentions to deeds, hope to actuality, Merlin's people to the last. But Christ, he was getting literary!

It took Jenny half an hour to get there. She did not have a car. The only person whom she could think of who might help, was Amanda Smiley. When they came, they entered the restaurant together.

Evans stared at them, their disproportionate size. Mutt and Jeff, he thought, the one as big as a Zulu, the other out of a circus. Still, they'd come.

'Mr Evans, I'm terribly sorry. This is Amanda Smiley.'

'De do,' he said. She did not offer to shake hands.

'Pissed,' Amanda said. 'He was pissed before he left.'

Evans flushed. From the moment he'd stepped off the train, there seemed to have been a conspiracy to embarrass him. Language now...

'I told him not to come,' Jenny said. 'You'd have understood.'

He wouldn't have, as it happened, but he got to his feet. First things first.

'Charge it up to accounts,' Amanda said.

'I'll go and see them.' Jenny said. She went off to the rear of the restaurant.

By now, they were the centre of attention. Dexter had not moved, snored away blissfully, but people had again stopped eating to watch.

'You've got a car, Miss?' he whispered to Amanda.

'Naturally.'

'Oh...' She looked a right tart, the big one. Dig that *naturally*? Cut glass accent, probably said 'Super!' when you'd done it.

'I'll take one arm?' he offered lamely.

But Amanda was quite unembarrassed, caught hold of Dexter's hair and lifted up his head with a savage little jerk.

'Dexter, you're a silly ass!'

Dexter came to life momentarily, shook himself like a stupefied walrus, but when he saw Amanda a foolish expression of immense ga-ga sloppiness came over his face.

''Manda, darling!'

'Oh, fuck,' Amanda said. 'We're not going to have an outbreak of that again, are we?'

Evans flushed beetroot red. He wished he was dead. If this was what they were like, these people, then that Whitehouse woman was right. Language in public places. She seemed, this posh bird, to take away from his masculinity. He was grateful, of course, that they were in charge of Dexter, but at least, they could watch it in front of him. He saw himself in the rôle of customer, not accomplice.

Amanda seized Dexter by the shoulder, and humped him to his feet.

'She's a sweetie,' Dexter said, but he was fast falling asleep once more.

'Get this other arm, you burk!' Amanda hissed at Evans as Dexter swayed once more.

He moved forward anxiously like an attendant ambulance man. He felt sorry for Dexter.

'Easy now, boy.'

While Jenny paid the bill, they manoeuvred Dexter to the door. People were openly laughing now and Evans couldn't get away fast enough. When they got outside, Amanda opened the rear door of a parked Volvo and they pushed Dexter into the back seat. He remained asleep, but still had life enough to tuck his feet together comfortably.

'Hopeless,' Amanda said. 'Absolutely hopeless.'

Evans nodded, but could think of nothing to say.

'Always doing it,' Amanda frowned. 'Contract's not going to be renewed.'

'The poke?' Evans said.

Amanda giggled, looked at him interestedly. 'Yes.'

'But what'll he do?'

'Oh, they'll probably have him over in ITV for an Arts Programme. Dexter always falls on his feet.'

Jenny joined them, then apologized again.

'I'm sure he'll be writing. He's bound to commission you now, I should think.'

Amanda went round to the driving seat and Jenny smiled limply. She seemed genuinely distressed and to understand how bewildered he felt. Tiny little Geordie hinny, he thought.

'Well, thanks for helping,' Jenny did not seem to want to leave him. He nodded. She smiled again, nodded once or twice, then got into the front seat of the car, but no sooner had she done so, than Amanda opened the far side door and stepped out once more. She came around to the car and stared down at him.

'It occurred to me, we've got a do on tonight in the Pickwick. Then we're all coming back to my place. There's eats and things. You wouldn't like to come?'

'*Me?*' Evans said. As soon as she approached him, he wanted to back away. It seemed impossible for a girl like that to want to be genuinely friendly. Despite her attitude, she spoke with the accent of visiting officials, lying cabinet ministers, inept bishops. Foreigners all. 'They' spoke like that, and he had no experience of them which might lead him to contradict his prejudice. You only had to look around the valleys to see how little things had changed in thirty years. There was a surface gloss, people had left; that was about all. The people remained victims, and he could not escape his conviction that it was somehow not right for him to mix with these others. It was absurd, illogical, and he was a free agent, but she embarrassed him, her manner bringing so many other things to bear, adding to his confusion. At the same time, he was aware of how wrong he was. His feelings drove him one way, his mind another. Why was it that a South Walian could never become or do anything without the apprehension that he was treading on somebody else's face? That occurred to him too. People talked about the chip, but it wasn't a chip. The chip got to the surface, but it was only a surface cloak for a buried anger that seemed to survive the centuries. Look at her. She wasn't angry. He must say something.

'Will he be there?' Evans said, nodding through the car window at the prostrate Dexter. It might pay to chat him up when the remorse set in.

'Christ, no!' Amanda said. 'Will you come?'

He hesitated. The comission remained uppermost in his mind. It was why he'd come to London. Perhaps he should stay up and — what was the word — circulate. That was what they did. He'd read about it, even seen it in the pictures. Lousy, it was too. Lousy stories, lousy pictures. And anyway, it wasn't him. He wasn't going to be on offer on anybody's plate. And he didn't fancy her, big tart. Even her eyebrows had muscles. Man-eater, no doubt.

'No thanks,' he said moodily. 'Anyway, I'm married.'

Amanda snorted incredulously.

'It's not an orgy, darling. I just thought you'd had rather a trying day.'

'No, thanks,' he said again. 'Thanks very much for asking anyhow. Ta.'

She suppressed a giggle, gave him a final amused smile, then got back into the car and slammed the door. God knows what she thought!

Jenny had been looking stiffly ahead, but now turned to wave good-bye.

He waved back, then lurched forward.

'Hey, you're not going anywhere near Paddington, are you?'

But they did not hear and the car vanished in the afternoon traffic. They could have offered him a lift.

On the Tube, he summed it up. A fracarse, he said to himself, a right how-do. The little Geordie, he liked, but the big tart was too frightening. Whatever she said, she made him feel like a doorman. His fault, of course, he had to admit that, but it was all outside his ken. As for that Dexter Tustian, he was a wet and no mistake. Art and fart, and nothing at the end of the day. That was it: nutshell. Finally, the absolute condemnation, was his drinking on the job. That was the full stop as far as Evans was concerned. You didn't turn up pissed when there was work involved. There was something serious about work, a holiness about the effort you put into it. It didn't mix with pleasure. It was grim some days, grim, awful, but it was still work and it kept you going. You couldn't do without it, and the thing was, never to mess about with it when you were at it. Head down, keep at it till the hooter went. It was what all the men in his family had practised for generations. All this cock about the Welsh language, the pit had formed them, the pit, work, the clammy old religions to keep their horns down, the fights and rows they had as a community, the anger that was buried within them, the sense of self and the need to walk upright that they'd never yet seen fulfilled. They were a hard, taciturn lot, Evans's folk. They had an insistent conviction that only the rubbish came to the surface so finally his day of failure ended with a grin.

At Paddington, he saw his story in the magazine which was still on sale at a bookstall. He bought yet another copy and carried it on the train, hugging it to himself. It was called 'Block Day', and to those who knew, it conjured up pictures of grinning colliers carrying free firewood under their arms, the one perk allowed. It was old stuff now, gone forever, but he could just remember it and it was part of him. More importantly, it was *his* story, there in the hand. It did not disappear in one night beside a lot of ads, or *Come Dancing*. It was there, and it was his, as ever-present as the street in which you lived, a solid thing, your very own.

On Location

Jimmy Reeve leant over the stile of the farm named after the long decayed nunnery — where lived 'the only virgins that ever lasted in Aberdarren' according to Jimmy — and did not like what he saw. Up to the path came the television people, Moelwyn Hughes, who was Aberdarren born and wearing a bright yellow duffle coat with brown leather trapper's hat complete with ear-muffs, and beside him the man-woman with the Eton crop and long pendulum Scandinavian earrings which 'swung right down to her moustache', as Jimmy told his wife.

Both wore gumboots, Moelwyn carrying a walking stick and a plywood clipboard on which yellow sheets were flapping, and even though they were still a hundred yards away, Jimmy could see that the man-woman, whose name was Etta, had a shawled bottle of Scotch in her arms which she nursed like a baby. Jimmy'd caught sight of them the day before and there'd been a piece in the local paper saying, 'Author Returns to Aberdarren', but for all Jimmy cared, they could go right back again to London or wherever it was they were from now. His wife Henley watched the television regularly and often praised the plays of Moelwyn Hughes which had heart according to Henley, but Jimmy didn't know anything about that.

Moelwyn Hughes had no heart as far as Jimmy knew, nor his father, or any of the Hugheses that Jimmy remembered. If there was any one characteristic of the Hugheses, a strain that ran in the breed, it was their family carefulness and eye on the main chance. They'd walk the length of the town to get a ha'penny off the price of a loaf, Jimmy's mother used to say. Maybe that was why they'd all got on, all left the town, and all made money in one line or another, but as far as Jimmy was concerned there was something not quite right about them. Whatever they touched might turn to gold, but something always went wrong eventually. And if the evil genie didn't hit them, it hit others.

Take the old man who'd made a fortune laying piped radio up the valley before the war when the mountains were said to interfere with the quality of the reception locally. The sound was better with this piped radio, people said, and you didn't have valves or tuning to worry about. Not that Jimmy ever worried about valves either, but they reckoned Old Man Hughes had bribed his way everywhere, wires sticking up all over the town, passing illegally over tram cables, up the sides of public buildings, under the ground, over the ground, any place he wanted them. He got himself on the council fawning over the pensioners, and on the Magistrates' bench, *in* this and *on* that, just to put his radio wires where he damn well pleased, according to Jimmy. And when television came, if he didn't go and do the same thing again! Must have made a cool half million, they reckoned, a house you could quarter a regiment in, three cars, and two Lord Mayors at his daughter's wedding — and all through sticking wires illegally in public places, in Jimmy's view.

Old Man Hughes had quarrelled with one of his sons, the story ran, chucked him out of the house and when he saw him in the gutter years later, the boy's sole had parted from the welt of his shoe.

'How're you getting on, son?' Old Man Hughes said.

'Rough,' the boy said. 'Dog rough. Look at my shoe.'

The old man bent down, took a look at the flapping sole, then pulled his money-kick from his back pocket, a real bookie's kick — Jimmy knew, he'd seen it — and it was white fivers then, fifty or a hundred of them all held together with a thick rubber band, and Jimmy could just see the boy's eyes as the old man fingered that kick. But the old man just took the rubber band off the banknotes and handed it over on its own.

'Try this,' Old Man Hughes said. 'That'll last you the day out.'

That was the story and as far as Jimmy was concerned that was the Hugheses for you. He believed it implicitly, but the trouble was — and Henley'd told him this a hundred times — he never showed it, his feelings and what he really felt about things. He was just too soft for words when it came to meeting with important people, and there were even colliers' houses up and down the hill where he was owed a fortune for milk and never bothered to collect it. He was too busy talking or too busy listening. Three ha'pence short of a shilling, his wife said, half-soaked by nature, and even if he didn't care what he looked like and had the one good suit, the one good cap and the one good stout pair of Sunday brogues, they had their children to think of and a house looking like a pigsty compared to some people's Henley knew.

Where was his urge to get on and make something of himself? she'd asked all those years ago. 'Do you want to stay with a milk round and stealing coal off a tip for the rest of your life?'

'Yes,' Jimmy said. Mooching was about his dap. He wasn't a shifter like some, and he was happy enough always.

But not when the Hugheses were mentioned. There was just this kind of Hughes quality which rubbed him up the wrong way inside, and he was soft enough never to give any indication of his irritation to them. If he had, maybe they wouldn't ever bother with him and this apparition that was approaching now and getting nearer and nearer wouldn't think that he spent his life waiting to hear from him.

They met about every five years, less if Jimmy could help it, but there it was, he always gave this impression of being glad to see anybody. It was his thing, he supposed, the easy-going countryman's way of his which was rare since Aberdarren hadn't really been country for a century, and the few farms that remained did so by courtesy of the Coal Board or the Forestry Commission, and there wasn't much of a living to be made, only milk and pigs, and new things like ponies for riding which was another thing Jimmy hadn't taken up as Henley'd urged him to do. The fortunes he'd lost in his life through having no go in him, according to her.

She would go on and on, and as the visitors broached the field below the stile at which he stood, he wondered if he should shout and tell Henley they were coming, but he knew if he did she'd get in a lather and start dusting the best china and run upstairs to change, doing all the things he never did for anybody, not even on the day he got married when she found two pairs of old socks in his going-away overcoat, which also had a ball of tarred twine and a clasp knife in the other pocket.

'What's this for?' Henley pointed to the twine. She knew about the socks because he'd simply forgotten about them.

He couldn't remember how anything got anywhere as it happened but he had an answer for the twine.

'I thought I might have to tie you up,' he said.

'You wouldn't?'

'You don't know. Maybe I got a bit too much for you?'

'Now, James,' Henley said. 'I don't like that kind of talk.'

'Well, there's a lot you'll have to get used to,' he said, pushing his cap back. She didn't like a cap on a honeymoon. But the cap was him and it stayed.

Still, that was a quarter of a century ago and there was a lot she'd got used to, fair play. They'd brought up five kids, lost the chance of buying the farm, but he still had the milk round and still lent a hand with the hedging on the neighbouring farms which was a skill that was going out now, one of the few things he did with an unmatched excellence which was valued and praised, his knotty brown arms with their bunched and powerful elbow muscles revealing another side to him which again he did not talk about.

Now Moelwyn drew within hailing distance and Jimmy could see he'd grown a beard since they last met and, although he was in his fifties like Jimmy, he wore his hair long in the youthful fashion, lank strands sticking out from under the ear muffs of the trapper's hat. Moelwyn had his country clothes on, Jimmy noted, a bad sign since it indicated that he would be staying a few days.

Moelwyn pushed the fur-lined peak of his cap up and bawled in that loud, come-back-home-and-doing-everybody-a-favour voice which Jimmy detested.

'How's Jimmy? How are you, boy?'

The man-woman raised the bottle of scotch so that it was clearly visible.

'How are you, Mr Reeve?'

Jimmy nodded, not shifting his position from the stile. He wore an old brown tweed suit with a collarless flannel shirt, a white silk muffler crossed about his neck and held there by a shabby blue waistcoat belonging to another suit. He was capless for once, his short cropped grey hair clumped above his lined forehead and puckering his eyes so that their startling blueness was immediately emphasized. They remained clear and youthful and people sometimes made a point of remarking about them. Once he had been driving along the road and a woman visitor had passed a remark in his hearing.

'She said I'd the most remarkable eyes,' he reported to Henley. 'Remarkable...'

'Dai Bo-Peep,' Henley said once. She said it as if it were as good a name for him as any. There were days when nobody'd leave him alone, not even in their minds.

Moelwyn took longer strides and joined him excitedly, inhaling mouthfuls of air as if he were stealing it.

'By God, it's good to be back home. How are you, Jimmy?'

'So-so,' Jimmy said. 'And yourself?' He merely nodded to Etta whose loud upper-class English voice made him feel uncomfortable.

'Problem, Jimmy,' Moelwyn said.

'Ah,' Jimmy said.

'So I said, if you've got a problem, come to Jimmy.'

'And don't come empty-handed,' Etta said, holding up the Scotch.

'It's a bit early in the day,' Jimmy said.

'Oh, we've got heaps of time,' Etta said.

'Brains, Jimmy,' Moelwyn said. He tapped his large domed forehead solemnly with a thick ringed finger. 'Come to pick them.'

He gave an ever wider grin, his regular false teeth glittering through the fronds of his straggly beard. The width of his smile seemed to indicate Jimmy was a huge joke as well as a friend.

The dogs from the farm had scented strangers and now Jimmy could hear their yapping in the yard behind him. The stile was in a field below the yard and not visible from the house, but their voices had carried and Jimmy knew that Henley would have got up from the chair where she had just had breakfast and would be standing in the porch looking towards the brow of the field. He knew that the moment she saw them she would run indoors to tidy her hair. Moelwyn always had this effect on her and, as Jimmy led the way over the stile and up the brow of the hill, he wondered why it was that Moelwyn of all people should be thought attractive to women.

He'd had two wives but Jimmy'd only met the first one who was Welsh. The other was an actress, Henley said, and she'd been somebody else's wife before that, some film star or other, and before that again, Sir-somebody-or-other's wife, even Henley couldn't keep up with her. Jimmy couldn't understand how people could get through wives like calendars and often said so. A bit on the side he could understand, or marrying again if you wore one out and they died, or even one divorce if something went wrong with the vitals and you needed a rebore, but three was taking it too far. What did they say to each other when they started off with that track record?

'It's just show business,' Henley said when he asked her. As if that said anything. There was a more important niggle that still existed between him and Moelwyn as it happened, because the last time he'd spoken to Moelwyn five years ago, he'd gone off with a leg of ham for his wife, and promised to put a cheque in the post, not having the readies on him, but he hadn't done so. He must have forgotten, Henley said, all forgiving.

'You don't think he'd do it deliberately — break a promise? Not Moelwyn Hughes?' Henley said.

'Well, he's made a few promises in his time,' Jimmy said. 'The nuptials, I mean. If I can use that word in the house?'

Henley didn't have an answer for that and Jimmy felt like a preacher for once. When the Hugheses said 'to have and to hold', it was provided it suited their book. Like them radio wires, Jimmy reckoned.

The three of them made it up to the brow of the hill, Jimmy just recalling the ham and wondering how he might tactfully bring it up when Moelwyn said, 'By the way, I still owe you for that ham'.

'Oh, go on,' Jimmy said.

'No, it's been on my conscience.'

'Get away,' Jimmy said.

'I can't remember how much it was.'

'Nor can I,' Jimmy said.

'Anyway, I hope this trip will do you a power of good.'

Jimmy did not reply and saw Henley wave at them from the porchway of the house with a sinking heart. People who came to see you bearing gifts seldom came to do you any good, in his experience. It was usually what they'd come to get which was the stinger, but if he dared to say that aloud, he'd have Henley down his throat.

'Honestly, James, your attitude!'

As predicted, Henley bolted into the house to touch up her hair and remove her pinafore, which you would have thought was no disgrace in a farmhouse, but then the moment Moelwyn appeared, you'd think she was hoping for a part in a play. Jimmy grunted. Fat chance. It was not until they were seated in the farmhouse kitchen with the kettle on and the bottle of Scotch plonked awkwardly in the centre of the table like a little lighthouse of early moring sin that Moelwyn came to the point. Once the pleasantries were over and Etta had asked for the toilet, the wind getting right to her bladder, it seemed, Jimmy prepared himself for the real reason for the visit. Moelwyn was a Hughes after all.

'Right!' Moelwyn said. He now had the clipboard on his lap and took out a pair of thick horn-rimmed spectacles which he propped on the edge of his nose, then looked over them towards Jimmy who sat on the uncomfortable chair and smiled back for something to do.

'We're looking for a farm,' Moelwyn said slowly and deliberately in what Jimmy called his Chief Constable's voice, 'which has been spoilt by the coal industry. Ruined, I must emphasize. D'you know what I mean? Coal tips all round.'

Jimmy stared at him. There wasn't a farm within twenty miles which hadn't been ruined by the coal industry. In the room in which they sat, the sills of the window frames had to be shored up or trimmed every few weeks due to land subsidence caused by the colliery workings underground. Three hundred yards away, a coal tip covered a good quarter mile of pasture and the access to good watering streams had been gone for fifty years before Jimmy's birth. It was colliery country everywhere you looked, and although the inaccessibility of Jimmy's farm was the cause of it still looking like a farm and he had a few good acres for pasture, the land was bounded on all sides by colliery property. It seemed a typical

Hughes question.

Henley mistook Jimmy's silence for non-cooperation.

'You know what he means, Jimmy?' Henley's face was small and anxious and she flashed Jimmy one of the sharp, cat-eyed looks. 'Behave!' her ageing, puffy-cheeked milkmaid's face said.

'Well, er...' Jimmy scratched his head.

Etta had come back into the room. Jimmy noted she'd taken off her earrings. Progress, he thought.

'The theme of the play makes it visually necessary,' she said helpfully. 'Thrills and spills!'

'Ah, yeah... Yeah,' Jimmy said.

'It's got to put the frighteners on people too,' Moelwyn said.

'Scary?' Henley said.

'Exactly. Now where can you suggest, Jimmy?'

Jimmy scratched his ear, but at the same time tried to give the impression that he was giving the matter thought. He took out a tin of tobacco, selected a cigarette paper and began to roll a cigarette with slow, nimble fingers. The name he was hoping wouldn't come up did come up, and it was Henley who mentioned it.

'There's Blaen y Maes,' Henley said. It was a farm which was literally situated under a tip on the eastern side of the nearest valley. It had once been a private house and there was a drive running through the trees from which you could see the tip appearing immediately above the tree tops and right on top of you. The tip made noises at night, and after rain quantities of slurry came down, fouling the driveway with obscene creeping shapes. Once Jimmy had seen monkey trees half smothered with the mixture of small coal and mud, their branches protruding like weird and stunted arms reaching out for succour. It was scary all right, that drive up to Blaen y Maes, and as kids they'd always used it for dares, but then, that was not so much because of the dark and the noises, as the people who lived there. Then as now, Jimmy thought, recalling the inhabitants who were old Aberdarren stock, a strain in them that made the Hugheses seem as far removed from the pressures of living as royalty. That was them radio wires again, you can bet, he thought. They obsessed him. Making a fortune out of wires was getting something for nothing, wit and not effort, and therefore on the sly side.

'Blaen y Maes,' Jimmy said, unable to conceal his frown.

'It's funny you should mention that,' Moelwyn said. He was looking intently at Jimmy. 'I thought of Blaen y Maes myself.'

Jimmy rolled the cigarette over and over in his fingers. Henley would know something was going on in his mind since two rolls was normal, a turn forward, a turn back, then a lick along the gummed edge for the perfect tailored finish before pinching out the stray ends of tobacco, but now Jimmy concentrated on the cigarette to give himself time to think. The question was, how much did Moelwyn know about Blaen y Maes?

'I remember that drive leading up to the house,' Moelwyn said.

'Just trees though,' Jimmy said.

'I wouldn't walk up there on a dark night if I could help it,' Henley said.

'That's just the tip,' Jimmy said.

'You know what I mean,' Henley said.

Jimmy could delay with the cigarette no longer. He tapped it at each end and Moelwyn leaned forward, snapping an electric lighter so that the cigarette paper flared and Jimmy coughed as the acrid smell of the burning paper stung his nostrils. Now he invented a phrase in his mind. This Moelwyn Hughes had a club foot on every finger.

'Well,' Jimmy said. 'It's got the tip there, of course.'

'Who keeps it now?' Moelwyn said.

Etta leaned forward intently.

'Wacco,' Jimmy said.

'Old Watkins?' Moelwyn said.

'His son.'

'You know him well enough,' Henley said. 'I mean, you go there every day with the milk?'

Jesus, Jimmy thought. Listen to her! Then his reservation came, and afterwards he would remember it — this precise moment of alarm. It was as if, in every tip that slid, there was a woman's voice responsible for the first trickle. Either a bloody woman or a bloody Hughes. In reply, he said nothing; nothing at all. So whatever anybody said later, it wasn't him that wanted to go there. Not Jimmy. Not that day.

'I was wondering if we could go over and see him,' Moelwyn said. 'The son?'

'We've got a car,' said Etta.

'Car's no good.'

'You could take the Land-Rover,' Henley said.

Jimmy later wished he'd had the nous to put the block on it there and then. He could have made some excuse about the Land-Rover which would have given him time to think of somewhere else, but no doubt Moelwyn knew what he was after and knew something about Blaen y Maes for that matter. As kids, there'd been talk which must have penetrated even to the Hugheses and he must have heard a whisper about Old Wacco. Henley didn't know, that was for sure, and neither did the man-woman. It was all a game this telly-lark anyway. Jimmy couldn't see it was work, either what went into it when they did it, or what came out when they'd done it. If he liked anything, it was a good western, or maybe something to do with the sea, but these scary pictures they showed didn't scare him. Another thing he hadn't had the training for, he supposed.

One thing was certain, Young Wacco hadn't either, and it was just like Henley to insist they go over there straight away without giving him a chance to warn Wacco, or even talk Moelwyn out of it once he'd got him on his own. He controlled a sigh. Here they were again poncing about Hughes's business, not their own.

When the three of them got into the front seat of the Land-Rover, leaving Henley to make lunch, Jimmy's feeling of dismay remained.

'You remember the old man, then?' Jimmy said.

'Just by sight.'

'You could smell him too.'

'Eccentric,' Moelwyn explained to Etta.

She nodded eagerly as they drove off.

It had begun to rain and the wheels threw a fine spray of muddied water up from the road as they drove and Jimmy concentrated on the lane ahead as he looked through the semi-circle cleared by the windscreen wiper. Everywhere he looked, there was a familiar object, a branch, a post, or a gateway that had felt his own hands and was in some way fashioned by him. Perhaps he had never left his own patch because something had passed from himself to shape familiar unnoticed things that nobody else knew about, and which he alone did not take for granted because he knew the effort involved. Title deeds or not, it was his patch, and nobody else's.

'The story you've done,' Jimmy said. 'Horror, is it?'

'A police story,' Moelwyn said. 'You know the series? Everybody watches it.'

'Scary anyhow?'

'The film has got to be frightening.'

'With the tip omnipresent,' Etta said.

'It's just something I cooked up,' Moelwyn said. 'A man on the run.'

'But the tip is very important,' Etta said.

'Just a story?' Jimmy said. 'Made-up like?'

'All in the head,' Moelwyn said.

'Imagined,' said Etta.

Jimmy was relieved by that. Who wouldn't be, living where they did? It was some time before they could see the coal tip whose peak extended above the natural contour of the mountain and on which the remains of the hauling gear still stood.

When the tip was in use, buckets of slag would be wound up on the high aerial wires from the colliery a mile or so below. The buckets would come up laden to the peak where a trip mechanism was fixed and when the buckets struck the tip, they would overturn, discharging the slag hundreds of feet down onto the tip below. As children, Jimmy remembered that the buckets never seemed to stop unless there was a strike or a holiday, or when the aerial wires were moved higher up the tip. You could sit all day and watch them coming and going, half a dozen or so at a time, all spaced out, beginning as little dots far down in the valley, then growing in size as they approached and through your half-closed eyes on a sunny day they would appear like live things coming up the wire and then, when they were close to the trip, they would turn slowly over above you like great black beasts, discharging their filth in a cascade of dust that went down onto the mountain below. Of course, it wasn't just dust, since they contained great lumps of stone and slag as well as coal leavings, and very often there was good coal too and the farmers often went out at night to forage on the tip and although you were fined for it if you were caught, it was hardly an offence in the local people's eyes.

The aerial wires were also a prize if you could get hold of a length, but as kids they weren't so keen on filching, just on watching the slow monotonous progress of the buckets as they came up-up-up-and-up, and then emptied and made their detour round the mast and trundled away down into the valley again. The whirring noise of the pulley on the wire, the clanking of the tripper and the whoosh of the discharged slag falling were the sounds of growing-up to those who lived near and they got so they did not notice them.

But Old Wacco must have noticed, for in his lifetime the tip covered half his farm and there he was living down underneath it and it grew bigger every year, taking his mountain away from him, changing the skyline as those buckets up-ended themselves, day and night. He must have felt bad about that every minute of every day he breathed, or half-breathed since he never breathed properly since the First War and they reckoned that was mustard gas, whatever that was.

Jimmy thought of this now, relieved that Moelwyn's story was made-up. He had a reservation about telling certain stories to people you did not know. Better to keep old wounds to yourself. But then, somebody like Moelwyn came home and struck sparks to kindle old memories, and despite his reservations, and being in the presence of a Hughes, Jimmy felt a sudden need to talk.

'They gypped Old Wacco out of half that farm, you know? Him coming home gassed from France and all. After the First War.'

'I didn't know him.' Moelwyn said.

'Gypped him. He had a war with 'em all his life about that tip. Reckoned it should never have been put there. He never understood what he signed.'

'It's the old, old story,' Moelwyn said.

'You never knew anything about Old Wacco?'

'Never saw him.'

'Just as well,' Jimmy said. He had a sudden picture of Old Wacco's chalk white face bent in a snarl as he cursed up at those buckets overhead, his eyes yellowed, his strong shoulders bent by the weakness of his lungs, so that he was always out of breath and forced to husband it, and every part of his face showed his agony. It was a wound itself, that face, and Jimmy could not get it out of his mind. He remembered the face and the successsion of facts which he always associated with it — the face, the pistol in the cupboard by the fire, and then the son, Young Wacco — but it was always to Old Wacco that his mind returned first, the man he thought of as the cause of it all, this story which it was better not to tell. Well, not all of it. But again, he could not keep silent. Perhaps he would tease them. He would have, if they were going somewhere else. Old man, the pistol, the son, he thought. He'd tell them half, he decided. But he'd better dress it up.

'I remember Old Wacco well,' Jimmy said. 'He had a Mauser pistol that was looked after like nothing else in that house.'

'A Mauser?' Etta said.

'He brought it home from France.'

'A lot of people did,' Moelwyn said.

'I couldn't understand it then, but I understand it now,' Jimmy said. 'He brought it home to shoot himself if his chest got too bad.'

'You don't know,' Moelwyn said.

Jimmy felt relieved. He knew all right. He knew and Moelwyn didn't. If you knew Old Wacco and you knew Blaen y Maes, you knew exactly why he brought that pistol home from France.

'Did he shoot himself?' Moelwyn said.

'Yes,' Jimmy said. 'Well, they said he did. Death by what-you-

call... er... misadventure.'
  'Well, then?'
  'Only he used a shotgun to do it. If he did it.'
  'You mean somebody else shot him?'
  'I didn't say that.'
  There was a moment's silence as they drove.
  'What happened to the Mauser?' Etta said.
  'Oh, it just went somewhere, I reckon.'
  'Went?' Moelwyn said.
  'Well, I dunno,' Jimmy said. 'I mean, can you find the things you had as a kid?'
  'If I had a Mauser, I'd know.'
  'Horfficer's gun,' Jimmy said, using Young Wacco's phrase.
  'Pardon?'
  'That's what it was.'
  Out of the corner of his eye Jimmy saw Moelwyn exchange a glance with Etta and Jimmy enjoyed the little sensation his anecdote caused, but he did not add to it immediately.
  Instead he remembered the very first time he'd seen the Mauser years ago when he was about ten and they were sitting around, a couple of ragged snot-nosed kids, and it was Young Wacco's boast that his old man didn't just have a shotgun like everybody else's old man. He had an officer's gun, Young Wacco said, only he said, 'Horfficer's gun' in that hoarse, cracked voice of his, something strained about it even as a child. One day, when his old man was rum-struck and in a good mood, they got him to bring it out from the wall cupboard near the fireplace and Jimmy remembered the rags inside and outside the holster, and how stiff the leather of the flap was, and the special dinky place for the ramrod and the general good nick of it under the rags, not like some guns you saw which would fall apart if you fired them. You could see it was kept from the air and the damp, and even the little brass holding stud under the flap of the holster was clean and free from verdigris.
  It was the most prized possession in the house and Jimmy could remember Young Wacco's wet little lips pressing tightly together when he told them that one day it was going to be his, and then his own disappointment at not getting actually to hold it, because no sooner had the old man's good mood come than it went, in a burst of coughing and cursing, and the Mauser was put away again. But Jimmy remembered it as clear as anything, probably because he'd had occasion to recall it later; it was an important item in the life of those scratching a living for themselves down there in Blaen y Maes.

'Death by what-you-call!' Jimmy said and shook his head wistfully as if admiring the neatness of the phrase he could never remember to complete first time. 'Misadventure, yes. There was a time when the Mauser was mentioned and a time when it wasn't mentioned. You sure you don't remember Old Wacco?'

'No,' Moelwyn said.

'Nor Young Wacco?'

'No,' Moelwyn said.

'Part-schooled, he was, young Wacco. Never left the farm much and was worked by the old man. Worked and worked. Worked bad. But he never growed much in his mind. They reckoned he was *twp*, Young Wacco.'

'Simple,' Moelwyn explained.

'If the old man had a face you'd want to forget, well, the son had one that didn't work.'

'Didn't work?'

'Didn't show anything much.' Jimmy didn't quite know how to describe young Wacco's face. When he said that it didn't work, he meant that there were times when an expression tried to come on that face, but never quite travelled, so that even when he was looking at you, he seemed not to be seeing you, and whatever you said, did not produce much change on it. The till never rang in Wacco's mind, Jimmy thought. It was hard to explain. They were now of an age, he and Young Wacco, and although he had seen him most weeks for years, the immobility of Wacco's small pinched features had not altered. Now his features were hardened and coarsened and he'd gone to pieces through living on his own, but his stare remained, and always what you saw on that face seemed to be the in-between of a real mood. It wasn't just that the till didn't ring, but the register gave always the same blank reading. Jimmy hadn't thought about it in years and now he didn't try to explain further. Only one thing was certain and that was another indisputable piece of Blaen y Maes history. The son was another item in which Old Wacco was sold short. Items, Jimmy thought. They made quite a bill when added up.

'Probably deprived,' Moelwyn said.

'All that,' Jimmy said.

'As a child, I mean. Did he go into a home or anything? Institutionalized?'

Jimmy shook his head.

'He must have had a mother?'

Jimmy shook his head again, suddenly daunted by the turn of the conversation. If they'd just shut up, he'd tell them part of the story, but the questions forced him to think and the mention of the mother whom he had also not thought about in years brought the gossip to his mind again and, with it, a picture of Young Wacco sitting lumpily in torn daps and rags of clothes in the school yard, and the other children taunting him in their cruel way.

'Where's your mother, Wacco? Where? Where? Where? Where?' They repeated it again and again, and back the answer would come, always with that dull stare, 'Been and gone'. They did it day after day, and even forty years later, Jimmy still felt a twinge of shame that he'd been too small as a child to do anything about it in the face of the bullies. He also remembered a puzzled admiration because Young Wacco never cried, but then he didn't laugh much either and his response to the taunts was so wooden that he was eventually left alone.

But Jimmy remained curious and later he'd heard one of the servants describe the mother as a bit of a gipsy scrag who'd come to Blaen y Maes one day with pegs. The old man, it seemed, had bribed her to stay, kept paying, but then she'd upped and left soon after the child was born. There never had been a woman in Blaen y Maes for long. Old Wacco had to pay for his oats, the servant man reckoned. It was probably the only thing Old Wacco had in common with Old Man Hughes, Jimmy thought.

'Mother,' he said. 'Been and gone, they used to say.'

'Ah,' Molewyn said knowingly.

'Wacco reared the boy himself.'

'Plenty of stick,' Molewyn said.

Jimmy noted the condescending use of his own phrase and nodded.

'Just like them dogs he let run there. The dogs had leads that he looped to a length of wire he had from the colliery and they was given the run of the drive. Knocking wire, they call it. Them dogs gave it a hammering all right.'

'Brutalized, I've no doubt,' Moelwyn said.

'No, he took a pride in them dogs.'

Molewyn gave another knowing nod and although Jimmy knew he was not referring to the dogs, he could not get the dogs out of his mind because, savage as they were, a pack of three half-bred Alsatians that lived all their lives outside, being made to kill and eat most of the year, Old Wacco had them controlled and a special way of talking to them which they understood and obeyed. He could make them do anything on his own place and they never left it, never

worried sheep, never were a nuisance, and if people who had to go
up there ever complained, Old Wacco would take a pride in talking
to the dogs and backing them up the wire step by step like a haulier
with pit ponies underground, and there was no doubt that the dogs,
mean as they were, were Old Wacco's triumph.

With them he was happy, and he was good to see with them, the
snarl gone from his mouth and his talk soft and persuasive with all
the patience in the world for the dogs. You only had to see him with
them and, with any nous, you'd know that if things had been
different, he would have done something mighty with dogs and
animals. It really was remarkable because he could even joke with
dogs which was a strange thing to say but true and he could even
tell them off and somehow get it across to them that he was sorry
they weren't quicker. He could make dogs try, that was the thing,
and in the dog world he was a kind of king, no doubt about it.

But not with Young Wacco. As soon as Young Wacco showed he
couldn't learn, they went their separate ways about the place. Jimmy
just knew about it from the outside, but in his mind, he could
itemize the details. If Old Wacco did the pigs, Young Wacco'd do
the chickens. If Old Wacco was up the top field fencing, Young
Wacco'd be down below fiddling with the farmcart or on the barn
roof — anywhere, provided it was away from his father. Young
Wacco couldn't learn and the old man tried everything, but he just
didn't improve. He couldn't even knock a nail in straight and there
was a potcher's mess about everything.

There must have been days when Young Wacco felt the old man's
tongue and Jimmy remembered the silences between them when
Young Wacco was like a dog that had turned on his master;
although whipped and brought to heel, you knew if you knew
animals that something had gone between them and things would
never be the same again. Jimmy knew this, had seen it and felt it,
and he did not like to see a man whipped into that hang-dog state
that came upon the really beaten, whether it was Young Wacco or
the people who'd been gypped by that Hughes putting wires where
they'd no business to be, and getting the law to say that he was right
when people protested. That was a different matter but it was
putting people down, and as far as Jimmy knew, no one had ever
put one over on the Hugheses. Not ever.

He did remember one time, however, when Young Wacco had
the last laugh as far as the law was concerned. And if it were not for
the shotgun, Jimmy'd given him a medal for it. Now he grinned as
he remembered. A good local joke stayed good for ever, he thought.

But it was the Mauser which had got right on top of Moelwyn's mind and stayed there.

'Tell me,' Moelwyn said. 'Didn't they call all those guns in during the war?'

'Both wars, they did,' Jimmy said. 'They brought in nearly a dozen. Myself, I reckon the police kept them all.'

'But not Wacco's?' Moelwyn's voice was anxious.

Jimmy bit the skin of his lip to stop grinning. He wished he'd brought Henley. She didn't know about the pistol. He could just hear her. 'Jimmy, are you sure he's got rid of it? No, are you honestly sure, Jimmy? Well it's not very nice, is it? Not knowing. And you go there every day?'

Jimmy kept his eyes on the road.

'Not Wacco's, no.'

'So he's still got it?'

'Well, I'll tell you. The Sergeant went down to Blaen y Maes one day. Somebody must have been talking. The old man was long dead and most people who knew him had forgotten the Mauser. Not many knew, but somebody must have blabbed.'

'Did the Sergeant find it?'

'I'm telling you. The Sergeant went there and Young Wacco didn't understand. "Mauser", the Sergeant kept saying to him, and he kept pulling his finger like it was on a trigger and going "Bang-Bang! The Mauser your father had years ago? Where did he put it?" Young Wacco nodded at that and put his coat on and went out of the house, the Sergeant following. He thought maybe it was in a shed outside, but Young Wacco walked straight past the sheds and up the mountain. Then he walked the legs off the Sergeant for about a mile, rambling round the tip not saying anything, just having him on and the Sergeant getting filthy and then they came to a pond. It was an old shaft, the deepest pond in miles and had never been drained. Young Wacco pointed to it and looked at the Sergeant very helpful. "That's where he put it," he said.'

'But it wasn't there?' Moelwyn said.

'You tell me,' Jimmy said.

'You mean he's got it now?'

Jimmy shrugged his shoulders. He could feel their apprehension, but he knew it had no relevance to themselves, and did not consider it. They were descending into the valley now, minutes from their destination, and although the rough track was wooded on either side, ahead of them they could see the other side of the valley, slag heaps and coal outcroppings riven onto the mountains above the thickly ribboned terraced streets. Now there was no doubt that where they were was heavily industrialized. They were going down into the filth and Jimmy felt aggrieved because Moelwyn's prompt-ings had sent him deeper into the story than he cared to go. You thought of one thing and then you thought of others, and where Blaen y Maes was concerned, it nearly always ended in dismay.

Blaen y Maes, he said to himself. He had a sudden picture of the old man in his mind as he had last seen him, bent in his cane chair coughing his life away by the kitchen window, the gassing terrible in a man who lived by his lungs and needed freedom of movement. But it was all an ache, Jimmy thought, the effort to put meaning to the gossip about the gipsy scrag who took off, leaving Old Wacco with a child that could barely talk. There was the failure of that, the boy going moody and muttering and silent in himself until he became the man he was now, a child-man, bent and dirty and the place rotting away under his feet. In all the living there's ever been, Jimmy concluded, there couldn't have been no two like them two, father and son; and deep in his bones, he felt the wrongness of strangers going there now. He didn't think anything would happen, but it was memory again, things better not remembered, being remembered, stones unturned and, if you turned them, it was your own fault if you did not like what you found there. It was somehow an elementary lesson that Moelwyn, Henley — all of them — had caused him to ignore.

Finally, he turned off the hill, entered a clearing and brought the Land-Rover to a halt opposite a rough-hewn log gate.

'I'd better go in and have a word with him myself first,' he said moodily.

All three looked at the gate in the clearing. The farm was not visible, but beyond the gate they could see the driveway, dank foliage and clusters of ferns interspersed between the trees on either side. The tip rose sheer in the distance and the whole approach was gloomly and uninviting, the trees overhanging the drive so that, with the tip blocking out the light, the driveway was like a tunnel leading into the darkness. They could see for about twenty yards and there the drive turned where the monkey trees began, veering towards the house.

Just over the gate, Jimmy's eye picked out one of the rusted iron stanchions where the old man had placed the knocking wire to give the dogs their run. The dogs had long gone as had the wire, but the rusted stanchions remained, crumbling monuments of Old Wacco's one success.

'All we want is permission to film in the drive,' Moelwyn said.

'The drive's super,' Etta said.

'It's his,' Jimmy said.

Moelwyn looked peeved. 'Tell him I was born here.'

'I'll tell him.'

'The programme's for network,' Etta said. 'Not just the Welsh!'

'Look out for the Mauser,' Moelwyn said with a grin. He pulled the poke of the trapper's cap firmly down over his eyes.

'Shit on you,' Jimmy said to himself.

He clambered down from the Land-Rover, pulling an old oilskin jacket from the cab behind him. It was Henley's fault, he thought again. If he'd refused, she'd have made a meal out of it, his refusal. He climbed the gate, his thoughts beginning to dwell on his own failures which seemed to have increased because of his dependence on her and on this Welsh trait he had, of being obliging more often than not, a weakness of which he was suddenly becoming aware.

He went forward slowly into the gloom of the trees, smelling the dank smell of the tip, his boots squelching in the mud, noting yet another stanchion with a loop of wire remaining. It was uncanny but he could just see Old Wacco's hands on the wire cutters he'd also brought back from France. Wherever he'd been, Old Wacco'd been a looter, Jimmy remembered. He'd brought everything back from everywhere, boots, clothes, wire cutters, Mauser. Anything that could be lifted, he lifted it. But he couldn't escape the gassing. The gassing was the price he paid, the catch. To all who went away there was a catch, Jimmy was sure. Like this Hughes being devoid of feelings now. In his case, the catch was plain dumb ignorance and selfishness which made him into a user, the prince of users, Jimmy thought. Let anybody tell him he was wrong about that.

Jimmy came round the bend where the monkey trees began, dribbles of slurry spilling out between them from the extension of the tip where part of it banked steeply into the farm yard. There were old cowsheds, pig sties still in use, a dried-up well and a cluster of corrugated-iron lean-tos surrounding the little courtyard and the kitchen garden through which ran an old path still paved with coloured stones and with traces of a mosaic that must have been shaped by some feminine hand years before Old Wacco came.

The main dwelling house, an L-shaped building with kitchen and back door bordering on to the courtyard, faced the tip, and what must have been the front door and best room of the house looked down over the trees into the valley. Jimmy could never remember being in the front part of the house since he had to call there, and as far as he knew, it wasn't used. Whenever he saw Wacco, Wacco was either in the yard or the kitchen. If it was cold, he sometimes slept in the kitchen, never even taking off his clothes. Jimmy knew, since he'd been there when Wacco rolled out from under a ragged blanket by the fire.

Jimmy hadn't been inside any room since the old man's day, but the sight of it through the open door made you want to itch. There was so many things in it, bits and pieces of things, broken bits of furniture, old rags, bundles of clothes, even a mincer from the long decayed dairy where Wacco ground up meal by the fire in the cold weather, the remnants of bran smelling the room out and leaving a spray of meal over the floor covering. The old man wouldn't have had that, but Young Wacco just went from day to day, pushing aside his own mess, and living worse than an animal. If he'd had a child or young person there, the authorities would have closed the place up, but there was no chance of that. Nowadays, you wouldn't get a gipsy up the drive, let alone into the house. Not that he'd any call for pegs, Jimmy thought, but for the other, yes.

Jimmy's unease continued. For so long, he'd ignored Wacco and had done what everybody else did, shut him out of his mind, but now it occurred to him that if his mother'd been alive, she'd have made it her business to take a fowl over, or a bowl of soup, or just have called. No matter how dirty Wacco was, however gone in his mind, he was a human being.

But he'd done nothing for Wacco, Jimmy thought; and not only him, but Henley, the only woman he knew who still wore a dust cap for cleaning! Think of what Henley would do for this Moelwyn Hughes. If it was Moelwyn Hughes living nearby, Henley'd have taken in his washing and tested the water with a thermometer before she dunked his woollies! But not for Wacco. And not him either, Jimmy thought guiltily: he was just as much a dead loss to Wacco, and now Wacco'd cut himself off and stayed cut off. He'd gone right into his mind and put the barriers up. But they should have tried. They should have pushed something through the door, made the gesture in spite of Wacco. If Wacco'd had the ham that Molewyn Hughes never would pay for, he'd have been in his oils — like a kid on a Sunday School treat. Unreasonably, Jimmy blamed Hughes for making him feel guilty into the bargain. Why couldn't they all stay on their own patch and leave him alone?

In the yard, the studs of his boots made a new sound with their hard metal tread on the cobble stones. He gave plenty of warning, coughed and scraped his boots as he approached the back door. He seemed to be noticing new things every second. Now he saw — as for the first time — an old brass knocker in the shape of a hand which, although green with neglect, must have been screwed into the door sixty years ago, probably at the discretion ot the same hand which traced the delicate pattern of the mosaic path. But now it did not work and remained closed up to the bare wood of the door from which a proper coating of paint had long vanished. There were still minute streaks of red embedded into the grain of the wood, but the wood took on the grey pallor of rotting wood everywhere, and on it there was a rime of fine coal dust blown from the tip. The rime covered everything, even the stone work and you could not put your hand down on any single object without taking it away soiled. The dirt was also in the air and although you couldn't see it, Jimmy thought he wouldn't be surprised if even the pigs didn't have a case against the colliery for what they'd inhaled. Blaen y Maes, he thought, it was too much. You either laughed or cried. Preferably in some other place and well away from there.

He knocked with his fist at the door, three cheery taps.

'Wacco? Wac boy. It's Jimmy.'

He stood back to survey the upper window, surprised at not having started the old sheepdog which Wacco kept, but there was no movement from inside or outside the house and now, in the silence, he could hear raindrops dripping from the trees in the woods and then the minute tricklings and slitherings of surface dust on the tip. He was just about to leave, anxious to seize any excuse when he heard a low muted coughing inside.

Jesus wept, he thought. He tried to remember when he'd last seen Wacco but he couldn't place the day. It might have been a week before. He called for the milk money at the end of the month, and even then, always took care to receive the coins in a gloved hand. Wacco gave you that feeling. Jimmy looked miserably round the yard, then there was a movement inside and the door opened, dragging on one hinge. Wacco stood there stockily in shirt sleeves and greasy dungarees, his face red-eyed and pale, and his hair, which he cut to basin shape himself with a razor, tousled and matted into a grey mess. As usual, he smelt, blinking stupidly now, his drawn face always appearing to surface from somewhere, then not responding to what confronted it. He seemed to see Jimmy as bigger than he was and ran his eyes over him wonderingly.

'I just called, Wac,' Jimmy said sheepishly. An infection had begun in one corner of Wacco's right eye, drawing the eyelid down slightly. One more damn thing, Jimmy thought. Everything about

Wacco set you on edge, grated you.

'Not your day,' Wacco said at the back of his throat.

'Not for the money. The money can wait.'

'What for?'

'Just not seeing you.'

Wacco did not seem to understand. Jimmy looked over his shoulder where he saw the sheepdog lying in a makeshift cardboard cradle beside the embers of the kitchen fire. The dog was half-covered with Wacco's blanket and three shabby cushions were propped beside it. It was clear that Wacco had spent the night before the fire with the dog which now lay motionless with its eyes closed, and Jimmy could just hear the faint warble of breath coming from the dog's chest. Its coat had lost its sheen. Its hairs were spread over the blanket, the cushions, the floor, and thickly distributed on Wacco's clothes. There were traces of vomit on the blanket but Jimmy felt no repulsion, realizing that Wacco had been nursing the dog all night. He could just see the dog in Wacco's arms, the one gentleness shared by father and son, and that was another thing too, being made to understand that. One damn thing after another.

'Took sick?' Jimmy said.

'He can't keep nuthin down.'

'Colic,' Jimmy said. 'Did you try milk?'

'Tried him,' Wacco spoke past Jimmy, looking blankly out into the yard all the time.

'Warm milk?'

'Tried him.'

'Biscuit?'

'No good.'

'Biscuit in warm milk? On a spoon? Some sugar?'

'Tried him.'

Wacco's answers seemed to come by rota as if answering long remembered questions from the past. Jimmy looked in again at the dog. He knew that if he felt the nose, it would be unhealthily warm.

'I could take him into town for you. Get him a shot of something?'

Wacco spoke again to the yard. 'I tried them powders. Don't keep nuthin down.'

'Let me take him to town?'

'He's a goner,' Wacco said.

'Try him outside?'

'Can't stand. Not on his own legs.'

'Water?' Jimmy said.

'Can't keep nuthin down, nuthin at all.'

Jimmy shifted his feet uneaily. The stench from inside was pungent and he had an urgent wish to smoke. He turned his head sideways and noticed that the pig-feed still stood in buckets outside the pens. He felt a desperate need to make a gesture.

'Let me do the pigs for you?'

'Can't keep nuthin down,' Wacco said. 'I chewed it for him myself, but it come up again.'

Jesus, Jimmy thought. He did not know what to say.

They looked in again at the dog. It did not have the strength to raise its head and now gave an involuntary shiver, the wheezing of its chest getting noticeably fainter. Jimmy scratched his ear. He did not want to be there when the dog died. He could not have said why, and although Wacco's face was blank and his voice retained its curious cracked note with the flat monosyllabic utterance of those who seldom talk because they have no one to talk to, he did not seem particularly alarmed. But Jimmy could hear the pigs grunting as if they felt the disturbance caused by his presence. Again he shifted his feet awkwardly, then stepped back to shut out the sight of that limp shape under the blanket. He was on the point of capitulating already, his original purpose forgotten.

'Well, if there's nothing I can do?'

'I'll do them pigs now jest,' Wacco said. He seemed to be counting the buckets one by one, nodding his head sociably across the yard as if acknowledging familiar objects.

Again Jimmy felt Henley's presence pressing down upon him. ('And you didn't even try. You went there and left Moelwyn waiting in the car.') Jimmy licked the corner of his mouth, detesting himself because of the wrong he felt was being committed by his intrusion. But he'd better try. Just once. Try and fail, he thought, that was it. He thought of Henley not Hughes. Hughes would go and good riddance, but he'd have to live with her after. He'd try once, just to make the attempt.

He cleared his throat nervously.

'You er... you ever know a fella called Hughes — Hughes the wires?' he said as casually as he could. 'They put them radio wires everywhere years ago.'

Now Wacco looked at him slowly and carefully as if hearing a new voice which was saying something social, a quite rare occurrence and happily free of barked reminders of duty.

'What do he do?'

Jimmy scratched his head.

'Wires.' It was natural that he should first think of Old Man Hughes.

Wacco's eyes passed over Jimmy's face slowly like a traveller's over a terrain.

'Do he know anything about dogs?'

Jimmy suddenly felt an immense cheerfulness, the creases appearing momentarily on his face and deepening as he grinned happily.

'Nothing!' Ask a bloody silly question and you get a bloody silly answer, he thought. Well, he'd tried, tried and failed, and now it was all buttoned up.

But his relief was momentary.

Wacco's eyes wandered back to the motionless dog. He looked at it carefully, pouting with the effort of concentration.

'Best to shoot him,' Wacco said.

'Shoot him?'

'He's a goner,' Wacco said.

There was a silence as still as the tip. Jimmy felt his heartbeats.

'You still got the Mauser then, Wac?'

The silence continued as Jimmy heard the crows far off in the woods, the crack of a distant branch, then a pit hooter far down in the valley, all sounds slipping into limbo as the pigs began to grunt hungrily for their feed again.

'Mauser,' Wacco said flatly. Again that face gave the impression that he was trying to remember, that something would soon be conveyed, given time.

'You remember?' Jimmy tried to sound casual. 'When we was kids? You showed it to me once.'

Wacco looked intently at Jimmy for the first time, then suddenly began to shake his head rapidly from side to side, a vigorous movement like a child's, a frown of denial — an actual frown seeming to be willed on to his face. He continued to shake his head for seconds, his lips opening and closing, then pausing as he began to expel breath in a soft continuous *nooo*.

'Nooo...'

But he did not actually say anything; no single word came forth for which he might be pinned down and cross-examined later.

'Nooo...' and that was all.

Jimmy stared at him, suddenly seeing what must have happened all those years ago. The little act must be the one poor deceit which Wacco'd learned the hard way, cowering in some darkened shed away from the road when confronted by his father and the terrible side-of-the-mouth cursing that came when the old man's patience snapped. It was the one expression — this head shaking and soft expulsion of breath — which fear, forty years later, still had the power to shape on Wacco's unresponsive features and now Jimmy felt sick to his guts. He felt it so badly that he might at this very moment be witness of the beating, or worse, spectator and party to some dark unnatural act whose cause and effect had continued to live over the years only to be brought out into the open for the first time by Jimmy's curiosity. Well, he'd had his answer, he thought, and now he knew. There was no doubt as to who had murdered whom. But what did the truth matter?

He stepped back, his third pace away from the door.

'No need to shoot him, boy,' he nodded at the motionless dog, embarrassed by the shakiness of his voice. 'Won't be long. They go very quick like that.' He felt the dryness of his throat and cleared it.

But it was his alarm that remained, not Wacco's. Wacco grunted, shrugged his shoulders twice, an awkward movement that might have been a gesture he had copied from others, then went silently back into the house, dragging the door shut behind him.

Jimmy stared at the door, knowing that the Mauser, oiled, black and sinister beneath its mound of protective covering lay exactly where it had always been in the wall cupboard beside the fire — and next to it, in the ancient faded tea canister, the ammunition, also protected in the driest place in the house. The wound remained and so did the weapon.

Jimmy turned and hurried away. He knew they would never be allowed to film there, whatever Moelwyn said. All the way down the drive he expected a shot, but the shot did not come then, not that month, not that year, and when it did come, it was Henley who made the most of it, even seizing on the opportunity to latch on to Moelwyn Hughes, who was in town again addressing some function, and actually inviting him up to the house once more.

The expected had happened, but people liked to pretend that the details were beyond belief.

'The police has to break the door in,' Henley said excitedly. She'd been saving it up for a year as if Moelwyn of all of them, would care the most. 'They got Jimmy to go down with them. Wacco'd been dead for a month. They found I don't know how many bluebottles on the stairs and the pathologist went sick for weeks. He'd never seen anything like it in all his life. Tell Moelwyn, Jimmy!'

As ever, Jimmy controlled his irritation.

'He had the Mauser,' Jimmy said flatly. 'The dog died the day after we went there. I offered him a pup, but he wouldn't take it, and then he stopped the milk so I didn't go there. Nobody did. He didn't want it.'

'You know more than that, Jimmy,' Henley said. 'You told me he killed his father?'

'It don't matter now,' Jimmy said.

'But why?' Moelwyn began to say.

'Go on, Jimmy,' Henley said.

'Well, it was the dog-thing and the woman-thing,' Jimmy said.

'Tell him everything,' Henley said.

Moelwyn Hughes had shaved his beard and cut his hair so that now he looked more like a chief constable than ever. In addition, he sported a cherry pipe which kept on going out and having to be relit and Jimmy hoped it would burn the tongue off him.

'What about the Mauser?' Moelwyn said.

'He took it from its place.'

'Place?'

'Where the old man kept it in case the gas in his chest got too bad.'

Jimmy wished now that he hadn't voiced his certainty that Young Wacco had murdered his father but you only had to think of Old Wacco out in the mornings after rabbits with rags around his boots to soften his footfalls and a scarf over his mouth to deaden his coughing to know that he wouldn't make a mistake when cleaning a gun, which is what they said at the inquest. Probably the old man drove Wacco too far and the boy turned on him, and had the guilt with him all his life. It did not matter now and, if there was any one reason he'd plump for, Jimmy thought, it was the woman-thing. Poor Wacco had no woman, not ever, and this Hughes with that yew-tree of a pipe and yet another suit of country clothes had three women that Jimmy knew of. One extreme to the other.

'Tell him the rest, Jimmy,' Henley said.

Jimmy poured himself a drink, mildly pleased at being the man in the middle and even more pleased that everybody, including Henley, had finally cast him in the role of knowledgeable celebrity. There was no doubt that his status had grown but that was probably because the police got windy and wouldn't go there without him.

'Tell us what they found upstairs,' Henley insisted. 'The rats and women's underclothes!'

'Not that, I couldn't, no,' Jimmy said at once. 'They asked me not to.' His eyes fastened on the burnished bowl of Moelwyn's pipe. 'I mean, not to the general public.' He emphasized *general* as if 'General Public' were a person.

'Jimmy!' Henley said. She couldn't take her eyes off him.

'Well, I daresay everybody gets up to tricks sometimes in their lives, I mean,' Jimmy said to Moelwyn. 'Look at your old man with them wires.'

But Moelwyn was stodgily silent.

'Blaen y Maes,' he said into his glass. 'What a location! I knew we should have filmed there. Trees, drive, tip — it had just about everything!'

'That was the Hugheses for you,' Jimmy concluded, Hugheses in general and Hugheses in particular, and that was what prospered, the strain that ran in the breed.

Beck and Call

Two large gins, a vodka and tonic, a half of 'E' and a tomato juice? Very good, sir. Er, in case you're looking, sir, the *Financial Times* and *Punch* have been taken on to the verandah, sir. Captain Bellamy, I think, or one of the young gentlemen. No sir, we don't take the *Express*, but the Suggestions Book is here, sir? Oh, very good, sir. Yes sir, I'll bring them up to the billiard room, the heating is on and I laid out the frame. It is snooker? Ah, I thought. A drink, sir? For myself? Thank you very much indeed, sir, but not tonight. I'm having a week T.T., sir. My presentation dinner, yes. Well, if all you gentlemen are doing me the honour after all these years, what I say is, well, I've got to be in form, sir. Tip-top, sir. Thank you very much, sir. Very kind, I'm sure, and you other gentlemen too. Angostura bitters? They were on the bar, sir, but I'm afraid Captain Bellamy and the Secretary... On the verandah. It won't take me a tick, sir. Excuse me, sir, gentlemen...'

A man's speech is only part of his life, expressing his present self at any given moment, but Freddie Feeley, veteran steward of the Royal Ocean Yacht Club was a man with a past. If he was in the plush now, a chirpy sparrow of a man with the climax of a lifetime's service awaiting him, it had not always been so, and all his life, he never regretted the first steps he'd taken in a cetain direction. In short, he thanked his lucky stars he'd got out of Dan y Graig Street all those years ago. What were the Welsh valleys anyway? Coal, misery, unemployment... From the time he'd declined to exercise his Uncle Bertie's racing greyhounds for a pittance and signed on as a junior steward on one of the old Ropner boats, Freddie'd begun a new life in the catering trade.

'Beck and call', Uncle Bertie'd called it, but Freddie'd had other views. Not that the Ropner boats were a picnic. Heartbreak hash in a shack of a galley on a red-leaded tramp steamer, hooligans up topsides, Yemeni Arabs down below, cork-fender soup and a donkey's breakfast for a mattress that could practically walk aboard, there were so many pairs of legs living in it! But it was the sea, it was away, it was all over; up to Bahia, or round the Gulf, Odessa for grain, Bilbao for nitrates, and Dan y Graig Street just a mention on the allotment note.

Freddie'd stayed at sea until the war came and then a stroke of luck had come his way. Giving up the greyhounds as his contribution

to the national emergency, Uncle Bertie'd got in as foreman with a
firm of builders working on air strips in inaccessible places, and
when they needed to expand their catering side, he'd remembered
Freddie, so Freddie had the best of both worlds. He avoided
catching cold as many of his old shipmates did, and on the buildings, he'd met Molly, his wife. It was still beck and call, of course,
catering always was, but there was not much difference between
rednecks anywhere, whether they came cursing out of the fo'c'sles
of tramps, or shuffling from behind concrete mixers, and Freddie,
with Molly beside him, had done all right for himself. It was the
meat and 'taters side of catering, but he'd reason to be grateful to
Uncle Bertie. When the war ended, however, he took a second
major step.

'Plum job this time,' he'd told Bertie. 'Down the coast. Steward
and Stewardess, Royal Ocean.'

'Why don't you come home?' Bertie said. 'The Shot and Shell are
looking for a steward. I know a good few on the committee.'

The Shot and Shell was the local name for the British Legion Club
which catered almost exclusively for working men. Bertie didn't
seem to realize that the Royal Ocean was a premier yacht club. It
was not only gents, but there was ample room for Molly to express
her talents on the catering side. Judges on circuit often stayed there
and liked a tasty dish. There was no comparison and Freddie had
a feeling there were new vistas in front of him.

Uncle Bertie sighed when told. He had reservations about everything outside of Dan y Graig Street. 'I dunno, our kid. It's still beck
and call if you ask me.'

But Freddie only smiled. They'd done all right out of the war. In
American camps, they'd had American rations, access to materials
which were in short supply to civilians. There'd been perks galore.
But you could put Bertie in Claridges Hotel, deck him out in a new
suit, heat him under the sun lamp, and he'd still look for a Dai-cap,
still cast a slate-grey eye on a slate-grey world. He was a real homer,
Freddie decided; of the terrace, fixed and rooted.

But not Freddie. If Uncle Bertie remained ageless with the lean,
loping stride and suspicious eyes of his precious greyhounds,
Freddie was eager, always ready to oblige. Short, light, deft and
quick in his movements, Freddie kept his energy, a currant bun of
a man, always on the go, always anxious to please, his friendly, red
face often held to one side with one ear cocked in anticipation of
his life's work, the service of the members. From the start, he'd
fitted into the luxurious, red-bricked premises of the Royal Ocean,

and relished the high white choker collar of his steward's jacket with its anchor-crested gold buttons. In the early morning when he was alone, he often opened the bow-fronted windows of the lounge bar and looked out at the gusty waters of the same Bristol Channel on which he had once sailed.

He breathed deeply then, long and deep, never forgetting to pat himself on the back, and for twenty-five years he'd never had a regret. The bottom had fallen out of the tramping market, but occasionally he saw an old tub, hull down, rusty funnels awash as she clanked away down the channel. It often put him in mind of his Ropner days, and he remembered the mounds of galley potatoes which were bought cheap, usually because half the load would be going off, and peeling them would be a race against time and nature. He'd known poverty, he'd known rock-bottom. He'd seen heat-crazed firemen dragged screaming from the engine-rooms of coal burners to be forcibly hosed down on the for'ard hatches, and others go out of their minds with prickly heat, or drink, or whatever madness possessed them. The poverty of the sea was no different from the poverty of Dan y Graig then, but somehow it seemed more wholesome. Anything was better than watching whole families go down one by one with tuberculosis, or listening to the day-long coughing of diseased miners through the thin walls of terraced houses. In his mind, the presence of the sea added a cleanliness to things, but these were but memories now, and for twenty-five years he had put them to one side. He'd got into a way of thinking. Unpleasantness in the past was what happened to other people, not oneself.

As Molly said when they took up residence in the Steward's quarters which had exactly the same sea-struck view as the members' lounge: 'Freddie... I think we've arrived.'

In some ways, it was a Cinderella story. Both of them had been born poor. Molly was Irish and he himself had more than a leaf of the four leaf clover. Grandfather Feeley had come to build the Glamorgan Ship Canal, and was by way of being an itinerant pit sinker and hard-heading man, until Grandma Feeley anchored him in Dan y Graig Street. Molly was also short, but round, tub faced with tiny hands and feet and a high complexion which was often aggravated by the pace at which she did everything. Indeed, on the few occasions when they served together behind the bar, the speed at which they worked was inclined to make you breathless. They were like two buttons, hands and feet in accord, a perfect team, inevitably cheerful and uncomplaining. Molly did not spend much time in the bar since her main responsibility remained with the catering. It was Molly's skill as a cook, the fact that she had once been a kitchen maid in the old Shelbourne Hotel, that clinched the job originally. She knew a thing or two, did Molly, and while Freddie was a reserve cook, his cooking was real red-lead, Red Ensign.

'Do you a chop and chips? Spotted dick to foller?'

But Molly was pastries and sauces, game and Sunday roasts, good old-fashioned, rather than continental. When she made a tart or pie, or concocted her special olive stuffing for the occasional salmon bass which a member might have caught himself, she not only excelled herself, she became a cause for discussion, a true artist, competing with herself.

'I'm damned if her apple meringues are not better than her apple pie!'

'Have you seen what the woman can do with a goose?'

'Don't tell me. I'd walk a mile just to sample her cottage pie.'

'Cottage pie?'

'Wednesdays. I don't know what she puts into it, but it makes me ill to think of going without it!'

There were some who said that Molly was more of an asset to the Club than Freddie, but whenever this was brought up, Freddie had his defenders. Both of them had aged, of course, but Freddie had never put a foot out of place. He was as willing as ever, but never pushed himself; was not the pushful sort. Damn it all, there were stewards these days in golf clubs and places who actually joined uninvited into members' conversations! But not Freddie. Of course, if you did happen to be in the bar on your own and wanted a chat, Freddie could be quite engaging. Sharp as a tack too. He knew all the members' birthdays, most of their wedding anniversaries and would always remind you. More important, if you were rung up, for example, you were never said to be there unless he'd consulted you first.

'Mr Bodega Jones? Hold the line, Madam, I'll just see if he's in the billiard room. Whom may I say is inquiring?'

'A Miss Irene Karsalis, sir. Yes sir. Very good, sir.'

'I'm afraid Mr Bodega Jones is expected but has not actually arrived. Would you be so good as to leave a number? Oh, very well, Madam.'

Good old Freddie. He'd a bit put by, it was rumoured. Some even said he knew a good share when he saw one! Of course, he must listen to what was said: the night there'd been that God-awful row when someone wanted to propose an Income Tax Inspector, he'd tactfully withdrawn from the bar. Bellamy'd squashed that.

'An Inspector of Taxes? We shouldn't be able to open our mouths!'

It was a cardinal rule of the Club that if you put up a chap for membership and he was blackballed by the Committee, you resigned. Thus there were no Jews, bookies, or inspectors of taxes, and apart from one or two sailing people pure and simple, there was a comfortable air of good chappery, tinged naturally with military and naval flavour as one would expect. There was limited accommodation and Freddie had pressed the trousers of many a High Court Judge who preferred the Club to the official judges' lodging house and the company of ghastly politicians. Anybody couldn't be admitted, but of course, membership was officially open to all, and after a rugger international, say, you might even hear a snatch of a hymn in the native language from one or two of the chaps who had come in from up-country.

Freddie, naturally, never spoke about these things. It was not his business. More to the point was that he had never had a cross word with anyone in the Club and for twenty-five years, he had been happy with his lot. When Molly, whose high colour had been so constant that it was unalarming, suddenly complained of heart pains, Freddie took no notice, but when they became more severe, Molly, like the members, had no need to suffer the indignities of a general practitioner's surgery. There were several consultants who were members, among them, Mr Bodega Jones. When Freddie approached him discreetly in the wash room, he was only too happy to oblige.

'Of course, Freddie. I'll pop in tomorrow before lunch. If we want any tests done, I'll run her back in my car. My dear chap, don't thank me. I'm the cottage pie king, remember?'

This was what the members would do for you, and whatever people thought about the Club, Freddie's feeling for it was hardly equalled even by those who practically lived there like old Bellamy. Twice divorced, once widowed, Bellamy was the elderly heir to a shipping fortune. He was virtually married to the Club, often stayed late, chatting in his cups to Freddie. He never failed to buy Freddie a drink, tipped lavishly, and as the oldest member took upon himself privileges as befitted a constant resident. He was given to pontificating in his cups and there were nights when he and Freddie, alone on each side of the bar, had high old conversations. Freddie never took too much, of course, but he had waited on Bellamy hand and

foot, through gout, divorce, re-marriage, widowerhood, three Labour Governments and an unsuccessful prostate operation. They
had a special feeling for each other. Freddie was 'a damn good
chap', and Cap'n Bellamy was 'a real gent'. His captaincy had been
in the Home Guard but no one was bothered. If he was now
grotesquely overweight, with a face so inflamed and pouchy behind
his eyeglass that he often gave younger members the apprehensive
feeling of being before some snapping bulldog, Freddie knew better.
Had he not heard of Cap'n Bellamy extolling his virtues?

'For God's sake, we're not going to shuffle up with a cheque and
a handshake. The fella's given his life to the Club. And Molly...
God, Molly's not had a Sunday off in years. No, damn it all, we'll
dine him properly. This is the Royal Ocean. We'll give him the
send-off he deserves.'

'But Molly?'

'Molly can't come, of course. We've never had a woman in here
yet and we're not going to start now. But she'll understand, probably knows the form as well as half the new members. No, we'll give
Molly a cheque as well, but Freddie's got to be dined. I'll speak to
the Commodore. It's got to be Freddie's big night.'

Freddie's big night... The anticipated occasion took on a glow in
Freddie's mind. When Cap'n Bellamy said things were to be done
properly, he meant properly. There was to be no fat-arsing about.
They'd engage staff. The silver would be glistening, new candles
ordered to fit the ancient candlesticks. There would be a specially
thought-out menu, trips to the west to purchase prime fowls because they wanted to be sure of what they were eating, none of your
wretched battery stuff. There'd be fresh asparagus, imported
French artichokes, local lobster and a paté that didn't stink of a tin.
Then there'd be the wines. On special occasions, the Club broached
its stock of ancient port and Bellamy himself would give two bottles
of his grandfather's Napoleon brandy.

'Two bottles?'

'There's to be no damned cheeseparing. I keep telling you, it's
Freddie's last night.'

And the instructions did not end with the food. Members still
serving in the Territorials would be encouraged to wear mess dress,
blues or a bum-freezer, and miniatures would be worn. There would
have to be an orchestra, of course. They could usually manage to
bring in a quartet of the soldiery from the barracks, but when he
thought of music, Cap'n Bellamy had a brilliant idea. The one
outside function he sometimes attended in the company of an old

crony, was Burns Night when the Welsh MacGregors, Mac-
Tavishes and McCalls got out their kilts.

'How d'you feel about the bagpipes, Freddie?'

'Bagpipes, sir?'

'Nothing like the piper's lament after a gutful. We'll play you out,
old chap. That's if you can walk, and if you can't we'll carry you! I
intend to see that it's a night the Club will remember. As well as
yourself, of course.'

Freddie beamed; stood gleefully first on one foot, then the other.
He was itchy with excitement.

'Bagpipes sounds all right to me, sir.'

'Splendid. You going to have one, are you?' They were alone in
the bar and it was midnight. A number of magistrates were members
and there was no difficulty with licensing hours.

'Well, I'll have a small scotch, sir.'

'Nonsense. Make it a large one. I'll have the same. It won't be the
same here without you, Freddie.'

'Oh, I wouldn't say that, sir. The new man's...'

'Not the same. Everything will change. I quite understand that
Molly needs to take things quietly, but well...it won't be the same.
I only wish we could have persuaded you to stay on alone.'

'Well, we're both getting on, sir. We've got a little flat nearby that
Group Captain Evans very kindly...'

'Know all that, but it won't be the same.'

Despite the ferocity of his appearance, the wrecked, puce face
with its bloodshot eyes and cyanosed nose, Captain Bellamy could
not disguise a genuine feeling for Freddie. It wasn't just that the
chap was so obliging and knew his place, but there was a continual
cheerfulness about the little fella. His discretion was legendary, no
praise was too great for him, but Cap'n Bellamy's affection went
deeper than that. They were of an age and generation for one thing,
both in their sixties. Both had seen the world changing and although
he never spoke of it, Cap'n Bellamy had no doubt that Freddie
disapproved of the flippant casualness of some of the younger
members, just as much as he did himself. Then there were other
things. There was not the drinking these days that there had been.
Chap actually asked for a ginger beer the other day. Imagine that!
And not ill either. The trouble was the damned Labour breathalyzer
which that bloody woman had introduced. It had changed the social
life of England, as Bellamy had once observed, despite the immaculate
Red Dragon which Freddie loyally hoisted on St David's Day. It
meant that members left earlier than they did. Wives got their hooks

on to them, and worse than that — as if that were not bad enough — in the presence of certain people you couldn't express an opinion without the danger of being contadicted, that was how much times had changed. They'd put a stop to scraping barristers bringing in Labour cabinet ministers regularly, but they were still to be seen at lunch on occasions, and that was also a sign of the way things were going. And if that were not enough, there were the arty-farties, by which phrase Cap'n Bellamy included some of the chaps who actually came in roll neck sweaters, youngish solicitors and accountants to boot! There was no end to the irritations, but more than anything, like Freddie, Cap'n Bellamy missed the dead.

Over the years, Cap'n Bellamy had seen the old boys off, stockbrokers, docksmen, merchants, the old civic leaders, the people who mattered, their hearts, livers, glands, tubes or whatever, popping one by one, and there were nights when he remembered them all. It was usually when the club was empty and he and Freddie were left alone over companionable glasses. Then he looked dismally over the handsome hide chairs, before which *The Field* or the *London Illustrated News* lay unread, and he saw their faces in the empty chairs, heard their good natured laughter, smelt the smoke of their cigars, the fellas who'd brought him on as a young member. Men of susbtance all, he reflected, most of them like himself, men who had inherited wealth, and had gone to good schools and done their bit when called up. Captain Bellamy had a marked aversion to the smart, or the jumped-up. There was still such a thing as tone and breeding and, although in his younger days he'd fallen by the way here and there himself, that was to do with the total incomprehensibility of women. But he'd never let a chap down and was known for it.

But his really deeply felt regret was that a sense of decorum had gone. Whatever anybody said, the chaps these days were too casual, not a patch on the old boys. They'd come in nightly and there'd be sessions and yarns, and many a tale told. More often than not, there'd be sombody home from the Colonies who would add lustre. You could sit in the Club and let the world come to you, and compared to these bitter days there wasn't the filth about, certainly not the dirty jokes. These had crept in, like the sex pictures in the newspapers which disgusted him, but in the old days, if anyone said anything that was more risky than sporting, he'd always insist, 'Taters before tit!' and it generally brought a laugh. Of course, they'd always had a few politicals, and a good few had bought their knighthoods from that Lloyd George scoundrel, but that was really before his day. The important thing was that men of substance had kept together, and the members had the feeling that they ran things. More warming still was the fact that in the hierarchy of the the élite, the awed respect paid to inherited wealth and family connections remained exactly as it should be. He hadn't had to keep himself to himself so much then, but nowadays, apart from occasional chats with a few chaps of his own age, his late night conversations with Freddie were the most rewarding and pleasurable features of his membership.

'D'you remember old Doc Harris, or Mr Malliphant-Edwards?' he might say of an evening.

And Freddie would cock his ear. 'Mr Malliphant-Edwards...'

'Ah, yes! Liked a good Havana did Mr Malliphant-Edwards...'

'And didn't he own a horse?'

'Barbary Shore!'

'That's him. He put me on that for the Cheltenham Gold Cup.'

'Marvellous chap. Was on the Gold Coast as a young fella.'

'Up and down double, I had on him. Him and Feathers Flying. Never failed to give me a nod and a wink when there was something good going.'

'And Doc Harris? "Bellamy," he said one day,' said Bellamy.

'"Go on the way you're going, you'll never live to see Gussies reach double figures."'

'Gussies?'

'Great Universal Stores. Made a packet in his day, did old Doc.'

On Freddie's part, there was the same veneration for the past which was felt just as intensely by him as Cap'n Bellamy, with the equal proviso that the past did not extend outside the Club. He too remembered the old boys. He had a special relationship with all of them, and had never failed to attend a funeral. Indeed, he had a bowler and a dark overcoat which he had purchased especially for the purpose, and although he was often forced to leave the graveside before the others, this was in order to hurry back to the Club, as there was an unwritten law that the bar should always be open to mourners. On several occasions, Freddie had been remembered in wills when several small sums had come his way. Once when there was a sudden crop of deaths, three in a week, he had mentioned his difficulties in returning to the Club to Bellamy who had promptly put a car and driver at his disposal. That was Cap'n Bellamy. All for Freddie. All for the Club.

'I expect you'll be coming to my funeral, Freddie?'

'Be more convenient if you could come to mine, sir.'

'Why's that?'

'There's less of me, and it won't take so long to park with only the one car.'

'Fill 'em up again, Freddie. At least we'll go with a certain style, what?'

'I hope so, sir.'

More than anything, Freddie shared Cap'n Bellamy's prejudices. Both were survivors of an age of stereotypes. Provided a man knew his place, he could get on in this world. He may be able to advance only so far, but at least he knew where he was. The catering trade had always had its malcontents, but they were losers all along the line. A gentleman expected service. It was what he paid for, and there was no reason why he should not get it. At the back of Freddie's mind was the memory of all the attributes which he had picked up from the gentlemen. They had affected his whole life, his manner of speech, not least his dress. Off duty, when he very seldom went anywhere, save perhaps for a walk along the sea front, occasionally a trip with Molly to the cinema if there was a musical on, or their annual holidays to Bournemouth, he dressed like a gentleman. With curly-brimmed brown homburg, a subdued check-tweed suit and stout brogue shoes he was indistinguisable from the members, and if his little face had kept its sparrow's perkiness, there were times when he could fix an offender with a cold eye that was quite unnerving. A barman who served gin without ice and lemon might be made to cringe if he were young enough. If Freddie was with Molly in a restaurant and a salad came ill pre-pared, they had no hesitation in sending it back. Not that they were uppish, but there were standards, standards which they themselves adhered to, and they saw no reason why persons in receipt of their custom should not conform. Freddie, of course, could not get away with it quite like Bellamy could. He did not quite have the air to carry it off, but by restricting his disapproval to a few choked sentences, he found that he could be quite successful.

'Look here... D'you call that a salad? 'Fraid not. Won't do.'

'Oh, go on, Freddie,' Molly might say, and he would reply: 'No, my dear. There are standards.' It was usually enough.

But that was Bournemouth, that was holidays. It was the club which formed the perfect setting, the air of a private select world which had never let him down. In twenty-five years, he had not a single regret, and when he thought back to all those years of hardship and penury in the little house in Dan y Graig Street, the yapping of Uncle Bertie's dogs, Grandfather Feeley's coughing, the inevitability of lodgers, damp walls and the dismal smell of stewed tea on the hob — he breathed a sigh of relief. How he'd come on! 'Beck and call,' Uncle Bertie'd said all those years ago. He was still alive, still in Dan y Graig, and he still, through force of habit, regularly inserted a clean sheet of folded newspaper to strengthen the lining of his cloth cap, a seventy-five-year-old greyhound fancier whom Freddie visited twice a year. He'd done him a few good turns, slipped him a few quid now and again, but you couldn't do anything with the chap really, he was stubborn and fixed in his ways. Chip on his shoulder, Freddie'd long ago decided; the sort who'd never got on; hadn't moved from the house in which he was born. What could you expect?

It was Molly who raised an eyebrow when Freddie insisted upon buying a new dinner jacket on the eve of the presentation. Her heart complaint was not serious in itself, but she'd have to take everything more slowly, and that was all. Over the years, she'd changed less than Freddie and remained a kindly body, less impressed with the world but more content with it. She expected less, and perhaps that was her secret. When the matter of the dinner jacket came up, she was quite surprised. Freddie had a dinner jacket which he some-times wore on duty at functions. It was old, but seemed perfectly presentable to her and she said so.

He did not agree, raised his voice irritatedly.

'It will never do.'

'But if you get a new one, you'll never wear it again.'

'How d'you know?'

'When do you wear a dinner jacket, except when you're working?'

He did not answer that question, but it did not matter. He was adamant.

'Well, I must have one. I can't go in that thing, and that's that.'

Away from the bar, he was less polite. His accent often slipped. There was the occasional grammatical error.

'The arms is shining, and it's green under the elbows. Second-hand when I bought it anyway.'

She looked at him hard.

'We've got a bit put by, but I thought we were going to go careful?'

The steward's voice returned: 'I cannot be dined in that thing.'

'How much is a new one?'

'It doesn't matter how much it is, I've got to have it. Thirty pounds maybe — with the trousers as well, of course.'

'*Thirty pounds?*' Molly remained frugal. 'And just think, when I was a girl, ten shillings would do to have enough on me, and for by!'

Freddie was not in the mood for the memories of an Irish girlhood.
'I'll need a shirt too.'

'A shirt?'

'They wear ruffles nowadays, and I can't have the old tie, it's made up.'

'Made up?'

'I shall get one of them you ties yourself.'

'You won't want a pair of fancy boots to go with it as well, will you?'

'It's got to be proper. They're taking all the trouble, it's the least I can do. Must look right. Besides, the cheque they're giving us won't be less than a hundred quid.'

That settled it. Freddie would be dressed discreetly, quietly, but absolutely correctly.

When the evening arrived, Cap'n Bellamy arranged to meet Freddie at the Steward's quarters in order to escort him formally into the Club as chief guest. The evening was to begin with decorum and there was not to be a hitch. Promptly at seven, Cap'n Bellamy arrived resplendent in dinner jacket, his two victory medals glistening in his lapel, and below them a scarlet cummerbund which he had acquired from an uncle who had fought in the Boer War and which was known as Red Sea rig. It amply contained his paunch and he felt it added dash, a ghostly reminder of a young buck with a waist. He gave three taps on Freddie's door, as solemn as Black Rod.

Freddie, equally resplendent, waited inside. He nodded to Molly who answered the door of the flat.

'Good evening, Molly,' Cap'n Bellamy gave a half-bow and managed a smile. He was not averse to a few condescending Irishisms. 'Is your man in?'

Freddie appeared, slipped a hand into the jacket pocket of his dinner jacket, his fingers comfortably warming an ancient silver cigarette case, the bequeathed gift of a member.

'Good evening, Cap'n.'

Bellamy expected him to come at once. They were all waiting downstairs in the Club, the Commodore and the hired Scots piper hovering at the main door, and the members at the ready behind.

'All set then, Freddie?'

'All set, sir. But you've been a good friend to me, sir, and I was wondering, well, if you might do us the honour of having a quick one before we goes down, sir? I've had enough drinks with you, heavens above.'

Bellamy blinked, taken aback. He had never been near the steward's quarters and had intended to return immediately. But seeing the serious look on Freddie's set little face, he could but comply.

'That's very kind of you, Freddie.'

'We'd like it, sir, as you've been such a special friend.'

Bellamy entered. It was a cosy little room, as you might expect, in apple-pie order.

Apart from a brandy after dinner, Bellamy stuck to scotch through thick and thin, but Freddie, with due regard to the proprieties, was going to begin with a fine, dry sherry.

Molly served them, declining anything herself.

Cap'n Bellamy was not sure whether or not he should sit down, so he remained standing. 'Here you are, Captain.' Molly was inexplicably nervous. Shrewder than Freddie, she had a sixth sense for disappointment, an in-bred nose which made her more reserved and cautious in her expectations. Or perhaps she just knew her place.

'The very best to you, sir, and our thanks,' said Freddie once more.

'To you both.'

Molly did not join them in the toast, but Freddie drank his sherry at a gulp. It was a gesture, inviting the Captain into the quarters, but one he felt he had to make. He had a dreadful memory of his mother inviting the police court missionary into their house when one of his brothers was in trouble, remembered her embarrassment and the phrase, 'Take us as you find us.' He wanted to clinch the fact that he had escaped all that.

'Well, then, skin off!' said Bellamy draining his glass. 'Very pleasant. But come on, Freddie, we're all waiting.'

Molly said nothing.

They made their way downstairs and Bellamy took care to see that Freddie should precede him. Every courtesy was to be extended, and indeed, the Commodore anticipated their descent and there was a swirl of bagpipes, warning members. As Freddie approached the lounge, the doors were swung open, and Freddie suddenly found himself the centre of attention as scores of faces turned his way. Almost every member had made it his business to attend, all of them wore evening dress and here and there, he could see the blues of the officers who had retained service connections, and one young man, a Lieutenant in the Royal Marines whose father Freddie remembered, wore a brilliant scarlet mess undress which stood out amongst the others. Even the younger members whose informality had been a cause for complaint had made the effort, and

all stood watching his entrance, their welcoming smiles enough to
bring tears to a man's eyes.

But Freddie did not blink. He had prepared himself well.

The Commodore shook his hand warmly.

'Commodore,' said Freddie, with a polite nod. But that was all.

Thinking him to be tongue-tied, Bellamy took Freddie by the
arm, and as they made their way to the bar, conversations began
again.

The new man had already taken over, and stood nervously
awaiting Freddie's pleasure. Other attendants had been engaged
and were busy serving.

Freddie stood to one side of the Commodore, a taciturn ex-naval
man.

'What'll it be, Freddie?'

'A dry sherry, if you please.'

'Bellamy?'

'Scotch.'

'Two scotch and a dry sherry for Mr Feeley.'

Mister Feeley... Freddie could not but notice. Exactly as it should
be.

There was some pleasant conversation. What was he going to do
with himself in his retirement? He'd given no thought to it. Molly
must take it easy, of course. Walking was the thing, the Commodore
said, but that set Bellamy off. He wouldn't be suprised if all the fuss
made about exercise was subtle propaganda on behalf of the shoe
manufacturers! The conversation was easily informal, but when the
time came to go into dinner, the Commodore called the members
to order, and again, he and Bellamy took up positions on either side
of Freddie and led him to be dined. Again, there was no shortage
of staff. It had been made plain to the outside caterers that this was
the Royal Ocean. The clear soup retained its clarity and flavour only
if served precisely at the right time and at the right temperature. As
Freddie said, there never was any hanging about.

Afterwards, he could not for the life of him remember what he
ate. Even though there were over a hundred present, there was still
a choice, and there were wines to go with each course. He remembered asking for a little of this and a little of that, but there was a
good deal of chat to take his mind off things. Members sitting near
called over and made jokes.

'I fancy that frilly shirt, Freddie. Touch of the Monte Cristos!'

He smiled politely, took care not to have too much to drink,
although he could not help mixing his drinks, but he stuck to the

grape when he could. The Commodore was a bore, but he was conscious of Cap'n Bellamy by his side firmly looking after him. Both refused lobster claws and Freddie was grateful for the choice here, as the instruments for extracting the meat seemed unmanageable. He had a savoury dish instead, proceeded to the fowl and on to the dessert, a tasty drop of creme caramel that Molly often served a home whenever he found his Rennies ceased to cope with his acidity. By the time they got to the 'Queen', and before the port was served, he was a little troubled by the fact that he had run out of his fund of small talk. Behind the bar, he had a cheery word for all and was an expert at following on another's conversation, but when he was the centre of attention, he was in deep water, he soon saw. He could think of nothing further to say. Best to keep his mouth shut then.

Cap'n Bellamy seemed to be doing the same, and the Commodore very seldom said anything. Of course, the meal took ages, despite the excellence of the service. There was simply so much to eat. Fortunately, his silence did not seem to bother anyone. But he still felt uncomfortable. He had locked up the beer pumps the night before after days of handing over to the new man, days when he had been so busy, so anxious to get things exactly right, that he had somehow missed the thought that he was doing everything for the last time. He'd counted up the bar chits, totted up his bits and pieces of accounts, advised on reordering, done such chores as marking the tankards of members who could not drink out of a glass, and even written certain instructions regarding the brewery callers and the temperature of the cellar — all without thinking exactly why he was doing it. He had done the same thing with relief stewards before going on holiday and this occasion did not seem much different.

But slowly, as slowly as the dinner progressed and one course followed another, he began to realize what he was losing and to understand the significance of the occasion to himself. He had heard many conversations about retirement. Some spoke of it as the ultimate; lazy days of doing nothing, being at nobody's beck and call. (There it was again, Bertie's phrase.) But others thought of it as a kind of creeping death, a slow dwindling into uselessness, empty hours before the grave. Of course, they hadn't put it in those terms, but he had never much minded work. Bar service might be difficult in these riff-raff places where they suddenly got coach-loads of trippers descending on them, but his life had been quiet enough. And he had a wholesome memory of real hard graft before he'd come to the Club which stood him in good stead. It wasn't the work side he minded losing, it was the company of the members. He had been so busy these last few days that he had not thought of it in such clear terms. They were not only dining him in a fitting manner, they were taking their leave. He probably wouldn't see them again, all these faces that now smiled so readily at him. He looked at them, and already saw them slipping away, moving into limbo, leaving him quite alone. It was like being present at one's own funeral.

'Freddie!' Captain Bellamy hissed. He had been staring into his own glass.

'Sir?'

'After the Loyal Toast, the Commodore and myself are going to speak, then young Miles-Morgan on behalf of the young members. Commodore's going to present, then you'll be expected to say a few words. All right? You know the form?'

'Oh, yes.' He had been previously told and had prepared something, but his thoughts had sudenly gone haywire. A veteran attender of other people's funerals, he could not rid himself of the image of the grave which had implanted itself in his mind. He had a feeling he was falling backwards, deeper and deeper into limbo. As the Commodore stood up, moving his chair back noisily to propose the royal toast, Freddie felt his stomach contracting. He felt sick and giddy. All round him, the faces of the members ceased to have understanding and blurred before him. Naturally, they were looking in his direction as he sat next to the Commodore, but they were looking at him and not seeing, he felt. It was quite frightening. Could the dead see who mourned them? They couldn't possibly. Then why had he gone to all those funerals? He had always believed that some feeling communicated itself. He couldn't let a member down, he had once said, and he meant it. But now, for a second, he felt he was himself looking above ground, straining upwards at a sea of faces, all peering incuriously down upon him.

'Gentlemen be upstanding for the Loyal Toast!'

He got to his feet with the others, relieved to feel blood still flowing in his arteries.

'Mr Vice — the Queen!'

'The Queen!'

It was ridiculous, this feeling. But it was real, he even heard the swish of wind in the trees, the droning of a grasscutter far away in the distance, the crunch of black shod feet on gravel, the slamming of car doors, the cars driving away, one after the other, the silence again — as if they were leaving him there to rot. He blinked them away, these awful sounds. As he sat down, he felt the sweat trickle under his armpits and his throat was dry. He tried to focus his eyes on the Commorore who had remained standing, an erect, firm-shouldered man whose taciturnity was in the style of the old time naval captain, a figure of fear living silently aft.

'Gentlemen, I need hardly tell you why we are gathered here this evening. We come to honour, we come to praise...'

Golden words, and well-chosen as far as Freddie was concerned, but he scarcely heard them. He'd escaped everything, the Ropner boats, the war, the graft of the buildings, even the routine chores of married life since he seldom had an evening free. They'd avoided having children, devoted their lives to other people, Molly and he. So what awaited them? Anything could happen with heart conditions. There was no guarantee they'd be together long. He had a riveting picture of himself sitting cold and alone on a park seat, children laughing at him, a solitary figure nodding away foolishly to himself, an unknown. Where could he go?

Bellamy had taken trouble with his speech.

'Now of course, there are seven Freddies. There is the Monday Freddie, the ever-present squire of the cardsharps! Tuesday's Freddie is much like any other, and Wednesday's Freddie is a very magisterial figure. It is the Late-night Freddie, however, for whom I have the deepest affection. What is seen in a glass darkly, often beats the light of day!'

Hearing the members laugh, a gathering communal chuckle accompanied by much slapping of the hands on the tablecloth, Freddie nodded automatically as he often did behind the bar when there was something said which he did not quite catch. He remained perfectly still, but his chaotic thoughts were forming into a conclusion. It was very simple. He did not want to leave them, didn't want not to serve them, didn't want them to be without him. There were times when he'd complained and grumbled and he had his likes and dislikes like other men, but now he experienced such a welling up of fellow-feeling that it caused his stomach to flutter. He couldn't bear not to see them. He owed them so much, fathers and sons now, and he had come to recognise family traits, nodding wisely to himself as a particular gesture gave his memory a jog. He couldn't be going from there forever. If they knew how he felt, they couldn't let him leave completely.

'And in presenting you with this cheque, Freddie, I want you to know that although it might seem unduly generous' — it was for two hundred guineas as Bellamy'd doubled it at the last moment — 'in our view, and I say this on behalf of all of us, it is poor reward for the service which you have given us.'

There was more of the same, spoken with utter conviction and much interrupted by deeply felt Hear-Hears. Indeed, Bellamy had a wet eye and removed his eyeglass, Freddie noted. Their generosity would put any other club to shame. It was handsome... handsome. But surely they couldn't let him leave entirely. They just couldn't. Out of the depths of his depression, a hope was born.

He got to his feet. He'd prepared a short speech with a little joke about Molly and how he was going to keep her cooking all to himself, another about his stock-exchange information, and a formal return of Cap'n Bellamy's funeral car, all personal jokes which they would understand. But when he got to his feet, he had the greatest difficulty.

'Commodore, members of the committee, gentlemen...' he managed, but then swayed slightly. His fingertips were numb. At the back of his throat, it seemed as if there were a tight knot of strained nerves. He became barely audible, speaking the absolute truth.

'It is very kind of you. I've done nothing for you that I haven't wanted to do. I've been as courteous to you, as you have been to me. I have been happy here.'

But he hesitated. There was a suspicion of a sob in his voice and Bellamy seeing his predicament, leant forward.

'Well done, Freddie.'

Freddie's voice grew more emotional. He tried to remember a phrase he had rehearsed.

'I know that Molly will join me in thanking you, but...' his voice broke altogether.

Bellamy tugged at his sleeve. 'That'll do, Freddie.'

But Freddie did not sit down to the tumuluous applause which he would immediately have received. He could not. For the first time in his life, he looked down upon all of them, the members in their finery, and his immense respect and goodwill for all of them acted like a current, a great surging stream of feeling that engulfed him, causing his little head to shake and his lips to tremble as his voice broke again. He recited his idea with a desperate urgency, the lazy slurred vowels of Dan y Graig thick in his speech once more.

'See, I can't bear to leave, and that's a fact. What I'd like more than anything, more than this money, all that, is for you to make me a weekend member or something, so as I could come in once in a while and buy you all a drink... 'Cos you bought me so many... I wouldn't let you down...'

The silence of the grave marks the end of a life, the final barrier, but Freddie had not yet come to it. For a moment, it seemed as if he had, and after the very real silence that followed what was later referred to as his temporary breakdown, no one spoke for a full thirty seconds. It was so embarrassing. Bellamy's thoughts were put in such a turmoil that it quite unnerved him. Fella'd fogotten himself completely. Cracked at the last moment... A member indeed? But behind his instinctive reaction to such a preposterous request, he had a more dismal feeling, a real intuition of the barriers that separated them and always would. The truth was, there was nobody he'd rather see on a boozy Sunday morning, nobody alive nowadays. There was no one who understood him better, nor who had catered for his needs with such kindly dexterity. He'd prefer Freddie's company to almost any single living member, that was the irony. It was like having a thing about one of the maids at school. Out of the question, but damned upsetting! Who'd have thought Freddie would overstep the mark?

But when Freddie returned to the Steward's quarters, Molly came straight to the point.

'How much was the cheque?' She had waited up for him to ask the question.

The swirl of the bagpipes continued below, but now there were louder noises as the furniture was sent crashing about and the younger members began their horseplay. Freddie had left as quickly as he could after the port was passed. No one said anything, but he had been left with the unmistakable impression that he had let himself down.

'Here...' he passed over the cheque.

'Two hundred?' she raised her eyebrows. 'Did they do you proud then?'

He nodded automatically.

'What's the matter?' She studied his face. It had taken on a bitter scowl.

'I've got a cob on. Bastards,' he said. He repeated it. 'Bastards...' There was spittle on his lips, a pounding of his heart that he had not felt for years.

She made him explain.

'Oh, Fred...You didn't?'

'I would have stayed at the corner of the bar,' he said indignantly. He was very near to tears. 'They always give the drayman a drink. And the Brewery travellers. I only thought, a Sunday now and again?'

'But Member's different.'

He shook his head confusedly. Perhaps he hadn't known how to express himself. His wish for company was the simplest thing. For the first time in his life, he had overstepped the mark, he supposed. And what a night to pick! He could imagine Uncle Bertie grinning, could see the grin, the knowing wink, the deep drawn folds on his thin face creasing as his lips curved downwards — the grunt that would follow.

'Beck an' call.'

But he would have a hard valley's answer:

'Since when did you make two hundred nicker on a straight take? Show me the dog can make that?'

He would never understand it, such a simple request, the grave-yard silence, the averted eyes, the refusal even to discuss it. Oh, they'd been jolly enough after. The moment he'd sat down, he'd had offers of drinks galore. Bellamy'd been tight as a tick and kept squeezing his shoulder warmly, there was no doubt about him. It seemed there was only one conclusion. It would never have happened with the old boys. Even if Bellamy'd put him up, he would have been overruled. Blackballed, they called it. He felt like a nigger, a real Kink, and he'd been born and brought up within twelve miles of the place.

But then Molly didn't see it either. You couldn't say she wasn't on his side. Oh, wasn't there someone — anywhere — who under-stood what he was feeling? How could you give half your life to a thing and then it kicked you in the face, the moment your real self was exposed? What was the answer?

It couldn't be that now they had done with him, they had no more use for him. It just couldn't be, they weren't like that, the members. They were standards, after all.

It must be the young members, he thought finally. They were increasing in number. And that Commodore, a real straight-striper he was, 'not granted' written all over his face.

He suddenly had a real need for an enemy, one person, anyone, just a face and figure at whose feet he could lay the blame.

Effie

"Please God let him be unsuccessful. Dear God, I couldn't stand to come back here. I daren't tell him, or anybody for that matter, but please God let him fail this time. I'll do anything, only don't let him come back here with a smile on his face. I couldn't bear it. Please God ... Please ... anybody?'

It had been five years since Effie had awaited her husband's return from a job-seeking interview, five years when their future seemed assured, five years of permanence, four-and-three-quarter years of bliss in their smart bungalow in the Karen district of Nairobi. There, the houseboys, the garden boys, the swimming pool and the mass of bougainvillaea over the terrace where they took breakfast after the rains — all combined in Effie's memory to form images of a style of life which they had now left quite firmly behind them. Kenya was memory; reality now was Dan y Graig Street.

The Morgan-Pritchards were home, staying for the time being with Aunt Morfydd in Dan y Graig's only detached house overlooking the Welsh market and mining town where Effie's husband, Barton, had grown up. Effie herself was English, a florist's daughter from High Wycombe, but she had met Barton when nursing in Queen Alexandra's Royal Naval Nursing Auxiliaries, and she had come to regard Dan y Graig Street as their U.K. headquarters since her own parents, like Barton's, were dead. Aunt Morfydd had brought Barton up, and still lived in the same house with her father who was ninety-seven. It was a large, if gloomy, house, and while theoretically there should have been room for them to escape each other, the problem with the Morgan-Pritchards was that, like many Welsh families, once the got behind the same walls their lives became impossibly intertwined. Goodwill and concern were omnipresent. You could not cough without solicitous inquiries being fired at you like bullets, and there were times when it was so claustrophobic that Effie wanted to scream.

Even the old man whom they called Dada added to the feeling of containment. He had survived a broken hip, countless pleurisies, two world wars, Aunt Morfydd, and ninety-seven wet Welsh winters, only to sit staring at her with that drooling concern which Effie found so depressing. Not that he was soft.

If his lips caressed that disgusting pipe, his eyes were sharp and bright, so shrewd in fact, that Effie wondered if he had guessed her secret.

Africanization was the reason Barton had given for the termination of their employment in the service of the Kenya Government. The Africans wanted their own in key places of employment, so it was Africans in, and Europeans out. At least, that was the story they'd decided upon, and as Barton said when he finally referred to the subject of their hurried leave-taking, once you decided upon a story, you stuck to it. Not that the real story was anybody's business anyway.

Effie sighed as she recalled, then ran her eyes over the chocolate brown wallpaper which the old man insisted on retaining in the living-room, and found a smile for him.

'Would you like a cup of tea, Dada?' Barton had gone down the valley to the County Hall where he was to be interviewed for a senior lecturer's post. What depressed her most, was that his qualifications were excellent and his background impeccable.

The old man stirred in his chair, twisting and untwisting a stained pipe cleaner.

'It should take a time. You know what these committees are.'

'Yes. Would you like a cup of tea?'

'Education,' the old man cackled. 'I always said, the most ignorant sit on Education Committees. The natural selection of the unfittest, I always said. They seem to recruit them on that principle. The councillors, I mean.'

He had been a colliery manager but his family were rooted in the area even before development of the coal industry, and his longevity seemed to confirm beliefs and prejudices he must have held seventy years before. His family had always been there and the rise and fall of the coal industry only confirmed suspicions which they must have held in the beginning. No good came from outsiders. In the past, firebrands like miners' leaders disturbed the natural distance between master and man, and as for these councillors, the Labour lot who had dominated the area since the First War, they were no better than scum who had risen to the surface and stayed there. He had ninety-seven years of observation upon which to draw, no one had contradicted him for thirty. He spoke as a man who knew.

All of which Effie thought a frightful bore, like most of the things which Barton's relatives did or said. Why they had to come back here, she would never know, she'd told a friend. But that wasn't strictly true, alas. Barton had come running across the world to Aunt Morfydd like a slighted child with a cut finger. He would never have explained himself, but he'd come home just the same.

'I'll make a cup of tea,' she stood up.

'Not for me,' the old man said.

'I feel like one myself.'

The old man smiled, studying her as she passed him on the way to the kitchen. She was aware of his scrutiny and did not like it. It might sound absurd, but the moment she turned her back, she felt she was being eyed in that unmistakable way. She clutched the silver chain which hung loosely over her tightly fitting trousersuit. If he was ninety-seven, she was thirty-nine, and with her straw blonde hair, arched eyebrows, wide knowledgeable mouth and large blue eyes, she had acquired a manufactured Swedish look that served its purpose in the number of men who turned around to take a second glance at her. It suggested if anything, that experience sat more obviously on her shoulders than the old man's. 'The dirty old Bee,' she thought now, but suppressed a giggle. If accused, the old man would probably have had a heart attack on the spot. And she was no prude. She ought to be grateful to him for taking her mind off Barton's interview. One healthy thought at least had penetrated her gloom, a hint of desire entirely free from the cloying odour of Welsh nonconformity which surrounded her. If her suspicion was true, that is. She made a charitable reservation. No one would ever know for sure.

She filled the kettle under the tap and looked up at the back garden, which like everthing else, seemed to be built on a slope. The garden, untended now and full of sour rhubarb run to seed, stretched up to a wall that backed on to a sullen tump of mountain behind which a distant, overgrown coal tip was visible. It was South Wales everywhere you looked; crowded terraced streets, coal tips, football pitches, working men's clubs, back-to-back houses, ugly industrial scars, a ravaged, played out country. Nobody would accept that, but Barton wanted to come back there permanently, 'back where he was from,' as Aunt Morfydd said. She seemed to glow when she said it. She was a maker of statements in the effusive South Wales manner.

'Well! Home now, is it?'

'Yes, Aunt Morfydd.'

'Back to where you belong?'

'Yes, Aunt Morfydd.'

'And Effie too, is it?'

'Settle in here a treat the moment she finds her feet!'

Not if she could help it, Effie thought, recalling the conversation. Barton said, 'Yes, Aunt Morfydd' mechanically, his accent returning as he buttered her up, keeping that soulful expression of glee on his Aunt's face, his yesses like the plucked notes of a one-stringed guitar. No sooner was he home than they were as close as close. Effie often wondered if the old man had any inkling of the destructive nature of that closeness.

'Woman, you'll strangle the boy! Give him a few minutes peace at least,' she'd heard the old man say several times. They hadn't been inside the house five minutes before Aunt Morfydd was clucking away, worrying about the suitability of the bedroom 'after the tropics'. Were three blankets too many? Did nylon sheets irritate the skin? Would they like a fan? There was one upstairs after an Uncle Bill who had come home from the wars 'riddled with tuberculosis'. Why he wanted a fan, Effie would never know. What she did understand was that Barton was on the run from her, but like everything else he did, it was to be a token run. She still had to be with him, following behind, witness of the direction his feet were going, and victim too, that was the hardest thing to take. As for Aunt Morfydd, Barton turned her on like a tap, awakening all the maternal instincts once more. No doubt they loved each other in their own way, but beneath the softly spoken concern for themselves, there was an intensity of feeling from which Effie shrank. Custard pie on top, if thwarted, Aunt Morfydd was huntress, tooth and claw, Effie was sure. She was a big, capable woman, her physical strength making her a superb layer-out of the dead, consoler at grave and death bed, a titan in troubled times. She had that Welsh expertise that came from familiarity with disaster which the valleys seem to breed, but there was another side of the coin which was less acceptable. Knowing her meant total involvement. There was no privacy, and privacy there had to be, Effie knew.

'Took your time over tea?' the old man said when she finally returned to the living-room.

'I let it stand,' she said evasively.

'In that case, I'll have a cup.'

He had changed his mind just to annoy her, Effie was sure, but she smiled sweetly.

'Of course.'

Her nursing experience had taught her that some old men would cheerfully wear you out with their fetching and carrying, and for a moment, Effie felt sorry for Aunt Morfydd.

'Three sugars,' the old man called querulously. As she poured the tea, Aunt Morfydd came up the back path. Barton once said that Aunt Morfydd used the front door sparingly. It might have been a Sunday-best door. Incomprehensible to any save the Welsh.

'Well! Making a cup of tea for Dada!' Aunt Morfydd exclaimed
as she entered. 'Three sugars, mind!'

'He told me.'

'He would.'

'First, he wouldn't have one, then he would.'

'That's Dada. Now you know what I have to put up with,' Aunt
Morfydd said. She never lost an opportunity of saying that, but the
moment she entered the kitchen Effie noticed that she immediately
took over the arrangements, pouring the other cup for herself
without even bothering to remove the large purple hat which she
wore for attendance at the numerous charitable committees over
which she inevitably presided. Presently, they were all seated in the
living-room.

'It seems no time at all since we sat here waiting for news of
Barton's scholarship.' Aunt Morfydd said.

'Scholarship?' the old man sucked his tea.

'Eleven plus, remember?'

Effie calculated. It was thirty-one years ago.

'In the war, yes,' the old man said mischievously. 'They reduced
the standards 'cos of the threat of bombing.'

'They did nothing of the kind,' Aunt Morfydd said indignantly.

'Not the bombing, but the sirens. The children were forever going
down the shelters in case?'

'They did lose a lot of time,' Aunt Morfydd conceded.

'So they reduced the standards?'

'You don't remember, Dada,' Aunt Morfydd said with a smile.

But Effie was sure the old man was right, and if he were right and
Aunt Morfydd didn't agree, then he didn't remember accurately. It
was Aunt Morfydd's technique.

But, whoever remembered, the living-room itself seemed to be
soaked in memory. Dada would not allow any changes to be made,
and there was such an aura of other people in the room that Effie
felt stifled by the past. There were brass shell canisters from the
First War, the badges of long forgotten regiments emblazoned upon
them. Then there were portraits of Barton's uncles, victims all in
one war or another. Inexplicably, these were fronted by a long
photograph of a Sunday School treat, a group including Aunt
Morfydd which had been taken outside a charabanc in the Brecon
Beacons. The photograph was at least forty years old. In returning
from Kenya, Effie and Barton had not only changed one continent
for another, but the present for the past, it seemed, and Effie could
not help but be affected by it. For all her apparent composure, she

wanted to scream. She clenched her fist, suddenly feeling her
hysteria return. How did she know that Aunt Morfydd thought her
a hard bit of stuff? She remembered that Barton had overheard a
conversation soon after they'd got engaged. But she'd been a hard
bit of stuff who'd lasted and kept her place in Barton's affections.
  Until Kenya...
  Effie dug her fingernails into the palm of her hand and hid the
hand behind her back. Why did these people never do things on the
spur of the moment? Why was everything so calculating? Why was
she herself not more charitable? Why did she have to reduce things
to such dreadfully simple proportions? She was not a hard bit of
stuff, had never been. Although her appearance had improved as
she got older, when she was in the marriage stakes she was much
more inclined to plumpness and there was a dowdiness about her
which she didn't fully understand. Nursing took a toll that showed,
and as soon as she'd realized that she wasn't going to marry the
inevitable doctor, she'd gone abroad with the Q.A.R.N.N.S., seeking to widen her experience, and it was in the Navy that she'd met
Barton who was doing his national service. She'd found herself a
husband but it was only after years of unsatisfactory affairs that had
never led to anything serious. Perhaps she'd been too easy going,
too ready for anybody's bed, even then? She'd never had a satisfactory
relationship that didn't involve sex, and then, after a month or so,
men tended to go off her. It was a crude way of putting things, but
then life was crude in her experience, especially for the plain girl. It
had taken seven years to find out there was no Prince Charming
waiting around the corner, only Barton, and Barton was serious,
concerned and needed her. If the truth be known, Barton was the
best she could get, but it was a dreadful truth. It made a human
relationship less than it was, and reduced her to the 'hard bit of
stuff' image which Aunt Morfydd had all along suspected.
  But Christ, what did Aunt Morfydd know about anything?
When she'd met Barton after a wardroom guest night in Trinco-
malee, he'd had — what did they call it these days? — a sex
hang-up that you could have used for a case history. She'd solved
that, and their marriage had been what an almoner friend had
called a working marriage. The candidate passed in some subjects but not in others, and that was a practical, commonsense
way of looking at it. But in her heart, Effie knew that she did not
want a practical, commonsense way of looking at anything. What
she wanted was to blot out the memory of those three afternoons
in the summer rains when Barton was away down in Mombassa

atthetechnicalcollege conference.

Three afternoons and three nights, dinners at Bobbe's bistro where they gave her a red rose and nobody ever raised an eyebrow at Donkor being with her, probably because he was in the police. Everybody knew the blacks could be worse than the whites where colour was concerned, but Donkor had a way with him, and moreover, his polished Police Commissioner's accent would have made even Aunt Morfydd sit up. 'You don't have to tell an African about sex,' Donkor said when Barton challenged him. She could see the sweat standing on Barton's forehead and clouding his spectacles now. He'd looked abject and ridiculous, whereas Donkor, caught in the act, immediately assumed a poise which would have done credit to a Home Office official at tribunal.

'Of course, you realize that we shall have to go home at once?' Barton said.

And Donkor'd replied, 'Isn't that taking things a little too far, old chap?'

Old chap. She remembered sitting silently in the corner, listening to them as if it was some other person who was involved. She didn't feel guilty then, only about the houseboy's sobbings in the kitchen. Barton had wrung his neck with a show of force that was quite unacademic, but he'd got the pertinent details out of him. Physically, the houseboy had suffered most of all, lost his job in the end, and Barton had unreasonably refused to give him a reference which was practically a death sentence if he wished to get employment with Europeans again. Poor Charlie, she thought as she remembered him. Charlie was a Luo but Donkor was a Kikuyu and gave him not a second's thought. Tribes covered the world, she thought.

But not the summer rains... If only she could get Barton to believe that her adultery was in some way contributed to by the climate? Africa was Africa after all. They'd often joked about the sexual potency of Africans before, and she had been curious, but no more. If she had sat chained to Barton on a desert island where he could not escape, she could never have convinced him that Donkor's attractiveness was rooted in the fact that he was so English, tribal marks and all! Donkor had a calm, droll, almost 'county' acceptance of the world in which he lived and ruled in a minor way. He was also considerate and what her mother would have called a perfect gentleman. And he spent freely, which Barton did not. Barton, in fact, proudly boasted that he had never given anyone a tip until he was twenty-six. It might be practical in Dan y Graig Street, but it certainly didn't cover Africa. 'Bit of a nose-picker, old Barton,'

Donkor'd said. She had not replied, but her silence was a chilling thing, she saw now. Barton would never have allowed anybody to have spoken out about her in that way.

'Oh Christ!' she said to herself. 'The messes you got yourself into!' Three afternoons of summer rains, then thirty years of Dan y Graig Street. What a future! She'd done all she could to persuade him to apply for a job in Maidstone where she had a relative on the Education Committee. She'd begged and finally wept, but Barton had remained his obdurate, wooden self. He was coming home where he belonged. Although he said that he'd forgiven her, he implied that home was all he had left. So finally, she'd accepted that and come home with him. Nobody knew, of course, and they'd invented the Africanization story which would no doubt hold up in the interview since Barton had impeccable references. Why had she come herself? The odd thing was that, having cheated on Barton, she now felt sorry for him. The stuffing had gone out of him for a time, but it also meant that he had lost that pompousness which came with his steady crawl up the academic ladder. Stripped of his lecture room omniscience and the accompanying stomach patting gestures that made her want to scream, Barton was almost young again, young, earnest and unsure of himself. He was also sexually more active, paying her more regular attention in a way that was not altogether unpleasant.

Life was a conundrum, she thought; quite without rules she could follow. You only found out about yourself when you had been truly yourself, for however short a time. Did that make sense? Effie had wondered about that all the way home on the boat. Perhaps human beings were like hermit crabs who inhabited borrowed exteriors, only to break loose when confronted with warmer currents of the blood which were stirred when the unexpected happened. It was an attractive idea if only she could forget Barton's wretchedness at the time. Hence her panic as she thought about the interview. She tried to order her thoughts, to put things into place, to sort out her real feelings. As a theatre sister, she had been brisk and efficient, but when it came to her own guilt and involvement, she was not above praying, a return to the habits of childhood above her father's little shop when all was well, provided the Saturday flowers did not go off over the weekend.

'Look, he must have some feeling left? He must have. I came home with him, didn't I? I could have stayed. Anybody would think I was the first? And he said, it's all forgotten. Over and done with. Finished! He said it. Well, does he think I'd do it again if we went to Maidstone or somewhere?

Hawk it all over the place? Well, I'm not that sort. Dear God, I've never worked in places where they talk any other way, men and women... Look, it wasn't me that didn't want children. It's him and his bloody meanness. I'm quite ready to start a family... Look, I said I'd stay with him, be a wife to him — everything, only dear God, let him not come walking up that path with a smile on his face. I can't do anything for him here, not with that woman, I can't. If anybody's responsible for anything, she is. She is, I swear it. She and this God-forsaken place...'

'Penny for your thoughts?' the old man said tremulously, interrupting her.

She blinked. They were alone again. Aunt Morfydd had gone into the front room so that she could look down the street and be the first to see Barton's car.

'Oh, I was just thinking about the interview,' Effie said unconvincingly.

'Very good in interviews, Barton.'

'Yes, I know.'

'Say enough, and not too much, that's the secret.'

'Exactly.'

'Myself, I'm suprised he's come home at all.'

'Oh?' Effie said. She looked the old man full in the face. The lack of collagen which came with age had caused the folds of his skin to multiply and his eyes stood out brightly like buttons against wrinkled parchment. Was there a twinkle in them now? If there was, it was more knowledgeable than compassionate.

'This place is dying,' the old man said. 'What's the sense of coming home for the funeral?'

'Barton doesn't see it quite like that,' she replied.

That was the other thing. How did Barton see it? Like many South Walians who leave home in their teens and never really return except on holiday, Barton retained a warm, myth-inspired image of a tumultuous valley community whose pre-war qualities of shoulder-to-shoulder empathy caused him to think of it with a nostalgic glow as a special world-defeating place. It was true that it had once been unique. Its name was synonymous with lack of deference to privilege. It was the birthplace of working-class folk heroes, and the ghost of an ancient culture still hovered about it, but now film stars and opera singers perpetuated legends which trade unionists were forced to forget. Like the film stars, Barton preferred the myth to the reality and retained the exile's enchantment with a never-never land, and nothing would shake it.

'Why come home then?' the old man asked her directly.

She shrugged her shoulders, indicating her own discontent. It should have been obvious that the decision was not hers.

'You want to put your foot down,' the old man grumbled, but then he said something which she did not quite catch and about which she would spend the rest of her life wondering. It sounded like, 'Stop his oats or something?' But it couldn't have been that. It just couldn't. The trouble was that the old man often mumbled away incomprehensibly. So she pretended she did not hear, and they did not continue the conversation because Aunt Morfydd entered the room noisily.

'He's come,' she announced excitedly, then hurried through the living-room to the back door.

Effie caught her throat. More than anything, she dreaded his smile as he came in through the kitchen door, but Barton astounded them all by using the front door. She heard his key scrape in the lock, then his footsteps in the passage. When he enteed there was a smile, but it was apologetic, flirting with his thin lips, puckering the corners of his eyes behind the thick 'interview' lenses which so distorted his appearance. He had grown a moustache on the boat coming home and now it added to the aggrieved expression above his hunched shoulders. He was defeated and putting on a front. He had worn that expression before.

'Granted,' he said, just the one word.

'What?'

'Your wish.'

Aunt Morfydd came rushing in, her arms outstretched.

'Well?'

She was prepared only for success.

'I'm afraid not, auntie. The qualifications of another candidate were preferred.'

'What?' Aunt Morfydd bristled immediately. 'Name him,' she seemed to be saying: *age, date of birth, family, religion, councillors canvassed, degrees, research, previous experience — any other business!'*

But Barton merely nodded. He sat down in the chair and began to remove his best black shoes which had remained at home during his African sojourn and now pinched his feet. 'But who?' said Aunt Morfydd.

Barton named the successful candidate and Aunt Morfydd immediately placed him, his family, his connections, even made a swift calculation of the number of votes likely to be pledged in his favour no matter who opposed him, but Effie did not listen. Poor Barton, she thought. He had lost his illusion about her, and now he knew exactly what he was up against at home. Two illusions shattered in his forty-second year. It was too severe to say that now he could grow up, but that was her hope.

'I'll make you a cup of tea,' she said to Barton.

'No, you won't. I will,' Aunt Morfydd said. She had been interrupted in mid-sentence; 'Councillors? — Don't talk to me about councillors!'

'I think he'd prefer *me* to make it,' Effie said firmly, and went into the kitchen.

She could picture Aunt Morfydd's face, her lips curving into a disapproving O as compact as the muzzle of a rifle, then biting her tongue so that she would not go 'too far'. But Effie did not care. She felt relieved, even elated, and checked an inclination to whistle as she stood by the kitchen window and waited for the kettle to boil. There were two other things that were also gone forever, Dan y Graig Street, and the long lean limbs and lithe muscular body of Commissioner Donkor.

'Hi ho,' she said to herself, looking out at the one, then finally dismissing the other. The act of dismissal had taken months, but now at last it was complete.

'Did you see her face?' she could imagine Aunt Morfydd saying when they were gone. 'Not a muscle moved on it. I always said she was hard faced.'

But perhaps, stamped on that big-boned, fresh coloured, Saxon face with its frank come-hither eyes and ironically parted lips, there was the clearest of all indications which only certain men understood. She was also English, and there were so many things about which she did not give a damn.

Bowels Jones

'Mr Bowcott Jones has the gripe,' Fan Bowcott Jones said to the Portuguese guide who had inquired. *'La grippe, n'est-ce pas?'*

'Sardines in charcoal?' the guide said with a charming smile and a fey waggle of his braceleted wrist. He was young, dark, and beautiful, with neat hips swathed in scarlet flares like a girl's. 'Cook in charcoal, no? Just the peoples from the hotel?'

'No, he's not feeling well. *L'estomac!'*

The guide persisted in not understanding.

'In a boat with fishermans, Portuguese style?'

'I shall come.'

'But of course...'

'But Mr Bowcott Jones is inconvenienced.'

'Vous parlez français très bien,' the guide said, and took out a handsome red purse. 'I shall require two hundred escudos for the two.'

They stood outside the bedroom door on the fourth floor of the Hotel Lagos in the Algarve. The guide had come all the way up the stairs since the lift was out of order, but Mrs Bowcott Jones could not make herself understood. The Portuguese were simple and charming, but the confidence with which they assumed they understood everything was profoundly irritating. They were grave and serious, more attentive than the Spanish, and the food, if you ate it in reasonable quantities, was infinitely more value for money. But this year, like the last, Bowcott had found a pub where they gave the impression of listening to him, and once again, it had led to excess.

Mrs Bowcott Jones sighed, searched her vocabulary, and finally said in a mixture of Spanish, French and Portuguese, overlaid with a sympathetic Welsh valley accent: *'Solamente uno!'* She held up one finger. *'Señor Jones — non! Pash favor, uno?'*

'Ah, jest one?' said the guide, flashing his teeth.

'Pash favor,' Mrs Bowcott Jones said again, returning his smile. They were extrordinarily sexy, these nut-brown boys. If you gave your mind to that sort of thing.

'One hun'red escudos for je..st the one?'

'Momento,' Mrs Bowcott Jones went into the bedroom and closed the door firmly behind her. Now her expression changed and her voice became harder as she looked down at the gross, fleshy bulk

of her husband who lay motionless on the bed, his chin bowed and thick knees doubled up over his comfortable belly in the attitude of an elephantine embryo. Bowcott was bilious again.

'No good asking me for sympathy. You're fifty-six years of age, very likely Chairman of the bench next year, but the moment you're abroad, you're like a sailor off a tanker or something,' his wife said sharply. The neat figure of the waiting guide had irritated her, and now the lump of Bowcott's heavy form reminded her of the white rhino in Bristol Zoo, the highlight of school trips when she was a child, and later a primary-school teacher.

Bowcott attempted to speak, failed, and said nothing. Years ago, he had thought his wife a little common, but it had the effect of increasing his self importance. He could condescend from time to time. But now he could just moan and was in danger of being sick.

'Oh, Fan... Oh, *Duw*...'

'Whatever you think you're doing, I'm going on the sardine trip.'

He opened his mouth once more but realized that his lips were partially stuck together, and gave himself an intelligence report. Booze *and* fags, he thought. He'd meant to stick to cigars.

'Just the people from the hotel. It's a deserted beach,' his wife said with some emphasis. 'And there's no need to make a face like that. The people on the tour are very nice people. English, of course, but they all asked after you at breakfast.'

Bowcott gave a little belch. He was getting old. One night on the tiles meant that there were days that got lost, slipped past the memory, notching themselves on to his stomach, however, like knife slashes on a branch.

'Where's your wallet? The guide is waiting.'

That was another thing. He couldn't remember where'd he'd put his wallet. He rolled over in a pool of sweat and felt under the pillow, but it wasn't there. He could not remember what he'd done with his shirt and shorts for that matter. Avoiding his wife's eye, he slid a glance in the direction of a nearby chair. But his shorts and shirt were missing too.

'I washed them,' Fan said darkly. 'Well, I couldn't send them to the laundry. I daren't. And your wallet wasn't in them. Oh, for goodness' sake, what have you done with it?'

She had been asleep when he had eventually got home in the early hours of the morning. He had been in the English Tavern in the village, a place he privately referred to as a hot spot, but things had got a little too hot, and now an extraordinary phrase kept repeating itself in his mind.

'For Chrissakes, the bogey's got his shooter out!'

It was such an alarming phrase for a man like him to have heard at all. There was a note of hysteria in it, but as he tried to fit it into place, he recalled incidents from the previous night, images floating into consciousness like the interrupted trailer of some incredibly seedy film. What had happened this time?

His wife turned impatiently to the dressing table drawer where they kept the passports. The wallet was not there either, but his passport was. Hidden between the folded pages, there were a number of high denomination notes which she knew he kept there for emergencies. They had always smuggled a little currency out of the U.K. You never knew when it would be needed with Bowcott. She took two five-hundred escudo notes and snapped them in his face.

'I wouldn't be surprised if I didn't really *spend* today. Some of that ornamental silver is expensive enough,' she said punishingly. She folded the money into her purse, put on the pink straw hat which she'd bought for the occasion in San Antonio, picked up her Moroccan handbag, and finally the Spanish stole from the package holiday of four years ago, and then marched to the door.

'The mixture is beside your bed,' she said at the door.

'Mixture?' he said hoarsely. He sounded like the victim of a pit disaster.

'The kaolin compound you had from Lucas Thomas the Chemist. Four spoonfuls a day,' she said, getting it wrong. *Two spoonfuls four times a day,* the instructions read, carefully written in Lucas Thomas's feminine hand writing. 'Although what Lucas Thomas knows about conditions here, I can't imagine. Portugal is not Dan y Graig.'

Her last words. She slammed the door which did not close and he heard her brave Spanish once more.

'Vamos a ir. A los sardinhos,' she said to the guide who had remained.

'Senhora is multi-speaking?' the guide said politely. 'In your absence, the lift is working.'

'Obrigard,' she pronounced carefully. She went to the first three lessons of the language classes in the Women's Institute every year. It gave her enough to be going on with, apart from prices which she insisted on having written down.

Still immobile, Bowcott heard the lift descend, feeling like an overworked seismograph. His stomach was so distended that each part of his anatomy seemed now to distinguish sounds, as well as record its own special suffering. Although by now the Bowcott

Joneses were veterans of the short quick trips all along the *Costas*, he always forgot himself sooner or later. If it wasn't the sun, it was the food or the wine, and although he usually reserved the big bust-up for the end of the stay when he could at least be in flying distance of Lucas Thomas's healing potions, this year he had gone over the top on the second night in.

Perhaps it was a mistake to come back to the Algarve? In one week last year, he seemed to get to know the town, and they had returned expecting to be celebrities, only to find that last year's crowd had moved on. But it wasn't only that. The trouble was within Bowcott himself. As his wirey, ninety-three-year-old mother said, 'Wherever we go, we take ourselves with us,' and it applied absolutely to Bowcott, just as much as did her other countless sayings: 'He would go too far...' 'Beyond,' as she said, using the word in its dark, Welsh sense; and she was right.

This year again, there was the extraordinary feeling of Welshness which came upon him abroad. At home, the valleys being what they were, if you'd had a dinner jacket before the war, and there hadn't been a lavatory 'out the back' for three generations, you were always minor nobility. Not to have had anything to do with the pits was blue-blood itself, and since the Bowcott Joneses had been wholesale fruiterers for years, he was a man of property and substance, and had always been so. But get him abroad, and the old ilk was still there, a wildness of spirit and a capacity for living recklessly that was now beginning to shake his fifty-six-year-old frame as much as it delighted his image of himself at the imbibing time. Fan, fair play, was as good as gold normally. A collier's daughter wasn't going to moan about a drop too much, or the occasional accident, hygienic or otherwise, but this time, there were additional complications. The world was changing, Portugal and Wales, and Bowcott had suddenly become caught up in a sea of feelings, even ideas, that were strange to him. If only he could remember, he was sure it was all very frightening. Something had happened which placed him on the map. But what was it?

It was not simply that he had taken too much to eat and drink. Not this time. And he doubted whether his condition could in any way be attributed to Lucas Thomas's fawning habit of dispensing without prescription. Both of them regarded the valley's solitary Indian practitioner with some reserve, and for matters of the bowels, Lucas was very good on the whole. But perhaps the streptotriad tablets, advised and dispensed as a prophylactic against gyppy tummy, were too strong. For Welsh mams with filial problems and an aversion to the smell of alcohol, Lucas actually kept animal chlorophyll tablets of staggering breath-cleansing propensities. Perhaps the strepto-what's-its were also out of Lucas's VIP draw? Perhaps between them, they had been too clever by far? Was the thin, anaemic figure of Lucas Thomas, pin-head ever bobbing and smiling obsequiously behind his affected Douglas-Home lenses, *a guilty figure?*

In fairness, Bowcott did not think so. Lucas had seen him right through a number of marathons in the last two years, Twickenham, Murrayfield, Dublin and even the Paris trip which was an exploder, a real gut-buster, yet Bowcott was still standing after sixty-four hours of playing and drinking time when former Welsh rugby internationals had gone under the table, triple crown and championship notwithstanding.

Talk about Bowcott and you weren't talking about a cauliflower-eared colliery fitter. As Lucas Thomas said, 'Old Bowcott knows his Raymond Postgate. Hell of a *bon viveur* ackshually.'

But others put it less delicately.

'By God, you've got a constitution, Bowcott!' a former Welsh centre had said when he walked off the plane at Rhoose before they drove into Cardiff. Alone of the party, Bowcott arrived clanking with duty free booze, fags and perfume for Fan, and walked, what is more, despite an inflamed eye or two, with a spring in his step. He might have been bringing the mythical triple crown home in his back pocket.

'I just keep in with Lucas Thomas,' he usually said with a snide tug at his clipped moustache. 'One needs a chap to look after one.' What he really meant was that he couldn't abide that Indian ghoul who didn't seem to understand the need for a blow-out or the demands of a palate like his own.

But now he was knackered. The wogs had got him in the guts. He slipped into the vernacular when he felt sorry for himself, and he lay on the bed like an infantry officer who'd been bayoneted against the trench wall. He felt as if they'd done for him good and all, his triple crown constitution notwithstanding. Once again, the hoodoo was down below the belt. It felt like snakebite and gave him second thoughts. Perhaps he should have gone to New Zealand anyway and followed the Lions? He would have, but for Fan, although when he read the advertisement, 'Six hundred pounds and two years to pay,' he'd felt tempted, but then decided against it. It wasn't so much that he couldn't afford it, but with payment on the never-never, it meant that a right lot would have been going on the trip. Of course, Bowcott was no snob on a rugby trip but, sport apart, he had a position to keep up as a magistrate. 'Out of town, we South Walians are all much the same,' he used to say with a twinkle whenever he addressed the Lodge or the Rotarians, but the truth was, New Zealand was too far for Lucas Thomas's ministrations. Lucas had always been his secret weapon.

His former adviser, he now thought bitterly. He wanted to think of anything rather than the muddied events of the previous night. But that damned voice returned. That incredible sentence...

'For Chrissakes, the bogey's got his shooter out!'

It was a common English voice, but for the moment, he could not put a face to it. He knew the police were involved too, but fortunately not with him. That was a relief. He closed his eyes and tried to trace back the roots of his involvement, but his mother's voice came back to him. She was always uncannily present after remorse-begetting situations.

'Bowcott, you will always be judged by the company you keep.'

'For Chrissakes, the bogey's got his shooter out.'

That was duologue for the record books.

'Your father was a man of substance. Admittedly, he marched with the miners in '29, but of course, they were a lot of rodneys, half of them, not Welsh anyway.'

'Welsh...Welsh...' he groaned. What memories on a Portuguese morning! Roots were always a problem, had bothered him when he and Fan had taken up their position at the bar near the swimming pool yesterday. Fan had put on her sun dress and he wore the khaki shorts and short-sleeved bush shirt which he still affected on these occasions. He'd also worn a straw fedora and the thick leather belt he'd bought in Malaga two years before. There was, as ever, the District Commissioner look that he cultivated before he let his hair down. Commissioned in the R.A.S.C., he'd been in Imphal later in the war and, now and again, let the phrase 'Wingate's mob' drop. It gave an impression that was not strictly accurate, but now most people did not remember, and he'd just qualified for the Burma Star so sucks to anybody who challenged his credentials. He was President of the local British Legion anyway, and his knees were brown enough in the old days. He'd been around, as they said, quite long enough to look after himself.

Why then, had things gone wrong?

He cast his mind back to early morning. A shaky day had begun beside the hotel swimming pool where English from Romford had arrived in large numbers. Previously, he and Fan had always found what Fan called 'a good class of people' on holiday. She meant rather far-back, posh accents, persons verging on county stock, justices of the peace at least. These, the Bowcott Joneses either accepted or did not. Ex-Indian Army people, they got on well with, anybody military who drank an occasional excess if you wanted a definition. In previous years, they'd met a very engaging old boy, Sir Philip Somebody-or-Other, and his wife from Bushey, and she'd also been nice with it. Nice with his full-time drinking, that is to say. In fact, on that holiday, she and Fan had had two spare time drunks for husbands if you wanted to put it in an unkindly way. It was what they had in common, a circumstance that immediately rose above geography and class. But now both these veterans of the bottle were dead, and over the years, the Bowcott Joneses had noticed that the people who went on package tours had changed, and that was the start of it yesterday by the pool, a decided lowering of the tone.

The irony was that they could have tolerated a Dai Jones, or a couple of Rodneys. In the previous year, they had taken to an Irish couple and been pleased to show them the ropes, but the Romford English were quite impossible. They were careful with their money, always checking their change, wrongly suspecting the waiters of robbing them, often shouting with those whining Home Counties accents, sometimes leaving the best part of the asparagus, drinking beer with meals instead of wine, moaning about tipping habits, and making no attempt to speak the language. Bowcott who always called all foreign currencies 'chips', tipped lavishly, and when tight, insisted he was *Pays de Galles,* and had little jokes with the waiters, like announcing as he came into the dining-room, *'El Presidente arribe!'* or *'Voilà la Chef de Policia!'* in *shoni*-foreign language, and the fact that he attempted to communicate delighted everybody. It told everybody that he was a large jokey man, and not mean, and the waiters gave them better service and huge, daily smiles. As at home, he felt a character and was the richer for it, but yesterday, for the first time, the Romford lot had put the kybosh on it, and more than anything, their voices infuriated him.

There was a child with freckles who did nothing she was told and whose parents could not stop talking. You did not take an early morning gin by the bougainvillaea to listen to them.

'Emma... Emma, don't go into the pool.'

'Emma, you'll get orl red.'

'Emma, if your brother's bein' a berk, there's no need for you to be.'

'You tell him, Dad. If he think's he's goin' to get away with that for change of a hundred 'scudos, he've got another think comin'.'

'Go on, Dad, tell him. You was in the Army.'

'Pardon? Pardon? Isn't the toilets' system rotten? Pooh...Raw sewage, I could smell. Reelly...'

Listening, Bowcott had never felt more snobbish. And years ago, if anybody had said Tom, Dick or Harry were coming abroad, he would have protested valiantly, but he sadly realized that now it was true, and felt vaguely ashamed. Unless they were careful, they were going to have a thin time of it. Very well, the thing to do was to cut loose from the package tour and investigate the terrain.

'*Emma! Emma, come and put your nix on!*'

That bloody child...To get away from Emma, and Emma's red-necked parents, Bowcott anchored himself permanently in the far corner of the bar, leaving Fan to snooze under the sun shade. He ordered a second gin and tonic (large), and looked philosophically at the glass.

'*Bom día,*' he managed to the barman.

The barman smiled, and in response, Bowcott showed him a trick with Worcester sauce. A minute drop cleared the rime from a grimy escudo and the barman was suitably impressed. Thereupon, for devilment, Bowcott sprinkled a little sauce into his third gin and tonic, no more than a drop, but enough to give the teasing, iron-man impression that broke the monotony of the morning. And, after that, he had to have another one to clear the taste away. Then there was the sun. Although his body was shaded by the canopy of the bar, his legs were burning, but the moment he decided to take a dip to cool off, what amounted to a Romford water-polo team arrived and made that impossible.

'To you, Georgie! Georgie! Not out of the pool! Oh, shit, you've knocked a bottle over.'

Bowcott woke Fan under the sunshade. She was a marathon sleeper.

'I think I'll have a stroll down the Vill'. I don't think I shall spend much time here.'

She blinked amiably.

'Be back for lunch?'

'Of course.'

'I should cover the back of your neck if I were you.'

She sounded like his mother. He nodded, found his fedora, buttoned his wallet pocket, and marched away, four gins down. The hotel, a hastily completed building especially created for the package trade, was surprisingly elegant with marble vistas and lavish copper fittings, reminiscent of the Spanish paradors. It would have been splendid if it weren't for the people at present in it, Bowcott thought. He now saw the Romford mob flitting in and out of it like fleas, their twanging voices affecting his nervous system so that he actually twitched once or twice. Getting old, he thought. Getting old and finding Buggins everywhere. He was pleased with that phrase. It was rather Army.

So it was in his District Commissioner mood that he walked down to the village, fat legs, heavy buttocks, belted girth and thick arms swinging as he affected a military gait along the rough, cobbled track. Several *burros* drawing carts passed him, their aged, black shirted drivers eyeing him inscrutably. It was a poor country, he noted once more. Every piece of woodwork needed a coat of paint, plaster flaked from the walls of the narrow cottages, and the burnt, arid soil behind them was lifeless and without green. There was not a flower to be seen, and the children ran about bare-footed in the streets while mangy dogs stretched out in the shade, and here and there, a caged bird sat lifelessly outside the houses. The few Portuguese pedestrians he saw, lowered their eyes when they passed him, or else paid no attention. They were neither surly nor obsequious, just there, passive spectators of the doings of the Lisbon speculators who'd brought the tourists there.

Poor peasants, Bowcott thought. Sad old men and women in black, unaware of the world that was changing about them. He felt vaguely sorry for them, but he was too much of a man of the world to entertain the idea that anything could be done for them. Two soldiers came around a corner, their shabby red berets, lounging gait and lacklustre boots catching his eye. For a second, he half expected them to salute, but they were just peasant soldiers, homesick boys without a spark of life left in them. He felt sorry for them as well, and at the bottom of the hill where he passed a small infirmary for the tubercular, he felt that half the soldiers he had seen might well have been garrisoned there. Once again, he felt sorry. Fair play, he thought, the old wogs never had much of a chance and didn't even look inclined to do much for themselves. Perhaps it was the heat?

By now, the back of his neck was burning. It was August and the wind that blew from Spain stayed there for the month, but he walked on masterfully, tipping the straw hat back. He never wore sunglasses on principle. You could never see what a man was thinking in sunglasses, and he detested people who wore them indoors which was scarcely reason for not wearing them ever, but he did not. The sahibs never did, he seemed to remember, so he did not either.

Presently, he came to a little square where there was a First War memorial, and for no accountable reason, he stood for a moment and doffed his hat in memory of the dead. If you'd asked him, he couldn't remember on whose side the Portuguese had fought in that war, but memorials always affected him. His father's two brothers had been with the tunnellers of Messines and had not returned, and Bowcott had an immense respect for military ceremonial, often stating that in the period of the two minutes' silence on Armistice Day, he resolutely attempted to remember faces of the dead he had known. It was somehow always an intensely moving experience to him, coupled with the thought of lives that might have been.

He stood for a full two minutes holding the straw fedora to his chest, then strode to an adjoining bar whose proprietor had noticed his little vigil.

'La Guerra?' the proprietor said curiously.

Bowcott gave a stiff military nod and sat astride a bar stool as he ordered a beer. From Omdurman to Mametz Wood, from Monte Cassino to Caen and back to Vimy Ridge, his mind had strayed to the accompaniment of ghostly bugle notes. The faces of the dead... How young they were... Callow boys for the most part, legions of them with no chance of living, the missing generations.

He switched his attention to the proprietor, erupted into two languages simultaneously, capping them with stern valleys posh.

'Las guerras lo mismo todo el mundo,' he said portentously.

'Ah, si,' said the proprietor with a wise nod.

A few more words, a few more beers, a good tip, and Bowcott was off again, feeling rather better. It aways paid to communicate with the locals. He passed the cobbler's shop where last year the cobbler had encompassed his extravagant paunch with a specially made belt from horse leather. 'Got a little chap I know in Portugal to run it up one morning,' he told Lucas Thomas the Chemist. 'Did it on the spot. There's such a thing as service left in the world.' ('That Bowcott Jones has been around,' Lucas told his wife.)

Bowcott looked in through the cobbler's doorway, but a different face greeted him, and rather than inquire, he backed away. There was still the same smell of leather and sawdust in the air, but the old man behind the counter was not half as jolly as the jester the previous year. It might have been an omen. But Bowcott went on up the street. He was heading for the English Tavern where an old Kenya Planter had set up a pub, English style, and where, the year before, he had drunk copiously with much good humoured joss in the company of like-minded fellows of his own age. They were exiles for the most part, chaps who had got out of England for one reason or another. He liked them best because they had given him the opportunity of playing up the Welsh side of his nature. 'Wouldn't think of living in England myself!' he had announced, and with his jokes and quips, the alacrity with which he bought his round, he was eminently acceptable, and indeed, the nights had passed in much the same way as they did in his local at home. The bonhomie of drinkers was an international thing, a safe and comfortable world in which to float.

The taverner's name was Matt, late King's African Rifles, a Kenya wallah with a prodigious thirst, and a joker into the bargain. Then, Bowcott had been *Bwana Mc'wber* Jones, and Matt was, *My man*, and they'd done a little Forces number, *Ten cents a dance, that's all they pay me!* to the delight of the Portuguese waiters. The company of old soldiers was the best in the world, Bowcott proclaimed, and what is more, Matt kept a good house: cockles on the bar on Sundays, always beef sandwiches to order, and it was a cool, clean bar with white-aproned waiters who knew their place, and a Victorian air to the china pumps with engraved fox hunting scenes and vintage dirty postcards in apple pie order on the notice board. More important than anything else, except the beer, was the lavatory, the cleanest in the Algarve, a shaded white light, English paper and the wholesome smell of disinfectant and none of your damned scent. Eight pints down and you knew you were safe with a beef sandwich to build up your bowels when sea-food got a bit too much. Bowcott, like an army, marched on his stomach, and in the previous year, he prided himself that he'd found the only place on the continent where you could drink like an Englishman and not rue the day. He'd told this to Matt who'd made him write it in the visitor's book. Last year, the lavatory, the pub, the fresh cockles and delicious beer and the primed ale had made it the best holiday Bowcott had ever had and he'd come back with the same expectancy.

Fatal...

District Commissioner Jones, *Bwana Mc'wber* Jones,Jones the Gauleiter of Romford had made a cock-up in coming back.

'For Chrissakes, the bogey's got his shooter out!' the voice returned.

As did his mother's: 'Figs and pancakes, Bowcott?'

Yes, by God, he'd done a burster. No wonder he had a mouth like an acrobat's jockstrap. Perhaps he'd swallowed a fig stone? Perhaps it was the oysters? He must be alive with shellfish. Shake him and he'd rattle.

'You will suffer, my boy. Yes, you will, you'll live to regret. Thank goodness Colenso isn't like you.'

Colenso! That was it! Now he experienced total recall. Colenso, his moody nephew. Pertinent point! As well as his guts and the wogs, the Welshy-Welsh had knackered his holiday. Trust them!

The Bowcott Joneses had no children of their own. ('Lack of greens,' his mother said.) But he had a nephew, Colenso, whom he'd attempted to take under his wing whenever allowed, a small, thin, bespectacled, intellectual boy who had got into the wrong set at one of the lesser Welsh universities and emerged a rabid Welsh nationalist with Honours Welsh and an interest in his country that amounted to fetishism, in Boycott' eyes. Despite all the gifts, the golf clubs, the fishing rods, the use of a salmon stretch, the wretch had become one of the interrupters of Her Majesty's judges, a demonstrator, a non road-tax payer who disappeared for weeks on end to summer schools and folk festivals where they ate, slept, breathed and dreamed Welsh, a way of life and habit which Bowcott found incomprehensible and which irritated him more than he could say. In his aversion to this recently reborn element in his country, Bowcott was quite unreasonable. There was something sickly and introverted about it, he was sure. There was nothing for the people in it, just milk and honey for training college lecturers and the like, another bloody cottage industry from which the few profited and exploited the many. Moreover, it excluded Bowcott entirely, with his long forgotten Welsh and what he called his international outlook. Fan, who was easy going, said live and let live, but if it were possible, Bowcott would have been a hanging judge as far as Colenso's lot were concerned. A number of the young were quite taken with it, even protested a patriotism that made Bowcott into a kind of quisling and that set him off to boiling point. A quisling! After the scraps he'd been in while in the Army, even going so far as to thump a paymaster and risking a court martial after one guest night.

'Welsh bastards,' the paymaster'd said. That was enough. Bowcott found a right cross that would have made Dancing Jim Driscoll cheer in his grave, and the paymaster had gone down in a heap in the corner by the ornamental-silver cupboard. The Adjutant had made enquiries and Bowcott had told him straight out.

'Can't have that, sir. It's not the "bastard" I object to, it's the slurring use of the adjective!'

The Adj had told the Colonel, and the Colonel (who was from Abergavenny) had a good laugh about it as it happened, and

everything had been quite all right, even lent a certain kudos to
Bowcott's reputation and the paymaster'd emerged as a shit anyway. Bowcott had struck a blow for his country, but it didn't register
with Colenso one little bit. When he'd told him with a certain pride,
Colenso's face had kept its intelligent, precious, rabbit look, and
then he'd gone off and married a girl who was even more immersed
in the Welsh business. They were like a pair of folk-weave Ghandis
together, often spoke Welsh in front of him, and brought him to the
boil more quickly than if they'd taken drugs in public. All through
the Investiture (to which, naturally, he'd been invited and now kept
his red, ornamental chair in the hall) he'd been on the lookout for
violence, but the fact that Colenso's lot weren't violent made him
dislike them all the more. Roots v. roots... It was a Welsh conundrum.

But to meet it here in Portugal! That was it, he'd gone into the
tavern to find that Matt had left, packed up and gone to Ibiza. A
youth stood in his place, a dirty, bearded, London wide-boy.

'Trouble wiv the Missus, so he scarpered.'

'Scarpered?'

'I bought him out February.'

Matt gone...The place was no longer the same. The china beer
pumps with their engraved fox-hunting scenes, exact replicas of a
pair in the cocktail bar of the Norfolk Hotel in Nairobi, were
missing, so were the comic postcards, the cheery publican's greet-
ings cards from home, the little saucers with crisps and olives in
them, even the waiters' crisp white aprons. Where there had been
a jar of the precious beef sandwiches, now there was a machine for
dispensing salted peanuts, and, as he soon found out, in the best
lavatory in the Algarve, there was now a contraceptive slot-machine
and a notice by the management proclaiming, 'This gum may taste
a little rubbery'. Not graffitti; by the management!

Worse still, there was Hair in the bar, by which Bowcott meant,
the young. Previously, it had been the middle-aged who had congregated there, giving the place the atmosphere of a cheerful, senior
officers' mess. But now girls in hot pants and semi-naked boys,
looking like aborigines in Bermuda shorts, draped themselves about
the place and the girls. There was not a soul there his own age.

'What'll it be then, Chief?'

'A pint,' Bowcott said, fragile suddenly.

'Sagres?' the new proprietor said, referring to the local beer.
'Anything else?'

'I keep a few Guinnesses for the old boys.'

The old boys... For some reason, the first phrase that come into

Bowcott's mind was a Welsh one, *Bechgyn y Bont*, one of the few
he knew. Translated, it meant 'Boys of the bridge', referring to a
group of old soldiers from his home town, survivors of near-deci-
mated regiments who had congregated together after the First War.
They met once a month, growing older over the years, finally
attending each other's funerals until they were virtually non-exis-
tent. Each of the boys of the bridge had a touching habit of leaving
a tenner in their wills, a tenner 'for behind the bar', when the
survivors would raise a number of solemn pints in memory of the
departed. But the time had come when they could not exhaust the
tenner, and the change was stuffed into a charity box. In the end,
the change exceeded the money spent. Farewell the *Bechgyn y Bont*.

Now Bowcott felt like one of them, and once again, seemed to
hear the Last Post sounding in his ears.

'I'll have a large scotch,' he said in his most cultivated voice.

'Right you are, guv. Old Matt had all the big spenders here, eh?'

The big spenders... Bowcott sat dismally upon a stool. No one
paid any attention to him. A young couple, draped around each
other at the end of the bar, changed hands soulfully. Why they had
to feel themselves in public, Bowcott would never know.

'Drop of splash, mate?'

Mate... But he nodded. It looked like a morning on the scotch, a
morning of silent reverie seated at the corner of the bar. He felt like
a colonial planter, recently returned home and completely out of
things. But it was not in his nature to sit maudlin anywhere, and he
soon struck up a conversation with the new proprietor, only to find
there was another blow to the stomach.

'I thought you was Welsh.'

'I beg your pardon?'

'*Iacky Da,* I gotta few Taffees comin' in here.'

Bowcott did not reply.

But he was to have no peace. Like a light skinned negro passing
as white, he had been spotted, and when he had downed another
scotch in stony silence, a newcomer entered the bar, nodded at the
proprietor who promptly sidled up to Bowcott and made the
unwanted introduction.

'Major Bowcott Jones,' Bowcott said grimly.

The newcomer was young, with dark, curly hair, a pale, nondescript face, and a slight stoop, unmistakably Welsh.

'It's hardly possible, but I don't suppose you're related to...'

Colenso, of course. Anything was always possible with bloody
relatives! But to come a thousand miles to Portugal and have the

dismembered limb of the family regurgitated. Bowcott could not surpress a dismal nod.

'I have a very great admiration for him,' the young man said.

Bowcott would have said, 'Good chap!' not, 'a very great admiration.' It sounded so fawning.

'Why?' Bowcott said sharply. His temper had risen immediately.

'His general militancy.'

'On whose behalf?'

'Why, the Welsh people.'

'He's never met any of 'em', Bowcott said unreasonably. 'But for Christ's sake, let's not go into it, I'm on holiday.' He felt so annoyed at this extraordinarily unlucky encounter that he was in danger of letting himself go. Questions of Welsh nationalism affected him in the same way as a wholly English counterpart might be similarly provoked by encounters with advocates of illegitimate birth, C.N.D., or permissive television. He cut short the conversation as soon as he could.

'Young man, if you don't mind... Look here, why don't you have a drink?'

'No, thank you,' the young man said. He turned away, but did not go.

Bowcott sighed. It was absurd to be standing in a Portuguese bar in the presence of obvious riff-raff, boiling about Aberystwyth University and it environs. He was on holiday, and now it was as if two worlds had collided in one person, and back his thoughts went like tired homing geese to the perennial open sore — Wales. It was a country of permanent ills, four countries rolled into one, and if you didn't get away from it now and again, you choked in the back-biting and rancour. Thank God he was a South Walian anyway. Thank God for coal and the Marquis of Bute. And a pox on the *Ychafi* Welsh and their road sign campaigns and eternal bleating.

He ordered another whisky and, by habit, asked for the morning paper, but when it came, it was in Portuguese.

'Haven't you got the *Express*?'

But they had not, and the young man smiled, Bowcott thought. He could not see, but he was sure he was smiling, smiling a young Welsh smile, and it was dark and foreboding, Bowcott was sure. Unreason leads to unreason, misunderstanding to further misunderstanding. Where prejudices foster, rancour is rife, and Bowcott now felt a wave of self-pity as he recalled that, sitting on this very stool the previous year, he'd felt like a proconsul. He and Matt had gone shark fishing with a drunken Dutchman, and with the wind in their faces, the rolling Biscayan swell beneath them off St Vincent, they had drunk whisky and eaten meat and recaptured a piratical feeling of freedom that had lasted a year. They'd brought in an ebony black Mako shark, its jaws snapping as they gaffed it, and later proudly laid it on the beach where the peasants came to inspect the day's catch. Bowcott had insisted on its being given away for fertilizer and then they'd drunk late into the night, wearing cowboy shirts and cutting slices of dried cod with sheath knives. It was a holiday of holidays, a reversion to primal living that had given him a new image of himself as an international outdoorsman.

All to crumble if he didn't shake off this Welsh depression. The young man had moved to another corner of the bar so Bowcott finished his drink, and with a curt nod to the proprietor, wandered out into the street where he bumped into an acquaintance of the year before.

'Jake!'

'Bowcott!'

'My God, that place has gone off since Matt left.'

'How long are you over for? When are you going back?'

They soon found another bar. Jake was large, sad and dyspeptic, a remittance man, odd-jobbing for the tour operators, an ex-professional wrestler with a villainous broken nose but with the temperament of an obliging spaniel, an expert hanger-on. He had gone native in Singapore when the Japs got in, had stayed out of captivity, a valuable workhorse worth hiding. But now he was ulcerated and hungry, occasionally delivering new cars from Lisbon, picking up what he could here and there. But an old soldier down on his luck could not wish for better company than Bowcott.

'How've you been?'

'So, so...'

'You don't say?'

'Place has got too full of people from home. Got very tight, it has. You haven't eaten by any chance, have you?'

Jake wanted a meal. Nothing but the best then. Jake had been around, that was the cardinal point.

'You had to get around,' Bowcott said happily, the moment they seated themselves in a restaurant.

'All over,' Jake said. 'All over.'

They ate through the afternoon and into the early evening. They ate oysters and clams, the fruits of the sea, and then gorged themselves on spiced meats and oiled salads. And they had to have a swallow with it, didn't they? And after the wine, the brandy — a 'tween course pick-me-up — they started on the fruit and figs. Bowcott had a passion for figs, as Jake had for *crêpe suzettes,* so that they did themselves proud, 'going round the buoy twice' whenever there was a course or a glass that took their fancy. By the time they lit cigars, Bowcott had shaken off his depression. Once you got a drop inside you, the world was a different place, no matter whether the drop included the anti-Romford gins, the War Memorial beers, the anti-Welsh whiskies, or the old soldier's litres, it was all a drop taken, and by the evening, he felt he just could not leave without a final pint at the English Tavern. Just to show there were no hard feelings. Jake did not mind, had looked wistfully at the tip which Bowcott left in the restaurant, but no matter, they'd have a chaser at the bar and drink to the vanished Matt.

But when they got there, the tourists had given way to the locals, including a uniformed Army picket from the fort. The proprietor had his eye on winter custom and encouraged the locals whereas Matt had closed in the winter, but a whisky drinker was a whisky drinker, and he greeted them cordially. Bowcott responded with a nod, at the same time aware of a certain tension in the air. Was it sixth sense that warned him of an atmosphere amongst the Portuguese? Jake and he were the only two foreign customers and it seemed as if people had stopped talking when they entered. Bowcott gave Jake a wink, lowered his District Commissioner's ear and raised Special Agent Bowcott's other antennae. He ordered two whiskies and chasers, sized up the bar.

The army patrol were standing uneasily in the corner, their glasses empty, but on the other side of the room by the panelled mantelpiece, there sat a large muscular young man with the stump of an arm protruding from his sports shirt. He was dark and thick-necked with an insolent flushed expression that separated him from the two nervous youths who were drinking with him. He wore his hair short, and from the way he put his good arm to the side of his head, seemed to have suffered a head injury as well. He kept tapping his head with his fist, a sombre demonstration indicating that there might be something inside which had gone wrong, and which he could not forget. But for the stump of his arm, his heavy, dark face might have protruded from the back row of a Welsh pack, Bowcott thought. It was absurd, but many of the larger Portuguese looked South Walian. They had the same quality of brooding, not quite a surliness, but an air of threat. There were even waiters in the hotel with aggrieved Tonypandy walks, hacking 'dust' coughs, and bad feet.

But here no one spoke. There was definitely an imposed silence, but the bar was so small, it was impossible to say anything without being overheard. Insanely, Bowcott wished he could mutter a few words in Welsh to Jake because no one else would have understood. The fixed glances of the army patrol in the corner left him in no doubt that their arrival was an embarrassment. There were so many things that it was better the tourist did not see.

The proprietor switched on the taped music and an ancient pop number came up loudly.

'*Quizas! Quizas! Quizas!*'

The atmosphere seemed to lighten momentarily.

'A *situarzione?*' Bowcott whispered inquisitively.

Jake shook his head nervously as if to compel Bowcott to say no more.

But Bowcott was curious.

'Punch-up, d'you think?'

Jake leaned forward and whispered with a convict's side-of-the-mouth grimace.

'The guy with one arm's loco.'

'Eh?'

'Mozambique.'

'What?'

'Caught one in the head. Bullet. I shouldn't say anything if I were you. Now he breaks up bars for a living.'

Bowcott looked around him with a distinct unease, and suddenly, the afflicted Portuguese rose unsteadily and wandered over to Bowcott who rose instictively.

'Engleesch peoples very good peoples,' the Portuguese said.

His eyes were troubled, perhaps unfocused. His breath was sour. he was very drunk and swayed once more. 'Naice peoples, no?'

'Well,' Bowcott said. It seemed a little inappropriate to insist on '*Pays de Galles*' as he often did.

The Portuguese put his only arm on Bowcott's shoulder and leant heavily upon him. He spoke with difficulty.

'Engleesch peoples fair peoples,' he nodded and smiled with all the air of definitive scholarship of an extremely drunken man.

Across the bar, the proprietor and the soldiers were tense, but Bowcott put his arm around the young man, gulping as his eyes met the obscene stump of the amputated arm. The flesh was red and puckered and strangely disturbing, a real wound beside all those phoney memorials.

'*Soldado?*' Bowcott said.

'Ye..s,' the young man gave a bitter smile.

Bowcott puffed out his chest.

'You'd better have a drink with me,' he said in a fatherly voice. 'Beer?'

The young man nodded, but the proprietor shook his head nervously. Bowcott ignored him. He knew he had skills with drunks.

'Two beers, *pash favour?*'

'I don't think...' the proprietor began to say.

'Nonsense!' said Bowcott. 'If two old soldiers can't have a drink together, what's the world coming to?' He was pleased he said that. A Buggins would have run out of the bar at the first sign of trouble. Even Jake was sitting there like a Methodist Sunday School superintendent.

The Portuguese lurched dangerously against Bowcott. The stump of his arm was barely concealed under the short-sleeved sport shirt.

'Steady the Buffs!' Bowcott said. He gave a friendly man-to-man wink, but it did not register.

The Portuguese looked into Bowcott's eyes.

'Me — crazy,' he said. It was a phrase he seemed to have learned to say, apologetically like a beggar's set piece.

The proprietor put the beers on the bar. The patrol had not moved and the sergeant held an empty glass in his hand like a weapon.

'We all have our off days,' Bowcott said, short of words suddenly.

The Portuguese nodded, deeply and mysteriously to himself, swayed again, then lurched from Bowcott's friendly arm and picked up the fresh beer glass defiantly, spilling half its contents as he raised his arm in a toast.

'A Ché Guevara,' he said loudly with a sideways glance at the patrol. He said it with reverence, a name that meant something, that was dangerous to say, but would be said always, secretly and in the open, a name for such young men to conjure with.

But Bowcott sighed dismally, reverting to his earlier feeling of dismay. Politics again... The bastards were everywhere, excluding him from their enthusiasms, waving ideas like flags, but always beating a hollow drum as far as he was concerned. It had taken him fifty-six years of his life to know his way around and learn the ropes of living, so why should he want to change anything?

The patrol sergeant, older that the boy soldiers beside him, was coarse faced and muscular, his leather shoulder-straps worn and comfortable, and the little gold wheel insignia on his beret was almost polished away with years of cleaning. He snapped a word of warning in Portuguese across the bar.

The young man spat on the floor.

'A *Ché Guevara,*' he said again, raising the glass and spilling the remainder of his drink.

Two young Portuguese customers left hurridly, a sweating youth tucking his shirt into his trousers as he went out through the door without a look behind him.

In order to quieten the situation, Bowcott raised his glass.

'*A Pays de Galles,*' he said, clicking his heels to attention.

No, *Ché Guevara,*' the young man said. '*Ché! Ché! Ché!*'

It was a tense moment.

A policeman appeared in the doorway. The flap of his holster was unbuttoned. He was a small, wizened, untidy policeman with the stub of an unlit cheroot stuck to his lower lip. His blue-grey uniform was shabby and his collar was unbuttoned below a podgy, unhealthy face. He drew his revolver apologetically like a tired male nurse producing a thermometer, but when the revolver was drawn and the safety catch removed, he beckoned at the young man and said one word.

'*Vivaldo...* '

The young man swayed uncertainly and turned towards him, putting down the empty beer glass. At that moment, seeing their chance, the patrol rushed the young man from the rear, the three soldiers, sergeant in the lead, coming around the corner of the bar like wing forwards. The knocked Vivaldo head first out into the street and as his head hit the cobbles below the door step, the policeman brought his boot down in a tired little kick that caused blood to spurt from Vivaldo's nose. But the damage was done by Vivaldo's head hitting the cobbles and he was unable to rise.

Across the street, a woman screamed.

Bowcott stared. The kick infuriated him. He drew himself up, brushed aside Jake who had risen to stop him, and marched to the doorstep, staring haughtily down into the face of the policeman.

'Look here,' he said importantly. 'There is no call to kick a man when he is down.'

It was then the proprietor called frantically.

'For Chrissakes, the bogey's got his shooter out!'

'Be quiet!' Bowcott snapped.

The policeman looked up at him confusedly. What business was it of his?

A sedan had driven up the street. At the wheel sat a large elderly man, deeply sunburnt behind dark glasses, the elbow of his light grey suit casually resting in the opened window. He lifted his arm slowly, a gold watch bracelet glistening then disappearing behind his shirt cuff. He seemed completely relaxed but as if by pre-arranged signal, the soldiers now picked up the semi-conscious body of Vivaldo and dragged him across to the car, bundling him into the rear seat and closing the door. The man nodded and drove away.

For a moment Bowcott was tempted to run after the car, but the proprietor had joined him.

'Come inside!'

'I demand to know where they are taking him.'

'That's his old man, you git.'

'What?'

'Come in before the bogey gets shirty.'

Bowcott hesitated. There had been no mistaking that kick in the face.

'Never interrupt the bastards when they've got their shooters out. If you was in the army, you ought to know that.'

Bowcott turned away confusedly. The soldiers were dusting themselves down in the gutter and the policeman lit his cheroot. Bowcott's interruption had been brave and meaningless, like a donkey braying in the dark.

'That Vivaldo,' the proprietor explained. 'The moment he's got a load on, it's Ché Guevara day and bloody night.'

'But...'

'Course, you can't normally do that in Portugal, but the joke is, see, his old man's in the police himself. So they come and get him once a month.'

'You mean, his father...'

'In the Chevrolet. Full up to here wiv him, he is. Must be.'

'You mean, they're doing his father a favour?'

The proprietor nodded.

'But what about the kick?'

'I 'spect the bogey's full up to here wiv him too.'

Bowcott could hardly believe it. But it was a village scandal and a village story into which other worlds had intruded, other worlds, alien ideas. The last thing Bowcott remembered before he mooched back to the hotel, were the Portuguese women drawing their black shawls over their heads as they came out into the street to discuss the matter, their sharp tongues cawing away like crows. He remembered enough to know that everybody's sympathies were with the father. An ordinary Portuguese would, of course, have been locked up at the mention of Ché Guevara, but Vivaldo apparently had connections.

'Influence,' Bowcott thought moodily. When he got down to it, the whole bloody world was like Glamorgan.

But how much had he understood? Had he behaved ridiculously again? He found his wallet finally, stuffed for safety on top of the Westinghouse air-conditioner, then examined Lucas Thomas's handwriting on the medicine bottle, *Two x 5m spoonfuls to be taken four times a day'.*

'Good old Lucas,' he said, forgetting his earlier animosity. He had a sudden intolerable nostalgia for grey skies, grey faces, grey terraced streets, the bustling conviviality of teeming football grounds and men's four-ale bars, and as if to salute them, he suddenly removed the cork from the medicine bottle, up-ended it, and drank copiously from the neck. He reverted to the vernacular finally, grateful for its protection. Bowels was buggers of things when you came to think of it. It was as if there was a particular danger that the slightest disturbance might make you think.

And he was spared nothing.

'Emma...Emma...' the voices began outside, floating up from the swimming pool as the Romford lot began to colonize it. *'Even if it is abroad, you can't run around without your nix.'*

He belched. There were days when it seemed as if his stomach was pressing against his eyeballs, and the way he now felt, it had all the signs of a real clogger. Lucas would eventually have to get the arrowroot out again, and Fan would probably enjoy herself for a day or two, mostly on her own.

The Scandalous Thoughts
of Elmyra Mouth

Elmyra Mouth did not like *BBC Wales*. Either on the box or off it. Although she dutifully watched the programmes which involved her husband as assistant camera-man, she was always conscious of a great disparity between them and her. She did not like the announcers for a start. The women looked like something out of a Sunday School vestry and the men sounded phoney, half-London, half-Welsh, neither one thing nor the other, with the most unacceptable of getting-ahead acquisitions, posh accents.

Then again, on the few occasions when she went down from the valleys to Cardiff and waited for Davie in the staff canteen, Elmyra had increased her dislike for what went on behind the scenes. Take the bosses. They treated the more lowly technicians' wives like dirt, either looking through you, or rambling on amongst themselves in deep, book Welsh. Always jabber-jabber, it was, never mind whether you understood or not. They had no manners, Elmyra concluded, but that was not the worst. From what she had heard from Davie who was inclined to exaggerate to please her, the place was a hotbed of sex. You never knew who was sleeping with who, and for all the air of sanctity which somehow got on the air, behind the scenes, Elmyra was sure, the place was like a rabbit warren.

Wasn't it full of strangers? Glamorgan people lost out all the way along the line. You seldom came across anybody from the valleys, or Cardiff even, just the *in* Welshy-Welsh, catarrhal BA'd North Walians down for what they could get; Ministers' sons from everywhere, and girls from farms by the look of them, legs like bottles, all sitting around endlessly in the canteen, heads bent together and the hum of gossip rising like steam above a football crowd. Some of them *lived* in that canteen. It was an unhealthy atmosphere, Elmyra felt, and definitely not her style.

But there was another side to it. Her Davie had a good job by valley standards. On top of what he was getting in take home pay, he always managed a few bob extra, what with car allowance, expenses and subsistence — it was as good as the Police from that point of view. But she had put her foot right down when there was any talk of moving down to Cardiff. Her grandmother had left her a furnished house, the corner one in the terrace, and where they lived, they had a view over the town that was worth waking up for.

From the bedroom window, she could see right down Dan y Graig Street, over the rows of terraced houses below them, right down to the memorial park where the trees formed an avenue beside the confluence of the Rivers Rhondda and Taff. Further away, familar grey mountains and brown tumps stood sentinel over other valleys, and everywhere she looked, Elmyra felt at home. Here she had a position and status, and although they used to call her Elmyra Mouth because of her not being backward in coming forwards in that direction, she was well content to be at home. She was a valley girl, was she not? She knew every brick of Dan y Graig Street, every blade of grass and *cwtch* on the bare mountain and tip behind, and although now you didn't hear the tramp of miners' boots in the mornings and the little front parlour shop around the corner no longer sold lumps of chalk for the colliers to mark their drams as they did in her mother's day, it was still home and here she felt comfy. So when Davie'd proposed moving to Cardiff as it would cut down his travelling time, she had a cryptic and typical answer.

'Travel you bugger,' she said flatly. 'You'll not move me an inch!'

For his part, Davie did not much mind. He was from further up the valleys, easy going, placid, glad enough to be in any kind of job when it came to it, and the extras that came his way from the travelling allowance allowed them an income that made life more comfortable. He had met Elmyra in a dance when home on leave from Malaya. One of Templar's boys, he'd caught a packet up the sharp end, a burst from a terrorist's gun that left him with a slightly stiff knee, and when Elmyra looked at him, handsome and sun-burned with the fusilier's dark patch hanging from his battledress, he didn't have a chance. She liked a man who was a man, and the wound, the campaign medals, the air of experience about him, and his close-cropped hair and enganging *shoni's* wink were enough. She also felt she could manage him, as her mother had managed her father, also an old sweat. Give the valley boys a good look at the world and it did them no end of good, and like many before him, Davie returned home from the wars with that certain air which Elmyra found irresistible. The best Welshmen belonged to the world. They didn't stay at home picking their noses in beautiful Welsh.

Of course, Elmyra was a catch herself. Now at thirty-two, she could still go down the shop without a bra under her jumper and nobody'd know for sure. When she got her war paint on, with her slim hips, long sexy legs and wide insolent mouth, she had her

mother's Saturday-night-at-the-Vic look, cocktail lounge, not the
Two-Foot-Six, a touch of the Lauren Bacall's, in short. And despite
her nickname, she never went too far with Davie. Marriage and two
children had calmed her in that respect. Now she thought more and
said less. She was perfectly happy, thank you very much, no need
to give her a thought. But she did sometimes worry when Davie was
out late. It was not that she feared competition — she'd go through
the BBC Canteen like a knife through butter if she'd occasion to —
but there was an end to her patience in waiting. She didn't mind
when he was away on location, but lately, waiting up for him had
got on her nerves. It was the age-old wives' complaint. It was when
he was not in when he said he was going to be in, that was the rub.
So when Davie informed her he was going to be late one Friday
night, she had a caustic reply.

They were sitting at breakfast, lolling about on one of his rest
days. Karen and Sabrina, their two young daughters, were in school.

'Oh,' Davie said, 'I forgot to tell you. Friday, I'll be late.'

'I thought it was your rest week?'

He took care to keep his eyes casually on the centre pages of the
Mirror. 'It is, but you know Fred Eckersley? He's off to London, a
promotion, and we're going to give him a bit of a send-off.'

'Fred-who?'

'Eckersley. You know. He's going to *Panorama*.'

'You don't have to kid me with none of that stuff,' Elmyra said
sharply. '*Panorama?* You can keep it. You know you usually take
me out Fridays?'

'Well, he's going on Saturday. It's just a send-off with the boys
from the Unit.'

'That Film Unit!' Elmyra said in much the same way as her
mother would have said 'That pit!' or 'That club!'

'Well, I could hardly refuse, could I?' Davie said mildly. 'Fred's
one of the best. It's just a get-together, that's all.'

Elmyra scowled. She knew the charm of that phrase. It could
mean anything from a few pints and a game of darts to the back
door stove in and him banished downstairs in a Worthington fug,
a bucket and sheet of newspaper ready beside the settee. Lifeboat
stations, as they said. About once a year, she knew, Davie let himself
go as her father had done and still did. They were both capable of
drinking without reason, stomach to stomach in the four ale, and
then returning home with flushed red faces, hoarse from singing
and as full as eggs. *BBC Wales* would be sorry to know that the songs
they sang were *Mexicali Rose* or *I have been a Rover*, but that was

beside the point. Where they got the capacity from, she did not know. She was a Snowball and Babycham girl herself. But she was careful to control her objections. If her mother had taught her anything, it was not to be a nag.

'Oh, well, I suppose you'd better go then,' she said resignedly. 'Just men together, is it?'

'Just the boys in the Unit.'

'Mind to be home at twelve then. Twelve *sharp*.'

'Oh, good Gawd.' Davie returned to the *Mirror*. 'I'll be home long before that.'

'You have to be up early Saturday, mind? I want to go shopping and Sabrina's got to have new pumps for her dancing lessons.'

'Rightho,' Davie said. And that was all.

But when the time came for him to leave and drive the twelve miles down to Cardiff, she noted he had his drinking suit on. It was an ancient Burton's Donegal tweed which he fondly believed did not show stains, but despite this optimism, she felt she knew the signs when it was produced. He wore it on the *beyond* nights and it looked like it, had stayed crumpled where he fell, spillages on lapels to boot.

'Twelve sharp then,' she repeated. 'And remember the breathalyzer.'

'Oh, if I have a meal, it'll kill it. A good hot curry'll do the trick.'

He went to give her a goodbye kiss. She'd done herself up. All the more desirable to come home to!

'So long then, kid,' he let his lips linger on hers.

She studied him gravely.

'You watch your bloody self. I know the signs.'

He repeated a family joke: 'It's not the drink, Auntie, it's the company.'

'I can see that by the veins on your nose.'

'Go on...' he gave her a playful squeeze.

'Stay if you want,' she kept her hands behind his neck.

'No, I can't. It's Fred's last night.'

She bared her teeth and released him. Men, she thought; animals. If he didn't come up the stairs cat-footed, she'd turn the tap off that night. Shut shop it would be, him and his drink and his Fred! As her mother'd advised, there was such a thing as frostbite after closing. But like her mother, she didn't want to be thought a bad old sort. So she merely grunted: 'Get on with you. And come home with more than your bracers!'

When he had gone, she heard the familiar clunk of the car's gears

outside and lit a cigarette before getting the children to bed. There
was nothing for her on the telly as usual. With all the money spent
on it, you'd think there might be a show she'd actually enjoy now
and again. Sometimes there was a serial or a play with which she
could identify, but it was never from Wales and usually had to do
with the Midlands or the North. Locally, she did not count, she
supposed. Not that she gave a monkey's. Davie said you had to go
to Bristol to get the Welsh edition of the *Radio Times* because
nobody took it locally. But why should they? It had precious little
to do with them any more than did the other commercial lot, who
weren't even worth mentioning, except for a passing sigh for the
Dorchester film stars worrying about South Wales on their yachts.
Mouths shut, remember the divi, and don't offend Bristol again.
Where were the valleys in that?

She finished her cigarette and went up to inspect the bathroom
which Davie had recently tiled. It contained a coloured bath, pink,
with matching accessories, and luxury of luxuries, a separate shower
attachment. Elmyra could remember what it was like not to have a
proper bathroom and she thought her coloured suite a whizz and
no mistake. Now she looked proudly at the hand towels, the
matching floor mat and lavatory cover, and thanked God for
Embassy coupons. It was the most hallowed room in the house.

Presently, she called the children in, and having bathed them and
settled them down in their nightdresses, decided to bathe herself.
If Davie but knew it, she spent hours in the bathroom, wallowing
in the suds, endlessly combing her hair, and surveying herself in the
long mirror she'd insisted upon. She often took her measurements.
Two kids and hardly an inch on or off at either end. Boy, she was
too good to waste, she thought. It was a good job she was faithful.
There were always plenty of chances. She couldn't go down the
market Saturdays without what seemed like a visiting team trying
to look down her dress, but she'd developed a look that killed, she
fondly imagined. And anyway, she wasn't interested. They said a
slice off a cut loaf was never missed, but not her loaf, thank you very
much. She was took, a one-man woman.

She did not dress after her bath, slipped a robe on and went
downstairs where she attempted to read her horoscope from a
woman's journal, but somehow she couldn't concentrate. She
didn't know quite what it was, but her mind was on the itch. Was
their marriage getting boring? Did they take each other too much
for granted? She'd caught Davie looking at pin-ups a lot lately, his
eye flashing to the ripe page of the *Mirror* before he so much as

crackled a cornflake. What if his eye was beginning to wander elsewhere?

At first, she put the thought out of her mind and turned to the broken hearts column which she also read avidly. People's troubles were incredible. The best required a stamped addressed enevelope for a confidential reply, but she was adept at reading between the lines. Some men were so crooked, they'd fox their own shadows. And slimy with it, pure slime. But not her Davie. She couldn't understand how she even gave it a thought. He was good as gold always. As open as the day is long.

And yet it nagged, this thought. For some reason, her natural confidence began to ebb away. It was the BBC that did it. Of course, it was ridiculous and the Cardiff lot were nothing like the London lot in any respect, but it was the showbiz world even if most of it was all in Welsh. Oh, why couldn't he get a job in the chain works or on the trading estate? Why couldn't he get a job at home? They said travel broadened the mind, even twelve miles a day, but there was all the difference in the world in those twelve miles leading to Cardiff. She saw them stretching out in her mind's eye: Treforest, the Estate, Taff's Well, Whitchurch, and then the environs of the capital city opening up like the red light district in some lurid American film. Downtown What-You-Call, she thought. She'd give him Downtown! Bloody Cardiff... It was so cold compared to the valleys. Oh, why couldn't he get a job at home?

Then suddenly, her mind began to panic. It was as if a spring had begun to unwind, a coil slipping slowly from its point of tension, then exploding, thoughts expanding like rings of steel and spilling into every corner of her mind.

What if he was on the knock? All those stories about Malay girls. What did they call them? Taxi Dancers. And what about the divorces in showbiz? The Boss of the whole BBC had had one and now he was working for the commercials! There was no such thing as bloody loyalty anymore. You only had to sit in the canteen to listen to them tearing each other's programmes apart to know that. Everybody got stick, and the South Wales boys who were coining it on *Z Cars* in London got the most. That was one thing, another was that she'd refused to go to the Christmas party on principle. The poor bloody technicians always got the raw end of it with the bilingual production staff and the bigwigs ruling the roost. She didn't fancy being squeezed, pawed or patronized in that crush. It was like Machynlleth zoo. If they had a zoo in Machynlleth. And if they did, Glamorgan and Monmouthshire people had to pay for it.

Like the bloody language. And as for what went on down in
Make-Up after some of those *Ychafi* programmes, disgusting wasn't
the word. Sometimes, they had actors there, and actresses, and the
Make-Up girls said anything went. It was no good putting in to see
Controller (Wales) either because he said London was worse and
Glasgow the best, according to what somebody had told somebody
who told Davie. At any rate, it was no place for a self-respecting
valley girl. Even if they didn't have queers which Davie said were
everywhere else. Like some places he knew where you had to stand
with your back to the wall as soon as you got into the lift, by all
accounts.

But what about Davie? If Fred What's-His-Name was on transfer
to *Panorama*, he'd be ready to let himself go, wouldn't he? They'd
probably have the riggers out drinking with them, and the scene
shifters, and there was a commissionaire who could tell a story or
two, she knew about them. Once they got the beer into them,
there'd be no telling what they'd do. If they weren't at it with the
Welshy lot, they might be down the docks and that was almost as
bad, if not quite. The trouble was, once you got near Cardiff, the
values changed. You could get drunk up the valleys like a man, but
after stop-tap, home you had to come, boyo, one foot behind the
other, or no place for you but the gutter. And there was something
very comforting about the gutter. There was seldom room for two
in it.

But Cardiff, the docks... She thought about them obsessionally
now. What she hated most was her sense of the city's anonymity,
those cold wide streets, actual architecture, people pushing, sometimes stuck-ups with yet another accent and the girls in the better
shops trying to sound like a lot of lezzes and looking down their
noses at you if you ever had to leave your address.

'Dan y Graig Street and up yours too!'

What was good about the valleys from her present pont of view
was that there was many a fly that was never unbuttoned because
it would be all over town the next day. You couldn't bend down to
straighten your tights without half the street pricing your underclothes. Walls had ears and bricks had eyes, and it was a good job
too, made you feel part of the family, and keeping the old Adam
down in all but the wilder spirits and they were usually Poles or
County School boys. There was no creeping off and having it on
the sly if you were married unless you were the Invisible Man or
something. What worried her now was the thought of them all
together, egging each other on. They said there were some rugby

clubs who actually had a competition when they went on the Cornish tour. Who'd be the first of the married men to click! Thank Gawd for that Malayan terrorist anyhow! He'd put the shot in just the right place.

By eleven thirty, Elmyra was convinced her marriage was threatened. If it could happen to Diana Dors, it could happen to her, couldn't it? They must be on the razzle. Must be.

As a matter of principle, she never kept drink in the house, except at Christmas. It was not that nobody called, but rather, that she knew very well who might call, and the men there were around here, you couldn't give them one drink. Oh, no. With them, it was one drink, finish the bottle. They were as Welsh as Welsh in that, out-and-outers, the bloody lot of them. It so happened that there was half a bottle of rum which her father had given Davie for his chest in the winter. She brought it out and poured herself a liberal tot and drank it with a swallow. She'd give him a going-over when he came in. If there was a hint of another woman, she'd give him a beating, the like of which the street had never known. There'd been some famous cases, one erring husband sewn in the bed sheets and laced with a broom handle in his cups, another wrapped up in wet wallpaper and pasted all over like a snowman before he got his. They didn't believe in sulking, the Dan y Graig women. Defiantly, she poured another tot, swallowed it, and then another. She'd give him sox!

But by one o'clock when there was still no sign of him, her rage turned like the weather cock to self pity. She was drunk now, wallowing in remorse. All these accusations. It was her fault, she'd refused to move to Cardiff in the first place. What was the good of blaming him if he didn't have a home handy? All the temptations were put in his way. He was a boy-and-a-half as far as his attractions went. A wife's place was to follow her husband. She'd jibbed at the first thing he'd ever really asked her. And now what was she doing? Never a quitter be, her father always said, true to the pit always; neither a quitter nor a squealer. Now she was both.

By two o'clock she'd finished the bottle. She got to her feet and staggered to bed. Now she was maudlin, disaster's victim. Dead, she thought, he was dead, neatly incised on the motorway, or crushed under some truck. He'd told her once he'd seen a man cut in half by a lengthy burst from a sten gun, actually in half. Now she transferred the image into her own mind, but it was too horrible. · He was normally the most careful of drivers, but then, they were the sort who copped it. She could not remember going upstairs, or

what she did when she got there, but she already saw herself as a
widow, pale and grief-stricken in black with the entire street turned
out for the funeral and perhaps a sight of one or two of the BBC
Celebrities who might be there. It was all over in her mind. Perhaps
they'd fiddle it to say that he was working so she'd get a pension,
no doubt Controller (Wales) would find a few words of English to
cheer her up, but she was a widow all right. She *felt* like a widow.
Thank Gawd her grandmother'd left her the house. She sobbed
herself to sleep finally, lying naked on the coverlet, her long, black
hair hanging down by the side of the bed.

It was in this position that Davie found her at three o'clock in the
morning. He smelt the rum on her breath with some annoyance.
There was no call for that, nothing wrong with her chest, but he
said nothing, stripped and eased himself in beside her, taking care
to throw the coverlet over her in case she would catch a chill.

In the morning, it was he who attacked first.

'You were lying there looking like a bloody book-jacket. What if
the children had come in?'

She felt dreadful, a mouth like a birdcage. Her temples throbbed
as she looked at him blearily. She'd decided on something before
she fell asleep, but now she could not remember what it was.

'You said twelve...'

'I was late because I had to drive somebody else home.'

'Twelve you said.'

'Well I wasn't much after, but before you go on at me, have you
seen the bathroom?'

'The bathroom?' she caught at her throat. She had a vague
memory of disturbance, a sense of sin.

'Were you swinging on the light cord, or what?'

'Swinging?'

'The plaster's flaked on the ceiling by the switch, and the matching accessories are stuffed down the pan.'

'The pan?'

'The lav,' he said accusingly. 'What did you have, an orgy all on
your own?'

In her frenzy, she must have tried to wreck her own creation!
Ychafi! And even as he accused, the fact that he did not couple her
with anyone else shamed her all the more. Thoughts was awful
things when you came to think of them: nasty.

'Oh, lor'... Sorry kid,' she said guiltily.

'I should think so too.'

She thought for a moment, then looked at him. 'It's the bloody

BBC I get worried. I don't know why you don't try and get a job at home.'

He looked at her startled.

'Hey?'

Then she said what everybody knew and Honours Graduates denied: 'You know you won't get on there. It's all clicks, and with your *shoni's* Welsh, what chance?'

He said nothing. They had discussed the matter before and what she said was right. It was just that he was easy going.

But now she pursued it.

'A little photographer's or something?' she said suggestively, as only she could. She slanted her eyes in a look she privately called The Japanese Goodnight. 'If you had a shop, you could come home dinner times. When the kids are in School. You know...'

He sighed. He knew the signs. From now on, she'd get her beak on it like a jackdaw at a nut. Might as well say yes to a shopkeeper before she dressed.

'We'll see,' he said comfortably. 'Leave it at that for the momeet.'

'Great,' she said happily, and later a sweet, intimate poem in monosyllables: *'Oh... Oh... Duw-Duw! Oh, help! Oh, Malaya! Oh, smashing!'*

Further up the street where the houses had bay windows and the occasional colour television they said Elmyra Mouth was as common as dirt, but the most endearing thing about her was that she thought him, her husband, the most desirable man in the world. He was hers, and apart from him and the children, she had but a single thought. 'If you was from the valleys, stay in the valleys.' Nothing else made sense.

The Ferryman's Daughter

1

There had been a preponderance of women in the Memorial Service, including a uniformed policewoman who had sat with one of Hywel's former secretaries at the rear of the improvised concert hall where friends and colleagues had gathered in embarrassingly small numbers when you compared the occasion to other such services held of late. Of course, Hywel had been much younger than the other distinguished broadcasters who had been similarly honoured, but that was not all, Delyth knew, not by a long chalk.

She sat at home in complete silence on the window seat of the drawing room, her small white face completely immobile as Hywel's mother began the attack.

'I expect it's taken you until now to realize the enormity of what you did?'

'The enormity of what I did?'

'You know very well what I mean. The time will come when even the children will realize. As it is, if there's a trust fund set up, none of the family will contribute unless you have no power over it whatsoever. T.J. told me himself this morning. He was horrified. He couldn't understand how you could have been so brutally callous.'

Delyth did not reply. Hywel's mother, like Hywel himself, had a way of speaking English that was so precise that you knew she was vain of her ability to choose such wounding words with care. T.J. hadn't said 'brutally callous', Delyth was sure. T.J. was a namby pamby, the elder statesman of Hywel's family, a former University Vice-Principal who'd inherited a good deal of money and kept it by shrewd investments and a private life of almost peasant simplicity. Having had no children of his own, he had spoiled his nephew all his life, Delyth knew, and T.J. who was over seventy, would understand nothing and provide everything when the time came, she was sure. He had nothing else to do. He also had a shrewder idea of Hywel's character than Hywel's mother. He could be managed but it was Hywel's mother whom Delyth was going to have to remove from the house. Today was the last time she would allow her inside the door and if she thought she was going to spend the night, she was mistaken. The last three days had been bad enough.

But before expelling the second body, there were still things to be done, the odd jobs that followed a sudden death like removing Hywel's clothes from the wardrobe. Although only in his early forties, he had never dressed like a television producer but spent extravagantly on clothes as if he had been some kind of executive (which, of course, he'd hoped to be) and there were at least half a dozen expensive suits from Austen Reed and Daks which would have to be given to someone. There was also a Dunhill cigarette lighter, various items of gold jewellery, sets of cuff links and one or two masonic watch chain decorations he'd inherited from his father, together with an assortment of ancient silver cigarette cases, propelling pencils, even a snuff box which were in the drawer where he'd kept his valuables. Each one of them would have to go, Delyth had decided. Before Hywel's mother said anything, she would make it clear that at present she did not want either of the children to have a single memento of their father. She would cleanse the house of him immediately and deal with the family when the occasion arose.

First, however, there was his mother whom she had never liked and had always refused to call by her christian name of Morfydd even when continually asked to do so. The Mason-Morgans were a grand lot anyway by Delyth's standards. Hywel's father had been an Army padre. Morfydd herself, as she would tell anyone within minutes of meeting them, was the first woman to get a first class honours degree in geography at Aberystwyth, the family returning to Wales from the sumptuous grandeur of Aldershot (according to Morfydd) only when Hywel's father retired. That Hywel had needed all T.J.'s influence to get him into any kind of educational establishment after a childhood spent on the move from one Army establishment to the next, that he had learnt Welsh only when it profited him, while his elder brother had run away from home and spent half his life in the Far East moving from country to country only a few steps ahead of the law — all these were Mason-Morgan problems, undeniable facts that would have buried themselves like slivers of glass into the conscience of any woman other than the woman who now sat preparing a second onslaught, having drawn not so much as a flicker of an eyelid upon Delyth's face with the first.

'I must do something about Hywel's clothes,' Delyth said.

'His clothes?'

'I thought you might take them with you tonight? There's a lot of junk as well. I don't want any of it in the house.'

Throughout the Memorial Service, Morfydd Mason-Morgan had

sat like a ramrod, her stiff back erect, her size dwarfing Delyth who had no alternative but to sit next to her. Morfydd had not cried as she threatened to do but as the eulogies were uttered by the Controller of the broadcasting station, she had nodded her head frequently, occasionally giving forth with a curious grunting assent like a sermon-tasting chapel deacon hearing familiar words of praise. She was a tall, striking woman with angular features, sharp eyes and pronounced cheekbones with a kind of statuesque dignity that was emphasized by her severe mourning clothes. A cartoonist would have drawn her with a mere two or three lines, that ramrod of a back, the flinty beak of a nose, the parabola of her downturned mouth, but the cartoonist would have missed the extraordinary brightness of her narrow set eyes which were blue like her late son's and gave to her face a look of singular intelligence. This was a woman who missed nothing you might think, and even in her seventies, there was not a hint of weakness or frailty about her. She had an abundance of white hair swept up in a neat bun and since she wore no jewellery, you had but to look at her and your gaze was somehow automatically swept up into her face. It was as if there was only the face and the forbidding image it presented, like that of an elderly Warden of an unduly strict Women's hostel where promiscuous girls were constantly under surveillance. What was extraordinary was that you could never imagine her being a girl herself and the few photographs Delyth had seen, seemed to be of another person altogether, as if that face had somehow been obtained half-way through life and bore no relation to anything that had gone before, certainly not to youth or frailty, or normal human weaknesses. The face, as Hywel might have said himself, was a production number!

Now the chin rose as Delyth's meaning was made clear.

'I wasn't thinking of leaving tonight.'

'I'm sure it would be much better if you did. And if you could take the clothes and things?'

'We normally give these things to the Salvation Army.'

'I don't even want to go through the pockets of his suits,' Delyth said firmly. But she bit her lips. She was already weakening. At first, she'd determined to leave nothing unsaid. She should have told her straight. 'God knows what's in the pockets!' But let her find out, she thought. Thank goodness the children had gone away to friends straight after the Service and wouldn't be coming home for at least a day.

'I just want to be on my own tonight, that's all.'

'I thought, in the next few days...'

'*And* the next few days if you don't mind.'

'Are you sure that's wise?'

Here we go, Delyth thought, hardening again. She hadn't forgotten the accusation of brutal callousness.

'There are some large cardboard boxes in the garage. They'll fit into the boot of T.J.'s car. If you'd just take the clothes, I'll deal with everything else before the children get home. We can pack them now.'

'I'm not certain T.J.'s coming.'

'Yes, he is. I asked him especially.'

'Without consulting me?'

'I thought you were too upset.'

That was a lie again. What she should have said, was 'Get out of my house, my life!'

'I don't understand you, I really don't. It's beyond me. You've changed out of all recognition. One of the things I was going to ask you was, how long is it since you've had any kind of medical check-up?'

'I'll get the boxes,' Delyth said, standing.

'Very well, but before you do, I should tell you that T.J. feels exactly the same as I do. We were all horrified. Horrified! How the French Authorities allowed it, I do not know!'

'It's very simple. I asked them. I was his wife.'

'But was there no religious service? Didn't you think I'd want to be there? His mother?'

'*I* didn't want anyone to be there.'

'But what if it got into the Press?'

'He wasn't important enough for that. Anyway, there was no service and I brought the ashes home. Now it's all over, I just want to be on my own. I'll put the boxes in the drive. You know where the bedroom is.'

'Give her something to do,' Hywel had always said. 'It's the only way to deal with her.' Delyth concealed a smile and left the room.

Soon she opened the garage doors, turning instinctively to find Morfydd had wandered out into the drive after her. By now, the pleasantries were entirely dispensed with and in the evening breeze, Morfydd's hair was ruffled and her striking figure reduced. Now she was about to break.

'I can't think what he ever saw in you,' she said querously.

Delyth smiled. That was the whole point. 'Someone unlike you,' was the true answer. But the hardest question was in reverse. Why, oh why, had she herself not seen through him, all of them for that matter, at the very beginning? What they had done — give or take a month or two — was their very best to ruin her life.

2

'Blame the Welsh!' Hywel would have said. It was what he always said when anything went wrong. 'The most paranoid people in Europe apart from the Lapps but at least they have the climate to contend with!' Hywel was never stuck for something to say and, for a short time, was often quite amusing. He had been so from the start whereas she herself was such a mouse and had once actually dressed up as the Walt Disney character Minnie Mouse in a college rag. The girl he had married was often tongue-tied and no match for the grandeur of the Mason-Morgans whose youngest son had quite swept her off her feet. Hywel, of couse, had a sports car while still a student. Apart from T.J. there were other uncles who also spoiled him, and the sight of him, his dark tousled hair and fresh complexion under a variety of sporty caps and wearing the kind of expensive sheepskin coat with the cuffs rolled back, made him stand out as a student pace-setter. He was never short of friends then and was already prominent as a leader, casting a kind of glow upon those who were accepted into his company. He had a laughing way of dismissing the responsibilities which blighted other people's lives. He was always laughing, his jutting family eyebrows often raised in jest, his rather thick lips invariably amused; indeed he treated everything as an entertainment. He did not so much arrive as descend, bringing with him an aura of gaiety so that nothing seemed quite as it was before he'd come. It was a very difficult thing to explain, and perhaps the answer really was that she was such a simpleton at the time.

She'd taken him home, his car, his clothes, his family name, and the street was agog. Her father was a bosun on the Irish Ferry and she and her sister lived with their semi-invalid mother in a terraced house without a view of the harbour, their upbringing hardly rural as Hywel had once suggested since they were bound by tides and there was never much to spare as long as Delyth could remember. But they managed, both girls became teachers, although, of course, beside the Mason-Morgans, the academics, the magistrates, the auctioneers, the landowners, all her people were out of a different drawer, despite the fact that Hywel always insisted that there were no class distinctions among the Welsh. Somehow, all the memories of the past always got mixed up with what Hywel had said and he was quite likely to make such statements when they suited him in the face of any number of incontrovertible facts. He had, for example, gone to public school, one of the few inWales and although the standards there raised a good few knowledgeable eyebrows, there was about Hywel that engaging charm that came from a kind of rootlessness for he seemed then to be free of the marks of any kind of place whereas she herself was a simple small town girl, the kind who was quite thrilled to meet anyone from the BBC or any of the Welsh television stations. She was in awe of such people and the family joke was that if she'd have been a boy and of another generation, she was the kind who might have run off with the circus, she was that impressed by anything that came from outside her own happy little world.

Like him, of course. He was slightly older than most of the students at the training college which they attended. There were unexplained gaps in his education, but he had ambitions even then. He was the kind who thought himself much too good for teaching. The children merely existed as material for him to show off his skills. Teaching was going to be a step towards the media from the very beginning. There was then as ever always an intangible hint of quite exceptional promise, of other, always unspecified things.

But it took her father to see through him at a glance.

'Well?' she'd asked after that first visit.

'It's up to you, my girl.'

'No, come on! None of that.'

'Up to you.'

'Don't you like him? What is it?'

'Your life's your own.'

Her father wouldn't be drawn. And it upset her terribly. Like herself, her father was small but broader with immensely strong arms and wrists, the kind of weather beaten, sure footed man who is seldom seen out of a jersey and who seemed to spend half his life with a tool bag under his arm, his wizened face under a crop of short white hair eternally sunburnt, a grin never far away. As a little girl, she'd thought he could do anything. He'd once cast the broken eye of a doll in perspex and set it so that it would wink at the press of a button, the tiniest eye of the tiniest doll and when he had handed it to her, she knew there was no other doll like it in all the world. And he was of the world too, a real traveller with tattoos to show for it. But he removed his cap when Hywel came into the room and she was mortified.

Then Hywel started speaking to him as if he were a local character, one of those old men who sat on the bench in the park, sucking their pipes and spitting on dandelion leaves. And Hywel wouldn't even let him buy a round in the pub.

'No, this is on me,' Hywel said, but everything about him said, 'I am aware that you are living in impoverished circumstances.' So much for the Mason-Morgan view of Wales and its absence of class distinctions.

But at the time, she'd blamed her father! He'd retreated into a shell she never knew existed. He made no effort, he was merely dangerously polite. And said nothing. Nothing at all while her mother waited on Hywel hand and foot and her sister was very matter-of-fact. Her sister was going with a boy who lost his foot in a motorcycle accident but soon after, her sister shrugged her shoulders and married him just the same. Her sister had her father's calm, but there was no doubt that it was she, Delyth, the youngest, who was her father's favourite. And it was her father whom she had hurt the most. When Hywel came to the house afterwards, he seemed to have acquired a knowledge of the tides, unerringly picking the times when her father was away. It was as if he had known what her father knew, had seen in a glance, a knowledge which had taken her the rest of her youth to acquire.

There followed the oldest of stories. Pregnant when she married in the summer they qualified as teachers, she did not know that Hywel already had an illegitimate child. What she did know was that the Mason-Morgans were extraordinarily welcoming. And Hywel would not leave her alone. It was a time when, like an exhausted traveller in the desert, she felt blotted out by the sun.

Later, she had many nights in which to reflect upon it all, those brief months, in particular the totality of his physical presence. Whatever you read, or viewed, there was nothing that ever explained the ferocity of sexual attraction, and there had never been anybody with whom she could discuss it, but years later, she believed her father had seen that there was in Hywel the kind of maleness that belonged in stable yards and while it excited her, it also upset her, in particular, the total dependence which it awakened in her.

'My legs are shaking!' she'd cried one night. 'They're shaking!'

She supposed in her ignorance that it was because she was so small and he was so big, but there was more than that. There was something about him that came alive in her presence. He couldn't wait to look at her, to touch her and it was as if his eyes fed on her — as if every part of her must be scrutinized as well as owned. And he made her limp. She seemed to have no will and things seemed to be happening to her that she could tell no one about. And then she was pregnant and immediately overwhelmed because not for a second did he hesitate and there was not the slightest regret on his part.

They would marry at once. The Mason-Morgans too were equally welcoming, Morfydd clapping her hands when they announced the date of the wedding and Hywel's father who was still alive then, hoped very much that her family would allow him to take part in the service. Within a month she was whisked around the family and met them all, including T.J. who made it his business to call on her parents to tell her father what a lovely boy Hywel was and how pleased they all were. The pregnancy was not at all obvious but she got the feeling that they were so relieved to see Hywel married that they wouldn't have minded even if they'd known. And that was that, the invasion of the little chapel, the day over as quickly as a flower carnival, the honeymoon in Rhodes where she miscarried, a house immediately provided for them together with a job for Hywel in a nearby Welsh county town and the march towards the media had begun.

And she'd thought she was as happy as it was possible to be!

There were, however, as ever, things she did not know, little items on the agenda that added up to make her education a total experience. What she did not know then was the Hywel had been given an ultimatum. Marriage was very much on the Mason-Morgan agenda. Morfydd had had her difficulties with her children. There had been problems with the vanished elder brother, little peccadilloes involving cheques, but since most of them had taken place in England they did not concern the family in quite the same way. The brother was no longer mentioned. Now it was Hywel who needed to settle down. Fortunately, Morfydd saw nothing wrong in getting married at a young age. She thought Delyth a pretty little thing and said so. So did T.J., who spent half the reception yarning with her father. And the whole tribe appraised her jovially, the ferryman's daughter. They were delighted she could speak Welsh and thought the fact that she was a qualified domestic science teacher an accomplishment that provided her with a reason for living.

'There'll come a time when Hywel will want to entertain,' Morfydd said warmly.

And her father said nothing.

She was pregnant again when she learned about the ultimatum. They were living then in a comfortable terraced house, purchased through an estate agent who was also a relative. Jobs were hard to come by but Hywel had experienced no difficulty and had walked out of the interview saying that after a few years in a comprehensive school, he could begin to look for something better. He was a well connected young man with a young wife and an old way with him, and, as ever, there was a feeling that he was at the start of a very distinguished career. Far from feeling he had been given a chance, he gave his seniors the impression that he was allowing them an opportunity to participate in a wondrous future. Of course, there were governors as well as politicans on the selection committe, but even the politicians were impressed and the estate agent had been quietly confident.

In fact, he said so.

'I won't say any more, Morfydd, but I am quietly confident. You can tell T.J. from me. Quietly confident...'

Three months later, Hywel was working late on a school drama production when T.J. rang, his voice betraying the urgency of the call. At first, she'd thought it was Hywel's father who Hywel said was suffering from a deliberately undiagnosed cirrhosis of the liver, but it was not, and T.J. would not leave any message except to ask that Hywel should ring back the moment he came in. As it happened, Hywel was already saying he was being delayed by various production difficulties even then, and she was asleep when he came in so that T.J. rang again on the following morning, missed him, and then asked for the number of the school. It was the first time she'd heard the strain in T.J.'s voice.

When Hywel got home that night, there was a weariness on his face which he could not conceal. He was still slim then, handsome in an old fashioned swarthy way with dark, smouldering good looks, but his voice was slightly hoarse when he answered her questions. He said he was using his voice a good deal in school.

'What was it?'

'Oh, T.J.'s fussing. We've got some shares in an investment bank and he thinks my brother's after them.'

It sounded plausible enough. Delyth knew nothing about money. The brother existed as a shadowy spectre, and anything could be attributed to a spectre. Now Hywel seemed troubled, so she did not ask any questions, although much later she became very curious for different reasons altogether. But that night T.J. rang again. She could not help overhearing the conversation since the telephone was at the foot of the stairs in the little hallway.

It seemed the family had offered something and something was not enough. But the irritation in Hywel's voice increased until he was saying simple words like 'yes' and 'no' in a screaming frenzy. Then it appeared that T.J. had mentioned a likely visit.

'How has she got my address?' Hywel said hollowly. This time there was defeat in his voice.

At the time, Delyth had no inkling of anything untoward. Hywel's ardour had not cooled. After the miscarriage, their GP had laughingly suggested 'a little bit of what you fancy', but pregnant again, she had never felt stronger. She also looked stronger. She had lost the bewildered look which Hywel's attentions seemed to have induced. She had once been a competitive gymnast and now went to Keep Fit classes where her figure won admiring glances and she had started to teach on several afternoons a week before she found she was pregnant again. Hywel was glad and, as usual, they seemed to be unduly well off. He dealt with all financial matters and she had not yet learned to drive. In all respects, she supposed she was an old fashioned wife in the way her mother had been, leaving everything important to her husband. They had been given the house, which made Delyth a little ashamed when she heard other young couples complaining about mortgages, but she was enough of a realist not to let it weigh on her conscience. If she had any complaint, it was that she had not yet had the opportunity of showing off her domestic skills. No one came for a meal, Hywel explaining that he had not yet met anyone worth inviting.

Now when he came in from the hallway, the colour had left his cheeks. He was clearly shaken by something. She'd been ironing one of his shirts on the large Harrods' ironing board which yet another of his relatives had given them and she put the iron down on an asbestos mat.

She attempted a joke.

'Don't tell me T.J.'s lost all his money?'

He looked at her blankly. It was only later that he developed the faculty for remembering his own lies.

'The investment?' she said. 'Is it shares or something?'

'I was hoping not to have to tell you.'

'What?' she laughed. 'We're broke?'

'No, no, it's me... Well, it's a spot of bother I got into a few years ago. It's going to come as a bit of a shock, I'm afraid.'

Years later, she would learn that his brother used such phrases, 'a spot of bother', 'a touch of the deficits'. They both sounded so un-Welsh, but then Hywel's normal speaking voice had convinced the people they met in Rhodes that he was English. The spot of

bother was an illegitimate child, an Irish nurse who refused to be
silenced and for whom a financial settlement had been arranged, a
settlement that now had to be improved on the advice of her brother
who was a solicitor and who had only just learned of it. It seemed
that Hywel had a past.

Somehow she understood her father's look at that very moment
but Hywel was very plausible and she was soon convinced. Wasn't
it possible for him to have got involved with some hard-faced Irish
hussy who knew exactly what she was doing? He'd never seen the
child. He thought it his duty to marry her but then someone had
told him that she'd been married before. There was even some
doubt about the paternity. He said he'd broken down and confessed
to his mother and T.J. had been sent to fix things. You would not
think even T.J. could be so foolish but at the time, it had seemed
as if everyone were anxious for a settlement. It had been made,
Hywel said, for the child's benefit. It was not as if it had been a
lasting relationship. But now she was determined to screw every
penny she could from them. Hywel hoped he'd done the right thing
in telling her at last.

She remembered sitting motionless on the arm of the chair, the
iron still switched on, its red warning light blinking like a traffic
beacon — it was a Harrods' iron with every safety device. She didn't
know what to say. She'd felt herself go cold at first, but then, very
soon, she had every sympathy for him. It was the way he had of
putting things.

'I wish you'd told me before. I wouldn't have minded then.' She
meant, before they were married.

'I know. I should have told you.'

'And not lie to me, an investment.'

'Don't you see? I didn't want to hurt you.'

All the time, he had never relaxed the pressure of his hand and
very soon, they made love on the floor, the red light of the iron
winking like a warning beacon above her. The woman did not come,
Hywel's father died, his death releasing certain funds in mysterious
ways and everything was settled. Later, she suspected that once she
had been told the threat of exposure vanished, but anyway, the
matter was closed' Hywel's drama group won the county champion-
ships and at a staff party, the deputy Headmistress told her that
Hywel was doing wonders with the children, but the Headmaster,
who had opposed Hywel's appointment, was not so forthcoming.
Then a month later, their son was born, a difficult birth necessitat-
ing a Caesarian and she felt her body would never be the same again.

Three months later, the headmaster visited when Hywel was ill with flu. Hywel tried to order him out of the house, but the Headmaster was grey-faced.

'If any charges are brought, it'll concern the two of you.'

The parents of a seventeen-year-old sixth former had complained. Hywel had spent the night with the girl at a hotel after a Drama Competition and from that night, Delyth took away the ugliest phrase which remained in her mind like a talisman and which she frequently recalled every time Hywel went off on one of his long explanations. Again, after denying the accusation, he attempted to describe a half-caste girl who would not leave him alone, but the Headmaster who'd either seen a medical report or had one quoted to him, said, 'There was vaginal haemorrhaging for several days'.

This time she could not speak. She knew. Fortunately, or unfortunately, there were no changes brought and Hywel left the school at the end of term, and they moved to the capital city where Hywel found a job in a deprived area, a dockside school where, despite all expectations, he was very successful.

'Why didn't you leave him then?' a friend had once asked her.

It was very simple.

'I'd just had a baby.'

But the truth was, she didn't want to meet her father's eyes, didn't want to confess failure. It would have been more understandable if her father had argued or if there had been some terrible scene, but he'd never said a word, just that single glancing look before he covered his own hurt. It was quite extraordinary but her feeling for her father kept her chained to a sense of duty which she could never have defended. So she made the best of things. Later, thinking of her father's influence, she compared it with the disastrous effect Hywel's mother had on her sons, but she could make no sense of it, any of it.

And once in Cardiff, everything changed for a while. 'Blame the Welsh!' Hywel would say every time anything went wrong. But he didn't include Cardiff. Its very cosmopolitan nature was as strange to him as it was to her and while they discovered it, it was as if, for the first time, they were doing things together, like foreigners in a new land. Or so it had seemed at the time. There were even — dare she admit it? — days when she was happy.

3

After three years of marriage during which a second child, a daughter, was born, the birth equally difficult, Delyth began to take stock. At twenty-four with two small children, she still felt bruised enough. But she'd recovered her natural optimism. They were still young. She hadn't, as her father would have said, jumped ship at the first sign of trouble, in exactly the same way as her sister stood by her fiancé when he lost a limb. Neither of them were that kind of people. Now Hywel came home nightly full of tales of the school where he taught. He spent most of his day in a condemned secondary modern building incorporated into a comprehensive complex which was still in the process of construction. It was a grim, prison-like building with an asphalt yard backing on to a glue factory. The staffroom had been in use as a morgue during the First World War and some of the classrooms were merely spaces in an ancient assembly hall separated by wooden partions so that you could never escape from noise and it seemed the things the teachers said were quite as outrageous as the unruly behaviour of the pupils. Thus he would report on the scripture teacher's latest gem. 'God doesn't want you to be a clock-watcher boy!' Another member of staff, on being introduced to Hywel, made no comment but remained seated at the staff room table with his head held in his hands, later to announce mysteriously that he was 'Up before the Committee on Thursday'. Thinking he was applying for a new post, Hywel politely offered his good wishes, only to be stared at. 'No,' his new colleague said, 'Whitchurch British Legion. Fighting, foul language and threats!'

Daily there was some such anecdote which Hywel reported and it seemed he had found himself a niche amongst a collection of derelicts, many of whom, like himself, had things to hide, but far from becoming resigned, he now began to plunge himself into school activites with an enthusiasm that immediately brought a response from children who had long been deprived. It wasn't long before his drama groups and clubs came to the notice of the Authority and when he reported that the Inspectorate were interested in what he was doing, she knew that it wouldn't be long before he turned things to his own advantage.

For her own part, when she looked back on this time, her sole problem seemed to be to get enough sleep. Both children were fractious and she would later say that Siân, their youngest, did not have an unbroken night's sleep in three years. Days seemed to pass in a blur, days that she could never after recall, but days nevertheless when their lives seemed to have an entrancing normality about them. Then, she was just like everyone else when her only companions, apart from the children, were the other young mothers whom she met in parks, tied like herself. What was odd was that she and Hywel seemed to avoid those who were Welsh-speaking like themselves and for a time, Hywel deliberately kept away from anyone who might remotely have any knowledge of that incident in the Welsh County town they had left. It was as if he was doing penance in the worst area of the docks and although it was never mentioned again, she noticed how disinterested he had become in things Welsh. There had been a time when he was at the centre of various nationalist groups, when many of his conversations were political, when he could be relied upon to give his support to the multiplying Welsh causes, but now he, like herself, seemed to be deliberately removed from almost everything they had known. She herself was so busy and involved with the children and the house that it was understandable, but Hywel even avoided the pubs which were becoming increasingly colonized by outsiders as the Welsh language media grew in strength and little areas of the city seemed to be taken over by people from much the same background as themselves. It was as if he was dropping out of sight and awaiting his chance.

The chance came with yet another telephone call from T.J. Now there were magical words uttered for the first time, 'Educational broadcasting'. It seemed that a Welsh broadcasting station was looking for produciton assistants with teaching experience and T.J. happened to be speaking to the newly appointed Controller about his nephew who was doing missonary work in the docks and quite wasted from the point of view of the nation's needs as a whole. T.J. always spoke in this way and although Delyth was inclined, at last, to bite her lip when he said anything at all, she was well aware of the implications. The young mothers whom she met daily in the park always referred to Welsh language televison as Telly Welly and never watched it, but of course, she knew that while they might regard it as a joke, they were quite wrong and she herself was a warm supporter of all the causes which Hywel had seemingly abandoned. If she was not as active as she might have been, it was because she was preoccupied.

But one night she felt a particular apprehension. Hywel had gone to talk to a cousin who had carved a niche for himself in religious broadcasting on T.J.'s advice. She had a feeling that the cousin would emulate the role played by the estate agent previously. She had no doubt that Hywel was interested and while they discussed the post about to be advertised, they had thought merely in terms of salary which was expected to be more than his present meagre teacher's wage. With the children and the recent purchase of a car, they were not as well off as they had been and although they did not have to pay rent, things were still tight. She was not sure but it seemed that the Mason-Morgan benevolence was not quite so forthcoming, partly, she suspected, because she always put off Hywel's mother from visiting. Now, more than ever before, they were on their own.

But that was not the cause of her apprehension. The proposed job would, it seemed, involve irregular hours of work and periods away from home and now, for most of their married life, she had got used to Hywel's regular habits. There was no doubt he worked hard, no doubt he was appreciated, no doubt that he had done well and the very fact of sticking a job in that terrible area was itself a mark of character. Sometimes when she had to get up in the middle of the night to attend to one or other of the children, she did so without disturbing him and often when feeding the baby, she would sit in the armchair with a strange feeling of contentment, knowing that he was asleep upstairs with the front door locked against the outside world. She imagined her mother must have felt like this when her father was home from sea and the more she thought about it, the more she began to appreciate the regularity of their lives. But, of course, there was more to it again. For some reason, she did not see Hywel as a man behind the scenes despite the fact that he was considering a lowly production assistant's job — she didn't quite know what that meant exactly — but instead she saw him as a performer, a personality, one of those household names who were steadily increasing in number. And it was not just the regulars who crossed her mind, those instant opinion givers who appeared on programme after programme with monotonous regularity, but the real stars, those professionals who fronted programmes of every kind and had a kind of glamour that was evident in the way they dressed, the company they kept, their habit of attaching themselves to more famous people, particularly actors or singers, their attitudes seldom critical and often displaying that lugubrious fawning servility which somehow seemed to her the hallmark of such people. It was very noticeable on the Welsh language channels as if minor stars were seeking some of the glow cast by those who populated the major constellations. But she simply thought it greasy and unpleasant. She wouldn't want Hywel mixed up with anything like that. To tell the truth, despite everything, she was rather proud of him for having done so well at a very ordinary job. In a way, it was rather like being a bosun. In Tiger Bay too, she thought. Her father had mentioned that with a wry smile, very surprised when she'd told him.

So she completed her chores and awaited Hywel's return, deciding at the last minute to wash her hair, finally using a blow dryer and ruefully fingering a clutch of grey hairs and noticing for the umpteenth time that although she had recovered her figure, there were marks appearing in the corners of her eyes, the pronounced crow's foot lines that would one day become permanent. She remained a bit of a Minnie Mouse, especially when she was tired and the wrinkles showed.

She was seated in a dressing gown when Hywel came in.

'Well?'

'I'm not sure.'

She felt an immediate relief.

'It's for you to decide eventually.'

Her relief vanished.

Of late, the old ebullient Hywel had returned, the air of promise and unspoken things to come, and with it, a filling out of his stocky frame. He was not only beginning to put on weight, he was putting it on in the wrong places and when he sat, poised on the edge of the settee as he did now, he reminded her of his father, that mysterious simpering grey-faced man who agreed with everything everybody said, whom she had met so briefly. But where his full face was long suffering, Hywel's was eager for approval.

'It's not just that the money's more, it's the long term prospects. I'm not going to get much further in teaching without much better qualifications.'

It sounded reasonable. He went on to describe the likely growth of Welsh television and very soon, it was as if he was rehearsing a speech for his interview. There were things he felt he could contribute, and then she knew, he had already decided. Of course he would be starting at the bottom, he said. There would be difficulties, but they had the children to think about. They lived in what by middle-class standards was rather a shabby neighbourhood. Very soon, they would have to think of schools for the children. Whatever course the future took, it was only right that he should do the best he could for them. But it was for her to decide.

Much later, she would think that half of what he said to her on such occasions was like a private sharing of what would later be a public utterance, and yet, she still listened, still felt that she mattered, still went along with him. But later still, she realized that this going back to what he thought were his own kind, far from being a healthy thing, was a death sentence. They were not his own kind, they were a new kind and he was entering a world which had never existed before. That night, and the night he came home to tell her that he had, of course, been successful, she felt an apprehension that she could not precisely articulate at the time. It was very odd but she felt there was an immediate parallel in the sudden departure of a Methodist Minister from the town they had just left. Thought by most of his flock to be a complete non-entity and a back-slider, he had suddenly emerged a television personality and was constantly seen on Arts programmes, his face flushed and gestures expansive, rumours about his drinking and private life circulating freely while he became more and more prominent. It was laughable in some ways, disgraceful in others, and yet she could not help but feel that the very act of becoming such a public man was in some way an act of frenzy — as if the urge to be on public display was a new disease. It was what her father would have said. There was also the strange feeling that Hywel would be leaving something decent for something indecent. Above all, what was quite extraordinary, was that now for the first time she seemed to be thinking for herself.

4

The suicide attempt came five years later. They'd moved again. Everything promised had been realized as far as Hywel was concerned. With the expansion in Welsh language broadcasting, there was a sudden demand for personnel, despite the fact that more and more aerials in the city were becoming permanently tuned in to English programmes transmitted from Bristol and the West Country. But Hywel had been in the right place at the right time. Now regular programmes were beginning to go out with his name prominent amongst the credits. The children were growing up. She learned to drive in order to transport them to a distant school where Welsh was the medium of instruction. Now she had different friends, among them the wives of people who worked with Hywel. Now they spoke Welsh constantly, and Hywel had been on a crash course to improve his knowledge of his mother tongue. They were part of a group largely composed of people much like themselves. 'Upwardly mobile', Hywel said, but it was a very exclusive curious world and she did not quite feel at home in it for reasons that took some time to become clear. Sometimes she went across to the park where she had earlier wheeled the pram and met some of her old acquaintances, the young mothers who had lived near them previously. A few of them were rather jealous of her, the new house separated her from the old neighbourhood, but others were welcoming. For other reasons which she could not explain, she was sometimes glad to get away from Welsh-speaking people, or rather, the wives of media people, for she was becoming aware of a certain condescention which some of them invariably showed her — as if, despite Hywel's success, there was something about her which had not kept pace with him. Or that was what she at first thought. It was a feeling shared by Hywel's mother who now, more than ever, had to be kept from visiting. It was not just the extra work involved since she was the kind who ran her gloves under window ledges in search of dust, nor even her complete spoiling of the children, but this view she had of Delyth as a pretty little thing, the emphasis always being on the 'little'.

It was not only patronizing, but as if she was being compartmental-ized as a person, hopelessly cast in the role of *little* wife from whom nothing much else could be expected. The entertaining they hoped to do never quite materialized. If they went to dinner parties, they were invariably media people and the only people Hywel ever suggested inviting back were much older than them, invariably men who might advance his career and although Hywel thought about the invitations, he was not quite secure enough to press them with the result that the few people they entertained tended to be rather boring. Very soon, Hywel began to travel the length and breadth of the country and it was then that the condescending looks of the wives of his colleagues began. Only a fool wouldn't have put two and two together, she thought later, but then, that was how she thought herself for a period of time that seemed never-ending — the fool and the victim.

One day when Hywel was away directing some programme in Builth Wells, she had safely delivered the children to school and was driving home through an unfamiliar district when she saw Hywel, or somebody who looked exactly like Hywel, emerging from a house and getting into a taxi at the corner of the street. It was but a second's glance and when she looked into the driving mirror, she could not verify her impression because the taxi immediately pulled away in the opposite direction. Hywel had now put on weight and his regular drinking had begun, but above all, his appetite had become gargantuan with the result that slim figure of old was already quite unrecognizable. Since he had specialized in making programmes about agriculture recently, he also at this time affected a countrified look, frequently wearing thick tweeds and sports

jackets which made him look even more overweight and it was the
thick herringbone tweed of the overcoat which had caught her eye
more than anything else. It was not the kind of coat you saw often
in the city, and, as it happened, Hywel had regretted buying it when
there were much more servicable coats available. It was somehow
typical of him to make such a foolish purchase, she'd thought, as if
once more, he was taking on the colour of his surroundings. The
expensive sheepskin had gone with the sports car, then in school he
had for a time worn tracksuits and trainers even though he was the
most unathletic man imaginable, but he felt they had given him a
certain image as an active drama teacher which no one but himself
could have explained. It was the coat that caught her attention, the
coat with which she taxed him when the opportunity arose.

But that night, he telephoned as usual from the hotel in Builth
Welsh as he had done on the previous evening. This was at a time
when he telephoned home nightly.

There were the usual pleasantries, the dutiful enquiries after the
children, his apologies because he might have to be away over the
weekend.

'What's the weather like?' she said lightly, the casualness of her
enquiry the first act of deception in her entire life.

'Quite mild. What's it like with you?'

'The same.'

'Is anything the matter?'

'No, no, I just wondered.'

There was a coolness about her which later disappeared altogether. It was not that she wasn't sure, but that some part of her
wanted to confront him in person. She wanted to see his face when
she challenged him. And this time, she wouldn't allow him to touch
her. Somehow the touching was a part of her defencelessness. So
her calm was a progression from the simple casualness of his first
question.

'Are you sure you don't mind about the weekend?'

'If you have to be there...'

'If there's any chance of me getting away, I will.'

'Not if it means spoiling the programme.'

Now she felt like an actress! When he rang off, she went downstairs and poured herself a stiff whiskey but the unfamiliar taste
revolted her and nearly made her sick. What was strange was that
there was no doubt in her mind at all. She just sat there motionless
and it wasn't long before she began to wonder what she would do
when her suspicions were confirmed. Again, she thought of her

father but now there were the children to be considered. There were problems. Both were small like herself, Geraint the eldest had inherited her mother's ashtma, and already showed signs of frailty, but more than anything she had a horror of divorce that was quite unreasonable. In the first place, she could not see herself returning home, an abandoned wife with two children and all the talk that would involve, and secondly, there was a dismal feeling that getting money out of Hywel would be a tortuous process and she had a vivid memory of one of her park acquaintances who was in just that position, legally separated and made ill by the simple business of staying alive. At the same time, there was a further thought, one that would later amaze her, and this was the incredible perception that a divorce would not help Hywel's career since there remained vestiges of the old puritanical traditions to which his bosses still paid lip-service. She was even at this moment still thinking of him.

But oh, how could he? she thought. She wept finally, tasting her own tears in the whiskey. That was the first night without sleep. When the second followed after a day of losing her temper with the children, she spent a night trying to put faces to the half-caste teenager and the Irish nurse and before long she thought she'd begun to understand some of the condescending looks which the media wives had given her. Of course, they knew him, or knew about him. Everything was known. Wales was such a small place, there were no secrets, and she had heard enough talk about others, the real celebrities some of whom had the morals of farmyard animals, she'd heard somebody once say. But that put her in mind of Hywel again. It was not just that there was something in him that couldn't leave any woman alone, it was more; he couldn't exist without the kind of admiration that she had given him, the total belief and abandonment of everything else for no matter how long, an hour, a night, a week. And it would go on and on, no matter what she said or what he promised. That was Hywel and how he functioned.

When he finally returned, he had not come in through the door before he announced that he had to return. There were camera problems, lighting problems. They'd got nothing in the can, he said. He'd only come home for a change of clothes, and, of course, to see if she was all right.

But she clearly wasn't all right. She wore no make-up. There were black patches under her eyes as if she had some kidney disease. She was haggard and pale. When she spoke her voice was tremulous and her hands shook. She couldn't even conceal her distress from the children. He had not noticed in the darkness of the hallway but when he came into the living room, busily shuffling through his mail, he looked up and saw her gripping the edge of the table.

'What is it?'

'I saw you on Thursday.'

'Thursday?'

'In Cardiff. When you were supposed to be in Builth. I saw you get into a taxi. Who was it this time?'

There was not even a flicker of annoyance in his eyes, certainly, not surprise either. He was merely irritated.

'Barbara,' he said. 'We didn't get back till three and I didn't want to wake you.'

Barbara was his secretary, a rather drab spinster who was temporarily allocated to his department.

Unfortunately, he'd forgotten that he'd telephoned that night and the previous night, saying he was actually in Builth Wells. She told him, but just before he could answer, the telephone rang. This time it was Builth Wells and there were problems.

'Real problems,' he said. 'Look, can't this wait? I've got to go. I've driven two hundred miles today already.'

She stood motionless by the kitchen table, then Siân fell over in the yard, the telephone rang again and he was gone, forgetting the change of clothes he'd originally come for, gone, hurrying away back to the car and away from her, sweating in that huge tweed coat, she could see. There was no doubt whatsoever.

Then the children's questions began, as usual making her feel guilty for the way she looked, for not covering up, for communicating her own misery to them. It was not that night but the next night, the fourth without sleep that she took the soneryl tablets and the whisky which were conveniently to hand. They were his tablets and his whisky and her exhaustion was of his doing. But fortunately, she did not take enough, vomited in her sleep and awoke in the middle of the morning to find his mother downstairs ringing at the front doorbell. She'd come unexpectedly on a coach with a party of women on a shopping expedition and also to see *The Sound of Music*. The film was apparently receiving its fifth showing.

'Of course, it's very sentimental but it gave me the opportunity to pop in and see how you all were!'

The children, still in their night clothes, were huddled like casualties in the corner of the kitchen, a trail of milk and cornflakes across the floor. At the time, she'd thought they hadn't been into her bedroom.

Covering up automatically, Delyth knew that Mrs Mason-Morgan thought she'd taken to the bottle and when Hywel came home later that week, he said there were certain things she had to understand about his job. He was suddenly hard and cool. He did not touch her. She could take it or leave it, he implied. He knew of some marriages that had been ruined by constant unnecessary accusations. The world was changing, he said, and he was changing with it. She sat and listened in a dumb silence. There was neither rhyme nor reason to her acceptance of everything he said, but accept it she did, and it was only when the children were older that he actually started to make excuses again, his lies then aimed at them as much as at her. It was as if something in her had snapped, as if she had forfeited the right to be a human being at all. She went about her daily chores like an automaton. She simply got on with things, a shell hardening about her, as they moved further and further away from each other until in the end, she neither cared where he was, nor what he did.

5

It was at this time that she began to discover the City. She'd already explored the nearest parks, and now she was at last able to get some supply teaching, invariably moving as Hywel had done to the roughest schools in the worst neighbourhoods. It gave her a purpose and she slowly began to discover a long forgotten self. But it took an age to make up her mind. Most of all, she lacked self-confidence.

There was a time when she couldn't even see herself standing up in front of a group of unruly children. She couldn't control herself, never mind anybody else. There were problems with references, referees, the Ministry of Education itself since she'd never even completed a probationary year. Then she became preoccupied with her appearance. She might have passed muster in some country school but now there came a time when she couldn't bear to look into the mirror. It was not just her scarred body, it was her face. She was already greying, the crowsfoot lines were becoming permanent and her thick eyebrows arched above her startled black eyes and her sharp, pointed chin giving her the look of some tiny forest animal in a permanent state of fear. If she was not actually always on edge, she looked it. The Minnie Mouse tag returned to her consciousness. She felt she could never muster any authority and there were such louts of children about.

Then a bizarre happening occurred. There was a long wardrobe mirror in their bedroom and she was changing one morning in preparation for a visit to an old college friend when she could not get her skirt to hang properly. It was a pleated skirt but she had altered the hem line and there was something she'd done which made it irregular so at the last minute she'd decided on a complete change, removing her blouse and examining her hips in the mirror. She was not completely naked but she turned once or twice in what she supposed might be a rather provocative way had she been in view when she suddenly noticed that she was observed. Resting against the window, and appreciatively puffing at a cigarette was the window cleaner, a tousled ginger youth with a pock-marked face and a denim cap jauntily perched on the back of his head.

Startled, she jumped, but the grin on his face and his appreciative nod might have been that of a spectator at a horse show. The window was open and before she could say anything, he winked in as friendly a way as could be imagined.

'Very nice too!' he said with all the authority of a connoisseur. 'Off out, are we?'

It was not in her to tell him off.

'Make sure you do the children's windows,' she told him.

'Oh, I don't come all the way up here to pick my nose, Missus!'

She pulled down her sweater examining herself, conscious that his eyes were still on her, finally slipped into her shoes with a flush settling on her cheeks. There was no logic to it, but it was as if everything had changed and after that the window cleaner often teased her, 'Not into the Miss Worlds this week then?'. Whenever she saw him, she felt cheered as if he was an ambassador of another world out there.

It was the same when she finally began to get the supply teaching jobs which she eventually sought. It was not the problem she imagined, and although her fears remained, eventually she found, as Hywel had, that she was needed. She soon developed a brisk no nonsense way of keeping children busy, and by preparing everything thoroughly, broke her day down into small acheivable tasks. Eventually, she found herself being asked to return to the same schools and while she did not immediately think of a permanent job, she began to feel more and more optimistic. She had recovered her independence. More than that, her conversations with some of the children brought her into contact with other lives, some of them so disturbed and frought with dificulties that she had a further sense of the ills of the world. There were those who were maimed and deprived, there was a shiftless seedy other-world where vile happenings and cruelties were daily events. Whatever had happened to her, she was not alone. She was not too badly off.

Within the space of a year it was as if this other world was giving
her names. She was Minnie Mouse, Miss World and Our Miss, but
then a series of minor ailments caused her to stay home with her
own children and this broken winter was capped by a car accident
when she broke her ankle. No sooner had she begun to make
another half-life for herself when she was returned to the old. Now
Hywel was promoted. Now Hywel had reached a point, he said,
where he could not go on without her support. What he meant was
that he could not stand her coolness. Other people were noticing.
His promotion also meant, she suspected, that for a long time he
would have a desk job. It was at this time when she had begun to
attempt some understanding of the Mason-Morgans and their
children that she had begun to worry about her own. She was now
sure that Hywel's childhood had been a kind of battleground with
several wars being fought at the same time. Whatever had passed
between Morfydd and her husband was somehow beyond compre-
hension at this distance of time. That weak silent man and the
domineering, forceful woman, always insisting on her accomplish-
ments, should by all logic have been the result of some inferiority
or insecurity but there was no evidence of it. Unless the padre too
had constantly strayed? It was an alarming thought. Then the simple
primitive concepts of right and wrong, obviously hammered into
the children at every possible opportunity seemed to have had no
effect whatsoever. Normally, people had a conscience, they suffered
guilt feelings in varying degrees. Delyth herself could not lie. She
simply couldn't. It was unthinkable and while she was not averse to
winning people's affections and scoring off her sister, for example,
she was ever-after conscious of her sister's hurt. But Hywel was
completely different and she knew now that he was different even
when he was articulating precisely the things he thought she wanted
to hear. He could describe anything, any single feeling, and over
the years, he had become even more expert than when she had first
met him. When he was there, he was marvellous with the children.
He had the capacity to seem genuinely interested in what they were
doing. At the drop of a hat, he could become a child and see things
from the child's point of view. It was the same with people, she
supposed. He had the habit of intense concentration on other
people's wishes, needs, their aspirations for themselves. He gave
them his full attention and he never forgot important details, but
only when he wanted something. Perhaps he had learnt it, practising
on his mother and on T.J., on all of them since people like that
encouraged it. She did not know.

What she did know was that he was on a Welsh bandwagon, and
he was a clear example of what one of her sardonic colleagues had
described as the contemporary disease. He suffered from Wales-in-
the-Head. This consciousness affected his every idea and dominated his life which was understandable as far as his work was
concerned, she supposed, but she was beginning to realize that it
had very little to do with the daily realities of most people's lives.
But like every other idea Hywel held in his mind for long, it was
very profitable, although she had a longing for someone to stand up
and say there was no such thing as a purely Welsh germ! Except
Hywel himself, of course. This was how she thought now. He wasn't
going to get round her, and one day, coming across an old school
geography textbook which dated to the 1930s, she found that the
word Empire was mentioned so frequently that it struck a chord in
her mind. People then, it seemed, were always doing things for the
Empire. They built roads, bridges, sacrificed their lives, their health,
their children, all for the Empire. If you substituted the word Wales
for Empire it was almost exactly the same kind of thinking. It was
quite extraordinary for her to have noticed something like that, but
she didn't dare say anything to anybody. She hoarded it all away.

She said he wouldn't get round her. The way he got round her
was by asking her things now in front of the children so that any
refusal on her part put her in the wrong. He had now reached the
stage where there were people he wanted to invite to dinner, and
they suddenly began to receive more and more invitations as if those
on the echelon below them had also realized that Hywel was worth
cultivating. Some of them were the same wives who had given her
such looks previously. But now there was a more obvious regard for
Hywel, a slightly different appraisal of her but always as if she had
somehow miraculously survived and kept pace, quite a surprising
little thing. She had gone to one or two houses with the grime of
the classroom barely removed from her fingernails. It was at a time
when confidential record cards were introduced in schools and she
was aware of daily realities in a way she never had been before, in
particular of the crimes visited upon children, the beatings, the
sexual assaults, the shouted scenes behind locked doors, the visible
evidence of hurt, worst of all the silent children who said very little
but whose eyes confirmed things she would never have believed
possible. And she would sit smiling as the conversation buzzed
around her, seldom contributing but saying to herself, 'Ah yes, the
Empire. We must keep the Empire, the jolly old Empire!'

'Delyth teaches,' Hywel would say, and then he would say where, naming the shabby districts as if she, in T.J.'s words, was doing valuable missionary work and people were suitably impressed. What nobody understood was that her teaching was the lifeline from the lot of them!

On some nights Hywel would look at her with warm regard as if he too was in some way infected by this view of her as a person who had come on. Now they slept in separate beds. If he touched her, she turned away. But soon, he was wooing her again. But it was the one thing he could not do in front of the children, so he had no chance.

Entertaining was another matter, however. Entertaining was part of his career now. So, it seemed, was keeping on the straight and narrow for he seldom went away and even offered to take her with him on one or two trips. He'd used the children as blackmail before they went on holiday, and she'd been available, as she'd learnt to put it, only because she knew that the children wouldn't have had a father on holiday with them otherwise. That was one for the record cards, but her lack of response made him drink all the more and she didn't care. But entertaining outsiders was not like entertaining him in her bed. That was no longer part of the grand design. But entertaining would produce him another colony.

So again, she went along with it, shrugging her shoulders and setting out to prove something to herself. She was not a prude but gluttony seemed to be an undiagnosed industrial hazard of the media people Hywel knew. It was no good doing wonders with coriander or trapesing to the market to get fresh artichokes, they didn't want subtlety, they wanted quantity, stuffing themselves over Normandy pork with rich puddings to follow, all the things she despised. And they drank like fish, one or two often using Company drivers as they went about their hogging, and just as Hywel had years ago been a great maker of statements about the Welsh (he'd dropped it recently) now she took up the same irreverent strain.

Like her empire thoughts, these other irreverences remained buried, although in one of the schools in which she taught there was an old, exhausted, permanently hungover Welsh teacher, a Cardi like herself who could not face a class until he had read the *Western Mail* from cover to cover and was the last exponent of 'silent reading' and to whom she often reported on the young notables who now began to come to her house. Like T.J., he was also known by his initials, a white-haired old soak with a country turn of phrase.

'Well?' O.O. would say, 'who did you have last night?'

She would report whereupon O.O. would shake his head in mock sadness. 'That beauty! The pee's not dry on his legs yet!'

And of another, he would add, 'I knew his father. Very few Ministers could empty a chapel, but by God, one look at him was enough!

She was never without one friend.

The entertaining continued, so did the entertainment. Now Hywel, portly and presposterous, began to cultivate even more important people. He affected waistcoats on occasions and got out his father's gold watch chain and once, when she was required to attend the Memorial Service held for a famous sporting personality, she'd trotted beside him wearing a cloche hat and feeling like the maid. This was the final period before he got the job he really wanted when the lies began again, and eventually he had become so gross that she could not imagine any woman, certainly a woman younger than him, being interested in the least. His belly sagged and his thickly bearded face had now begun to resemble that of some debauched Old Testament prophet, the eyes often inflamed for, despite his workload, he was never without a glass in his hand. Now the wives looked at her with sympathy once more but also with a certain unmentionable curiousity as if they could not imagine how she endured such a gross physical presence.

But she had already calculated a date for leaving him when he died.

6

She faced them all in the Memorial Service like a celebrity. No one could understand why. She wore a sheath dress, patent leather shoes, her highest heels, a black suspender belt, and sheer, seamed stockings, the tiny bulge of the clip of the suspender belt visible through the material of the dress when she sat. She knew because she could see Hywel's mother staring at it. She also wore a hat which was hardly a hat, more like a half-formed butterfly perched on the top of her head with her hair, neatly curled up, coiled around it. She'd recently been to a beauty parlour in France and had her eyebrows plucked and she wore the slightest tint of dove grey eye shadow, all of which gave her face an altoghether more interesting aspect. If anything, it looked thinner, but since she was handsomely tanned, not only had she never looked healthier (as some people remarked) but there was now, for the first time in her life, a certain air about her, a chic that was quite devastating. Had she been a model, you would have expected the ferryman's daughter to appear soon demonstrating what could be done next with a fisherman's slinky jersey! And now her face was quite inscrutable. The re-shaped eyebrows had removed the Minnie Mouse look completely and the marks etched below her eyes merely made her look experienced. There was not a hint of her former self.

She'd told her father and sister not to come and she hoped there was no one there from her family. Up until the last minute, she wasn't certain she would go herself, and, as usual, it was only for the sake of the children that she'd agreed, one of the many problems faced by the harrassed Controller of the broadcasting station who wasn't at all sure that the Memorial Service should be held, but had given way himself to departmental pressures. He seemed to be aware of his mistake since there were so few people present and began the customary eulogy with a nervous clearing of the throat, his thick North Walian accent making his ill chosen words seem all the more ponderous. Once you got these people away from their desks you realized how inadequate they were. Throughout, Delyth kept her eyes riveted on the bridge of his spectacles, her chin tilted pertly, allowing herself neither a glance to right or left. The gist of his peroration was soon revealed. Hywel was a man who had given Wales to the world. Of late, his speciality as a producer was what might be called The Welsh Connection, with distinguished exiles, with foreign lands, with those industries that had taken Welsh people the length and breadth of the globe, not forgetting Hywel's other preoccupation with the vanishing past.

But Delyth soon stopped listening. It was the mixture as before. It might even have been Hywel speaking himself. The Vanishing Past, she thought. By it, the Controller meant images concocted from obscure farm ploughs or the hulks of derelict schooners which had once plied their trade to long forgotten harbours. As for crossing and re-crossing the length and breadth of the world, while it was quite true, what he should have said was that if Hywel had found a Chicago gangster involved in the St Valentine's Day Massacre with a name like Evans, it too would be good for a programme, together with the expenses and the month-long booze-up that went with it. They would do anything rather than address themselves to the present. Later, during the final hymn, Morfydd clutching her throat beside her as she sang querulously, Delyth stole a glance at the assembled congreation. Besides the top brass — the Empire builders — there seemed an unusually large number of women which was a surprise. He couldn't have gone through them all, especially the policewoman, she thought ironically. At last, she felt uninvolved.

When the service ended and the procession of people came over to greet her, she had but one image in her mind and had she revealed it, she would have horrified everyone. She knew exactly what everyone was saying. 'Isn't she bearing up splendidly? She's looking so well considering... I always knew she was a brave little thing!'

But it was all she could do not to giggle. She'd fixed the lot of them. What had upset Morfydd so much, was not just the suddenness of her son's death, but the fact that she had not been informed of it for several weeks. They'd gone on holiday to the South of France and on the very first morning, Hywel had been playing football on the beach with the children when he'd suddenly put his hand to his heart and dropped down dead. There'd been a doctor nearby who told her he'd had a massive stroke. Then with three weeks of the holiday remaing, she determined to carry on with it, making up her mind on the spot since they were touring and had a number of places booked. They'd not had a family holiday for four years, by now Hywel scarely saw his own children for any period longer than half an hour so she'd come to an abrupt decision. The hotel had been marvellous, arranging the crematorium in Marseilles and eventually, she'd driven home, refreshed and tanned with Hywel's ashes in the back of the car, only informing his mother a few days before they'd got on the ferry. But although it was a decision taken quickly, it was not taken lightly and she had no regrets whatsoever. She'd even had a laugh that she could never communicate to a living soul. Hywel's ashes had been placed in a plastic urn and once, when she'd been stopped for speeding, she'd inadvertently produced the cremation certificate with the other documents and the incredulous look on the faces of the gendarmerie had made her feel like a celebrity. The gendarmes had asked to see the urn and when they did, saluted with that thrilling French precision, even escorting her away from the intersection.

That was the last of Hywel really, sliding about in the boot of the car.